I0614310

Eden's Charms

by

Jaclyn Tracey

Eden's Charms

Cover Art by *Rae Monet, Inc. Design*

The Wild Rose Press, Inc.
PO Box 708
Adams Basin, NY 14410-0708
Visit us at www.thewildrosepress.com

Publishing History
First Black Rose Edition, 2014
Print ISBN 978-1-62830-192-2
Digital ISBN 978-1-62830-193-9

Published in the United States of America

"Excuse me," came out countless times as she wormed her way to the front of the queue. "Please, that's my husband up there." She lied. Once behind him, she slapped his shoulder hard.

Startled, Ethan jumped. "Persistently pesky, aren't we? What now?" he asked. Seeing his reflection in a pair of black shades, he immediately began touching up his hair.

What made Savanah even crazier was when he pulled his lips back and started picking at his teeth as if she were a mirror put on this earth just for him. "Narcissus, some people never change," rolled from the tip of her tongue. "You're rude, arrogant, pushy, and it's more than obvious you don't care about anyone else."

"Then why the hell did you marry him?" Someone asked.

Ethan choked on laughter. "What?" he asked again.

This time Savanah noted a distinct edge of amusement with his sugar-coated tone.

She put a silencing finger up to the man's face behind her and mouthed, "Shush!" Turning back to Ethan, she demanded, "I want an apology. You pummeled my toes and had no right flipping me off."

"I can see why he did it," Mr. Nosey, from behind, added his two cents.

In a heated tone, Ethan yelled, "Don't you talk to my wife like that," right before he grabbed her and pulled her close enough to whisper, "Who are you, woman?"

Dedication

To the one man who shared the vow
"'Til death do we part,"
please stop singing the last line of
the Meatloaf song, "Paradise by the Dashboard Light,"
to me.
After twenty seven years you still share my soul,
invade my thoughts and make me smile for no reason.

To my Editor, Callie Lynn—
once in a blue moon you meet someone
who's changed your life~
for once I'm not talking werewolves, but someone
who gives of herself asking for nothing in return.
You are that person, and I am forever grateful we met.

Chapter One

London, England

"Harder," Savanah St. James grunted as she eyed her *oh so* handsome partner's lean, well-defined muscular body. *Uhm!* Hungry, she licked her lips. His complexion reminded Savanah of a model who'd been airbrushed to perfection; not one freckle, pimple or wrinkle to be seen by the naked eye. It wasn't fair. Currently, she had at least one of each. His blond, unruly curls sprang out from under his baseball cap and framed his kissable face. The black T-shirt with the logo *Define Girlfriend* stretched paper-thin across his broad chest. And his shoulders made her want to run her fingers in circles around his nipples to see if they weren't the only thing to pop up!

"Harder? Are you sure?" he asked.

Savanah glanced down at his knuckles, white from pressure. "Yes, please—give it your best shot!"

"I think I hear a song in there somewhere. Nothing's happening. The old tool's just too big." His grin hinted of roguery.

Savanah rolled her eyes up every delicious inch of the man.

Music to her ears. Her mind digressed to her last encounter with the opposite sex, and she scanned her pinky finger. Yes, too big would be a welcome change.

1

"You can make it fit. It *has* too." She cringed. Was that desperation in her voice? Savanah gripped and wiggled the solid mass back and forth to no avail. Her reflection in his black-rimmed aviator shades screamed diva, and even though nothing else was going as it should, she smiled. Hopefully, she wouldn't be the only one to notice. Her eyebrows did a little dance catching her partner's attention.

Mr. Ray Ban gave a smug smirk. He suggested, "*Gently.* You're too rough. Why the hurry? We've got all night."

All night wouldn't cut it. She wanted eternity. "Me? I can't believe this. We're so close. Wait, hold this." Savanah winked, placed the rod in his grasp, got up and left the man hanging. She returned waving a bottle of massage oil in the air.

He snatched the bottle and read it. "A woman after my own heart."

Indeed I am and that's not all. She gave him a playful grin. "If this doesn't work, you're on your own. I wish you'd take off your shades. I'd love to be able to see your eyes. I'd like it even better if I knew your name."

"Isn't this more intriguing though? Leaves some mystery… Don't you agree?"

Savanah watched with eager enthusiasm as his soft, sensuous lips puckered and he blew her a kiss. Oh, the areas she wanted those lips to travel! "You could say that. Hey, you're in. Oh, it's snug."

"So…Savanah, do you do this often?"

"Nowhere near as often as I'd like."

****

After an incredible, long, strenuous night, Savanah

stirred when the bed shifted.

"Savanah? Wake up. For the love of magic, what were you conjuring up last night? No—never mind. I heard enough. I didn't know you had company, or I'd have gone to a flick."

Savanah opened her baby blues to find her best friend and business partner, who just so happened to be her uncle on the side of her bed, his legs crossed, eyeing her. For some reason he had a mischievous smile on his face. The smile suited him. Shame she rarely saw it. He'd pulled his long reddish-brown hair into a braid today, away from his face, which showed the rugged contours of his cheeks and chin. His deep maroon dress shirt, green cargo pants and a pair of tasseled loafers with no socks, told Savanah either he'd gotten up way too early or she'd slept way too late…again.

"Jules?" Scratching her head she prattled, "I was alone all night."

"No—I heard a man's voice."

"Oh no! Don't tell me I had an out-of-body soul date. God, I didn't even get his name. This seriously hot blond and I were putting together a baby's bassinette, and we couldn't get the thing together. None of the pegs, legs, whatever they were, would fit together. Square peg—round hole syndrome! I'm rather confident you've been down that road." She slapped his arm and gave up a toothy grin. "I won't tell you what I used to get it to work."

"Savvy, you were screaming something about getting some lubricant while you charged through the flat last night into the bathroom and then back to your *boudoir*."

"I really ran and got the oil?"

Julian nodded. "Been a while since that bed's got some action…other than you, alone."

"Ewh! Absolutely uncalled for!" Savanah slapped his arm again. Harder. She countered, "Who's calling the kettle black? It's your own fault you have no lady keeping you company, Mister overbearing, egotistical, anal, compulsive werewolf who has more hair on his feet than I do my legs." Savanah pulled at a few strands on his foot.

Julian raised one eyebrow toward her, baring a different grin worthy of backing up a step or two. "You make me sound like the boy next door or Donald Trump. Get up, woman. We have to get the museum ready for our treasures and get an agreement written up between the UK and Egypt before we can ship our things here."

She mumbled through a yawn, "Ten minutes tops."

"Translated into Savanah standard time, one hour. I'll walk to the bakery and get you a scone and some Earl Grey. Lemon glaze or raspberry?"

"Lemon. You're the best. Love you more." Eyes closed again, Savanah flopped backward onto her bed. "That dream-date was so real, Jules. I feel I've known him all my life. We really connected. Wish I'd seen his face. Body was a scorcher." Savanah licked her index finger and tapped her rump as she made a "Szzzzz" sound.

Julian chuckled. "Sounds like you're more like your mother and your aunt than you know."

"And maybe I'm just a dreamer."

"A beautiful dreamer, Savanah. But now we need to make our dreams a reality. Get your lazy bum out of bed. It's eleven; the day's going fast. You and I sure as hell aren't getting any younger."

"Sweet of you to mention that. Oh, don't forget a lot of sugar," she yelled as he left.

Out of bed and in the living room of their tiny five-room flat, she looked around at all the boxes of artifacts she'd collected over the years and no matter how many times she perused the items it amazed her that she had some of the most sought after antiquities in the world at her fingertips. Treasure hunter extraordinaire and superb preternatural archeologist!

"Soon people will know the name Savanah St. James and never forget it." With a quick pirouette, her reflection caught her attention in the mirror. Mid spin she stopped and fluffed her skewered, thick jet-black curls. "Mirror, mirror on the wall, laugh at me today and I'll hang you from the banister and watch you fall." Without further ado she headed to the shower.

One hour later, she and Julian were sardined into the tube—destination—Trafalgar Square Station. No more than a hop, skip and jump from the station stood, The National Gallery, where world treasures graced every wall. As she dangled from a handrail hook with a complete stranger, Savanah felt certain she resembled a slab of meat in an oven. The underground sweltered. The place acted more like a slow cooker than fast, easy transportation. The air conditioning systems were off…again. She wondered why she even took the time to do her hair. The curls were rising faster than the flaky little doughboy getting kneaded by a set of strong hands.

Savanah knew all too well the inside workings of the I-PEON's, International Preternatural On-sight

Neutralizers. The legalized, murdering scoundrels believed turning off the air coolants would smoke out anything non-human because rogue vampires tended to attract flies if left out in the heat too long and shape-shifters looked like rabid St. Bernard's, drooling buckets of thick mucus. Updates needed to be made on their Intel because not all vamps turned into beef jerky in the sun and not all lycans looked like they needed distemper shots. Her family was death-defying proof.

Savanah chatted endlessly to the older gent and told all the details of her life's work. "—the exhibit is a first. It showcases artifacts and an actual mummified vampire. You must really come see her. She's beastly, but she's my baby," she suggested, her enthusiasm piqued as she widened her stance and braced for the train to stop.

The older gent, in return, patted her shoulder before he exited. "Dear child!" He shook his head. "You need to find a husband and have children instead of chasing demons. Chase the little monsters. You're much too pretty to waste your youth on the dead."

Savanah watched the doors close, she on one side and he on the other, two very different worlds apart.

****

Other side of the pond, Boston, Massachusetts

Raven St. James eyed Filenes's basement from every angle—chaos in the making. Her enthusiasm hit a new high. She'd gone with one mission and one mission only—to conquer and rack up the national debt in the process. She scanned over the mountains of unfolded clothing, the shoes strewn across the floors with no mate to be found, perfumes clouding the isles like fog in the moors of England, women sneezing and red-eyed because of it, and busy little fingers franticly tapping out tunes on cash-registers to the sound of money, and she realized she'd done just that. She'd conquered the store. The only thing missing was a song from the early 70's sung by an acid-rock era band rambling on about money blasting through the airways. It would have been a welcome change in place of that all too cute little *Red-nosed Reindeer* ditty. She'd heard the little track one too many times and had ill-fated feelings for the holiday tune, thinking a nice bloody venison steak would hit the spot. She licked her lips and groaned at the same time. *If only I could kill you all over again Jasper Black. The damned curse you bestowed upon me will be the death of me, or someone else if I don't get some nourishment soon.*

One hundred years later and Raven still loathed the two dead monsters that had turned her. The other ghoul, Xavier Sinclair. Not only did he turn her, but he'd raped her. It couldn't get hot enough in Hell for him.

Her dents poked through. Against the odds, she jammed her fingers into her mouth and pressed hard on her fangs, praying they didn't hang over lips. Nothing worse than looking like a desperate vamp, although—it would clear the isles and give her some much needed elbow room!

Her sister-in-law, Serina St. James, she'd lost between the racks of clothing. Not much taller than said racks, Raven seemed to lose Serina every time they ventured out. Raven suggested she wear a cowbell when they shopped. Serina in return, suggested something to do with turning her into a fat cow. And the fact that Serina could, worried her.

"This store is insane, Serrie." Raven pilfered

through the dresses, her voice raised. "Would you look at this? Oh, my boys are going to love me to death in this little number. And look at the price tag! It's almost a negative number." Raven held up a black, silk dress to herself, shaking the slinky little thing to show Serina once she popped her hand up and waved a silky black thong in her direction.

"Over here!"

The dress was a mini. Almost too short to be called mini. *Swatch worked*, Serina thought. Serina gave up her smile at the last second; she liked the dress as long as she didn't have to parade around in it. At five-foot-seven, Raven could pull it off. At five-foot-three Serina couldn't pull off a box of cereal from the top shelf of a market! It wasn't fair!

Raven added, "Jonah, Payton's and mine one hundredth and ninth year anniversary is this week."

"You amaze me. Most people can't hold a relationship together one year let alone well over a century, and you do it with two men, mind you. Just think Raven, if we could be on one of those daytime talk shows you could tell your story to the world. Of course, we'd all be slaughtered shortly after, but you'd have your fifteen minutes of fame for what it's worth."

"Sounds more like trash telly where they all go about claiming someone else is the baby's dada. Repugnant truly, that phrase."

Raven's brilliant grin faded before Serina's eyes. Irritated now, the few wrinkles Serina owned were cast in stone. "You'd think by now public opinion would have changed about us."

"Serrie, give it up. Vamps are the scum of the earth. I heard there is to be another godforsaken reality show featuring the hunts and kills of anything non-human. There are way too many fanatics running the streets starting wars, both vamps and vigilantes. Hollywood and science have taken art imitating life well past the point of ridiculous. Our little family is going to have to be flawless or else…" Raven dragged her finger across her throat. "Hey speaking of our little family, when is Savanah due home?"

"Right about the time I'm due. Thank the Goddess she's finally out of that dreadful relationship with that antique of a thing. He always smelled like mothballs." Just the thought of the bony man made Serina cringe. *Odd couple?* She believed Savanah and the crypt keeper—his not-so-affectionate nickname—made Bill and Hillary look like Ozzie and Harriet.

"Raven, your cell's about to chirp. It's Savanah. Her ears must be ringing."

"I hate it when you and Jovan do that. It takes away the mystery." Raven gave her sister-in-law the evil eye and flipped open her pretty pink phone. Before she got it to her ear Savanah's voice hit the airways.

"Hey, you two, you talking nice about me?"

"Savvy?" Raven glanced at Serina. "You were right."

Serina winked. "Am I ever wrong?"

Raven shoved Serina off balance in a playful gesture as she spoke to her niece. "Where are you?"

"London for the next few hours then Jules and I are headed to Cairo on the red-eye. We're on to a few leads about some vampire's artifacts."

"Peanut, I think each one of us is old enough to qualify as an artifact. You could put your entire family on display. When will you be home?"

9

"Definitely could put *you* on display, Aunt Ray," Savanah teased. "This summer. Come see me. You have no excuses."

"Other than I hate flying. And your Aunt Serina gets seasick with just the mention of getting on the raft in the pool. And since neither one of us mastered time travel or evanescing, we're stuck on this side of the pond. Don't get mad at us."

"I'm not. I just miss everyone. A girl gets lonely. My parents are coming over soon."

"Have you met anyone worthy of bringing home yet?"

"Give Auntie Serina a giant hug. Love you guys."

The line went dead. Raven glanced at Serina. "You heard her. And she evaded my last question. Rudely." Raven shoved her phone back into her black, patent leather abyss. "This summer! That's a lifetime from now."

"Definitely one life!" Serina rubbed her belly. The one hundred year childless hex her mother condemned her to had finally ended! With one helluva good bang.

Standing with her back against the wall, Serina waited for Raven to make it through checkout. She watched as a man hidden behind dark sunglasses and a red baseball cap sporting the 2004 World Series Baseball team, shove people out of his way, all most tripping over Serina's feet in his wake. He was on the heels of a pretty woman with long dark hair; following her obscenely close out the door. If the woman put on her brakes she and the gentleman were going to need formal introductions of sorts after being removed from her delicate derriere. Serina did a double take thinking the woman was Raven, she resembled her that much.

"Serrie, I'm sorry. Oh my God! Some guy just grabbed me from behind, swung me around and kissed me like I haven't been kissed in a long time. After an awkward minute of swapping spit he licked his lips, then apologized. He said he had the wrong woman. Whew! Sweet!" Raven readjusted all her bags under her arms and blurted out, "Do you remember the guard at the manor that always spied on us just before André almost got crowned king?"

"It wasn't us he watched. It was all you, dear." Amazing how one hundred nine years had flown by in the blink of an eye.

"Remember Donovan?"

Serina nodded. "Hard not to. He had the dark hair with mysterious olive eyes and a tight tush. I'll bet Payton and Jonah remember him as well, although, not as fondly." Serina nudged Raven's arm.

Raven grunted. "Anyway, that guy reminded me of him. My tummy's rolling. I'm famished, and yes, I mean that. I brought a few spare pouches of type O neg. They're in the limo, on ice."

****

As she stared out the window of their limo, Raven frowned. Once she gathered her courage, she confessed, "I bit him you know, Donovan." The weight of Serina's gaze crushed her. "Desperation took over one night, and he was there."

Serina's voice cracked. "I'm listening."

Raven readjusted herself in the seat to face Serina. She took in a large breath and released it slowly. "It was fantastic, Serrie. I remember it as if it were yesterday." Raven touched her lips. "We ended up naked so fast." Raven searched Serina's face. Not even a twitch. "Well are you going to say anything?"

"Raven, you're an adult. You're not married, although it seems like it even if it is to two men. You explored other avenues of your life. There's nothing wrong with that, and the fact that it only happened once—"

"Higher," Raven cut her off.

"Two?"

Raven's fingers pointed upward. "Keep going."

"Twenty?"

A cacophonous grunt echoed through the car. "It happened four times. God help me, I couldn't say no to him. I didn't want to."

"You had sex four times or bit Donovan four times?"

"Both."

Serina rubbed her jaw. "I'm not certain I want the answer, but is the man who just had his tongue down your throat Donovan?"

Raven closed her eyes in hopes to hold back the tears. It never worked. She blindly reached for a box of tissues in the console, her hand grasping at air.

Serina jammed a wad of tissues between her fingers. "Oh, Raven!" Serina cajoled, "We have to find him. You're his bloodline. You sired him."

"Serrie, I'm pretty sure when he's ready, he'll find me."

"What do you mean?"

Raven dabbed at her nose and eyes and then pulled the sweater just below her collarbone. "He nipped me in the store." Ashamed, she turned abruptly back to the window and watched people along the sidewalk meld into one long stream of legs, heads and torsos as the limo sped up. "What have I done?"

Serina laid her hand on her sister-in-law's shoulder. Trying to lighten her mood, she asked, "Tell me he wasn't the one with the Red cap on sporting little red socks?"

Raven wiped her eyes and attempted a grin. "You and your Yankees."

Chapter Two

June 6
The House that Ruth Built, New York, N.Y.

Lucian St. James hesitated purposely, as he produced his best sexy smirk, which worked like a charm every time. "Who do you think will win today, M'sexy lady? The team that *finally* broke the curse after seventy-six years or the not-so-evil empire?" He egged her on as he led Serina to her seat behind home plate.

"You're not the least bit funny, St. James."

"Luce, you can't say stuff like that to her. She'll get mad and try to juju ya, and we all know how well that goes—or doesn't!" Payton whispered as he, Raven and Jonah settled into their seats beside them.

Lucian's eyes went wide. He put a silencing finger to Payton then wrapped his arms around his wife and pulled her to him. As he slid his hands over her ripe abdomen, her stomach went rock hard and then relaxed. One minute later the same thing happened, each time his wife's face reddened. Concern crept in.

"Serina? What is that?"

"Braxton-Hicks contractions. Been getting the annoying things on and off for the past few days."

"You're certain that's all they are? Not the real ones?" Lucian asked.

"No worries. These have no rhyme or reason. And

we're still a few weeks out. M'lord, the baby wants a hotdog with the works, a pretzel slathered with cheese and some water. Ooh, and some cotton candy. I'll lick your sticky fingers after we're done." Serina lifted her eyebrow in a non-prim, non-proper fashion.

"Would you stop all ready?" Raven teased. "Dear God, woman, you're pregnant, act like it!"

A wave of scorching heat blazed a trail to Lucian's groin with the mere thought of his wife's lush lips anywhere on his body. Nine innings suddenly seemed a little too much like eternity and although he had eternity on his side, he didn't feel like waiting to get steamy and naked with his wife. His very beautiful, very pregnant wife. The same little devil that put a restraining order on their conjugal visits until their wee one made her grand entrance into the world. Serina worried he'd poke her head with his penis. Yes, that comment did wonders for his ego.

A mere two strikes away from the seventh inning stretch, Serina stood in her chair and screamed at the home-plate ump for a bad call against the newest member of the team, number eighteen. She didn't have to like him in pinstripes, but if she rooted against him? She couldn't go there. Superstitions were like bad hair days; you had no idea when they'd pop in to haunt you. "Come on eighteen. *You can do it*." Serina yelled trying to sound just like one of the characters in the movie, *The Water Boy*.

"Ah, so you do like *número* eighteen."

Serina bit her cheeks before spewing, "That's blasphemous." She stuffed her last bit of her pretzel into her mouth and then licked her fingers clean.

"It is not, M'lady. You like him. Admit it."

"No—I do not. He's a transplant a—a—a spy from another team," she spewed flustered.

"I agree," Jonah added.

"So what if he looks awesome in pinstripes." That last part she mumbled as she smacked her lips together.

"I agree," Raven tossed in. "Love a man in uniform!"

"I do believe this is a case where the lady doth protest too much. He's a great player. He was great when he played for Boston. He's just better now that we have him on our side. Face it, luv, you'd even like a few of the other players on Boston if they were in stripes, specially the one with dreds."

Serina laughed as Lucian jerked back away from her just in case she swung at him with the pink, fluffy ball of fairy floss. *Like I'd waste this scrumptious little confection on him...*

"Jail-bird stripes." Serina never turned to see her husband's reaction.

With the next pitch careening backward toward her, Serina waited with the patience of a lizard, his tongue ready to snag the first bug that buzzed him. Net or no net between she and the players that foul ball had her name on it. Out of seven innings this was the closest a ball had come. Nor was she waiting for Skippy, the ball boy, to bring it to her. Seemed his interests were well occupied with all the pretty young things who weren't bursting at the seams with child. Serina jumped non-to-eloquently as only someone eight and half months pregnant could do, over the sidewall and proceeded to waddle as fast as her puffy little feet could carry her.

"Doc, stop!" Payton yelled, his amber eyes ready

to spark. He turned to Lucian. "She's your wife, get her off the field before we have to go bail her out."

Serina took chase after the ball where she found— she too was being hunted down by security. She stopped, picked up the ball—triumph plastered on her face in the form of a giant smile as the guard closed in on her, then changed her smile to a frown, dropped the ball, grabbed her stomach, and looked down at her feet to see a flood of water spilling from her body. Her new comfy shoes that expanded to accommodate her swollen tootsies were now soaked in amniotic fluid.

"Oh my God, Lucian!" Serina yelled, with a protective hold on her abdomen. "It's not what you think," she shouted to the guard. Fear swiftly replaced embarrassment. "Lucian!"

Lucian got on the field before she finished screaming his name a third time. He approached the camera operators and asked them, "Please stop filming my wife. Doesn't the team have a policy of not filming crazy pregnant ladies jumping on fields?" To no one in particular he mumbled, "One hundred years of keeping our identity a secret—blown in a New York minute and on national television to boot. *Fuck!!!* I can say that coz they're only bleeding gonna bleep it anyway."

"Lucian." Serina panted. "We're about to have our baby."

"So it appears, my wild rose. So, Doc…Braxton Hicks or the real thing?" Lucian shook his head. Once beside her, he lifted her into his arms.

"Ouch! Oh, Lucian, put me back down," Serina whaled. "I think the baby's got other plans on where she wants to be born. Ah-hoo-ah-hoo…" She practiced her Lamaze breathing.

"Oh not here, Serina. I knew you wanted to meet your number two, but this?" Lucian gave himself the hand-to-the-forehead slap.

Just then, as if hearing his name, the team's illustrious captain and a few other team-mates came out of the dugout to see what the hold-up on the field was about. Serina shrugged her shoulders and gave a little waggle of her hand to them. It was all she had.

"Ah, just a pregnant lady behind home plate delivering a baby," One of the players yelled into the dugout.

Her knees buckled. Lucian caught her before she hit the ground. Was it seeing her all-time favorite baseball player this close up or the ensuing baby? That little devil Mr. "J" probably had women swooning at his feet on a daily basis.

Out of every scenario Serina had ever played in her head on how to meet the man…this so wasn't it—breathing heavily, sweaty, and soaked from the waist down. That was supposed to happen *after* she'd met him! With her dignity barely intact, she managed to squeak out a tight-lipped grin in his general direction. That grin flew out of the ballpark with the next contraction.

"The baby's head is coming—*now!*" Serina panted. She heard people in the stands chanting, "*You can do it*," and if she weren't so scared or embarrassed she'd have laughed, but right now…laughing wasn't an option. Pain medication… *Now that would have been a beautiful thing*, she thought, *if only it worked on vampiric witches.*

On the ground, surrounded by news cameras fighting for every angle of the lens they could get,

Serina pushed, regardless of the stadium filled to capacity of people watching her deliver her child, as others watched from the comfort of their own homes. Lights, camera, action! The first thing to come out of her was a brown torpedo.

Her dignity was no more.

She did not just go pooh.

She'd always laughed when she heard of other women telling of their delivery stories. Funny thing, she wasn't laughing now. Lucian was though! Until her fingers tangled in his hair and she jerked his face to within inches of hers.

"I didn't see a thing," he said, hidden behind a smirk.

When she doubled over with the next contraction and the baby's head came out, he lost the smirk. Lucian sat with his wife between his legs and stroked her face. At the first sight of his daughter, tears flooded him while the team's sports doctor delivered the wee one. Lucian gazed into Serina's eyes and in that moment in time, he saw the most beautiful, ethereal vision—his wife and daughter laying there both smiling up at him. He bent over, his lips on his wife's forehead, the happiest man alive.

Sex!

The thought slammed him over the head just as his wife would soon enough for even daring to think such thoughts. He couldn't help it. He looked around in search of someone wielding a baseball bat. *The entire team. Shit. Alibis for them all.* The smirk resurfaced.

He was about to get his sex life back. This day couldn't get any better from his point of view. Suddenly Lucian understood a shopaholic's euphoria wandering into a dollar store loaded with singles.

Typical male. Serina sent her husband that thought.

Lucian wiped a few stray strands of hair from his wife's face. "Pretty lady, there is nothing typical about me. She's perfect. Thank you for such a gift." Lucian kissed Serina's lips with every ounce of love he could pour into it. He made love to her with that one kiss in front of the world, with no one the wiser, except for every bleeding heart, romantic out there. Passion burned in his eyes. He pulled away from Serina and kissed the tip of her nose. "M'lady, *je t`aime tant.*"

Serina mouthed the words, "I love you too," back to him as she wiped the tears from his cheeks.

****

"Oh Maestro, I'll give you one guess what just came across the telly." Xanti Sinclair skipped across the penthouse from the television to the window, to glance at the statue of Eros in Piccadilly Circus. Finally, he'd found them again. And where Lucian St. James could be found his twin sister, Raven, was sure to follow.

"The supreme court finally got the wording, *IN GOD WE TRUST,* out of our lives forever?" The older man with a neatly trimmed salt-n-pepper beard asked as he slurped at some fluid stuck to his lips.

"Not yet, but think back to a time before cars, before cell phones, computers… Hell before most of the fodder about us had electricity. Remember any one family disappearing into the night?"

The Maestro dipped his head between the thighs of a woman spread out on a table and dragged his tongue down the inside of her smooth, curvy leg. The closer he moved toward her more delicate parts, his two inch ivory posts descended. He'd worked up an insatiable appetite and wanted dessert. He'd given her, her treat, now it was time for his. Completely engrossed in what lay before him, it took a minute to register what Xanti said. Xier looked up. "You've my complete attention, son."

"A birth marking of nobility has appeared on the big screen," Xanti chirped.

"Lucian St. James and Serina are still of this world? Or is it André and Jovan? And in the name of all unholy things, how did those two men end up marrying two of the most powerful bloodlines of witches? That's beside the point, what do you know?"

"You knew they're half-sisters, didn't you? They share the same father. Anyway, Serina just birthed a daughter for the world to see bearing the royal mark along with her royal fluff."

"Are you positive?"

"I'm not stupid, Father. I know fluff when I see it." Xanti pointed to the woman on the table and watched his father's black eyes glisten. "I would stake my heart on it, Sir."

"Trust me, if you had one, I'd have done it long ago," The Maestro remarked coldly as he fondled the woman's private lips, and she squirmed with delirium.

"I've more news. Father, can you feel the vibrations in the air this eve? A ripple of powers to be?"

"Explain yourself, Xanti. Do not tell me the St. James clan will regain power after this long abstinence."

"He is born today. Xavier's and my son has been born today as well."

"Oh this is delicious." The Maestro shook his head back and forth with his face buried in the woman's minge. When the words registered he asked, "What the hell are you speaking about, Xanti? Who else was born?"

"What is the date? Three sixes hold this day. I personally saw to it Xavier's and my son would be born to Raven St. James today. The birth date of our lord and master."

"How, Xanti? Your brother has been gone over a century."

"Xavier and I shared a woman, the day before his untimely execution. We bed her then I cleaned her insides out afterwards. I stuck all contents in the icebox including our semen and the rest is history."

"Xanti," Xier skeptically asked again, "how do you know Raven St. James bares your child?"

"I found her in Boston shopping, drugged her so she'd have no memory of me and implanted Xavier's seed into her, along with mine."

"So, let me get this straight, Xanti. First you evacuated the seed from a woman you and your brother fucked eons past, froze the contents, and then you drugged the illusive Raven St. James, and you of all people, had sex with her and implanted Xavier's sperm inside her too? You—a son? I'll be damned. Well, actually, I suppose I already am, but I always considered you a poofer. Humph! And you're positive beyond a doubt that it was the St. James wench? Did she wear the royal birthmark as well?"

"For the record, I said I implanted the seed. I wasn't able to see her clearly, due to the dark hour. She had some celestial splat of ink. But it had to have been her."

"So chances are good that you bed a woman with a

tattoo, impregnated her with rotten seed, yours, and now my grandchild is out there somewhere in the world alone."

A silver cleaver whizzed past Xanti's head.

"I will be on a flight as soon as possible to end this. I will bring respect to you."

"Or I'll stake you, Xanti. You'll beg me to really kill you. Take Ethan with you."

"Not the wolf, Maestro. He treats me like a child."

"If the shoe fits Xanti…" Hearing the door open, Xier turned. "Speak of my devil in disguise.

Ethan Kitt sauntered into the spacious fifteen-room flat, picked up one leg, yanked off one foul, worn-out sneaker, chucked it across the room into a basket and then did the same with his other and headed straight for the fridge. Hungry? He lost hungry about ten miles back. He'd hit stage four. Not good. Stage three was bad enough if he hadn't eaten but anything beyond this and he got ugly. A fifteen-mile trek, being chased by the cops didn't seem fair, especially when he traveled the heel-toe-express route and the cops followed in a car, but he lost them. Passing his boss, he gave him a high-five. "Nice catch, Boss," he said without thinking twice as he passed the buffet on the table. The woman was an appetizer, dinner and dessert all wrapped up in one.

"Did you get it, Ethan?" Xier asked his hand outstretched, waiting.

"Sorry to say, Sir, no. Someone beat you to your treasured tome again." Ethan took one look at Xanti and choked back laughter. "Oh Christ," he said as he played with the blond bristles covering his chin. He opened the fridge and grabbed the leftovers of a sub he'd started for breakfast. His mouth full, he almost lost it looking at Xanti.

The son of one the most powerful vamps in Europe stood slouched in a ten-gallon hat, leather chaps covering his designer jeans. Today's florescent pink T-shirt pick read, *It's Better To Be Thought Of As A Fool, Than To Speak, And Remove All Doubt*. Either way, Ethan knew there was no mistake; Xanti owned the title of village pilchard.

The vamp even told Ethan he wanted his fangs capped in gold and that he'd found a dentist to do it. He'd told Ethan when he smiled, he wanted people to think of… Ethan had knocked him out cold and walked away before he sullied one of his favorite pirate's reputations.

"Howdy, Hoss." Ethan scratched his nose with his middle finger as he passed Xanti.

"Do you see what I mean, Maestro?" Xanti whined. "I don't want him to go to the States with me. I am capable of going alone."

"You're not capable of going to the bathroom alone!" Ethan blurted. He turned his attentions to the Maestro. "So where we going and why, Maestro?"

"New York, Ethan. It appears I am a grandfather." The Maestro shot a cross glare at Xanti.

Ethan looked at Xanti in a whole new light. "I didn't think you had it in you."

"Ethan!"

The Maestro's voice startled him.

"What?" Ethan asked holding back laughter.

The Maestro raised his voice one more octave. "Bring my grandson home. I want to raise him."

Ethan's lips twisted. *No babies, nope I didn't sign*

up for babysitting. Or kidnapping. Then out of the blue that random dream he'd had a few months back whacked him over the head. Tall, sultry creature with giant blue eyes left him dazzled. *Why couldn't we have been having sex instead of putting a bassinette together?* Could this lead him to her? "What about the mother?"

The Maestro turned his black eyes on Ethan and gave a subliminal suggestion using his voice and eye contact. *"You're a persuasive man, Ethan. You know what women want, and you know how to get it, unlike Hoss."*

"Father!" Xanti squealed.

Xier lifted a hand to his son that said, "Shut up," without words. He turned to Ethan. *"Use your charms, but don't come home without a baby.* Your money is in the account, and I believe your plane, you left at JFK Airport on your last jaunt."

"Come on, Xanti. I'll let you pack my bags." Ethan swiped the younger vamp's hat and headed back to the fridge, laughing.

****

In London, André St. James sat glued to his telly, his eyes widening by the second as he watched the day's highlights of the baseball games state-side, only baseball wasn't what came across the screen. The number one pick revealed his niece making her grand entrance into the world and his sister-in-law leaving nothing to the imagination about the birds and the bees and the end results.

"Jovan? Oh, Auntie Jovan?" André yelled with a lilt in his voice to his wife.

Jovan sauntered into their den wearing only long

blonde soaking wet curls. Most of her soft sensual curves were covered by the sun-kissed tendrils. Lady Godiva didn't look this freaking hot.

"This better be worth it. We're running late *mon mari*. And Savanah and Julian will be home any second." Jovan gave André a devilish grin that reeked of sex as she did a slow spin showing off her backside.

"*Cherié*, that was a cheeky shot, literally. We'll be running even later if you don't get dressed. Before I lose myself in you, look at the telly." He handed her a robe to cover up all the distracting areas her scrumptious body offered. And with her abdomen ripe with his child, her breasts full, firm and in his face, there was no better aphrodisiac.

Not a second after he wrapped Jovan up, Savanah and Julian raced in, spilling packages into an already crowded room of suitcases and travel bags.

"Did you hear the news or has anyone called?" Savanah asked breathless. "We caught it at the pub. Isn't it wonderful?"

Jovan put her index finger to Savanah's lips. "Shush, Peanut. Look someone just delivered a baby at a baseball stadium. How sweet."

"As I tried to say, Mum—"

Jovan clamped her hand over her daughter's mouth. Her face inches from the television, Jovan backed up a step. "Cripes, could they have gotten any bloody closer with the zoom lens?"

"Jovan, look closer." André tapped on the screen.

"Close enough, thanks." Jovan noticed her husband wipe his eyes and shake his head. "What?" She asked. "André, are those tears?"

"Oh, *mon amour,* anyone look vaguely familiar?"

"Sort of looks like—oh—my—Goddess—Lucian and is that—Serina?" Jovan swung around fast, her wet hair whipping her husband in his face. "I'm an aunt! You're an uncle!" Tears fell faster than spilled milk. She yelled, "Savanah, you've a cousin." Then she began to laugh. "Serina's going to be upset when she sees this and the extra ten pounds the telly added to her bum. She'll be more upset she didn't have a shave before going to the game."

Julian tossed in, "Please tell me that's a Tootsie Roll next to them on the ground."

"Jules! Mum! You're both so bad! I'll call home and check on everyone." Savanah headed for the phone.

"Hey, hold up! Is everyone packed and ready for the flight home? Passports? All those measly little bottles, pygmies would die for, all set to go? You know, three ounces or less, locked away in quart-sized plastic zip-up bags, so we can board our plane without getting yanked out of line? Stripped naked? I wouldn't mind seeing you naked again." André pinched Jovan's butt as she passed him.

"You had your chance, Mister." Jovan bared her teeth.

Savanah enjoyed the antics between her parents. Their love for each other never faltered, in fact, it only strengthened each day. Oh, how she wanted to find love like theirs. Her face twisted. *One-hundred-thirteen-years-old and not even a bloody boyfriend.* "If, the airlines so much as lose one item I've packed, Papa, I'm turning them all into hotdogs and setting them in front of *Takeru Kobayashi*. Mum? Don't pack your blow-dryer 'til the very last sec. Jules, same goes for my transcripts. I've got some work to do on the flight."

"You mean this one?" Jovan wiggled the red dryer in her face. "I thought you bought a romance book yesterday to read on the plane." Jovan paid her no heed and packed the blow dryer right under her little nose.

"Mum!" Savanah yanked the life-saving device out of her suitcase. "That wasn't funny. I can't walk out of here with my hair wet. God forbid it's humid. My hair alone will take up more space than your belly." Savanah ducked as her mother tried to swat her. "I packed that book. A person could die of a broken heart reading the first chapter. I'm already in a mood."

"That you are." André grabbed Savanah's hand. "Come on, we've got a few hours to kill before we head to Heathrow. Let's get some air, and we'll bring your Mum home some chips."

"You brown-noser," Savanah teased.

"Savanah, at one-hundred-thirty-four years of age, I've learned how to stay on top of your mother and her moods."

"That's more than obvious, Pops." Savanah giggled when his hand connected to her backside.

****

At a brisk pace, André and Savanah kept up with the hustle and bustle of the crowded walkways along King Charles Street, Parliament Street and before they realized it, they'd landed on Victoria Street in front of Westminster Abbey and just like the surround-sound of a theatre, clicking sounds amplified the airway as cameras flashed and tourists took their memories home with them.

"No matter how many times I see this place, it awes me."

"Me too, Papa. Are you sad that you were never

crowned king?"

"No. Are you? You'd have made such a generous queen, Savanah, so beautifully loyal to those you love. Some days regrets fill me, never for me, but for you. My selfishness took that option from you before you even understood what it meant."

"Papa, your sacrifice kept Uncle Lucian, Aunt Serina and Aunt Raven safe. I hold the greatest respect for your choice. It must have been difficult to turn down such an offer from Queen Mattie in her time of need. She was beside herself after the fiasco the night they tried to stone Aunt Serina. Thank Goddess Aunt Serina's mother turned back the sands of time to save her daughters and find Devona."

"Pregnant, let's not forget, by a vamp. 'Tis such a shame the baby was kidnapped and never found. And please, Savanah, never mention that woman's name again. She cursed us for a century. No children. What type of hag does that?"

She squeezed her father's hand and dragged him toward the church. "She's got issues. Come on, Papa. 'Tis been so long, since you and I were here together."

Inside the Abbey, history closed in around Savanah like a dried up flower stuck between the pages of a diary. Surrounded by family and friends forever encased in different tombs, she found it hard to breathe, but as they passed through the Chapter House, to the centre room where the coronation throne sat she took a moment to enjoy the phenomenal craftsmanship of the stained glass windows. Each so different. Each a window to someone's soul.

Eyeing the renowned chair as they entered the abbey, Savanah lost her brilliant grin. It reminded her more of the electric chair. It would have been, had her father been seated at it. She knew vampires couldn't run a country, although she'd heard rumors France did just that around Louis XIV's time. Various stories surfaced that the Sun King proclaimed himself that to cast off suspicions of his family and their nocturnal, carnivorous habits.

And in her courtyard sat King George III with his porphyria and links to vampirism, so who was she to throw stones?

"Do you still have the tiara your uncle Jonah gave you when you were little?"

Savanah's smile hinted of devilishness. "Last time I saw it, one of my porcelain dolls wore it. I'm not much into the beauty queen routine anyway, and I've no need for it. I meant what I said—no regrets."

"You are my little queen, Savanah." He ruffled her hair. "There were days when I could have crowned you myself."

"Papa, you've never been upset with me a day in your life."

"That, little girl, is because you always flashed me with that damned light trick you and your mum do. I never stood a chance."

"Just so you're aware, you still don't." The smile she flashed could've won her the beauty queen pageant. Savanah stood to offer her father a hand up. Behind her, a hand tapped her shoulder. Her shrill screech ended the silence in the church. In an instant, she had become the object to gawk at by other tourists.

Savanah turned and ended up face to face with the one person she wanted vanquished from this atmosphere. Mr. Pinky finger in the flesh. Behind her now, André placed his hands firmly atop her shoulders for support.

"Hello, Savanah. I hear you're leaving soon for America. I'd hoped we could talk before you left."

Stringy blond hair, sunken eyes with no lashes and more cartilage than skin on his nose and no firm ass—hell no ass period, Savanah wanted to kick her own for actually dating this pencil dick. "How in bloody hell did you know we were here?" She backed up into her father's arms.

"I hate to admit it, but I followed you."

"Oh, so now you're stalking my daughter? Didn't we put a restraining order against you? Nowhere near her up to five hundred ridiculous meters or something? I suggest, Radcliff, you scurry your bony ass out of here before the ceiling comes down atop of you, or I do."

"Ah, the doting papa." Radcliff pointed between the two of them. "Isn't it funny you two look more like siblings than father and daughter?" The frail man scoffed.

"What do you want?" Savanah chided.

"Just keep in mind I want recognition in your display come opening day."

"You bastard. You did nothing to deserve it. Uncle Julian and I did all the work, the research, the hunts, everything. The only thing you did was plant your DNA into my mummy—and I don't mean mother!" Savanah balled her fists into knots, ready to take a swing at him if he got any closer.

"Savanah, Lord St. James, I've kept my mouth shut about your family secrets, including Uncle Julian's once a month fur coat and Lord Lucian's disappearing acts. I'll have my name on the credits come opening day or your family will be plastered on the front page of every tabloid."

André grabbed Radcliff's shirt collar in a fitted rage. "I'll plaster your emaciated excuse of a body across the rails and watch with a smile on my face as the trains roll over you again and again, severing you into tidbits for the stray dogs to scarf up."

Radcliff jerked out of André's clutch. "No *Princess*!" He enunciated her title slowly, as he bowed. "That's but a warning. You'll meet the real bastard if my name doesn't appear anywhere in the credits. I better get a piece of that display." And with that, he squared his shoulders, turned, and ran. All that was missing was the tail between his legs.

Eyes wide, Savanah turned to André. "Papa?"

"Let me take care of him."

"Can we leave? I can't wait to get out of here and get home and see the new baby." *And get the hell away from that moron.*

About to step into the tube, André warned, "Mind the gap."

No matter how many times she'd heard the phrase, it made her smile, and she did as asked. She peeked down watching her footing for the gap between the car and the railway tracks.

****

The engine's deafening roar came to an abrupt halt when the tires touched down on the tarmac. The 747 bounced twice, leaning left and then right before its balance was regained and it taxied back to the gate. The bottle of water Ethan had to his lips jammed into his frenulum with the jerky landing. It broke open the tender skin between his upper teeth and lip. The backwashed water in the bottle turned pink. Cursing under his breath and impatient, he waited for the light above him to flash saying it was okay to move around the cabin. Looking ahead at the bathroom/closet, Ethan tried to decide if he wanted to subject himself to the aromas and the claustrophobic anxiety he knew he'd get if he didn't have someone in there to distract him. Nature called regardless of what he did or didn't want. He made his way up the isle and stood outside the door. As he waited for the next available closet to open, Ethan eyed a blonde woman headed in the same direction. *Ah, company after all! Gorgeous. Long legs, tiny ass, b-e-l-l-y! Baby on board.* "Hello pretty, Momma!" Ethan purred in the tall blonde's direction, regardless of her maternal condition.

"Move your arrogant *arse*." Jovan covered her mouth as she shoved past him in a rush.

Ethan scratched his head. "I got here first." He smiled until he saw the woman gagging and then the loud wet belch a second before…

Jovan vomited down the front of Ethan.

"What the f—why?"

"I said move." Jovan offered no apology, shoved past him and closed the door in his face.

****

"Ouch!" Savanah yelled hopping on one foot.

A bottle of ginger ale in hand for his wife, André asked, "What is it, Peanut?"

"Some guy just drove over my toes with his carry-on." In the never-ending custom's line, she noticed a blond man with a cute tight butt that filled his jeans out nicely. He was tall enough for her liking and in a major huff to get through customs. Savanah noticed she wasn't the only one he bounced off as he budged the lines.

"Hey!" She yelled, her temper ruffled, "Watch where you're bloody going."

Ethan turned to face the music and the moment he did his eyes were drawn like iron to a magnet to a tall woman in a baseball cap with thick pig tails sticking out of each side of her head. Dark sunglasses rested high on her cheekbones. Looking at her from head to toe he wondered where she got the money to purchase her clothing let alone a plane ticket. Her jeans had to have been a religious relic, holier than thou. Both her knees peeped through, and all the way down the length of her long slender legs, more holes than material were noted. Her flip-flops weren't designer's, but he did notice her manicured, hot, neon-pink toenails. Hard not too. *High maintenance.* Maintenance he decided he wouldn't mind maintaining. Her T-shirt fit snuggly, sporting his team's arch rival, *The Evil Empire*, along with two *lick-your-lips*, sensuous mounds of flesh. *Opposites attract, right?* A second scan revealed she wore no rings on her delicate fingers. His eyebrows rose.

"Did you hear me?" Savanah raised her voice. "Watch where you bloody go, you giant bull."

"You watch where you bloody go, you giant cow," he mimicked in his British accent.

"That is by far the worst imitation of the British impersonation I've yet to withstand."

Beautiful or butt-ugly, he no longer cared. "Then don't talk to me." With a quick bow, he flipped her off, spun on his heels and got back in line.

"Tell me you didn't just do that!"

Ethan spun around and with a roguish grin saluted

her a second time. "This what you meant?" He headed back toward the customs gate.

That someone would treat her in such a manner—her blood roiled. *If he wasn't so rude or a giant moron… Oh, Savanah stop. You're desperate. Some bald clown with a giant, brilliant-red bulbous nose would probably look good right now. Or not.* Unwilling to give an inch, and having to get the last word, engraved into her very being, Savanah pressed through the lines of tightly woven people where she found no one willing to let another air bubble squeak by, let alone a body.

"Excuse me," came out countless times as she wormed her way to the front of the queue. "Please, that's my husband up there." She lied. Once behind him, she slapped his shoulder hard.

Startled, Ethan jumped. "Persistently pesky, aren't we? What now?" he asked. Seeing his reflection in a pair of black shades, he immediately began touching up his hair.

What made Savanah even crazier was when he pulled his lips back and started picking at his teeth as if she were a mirror put on this earth just for him. "Narcissus, some people never change," rolled from the tip of her tongue. "You're rude, arrogant, pushy, and it's more than obvious you don't care about anyone else."

"Then why the hell did you marry him?" Someone asked.

Ethan choked on laughter. "What?" he asked again.

This time Savanah noted a distinct edge of amusement with his sugar-coated tone.

She put a silencing finger up to the man's face

behind her and mouthed, "Shush!" Turning back to Ethan, she demanded, "I want an apology. You pummeled my toes and had no right flipping me off."

"I can see why he did it," Mr. Nosey, from behind, added his two cents.

In a heated tone, Ethan yelled, "Don't you talk to my wife like that," right before he grabbed her and pulled her close enough to whisper, "Who are you, woman? Go get back in line and get on the next flight back to jolly old England and see if it doesn't rub off on you this next trip. Want me to rub off on you? Put you in a better mood?"

Savanah went to put her finger in Ethan's face, only this time he caught her hand and held on. She fought back the only way she knew how; she sent him some burning, spine-tingling zingers that ripped down the length of his arm and back to his heart.

"Holy shit, Pippy, are you trying to give me a heart attack?"

Savanah cracked up laughing. "Pippy?"

"Longstocking? Look at you, woman. Take those glasses off. Great team you've got there." Ethan pointed to her T-shirt.

Savanah smirked. "You're a Yankee's fan?" Maybe there was hope for him after all.

"I wasn't referring to the shirt, Pip. Little deeper than that." Ethan eyeballed her breasts with a hungry expression. "Boston, baby, all the way to the World Series—again."

"Want to wager my team can knock your balls out of the park?" Savanah glanced to his loins. She laughed as Ethan cocked his head to the side following her gaze.

"*Touché*, Pip." Ethan licked his index finger and

gestured one point for her.

"Hey, newlyweds, the lines moving. I'd like to get out of this place today?" The voice from reason yelled.

Both Savanah and Ethan turned, and at the same time yelled, "Shut up." Then they looked at each other a bit stunned.

"I've got to go. You owe me an—"

"I'm sorry," Ethan offered. "Want me to kiss them better?"

"You should be. You needn't bother kiss my toes, but my a—?" Savanah turned away from Ethan and tapped her hand to her bottom, wearing a smile fit for the queen she should've been. With a delicate sway to her hips she walked back to her family.

He stood there both dumbfounded and mesmerized, his gaze glued to her sweet little *derriere*. *Oh, kiss it I shall, Pippy.*

Chapter Three

Going through customs Ethan chuckled. "Do you have anything to declare?" the customs officers would ask him as they did every other person.

No, today he declared nothing.

So what if it was a slight white lie? The two caskets were loaded onto his 750 Cessna CJ1+ plane. Ethan ogled over his plane. He loved it more than anything in his life. Materialistic? Him? Yeah, but it was all he had. The plane was his ticket to freedom whenever, wherever he wanted to go. It was his escape from reality and his reality over the past few years had taken a ride on the wild side.

After he'd made contact with the tower for clearance, settled into his cockpit, gripped his joystick (the actual controls), he hit the runway. Destination, Saratoga County Airport.

Ethan was on a mission. Not from God, but the exact opposite. But who was Ethan to complain? He was getting paid generously to do what he loved, to fly and along his journeys meet a few women, like the one he'd just met. Shame, he thought. *If I'd met her on the plane, we could have had some fun in the bathroom. Sure as hell would've beat getting puked on by the other lady.*

He loved women and women loved pilots. Synchronicity! A match made in heaven, or damn close.

He'd been told his light green eyes illuminated his face, but he always thought they were his second best feature. His first? The girls loved the one and only tattoo he owned.

Painted on the head of his penis, sat a hot air balloon that inflated, filled out rather nicely, he thought, and lifted up high to the heavens when the occasion rose. It hurt like hell when he had it put on, but the rewards after… The tattoo artist had kissed it better.

****

With his tiny bundle in his arms, Lucian looked toward the hospital room's door when it swung inward. Duncan Thomas peeked into the room. Lucian gave him a nod. Duncan was his best mate and as close as a brother.

Duncan glanced at Serina. "Out cold?"

"She's earned her sleep. A natural delivery with no medicine—ouch!"

Duncan tapped Lucian's shoulder. "How's it feel, Luce? Isn't it the most wonderful feeling holding your baby? Look how she watches you with those dreamy oceans of blue. She recognizes you all ready."

"Well I hope so. I've spoken, sang and read to her every night since I found out we carried her. It's been so long, Duncan since I've held a child in my arms. Sydney was three when we adopted her. This is so different. So wonderful. Look at my wife, old man. Is she or isn't she simply the most beautiful creature alive and to give me this gift." Lucian turned away from Duncan, tears filling his eyes.

"You're as bad as my wife, Luce. Don't turn away on me. I've waited a lifetime to see this look on your face, and I want to cherish it. And I want to see it in about thirteen years when you've gone gray because that little lady is plucking away at your last nerve like you're her personal fiddle."

Lucian snorted. "Where's Molly? Let me have this moment with my baby before we have her all grown and boys chasing her. God help them, Duncan. I'll bite them all to keep track of them. Can I do that?" Lucian's eyes smoldered at the idea of boys going anywhere near his daughter.

"And not get staked? Think not. Idle threats work though. You're big enough and intimidating enough to keep the boys at bay. And if all else fails introduce them to Julian. Molly's in Saratoga or did you forget you called me just as we arrived there today? She's getting the house ready for everyone's arrival home and picking everyone up at the airport pretty soon. I hate to change the mood, but have you done anything about the blood tests for Elyza and your wife? You know the risks we take being here."

Lucian kissed Elyza's forehead. "I love you, M'little lady." He kissed the baby again. "My dear friend, you doubt me? I evanesced, walked into a lab full of white coats, computers and worked my magic better than my wife could have. Don't tell her I said that though!"

Duncan laughed. "That's not hard to do. Serina messes up every spell she does!"

Lucian's eyes grew. "Shhhh! Don't let her hear that. There is no record of Elyza's genetic gifts. It's all good."

"Splendid." Duncan turned to Serina and gave her a light kiss on her forehead, to which she never stirred. "See you in the morning. Get some rest Luce, because once the bills catch up to the insurance you're gonna get bounced out of here and life as you know it, is over."

****

Upon arrival in Saratoga at his North Broadway residence, Ethan specked out the place, and made certain everything had been taken care of for his two companions before going to the carriage house. The Maestro told him there was a gift waiting. Inside, resting on an old-fashioned turnstile, once used for washing horses and carriages in the late nineteenth century, sat a sporty little convertible, two-door, black on black leather, six speed with a thank you note and a big blue bow. The card read, "No more running around town unless you take this. Xier." The car had two miles on it and a full tank of gas. As Ethan slid his hands over the paint job, his groin grew rock hard. Couldn't help it—guy-car thing. He loved his new car almost as much as his plane. He plunged his nose deep into the leather seats and inhaled that *new car smell.* For the briefest moment a giant moue worked its way onto his face. What if—once he found the Maestro's grandson, it had a leaky diaper or spit up on—or god forbid, inside his new car? His heart raced. What had he gotten himself into and why couldn't he just say no? No to the Maestro? Then he remembered who he was dealing with. A crazy man. No, a crazy vamp. One that had him strung up better than a puppeteer with his marionette playing a game of Twister. After he slipped behind the wheel of his car, he stroked the steering wheel. She needed to be treated with kid gloves, worked up to a slow pace then taken for the ride of her life. He pulled out of the driveway and trolled North Broadway, swerving to avoid potholes.

Saratoga had grown since he'd last been here. New buildings, homes and businesses seemed to have sprouted overnight better than Chia pets could grow green fuzz, but the town retained an attractive quaintness. The over-flowing flower baskets that hung from the old-fashioned streetlights and beds of colorful flowers that spilled out onto the sidewalks reminded him of home and his mother. A pang of longing struck a distant chord. Home was no longer where the heart was or a place for him to hang his baseball hat.

All along Broadway, musicians played their hearts out to couples hand in hand that strolled by. He actually thought he might like to settle here, but that would require a woman and he wasn't ready to commit to one woman yet, if ever… Unless Pippy became part of the package. Random, no ridiculous.

Shaking her long, leggy image from his thoughts, Ethan focused on finding a spot in the parking lot in between Lillian's and Professor Moriarity's. He scoped out the area. His new car had to be safe. He parked her in between a Mercedes and a Jaguar. Three times he went back to the lot to check on her before he actually made it inside and to the restaurant. The term OCD crossed his mind on more than one occasion, but he scoffed the phrase, telling himself. "I'm not obsessive or compulsive. Diseased definitely," he chided as he hopped over the cracks in the sidewalk and scooped up a head's-up penny.

The aromas from Lillian's Restaurant found Ethan's nose an easy target. He hungered for food and companionship, and at the same time, jet lag followed him better than his shadow. The stress from this job seemed to hover over him like a nasty case of herpes. Not that he knew what they were personally.

Kidnapper? Me? No way. The Maestro's bonkers. He tried to push aside his gut instincts that this was a *really stupid* idea. No, it was worse than stupid. Catastrophic worked. His little voice of reason told him a woman's flesh would sate his needs. Sex: his cure-all, tell-all, and end-all answer to every problem he ever had. And in some cases the beginning. He knew better than to listen to it, his little nagging voice of nonsense. Thinking back, his anniversary for turning into a werewolf happened just over two years ago. He'd met a little woman who stood all of five feet tall, dark brown hair and sky-blue eyes. Spry little creature, and she liked things rough. Ethan found out the hard way why. During the full moon she lost control, and shortly thereafter, her life. July of '04 was a bitch. Not once, but twice the blue moon initiated him with a vengeance, almost skinned him alive. Ethan tried very hard not to relive that, but…like a dog with his bone, the more he tried to bury the hurtful memories, the more they resurfaced. No family. Nothing to lose. Except himself. Hearing his father, his best friend, mentor, example of a man who lived for his family say to the doctor, "Then pull the plug and be done with this," came very close to really killing him. Ethan met Xier the same day. It was his fate so it seemed.

What Ethan needed was a woman who could take the proverbial licking and keep on ticking. Then his head, the one that wasn't visible, wondered, *Where's Pippy? I could lick her all right and make her tick.* He groaned. If only.

How did she do that? Get inside his head or heart?

Why couldn't he shake the vision of her deep blue eyes or still smell her scent on his soul? This had never happened. Jet lag. It had to be. Didn't it?

Inside the restaurant's bar, he scoped out the best seat to see who sauntered in, to see if he would indeed get lucky here tonight or have to search elsewhere. He settled easily into his chair and made idle chitchat with the barkeep, until a woman wearing tarantula eyelashes that looked ready to crawl off her bounced in with a much-too-perky set of breasts he could happily smother within. She shoved the gelatinous knockers in his face and winked. He actually had to back up to see her.

Things *were* looking up.

"Penny for your thoughts."

He gave the brassy brunette his best-practiced transparent grin knowing he could do better, but what the heck? Ethan dug deep into his pocket and fished out the penny he'd found from the sidewalk then handed her the coin and kept his thoughts to himself.

The tall, buxom woman flashed him yellow, stained teeth. They screamed for the underappreciated skills of a dentist with his drills, chisels and happy gas. Would he need happy gas to get through this night with her? Couldn't hurt! Ethan did his best to ignore her mouth, paying complete attention to her, roughly eight inches southward. He now understood the phrase silicon valley.

The girl's panties are probably one steamy mess. He wasn't being arrogant—all right, maybe a bit, but he had that effect on woman all the time. He'd come to trust his instincts that he could and would get any woman he ever wanted.

After two drinks and appetizers, Ethan looped his

arm through Trixie's. Then he worried her name referenced her profession? Turning tricks? Diseased came to mind, but it didn't stop him. His visible head was no longer calling the shots. With Ethan's free arm he grabbed their dinners and headed toward the exit. About to say something to the possible tart, Ethan took a sudden vow of silence. He'd been *very* hasty in his choice of women.

A vision, no a goddess, breezed into the restaurant with black curls blowing around her face as she came in from the windy street. Sun beams cast a golden haze around her and left her to look like a life-sized angel.

His!

The tailored, white two-piece silk suit graciously clung to her body and revealed every finite point Ethan wanted to trace with his tongue. She wore nothing under the jacket and that suited him just fine. Her breasts were full, voluptuous, *all-natural* and in serious need of his uninterrupted raptness. He decided it must have been cooler in the restaurant because her nipples pressed tightly into the silk. He wanted them pressed between his teeth. When she took off her sunglasses, he stepped backwards. Her deep-blue, flaming eyes warmed the room. All that was missing was the fireplace and the bear skin rug with them entangled in one another's body parts. She stood his height, if not a tad bit taller, five-eleven or even six-foot in flip-flops. No pretense. He liked that. She wore what God gave her proudly. Her hips were slim and her legs long. Doing his once-over, he had trouble picking out which spot to stare at. Her lush lips had a perfect pout that needed to be kissed off her face. Black lace eyelashes covered her cheeks. Suddenly, all he wanted covering her was him. "Holy mother of God," he said, his eyes drawn back to the flip-flops and blinding-pink nail polish. "It can't be."

And then there were her two bodyguards. Ethan stepped backward again, took in their sizes and gulped down the salmon appetizer attempting to swim upstream.

His palms turned sweaty, his pulse picked up and he wet his lips just like a woman when she realized she had a man's attentions. One of the men had to have been cloned from Goliath. He stood six-foot-four or better, muscles spread across him like concrete road maps. A stream of professions went through Ethan's head, from bodyguard to pro-wrestler to hit man to center-fold for *Play Girl Magazine*, he was that freakin' pretty. Jet-black curls flowed freely down his back and accented his deep-blue almost black eyes. And he had the same pouty lips as Pippy. Shit, Ethan mused, if he swung both ways he would've tried for them both.

The other man appeared miserable like an ogre, a scowl shrouded his face. His eyes were uniquely puzzling. One large green eye, the color of jade fought for dominance with his big brown buck-like eye. He didn't look at people, he glared at them. He stood a few inches smaller than pretty boy, but he weighed more. Ethan figured Superman would have flown the coup if he'd come up against this guy. There Ethan stood, in shock and awe of the threesome wondering if he could survive the kryptonite this trio packed. His ego was big enough to take on the situation. His IQ, however, wasn't his strongest point tonight. Case and point, Trixie. He glanced at her out of the corner of his eye trying to think of a brilliant way to ditch her. About ten feet from his *vision*, Ethan stopped and faced Trixie. "Would you eh—ah?" He placed his finger in Trixie's face asking without words to hold up for just a second. He shoved the dinners into her calloused hands, turned about face and glided on air toward his dream girl.

****

Savanah rolled her eyes over every inch of the man the moment she realized his intentions were to devour her even before they'd been introduced. An instant recognition crippled her. Her gut gave off that queasy *I'm going to explode any moment urge* and her legs went weak. *Jet lag*, she thought. It had to be all the different aromas and no sleep getting to her. Then why did she want only the man in front of her for dinner? She had trouble removing her eyes from him. Hell, at this point a surgeon couldn't have done the trick. But as he stared back, she realized he did the same to her. Her tongue prepped her lips for whatever happened. His light peridot eyes had to have been snitched from London Tower. Then an epiphany slammed her. "Holy mother of God, he's the guy from the airport. And who's the bimbo with him?" *Why do I even care who he's with? Because he's mine.*

Wide-eyed with a hint of a grin, Savanah waited.

Before Ethan knew what he was doing he was inches from Savanah's face.

"Hey, Pippy," was all he said before he covered her lips with his.

His hands, by design, found her cheeks, his thumbs brushed her petal-soft skin. He kept his eyes closed. Since his attack and being turned, he'd vowed to never trust another woman and until today he hadn't closed his eyes when he kissed one. Savanah's lips moved with his. His pants tightened all over again. He pulled away from her as he opened his eyes and watched her looking at him full of wonder, especially when she went limp in his arms.

The two bodyguards approached as Savanah came around.

"What the hell?" Savanah asked, the words lackadaisically toppling off her tongue.

"I just ah—had to. Do you always pass out when you're kissed?"

"Only when it's by strange pilchards."

Trixie tapped Ethan's shoulder twice before he responded. Savanah stood, steadied herself and stepped back and away from the scorned woman.

"Who's she?" Trixie squawked. "I'm not into threesomes."

Ethan glanced at her breasts one last time and sighed. "Me either. Look Trixie, my plans changed tonight. I'm sorry. Dinner's on me."

"Yes it is!" Trixie spit at him, then spun on her three-inch stilettos and stomped out of the restaurant. In Ethan's next breath he met bodyguard number one—Julian.

Before Ethan could introduce himself, he hit the wall so hard his cosmopolitan blew out better than then a whale could spew water.

Julian ducked, and in a low growl barked, "You have no business marking our woman. I could kill you for such an act. This is the only warning you'll ever receive from me. Attempt to touch her again and I'll show you the true meaning of death warmed over. Do we have an accord?"

After catching his breath, Ethan ripped out, "An

accord? What are you…some outcast pirate? I kissed her *Shrek*, I didn't piss on her like she's some fire hydrant, marking my territory. I only wanted to meet her and get rid of the other one. I just—"

Julian tightened his grip, and held Ethan easily with one hand pinned to the wall, his feet dangling. Teeth clenched, the veins in his neck ready to explode he ordered, "You just leave her alone, boy."

Ethan didn't budge. Not that he could.

Savanah tapped Julian's shoulder. "This might very well be why I've had no action in my bed," she whispered. "You're so damned overprotective. I just flashed everyone in the vicinity to keep things status quo, well everything except our pin-up boy!"

"Mouth, Missy." Julian dropped Ethan.

Ethan ended up flat on his ass looking up at Goliath the second bodyguard.

"Who do you think you are and what the hell was that display?" The giant glowered ready to squash Ethan like an ant.

Ethan tried to figure out who or what the hell the man was. He wasn't a shifter, but he wasn't a vamp either, even though his aura screamed otherworldly in an understated, kick-ass tone. He'd been around the Maestro long enough to realize the vibrations the vamp gave off were unequalled to this spine tingling experience. "What are you? Her sentinel?" Ethan pointed to Savanah.

André raised his voice. "I am the very reason you hid under your covers as a child."

Blankly, Ethan offered, "I'm sorry, Sir. I meant no harm to your sister."

"Sister?" Savanah burst out laughing.

André continued to stare him down. Savanah watched in silence. Julian gave her father the gentleman's nod of acknowledgement, a gesture that reeked of arrogance and liters of testosterone.

"You have learned well from the master, André." Julian gave a roll of his hand from his chest—an upright bow.

Savanah gasped. "You two are so full of yourselves. I can't stand it. How has Mum put up with you both?"

"Your mum loves me to bits and pieces, little girl," André answered.

Julian added his two cents, "And I'd love nothing more than to see you actually end up in those bits and pieces." Julian's smirk held the slightest bit of truth to it. Yes, the two men were close, but there were days.

"Watch it, Grimmy," André snapped.

Julian laughed a hearty burble then switched personalities easier than Cybil. "So, Mister…You never answered us."

Mouth open and about to answer, Ethan noticed the hostess approach. Her belly ring dangled from under her shirt like a fishing lure, trying to catch someone's attention. Well it did, but he wasn't interested. His interests lay solely on the woman in the white silk suit.

The hostess rattled off a spiel with more accuracy than an auctioneer that their table would be ready soon and dinner was on the house because of the mishap at the front door with someone coming in and vomiting all over and starting such a ruckus. She vanished just as quickly, her ponytail bobbing side to side.

Once again the center of attention, Ethan offered, "Sorry, but if I didn't get body-slammed…"

Savanah rested her eyes on Ethan. "You going to tell us a name or do we play twenty questions?"

"I'll play more than twenty questions with you!" He raised his brows in a playful gesture toward her.

André grabbed him by the shirt collar and hoisted him once again off his feet.

"Oh, Christ! Not again. My name is Ed." Ethan offered.

"Liar," Savanah accused. Lies. She could smell one better than a cadaver dog could sniff out a zombie at the bottom of the lake. Her mother had the same gift, as well. Walking, talking lie detectors.

Ethan looked at her as if she had two heads.

"What?" she asked innocently.

"Lightning actually does strike twice, hey Pippy. How'd you know?"

"What does he mean calling you Pippy?" Vehemence saturated André's voice.

"He's the guy that ran me over at the airport."

"I didn't run you over, and you still have nine other perfectly pink tootsies." Ethan gestured toward her feet.

Savanah's smile spread across her face when she realized he'd noticed her toenails. She choked down the immediate gratification when she rethought her values and decided she might be just the slightest bit shallow. *It isn't all about me, is it?*

She smiled again. *Yes, by the Gods, it is.*

Dismissing the ridiculous grin plastered on his niece's cheeks with a slight tap to the back of her head, Julian said, "Your name. Now!"

"Ethan Kitt."

The hostess returned. "Should I have another seat set for four?"

Simultaneously André and Julian answered, "No."

Savanah pouted. "No?"

Ethan didn't look any better. "Why can't I join you?"

"We don't trust you. We don't know you, and we don't like you." André rested his hand atop Ethan's shoulder, and nudged him toward the door. "Young man, you should be running out of here with your tail between your legs. Might I suggest that you never come near our family again, because if you do there are no guarantees I'll save you from him." André shot his thumb over his shoulder toward Julian.

Ethan gave a half-court bow to Savanah. He turned to exit, but stopped short, and turned back to her. "I'm sorry. I mean that. You are no doubt, the most gorgeous creature to walk the earth and your lips…Ummm!" Ethan closed his eyes briefly then placed his index finger under her chin. "I got the awkward part of the relationship over with Pip…the anxiety over the first kiss. It's all downhill from here. You even look great with pig-tails. Oh, you know my name, but I don't know yours."

With a seductive sway to her hips, she pulled her shoulders back, which accentuated her natural gifts, and Savanah stepped in closer to him. Very gently she tussled his hair. "Leaves a little mystery behind the whole ordeal, don't you agree?"

"Yes, Ma'am, it does." Ethan winked at her then straightened his posture, squared his shoulders, turned briskly on his heels and left the restaurant. "I feel like I've had this conversation with you once. I know that sounds like a line but, I'll find your name before nightfall, Rapunzel," he yelled back.

Every one of nature's laws compelled Savanah to follow the man out the door. She followed her feet right up until her father blocked her advances.

"Never chase a man, Peanut." André advised, "Unless he's stolen your heart. Then shoot the bastard once you catch him."

"You're such a romantic, Papa. What was I thinking?"

The hostess led them through a maze of tables and up one step to the back of the restaurant by the fireplace to a nice, cozy table. "This is your waitress, Edan."

"Edan? Sinful name. A bottle of your finest Merlot? Please?" Julian's grin for the tall waitress with blonde curly hair and large, almond-shaped green eyes had her covered in a light blush.

Savanah kept a curious eye on Julian. *He's flirting. Go Jules*! "Papa, do you believe that man? He kisses me—and why? Then he lies and then when all else fails he tries for a lame case of sincerity?"

"Peanut, the only truthful thing he said related to your beauty. And about that kiss—don't tell me you didn't feel anything."

Savanah's fingers traced her lips, her eyes closed and, in that instant, she realized life as she knew it was about to change.

"I second that," Julian added. "I marked him. I'll smell him a mile before he gets near us. In retrospect, I don't ever remember being that naïve when I first turned."

"Uncle, you've never let your guard down a day in your life. You're always so well-reserved, it's rather frightening. So incredibly—what's that word you always call him, Papa?" Savanah turned away from her uncle, laughter so very close to the surface.

"Anal." André answered giving his daughter the shifted brow.

"Good. It's what I intended." Julian gave a firm nod to André.

Savanah rolled her eyes. Here we go again, she thought. "No, it's not good. One day you'll snap," She said as she reached into the basket and broke a breadstick in half, the crumbs landed in Julian's lap. "Like this did."

"Let's just get Lucian, Serina and the newest member of our family, Elyza, safely tucked away first? I can worry about my lack of a love life after that." Julian winked.

"She's right, Jules. You need to take a day or two off and relax. And I believe this waitress may be just what the doctor ordered."

"Papa, you're embarrassing. You're like some old biddy who's lost the filter on her lips and blurts out whatever she thinks." Savanah watched the waitress, Edan, uncork a bottle of wine, and pour a small amount into Julian's glass. Edan never took her eyes from Julian's as she handed him the glass. Her fingers lingered long after Julian's hand reached the glass. Savanah watched the woman wet her plump, deep red lips, one hundred percent mesmerized by her over-zealous, egotistical, *would-lay-down-and-give-you-his-heart-if-you-needed-a-transplant,* uncle.

Oh, my God! Did you see that, Papa? Could she have been any bolder? Why not just throw herself in his lap?

That's probably next on her to-do-list. Savvy, let him be. The same goes for our little shifter. He just did the same thing to you, except he threw himself at you and you caught him! Hook, line and lips.

Lips scrunched to one side of her face she agreed, "Point taken."

"Thank you," Julian said to the waitress, with a small nod. "Place a second bottle on ice and after your shift ends, we'll share it."

The waitress looked around and grinned. "Eleven, my shift is done," she offered casually.

"I'll see you then." Julian reached for her hand and chastely placed a small kiss in the center of her palm.

"I have to get back to my tables. See you tonight." The waitress hurried toward the kitchen where a few other women crowded the doorway. Small chatter and giggles erupted.

Savanah nudged Julian's arm with a nod toward the kitchen. "Uncle, stop staring at her. Why didn't you two let me take care of Mr. Kitt instead of manhandling the poor thing?"

"I can't put my finger on it, but something about him seemed fallacious." Julian put the glass to his lips and took one long sip. "Nice vintage. Savvy. I don't trust him. I'll guarantee you if he ever lays a finger on you, he'll be missing it and a few other things come morning."

About to clobber both her father and uncle for their Neanderthal logic, Savanah decided she needed air. "Would you two excuse me? I need to freshen up. To many pheromones in the air." Savanah stood and headed for the restroom. Once inside, she dowsed cold water on her face to relieve at least one part of her anatomy. Everything else on her body felt worse than a car with no coolant in its radiator stuck in the midday sun. One steamy mess. Her breasts longed to be touched, and she now found a tickle between her thighs she couldn't scratch in public—well, not without getting arrested for public indecency. *What the hell did he do to me?*

"What's got you two looking so serious?" Savanah asked as she sat down.

"Nothing a silver bullet won't fix. We were just talking about your new beau."

Savanah snorted.

Julian never missed a beat as he poured the wine and handed each of them a glass. Julian raised his wine. "We welcome Elyza Tracey St. James to our family. Our little treasure to be cherished for a lifetime. Cheers!" The glasses clinked and the three of them waited to see what else their little waitress could dish up, or at least Julian did.

****

His little roadster headed north on Broadway, Ethan pulled a U-turn in the middle of the busy road. Cars skidded to a stop and curse words filtered into the air in the same manner as the squealing brakes did. Even his charismatic grin didn't cool the other driver's overheated tempers.

Can't please everyone all of the time!

With a left onto Spring Street, a right onto Nelson Avenue and a left onto Union, Ethan found himself headed toward the Flat track and ultimately the house in which Raven St. James lived. The hustle and bustle as breeders and trainers got their horses ready for the racing season spread through the east side of town the same way manure did the stables. Local police cars hogged each corner, pick-up trucks, horse trailers and horses cluttered the sides of the roads making traffic bottleneck in areas. Security guards placed in strategic locations helped to cross the animals and patrons from the stables and parking lots to the track. With the St. James' home bordered on the track's property, Ethan realized this might work to his advantage. All the extra people milling around, he'd blend right in. And if he was caught snooping? He'd claim he was the accidental tourist. Yeah, he was an accident waiting to happen all right!

As he turned right onto the narrow unpaved road and passed through the main entrance, he read the sign posted: *Rose Gardens Close at Dusk.*

Pine trees, thick with green foliage, allowed only glimpses of sunlight to filter through. At the first sign of loose gravel, large beads of sweat formed on his brows. Worried a rock might jump up and scratch the paint on his new baby, he drove so slow the speedometer barely registered. This whole baby snatching ordeal would destroy his sanity. All he wanted to do was turn around and get the hell out of here but he physically couldn't. He felt as if he'd been brainwashed. Pretty certain he had been. He needed to grow a new pair and stand up against this lunatic.

And yet he continued, being toyed with like a broken emasculated Ken doll against his will.

A fork in the driveway with a sign pointed him away from the main home, to the gardens, where he parked. Ethan got out, locked the doors and walked to the base of a small incline where he took in the fortress. "It might as well have a moat." He counted five floors of windows. Chimneys climbed from the roof like dandelions popped up from the earth in the spring.

There were plenty. The solid, gray-flagstone castle all but dared him to try to breech its walls. The place reminded him of a time long ago when kings built fortresses to keep people like him out. Without so much as a game plan, he veered to his left, and wormed his way around the backside of the home on his belly, cutting through the grass with the stealth of the snake he felt like.

He stood, brushed the dirt from his clothing and peeped in the kitchen window. Ethan had never met or even seen photos of Raven St. James or any of her family for that matter, but he'd heard tales of her beauty, hence the nickname, little Beauty.

Not a lot to go on!

What I really want is the beauty I left at the restaurant. Shake that vision, Eth, coz her two side dishes bite back.

Standing on top of the air conditioning unit, he decided no baby lived in this monstrosity. The manor held a tranquil setting, more like a library or a morgue.

This is insane. I have to get the hell away from here. I'm so not a kidnapper. Turning to abandon this ludicrous plot, a cold, dry force-field encased his body like a layer of freezer wrap, prepared to suck every last drop of moisture out of him. He recognized the Maestro's calling card.

You will do this, Ethan, because, otherwise, I shall cut off your lifeline when we see each other once more. And I don't mean your bank account. Raven is not a fit mother. I will not have my grandchild raised with that family. They executed my son. Remember this.

Isn't that what family court is all about, Xier? That's why there's a judicial system. So people can spend their last hard-earned cent giving it to the lawyers and judges only to get screwed over legally.

You will not disappoint me, Ethan. Betray me once and you'll regret your very existence. They will thank you in the end. As will I.

About to tell the Maestro where he could stick his '*Betray me once*' bologna, a tall woman with thick, blonde curls walked right in front of the French doors he peered in and headed for the fridge. He ducked when Blondie cranked her neck back and stared at the back woods. Her light blue eyes looked like a husky's or wolf's eyes and then the belly came into view. "No freakin' way! She's the one that puked on me." Ethan retreated to the wooded area. "Could this night get much crazier?"

****

Jovan knew something or someone was in the woods watching her. If the hairs like cactus needles jabbing her neck were any indicator, she had only one choice. *André, I'm sorry to disturb your dinner, but we've company in the woods.*

André turned to Savanah. "Flash everyone. We're out of here." He tossed a wad of bills on the table, and headed for the exit.

We're on our way. Are you all right? Where is Molly? Is Duncan home with Luce, Serina and the baby yet?

Molly's in Elyza's room wallpapering. Raven's on her way up from Poughkeepsie with Jonah and Payton. Duncan, Lucian, my sister and the baby are still in the city.

I'm two blocks away, Cherié. Don't worry. Stay away from the windows and doors. I'm pulling up in the

59

drive now.

Just how fast did you drive?

Cherié, I always drive like a madman to see you.

You're an imbecile, just as your sister says.

That's Lucian she calls imbecile. Not me. Would someone please get this right?

André moved with a blurring speed while Julian circled the house from the opposite direction. He may not have been a vampire like his siblings or a werewolf like his brother-in-laws, but being a donor a few times a week to Lucian, he reaped the benefits of speed, strength, and telepathy with everyone in their family. There was an upside to this paranormal, supernatural, phenomenon André enjoyed most days. Right here, right now, he wasn't feeling it.

Julian met André on his hands and knees, his nose to the ground like a pit bull, sniffing out every grain of dirt. He looked up, his nose covered in grass and mud.

André shook his head when he saw him. "Why didn't you shift?"

"Didn't feel like ruining another good suit. You'll never guess who was here."

André gave an impatient glare.

"That stupid little mutt from the restaurant. I should've killed the ignorant bastard then and there. What does he want that's worth his life?"

"You already know it's my daughter. I get to kill him and bury him in the back woods," André added, baring no hint of amusement.

"Fair enough. I was going to turn him over to the police."

Pointing to the door, André whispered, "Jules, it's open." Both men were inside in a heartbeat. Julian took the back stairs from the kitchen and André, the main stairs in the center hall.

Jovan, he's in the house.

****

Ethan entered the nursery behind Jovan. "Ladies, hello. No need for panic. I realize it might be a bit overwhelming seeing a stranger in your home, but I really only need one thing and no one will get hurt, including me, but that's a whole other story."

Jovan took one look at Ethan, staggered backwards, and latched on to Molly. Her frantic brain tried to make the images in front of her make sense—or go away. Her eyes had to be playing a malicious joke on her. This man could not be *the one*. She'd never been wrong the rare few times she allowed herself her sightings. Scrying, she knew there was a reason she didn't do it and this idiot just made her case and point. Chattering teeth bit out, "Who are you and what do you want?"

"The baby and Raven," Ethan answered in earnest.

Molly dropped her brush to the floor. "Are you insane?" Defiant, the red head added, "There's no baby. Go out the way you came in, and we won't hurt *you*."

Taking in all the baby things, the cradle, the swinging chair, the changing table, the mountain of pink clothes with tiny satin hangers, the white rocking chair with lavender roses blooming all over it, and a zoo of stuffed animals, he tossed his hands out. "Really?"

André, he's here with us. He wants a baby and Raven.

Keep him talking. Julian's coming in through the bedroom window. When he comes in, I'll come through

61

the door.

"Really, Mister, there's no baby. We're just two contractors hired to paint. The baby hasn't even been born yet," Molly lied.

"I beg to differ. I know the baby popped out two days ago, and Raven and he are coming home, here, today."

"Then you're one up on us, buddy, because no one named Raven lives here and as you can see the crib's empty. And if you're not color blind everything is bloody pink and purple." Jovan said her jaw tense.

Ethan scratched his head. They certainly had a point. He knew if he had a son he wasn't going in a pink and purple room. *A little girl with jet-black curls and green eyes would though.* Ethan shook his head. *Christ, not five minutes ago I'd sworn off children. Now I've got a little girl? I've been hexed!*

Jovan shared the conversation to André. *What the hell does this guy want Ray for and why would he think she had a child?*

I don't know, Cherié. We met him at dinner. He planted a giant kiss on Savanah. Maybe he's lying to you to get to her?

He's not lying. He believes Raven had a baby, and he wants him. A son.

The look Jovan fired Ethan by all rights should have left him a giant ash pile. "Do you have the right address? Certainly somewhere, someone else had a baby you can go steal?"

Ethan held his heart, and with a little sarcasm added, "Ouch. First you puke on me and now you insult me."

"That was you on the plane?" A sardonic half-grin

worked its way onto her lips. "Trust me, it won't be the last thing I do."

Julian crashed through the window and flew across the room with unprecedented speed. André had his backside, with Ethan's arms crossed and locked behind him before his next breath.

So shocked at the sight of the two men again, Ethan lost the contents of his bladder down his leg, out his shoe and all over the floor into a sloppy puddle.

"Damn, he's not house-broken," Julian said one inch away from Ethan's face. A little closer and he could have kissed him...or bit off his nose. The latter being Julian's choice.

Actually everyone's but Ethan's choice. Not that Ethan wanted to kiss the man, but if it were a choice between his nose or his dignity? Well, having just peed all over himself, the point seemed moot.

"Ladies, Savanah's in the carport screaming obscenities because I locked her in there for her own safety. Would you please go release her?" André tried to scoot the women out.

Getting her last digs in, Jovan yelled, "I don't care what happens to you—" She poked Ethan in the breastbone "—as long as it isn't in this room. My paint hasn't dried yet, and I don't want any bloodstains or evidence. Do you hear me, Grimmy?"

Julian shot his hands into the air and mouthed, "What? Me?"

Ethan's rosy complexion took a drastic turn for the worse.

Watching him dry-heave she vowed, "If you even think of vomiting in this room I'll kill you myself. Swallow it. André, get him out of here." Jovan jammed

Ethan's mouth shut. "You ever touch my daughter again, I'll turn you into the bull she said you were. And you'll be castrated first."

"It's called payback, Mom." Ethan's salmon appetizer left a rancid puddle of pink chunks on the floor.

"Kid, you've done something I haven't seen in a century. You broke open a beehive and my little queen's about to take a chunk out of your hide," André chided.

"Who the hell are you people?" Ethan asked as he tried to wipe his chin off on his shirt.

"Raven is my sister, and she is neither pregnant nor lactating." André spun Ethan to face him. "Now, what makes you think my sister had a baby and why would you of all people want it? You're not leaving here 'til we have answers. Please, humor me, and tell me you didn't sleep with her."

"Me? No, but I know who did."

"Actually, Ands, he's not leaving here period. We can't let him go." Julian winked behind Ethan's back. *But we can have some fun with him until we figure out what to do. The kid reeks of vampire.*

André wasn't entirely certain he really didn't want the little twerp buried in the woods.

"Who's Savanah? Is she the beauty from the restaurant?"

André picked up a poker from the fireplace, and jabbed the rod's tip into Ethan's side. "It is not your turn to ask the questions. It is your turn to answer them. Who sent you here?" He prodded Ethan's gut harder.

"I'm claiming the fifth."

"He's all your, Jules. Take him to the tack room."

64

André stormed from the room, his temper ready to stick around and finish the kid off. He found his wife and daughter in the kitchen.

"Papa, what happened? Who's upstairs?"

André put his finger gently on his daughter's lip and kissed her forehead. "We need to find out where this kid gets his information. Why would he think Raven had a baby?"

"Who?" Savanah asked again.

Jovan reached out to André, and whispered in his mind. *We need to talk when we're alone. Something's very wrong. The boy's mind is tainted by a vampire. He doesn't realize his free will has been bought, and he's now an indentured servant. He's dangerous.* For her daughter's ears she inclined her head to the pantry. "We can make the truth serum up. Won't take but a few minutes. We'll meet you in the stables."

"Cherié, why the truth serum if you can detect lies?"

"Because he will lie 'til the cows come home to protect his master." Jovan kissed André on the corner of his lip.

"Here we go again." Savanah knew it. "One kiss leads to another, and I'll be waiting all evening to get to the stables." Savanah pried her mother from her father. "Come on, Mum. I want to see who we've locked up since no one's talking."

****

Ethan shifted halfway down the path to the stables thinking he could outsmart, out run, overpower this man. Not happening. Simply put, Ethan had been outdone on all levels. The mold for werewolves was cast from Julian.

65

From Ethan's vantage this scenario continued to spiral downhill. Getting dragged by the scruff of his neck to the tack room was the icing on the cake or so he thought until Julian secured him to an old wooden beam with a silver chain, and wrangled a loose muzzle on him. Panic escalated to level orange when Julian dug up as many syringes as he could muster then spread them out on a tattered, dusty horse-hair blanket. Nothing aseptic in these urine soaked walls.

"No freaking way you're poking me with those things."

"Good to know the wolf has evolved to communication in both life forms."

Julian winked, but it wasn't a warm, mischievous blink like the ones Ethan doled out. Ethan realized there and then Julian was probably more of a cold-blooded beast than the Maestro.

Both Jovan and Savanah sneezed in unison when they entered the musty barn. "Here's the mixture. Who's it for?" Savanah dabbed her nose with a tissue, searching. "Oh my, I don't miss this place."

Recognition of one angelic voice had Ethan crank his large head in the direction of freedom, the sliding stable door.

Taken aback seeing Ethan, she approached him with caution. "We meet again. No mistaking those green eyes. You got all dolled up for me? Nice coat! I must say you have a definite angle at getting to know people."

"Yeah, you'll never forget this, will you?" Ethan sat on his haunches and bat his puppy eyes at her.

"I don't think I'll let you forget it either." She smirked.

"Savanah! I know your name!"

"Well, Ethan, I'm not Rapunzel. And I sure as hell won't let my hair down for you."

Ethan's nose twitched as he watched Savanah hand her father a glass flask with a bluish concoction gurgling without the need for flames. Steam rose, and sweetened the air with a mixture of juniper, peppermint oil, rue, violets and raspberries.

Savanah passed another flask under Ethan's nose to which he grimaced. The second flask contained a burnt amber gel. "And yes, it is what you're thinking. It is my very own sweet and sour sauce." She didn't need to read his mind. The look on his face said everything. She ran her fingertips across his blond fur, then rubbed behind his ears.

"Lower, sweets—the itch is much lower," Ethan countered.

Savanah picked up a horsewhip, and cracked it. "Still itch?"

"Woman, I love the way you think." Ethan growled at her through the muzzle.

Picking up one the syringes her uncle had laid out, she aimed it at his back leg, daring him, without words.

In his sternest tone, André shouted, "Savanah!" She jumped and the syringe went sailing like a dart just missing Ethan.

"That was close." Savanah bent over and got in his face. "Next time I won't miss."

"Ha ha ha!" Ethan added sarcasm laced.

"What have I told you about becoming infatuated with creatures we have to put down?"

"Papa!" Her free hand atop her hip, she huffed a giant curl from her view. "Why can't I keep him? You always kill off the cute ones. *Always*!" Savanah turned away from Ethan wearing a smile her orthodontist would have appreciated. "I never freakin' get to have any fun."

Although teasing him wasn't a bad way to spend the night, for a brief moment Savanah's fantasies stole her and the wolf far away from her family where it would be just the two of them, her as Red Riding Hood and Ethan, the big bad wolf chasing her, catching her, and devouring her in a completely sensual, erotic frenzy—tongue, teeth, fingers, penis…The whole nine yards—ah…make that inches and yes, it was bigger than her pinky!

Happy dance time was moments away.

She wanted to make love to him, show him feelings she had no words for, only deep seeded desires. She wanted him to leave her breathless, exhausted under him. She needed his warm flesh against hers hard and fast. Savanah looked at Ethan and for a minute panicked he'd been able to read her mind. She broke out in a cool mist. *Crap, I inhaled my own freaking concoction.*

Ethan stared at Savanah, tongue flopped over the side of his mouth, with lethal picturesque choppers showing through.

"You're drooling, Mr. Kitt." Savanah pointed to his lips. "Quite the set of dents you've got there." The second the words rolled from her lips, she knew somehow he'd take full advantage of the opportunity.

"All the better to eat you with, my dear." His tail wagged in the dirt leaving him in a smutty cloud.

Rancor saturated Jovan's voice. "Why is that thing still breathing?"

Smothered by her mother's tenor, Savanah's saucy dream ended up watered down. Her mother was piping hot.

André answered, "We were waiting for you, Cherié."

"Hold up a second." Ethan barked. "Are you really going to kill me?"

Everyone answered a collective, "Yes."

"If I talk?"

"Yes." Jovan hissed.

"Probably." Julian weighed his hands like a balanced scale.

"If I give you names and places?"

"We'll see." André.

"What do you want?"

You, once you lose the mangy fur. Savanah eyed Ethan as if he were a one hundred-eighty pound chunk of eye-candy made to order just for her. *Oh! I'm in trouble.*

Yes, you are! Ethan's gaze began with her feet and worked his way very slowly up every delicious, lip-smacking inch of her body, as he took in everything the woman had to offer him. When his eyes rested on hers he smiled, still in the form of a wolf, but he smiled all teeth and tongue. *Yeah baby, I'm the big bad wolf, all right. And I am going to eat you for breakfast, lunch and dinner. Dessert, however, is on me.*

Savanah's eyes went wide. She stumbled and covered her ears. Ethan did a double take hoping it was coincidence and that the woman couldn't read his thoughts even as he read hers without conscientiously realizing it.

"The truth, Ethan."

Julian's stern voice nearly gave Ethan whiplash as he spun his head toward the man. "The man that sent me after the baby is Xier, or the Maestro known by others. His son said some unstable chic, Raven, had his grandson two days ago, and he wants it. Xanti Sinclair claims he and his brother Xavier had a child." With the mention of that name Ethan watched this family unravel. Purposefully, he said, "*S-i-n-c-l-a-i-r*," again, slowly, spelling it just to see if the same reaction happened.

Jovan choked. André held his arm up on one of the stables doors to steady himself and Julian, Mr. Rock of Gibraltar, landed squarely on his righteous rump.

Savanah ran to her mother's side. "Uncle Lucian beheaded that bastard. There was no way the guy had a kid. One century ago the science and technology wasn't born."

"Seems I've hit a nerve or two." Ethan bucked up.

Getting back on his feet, Julian asked, "What makes Xanti think Raven had a baby?"

"I'm just the messenger. I don't even know what she looks like. Xanti told me to look for Sleeping Beauty. Lot of help there."

"Then turn around and feast your eyes, Mister." Raven strut into the stables wearing dark sunglasses, skintight leather pants showing off long lean legs and three-inch heeled black boots. Her hair was done in a French braid. She avoided all the eyes except Ethan's. One glance at him, her jaw dropped. Raven faced Jovan, pushed her glasses atop of her head, her eyes wide. *Jovan the painting—werewolf or not, there was no mistaking the face behind the fur.*

About to say something, Jovan opted for a

silencing finger to her lips and whispered, "Not now, Ray."

Having that nasty sensation of eyes burning a hole in him, Ethan glanced between Raven and Jovan. "Why does everyone always get that B-rated Zombie look each time one of you sees me?"

"Because you're a walking dead man." Raven ran her fingers down the front side of her body. "As you can see I've no baby. So you work for the Sinclair's? Who in Hell did you piss off to get that job?" Raven's voice couldn't have held more sarcasm if *she* were made of spandex.

"Well I'm not surprised I was given the wrong info yet again. I apologize. So—if you'll all just untie me and get this tarnished silver off me, I'll be moving on. No harm done. Seriously, do I look like I have an idea what to do with a baby?" Ethan scoured the room, waiting, hoping to find an ally in any one of them. Not even his tall, dark beauty budged. The look she gave him reminded him of a lover scorned. Yeah, he'd seen it more than once. Just tonight as a matter of fact, from that buoyant little trickster.

Behind Savanah, a cyclone of black dust caught Ethan's eye as it gelled into a figure. The air pressure seemed to expand then shrink. His ears popped. Woodchips and sawdust filled the air. All the horses became restless; grunting and shuffling in their stalls. Out of the dust storm, a tall man with a deep olive completion and bristle-short, black hair emerged.

Ethan sat back on his haunches. *I knew I shouldn't have asked if this night could get any crazier!* Ethan held a paw to Savanah. "You might want to turn around."

The stranger brushed past Savanah to Ethan, and dug his long thin fingers into his fur. "Ethan, dude, you've looked better. I knew you were into bondage, but this is different even for you. I didn't know you were into putting on shows for crowds."

Ethan noticed Savanah's posture stiffen and if looks could kill, he thought he really might die tonight. *Little possessive there, Pippy?*

Savanah's snow-white complexion went green as a little thing called jealousy chewed through her epithelial cells. She didn't like the idea of Ethan being bonded with anyone, man or woman if it wasn't her. Visions of him handcuffed in silk restraints and being used as a sex toy bombarded her brain. Sometimes her imagination was her worst enemy. She couldn't help the hurtful look she shot him. And to add insult to injury her conscience began giving her grief. Part of her wanted the lying, would-be kidnapper with ties to the one family they never wanted to see again gone. But her hormone's conscience? *Is there such a thing?* She wondered. Each and every little wanton cell wanted the blond wolf/man to stimulate them. Just thinking of Ethan left a burning, licentious, desire scorching a path directly between her thighs. She attempted to reason with herself the damned man came here to kidnap a child her aunt supposedly birthed. What if Raven had the baby and he'd succeeded? Confusion reigned control between her head and her heart. Every instinct said this man would be the end to one-hundred-thirteen year drought, also known as her loveless life. *God, I know how to pick them.*

"Pip, you all right? You're looking a bit off color." Ethan asked his voice calm and soothing, sincere.

Oh, I wish he'd stop calling me that. Savanah crossed her arms, confused. *Could he be genuine with his interest? Or is this just a new angle?*

Ethan glanced upward. "Sorry, Pip, but the name suits you. Really, you okay?"

An epiphany hit them. Both gasped in unison as they locked eyes, realizing privacy just became a thing of the past. Savanah's hand flew to her mouth but, "Oh shit," flew out regardless.

"Mouth, Savanah," André warned.

"Sorry, Papa." Her eyebrows pinched at Ethan she answered, "I'll be fine, thanks. Anyone remember that Mel Gibson flick where he wore tin foil around his head to block people's thoughts? I need some. Now!"

"Oh Jesus!" Jovan mumbled.

Ethan howled with laughter. "I was thinking the—"

"I know. This can't be—"

"But it is, Pip. Deal with it. Vonnie? Were you the other passenger on my flight? I never did check the second box I brought over."

"No, Eth. Been in town a while on business," the man answered, stalking Raven with his eyes.

"Donovan?" Raven barely got his name out. She turned to see if Jonah and Payton were near.

André rubbed his eyes. "Donovan, as in the old guard at our estate in England last century? We haven't heard hide nor hair of you in a lifetime, literally."

"Hello, Ray, André," Donovan bowed before André showing an old respect for the man that came within minutes from being crowned King. "Jules, Jovan." Donovan waved. "You two look the same. Savanah? Is that you? Wow! You grew up. You're beautiful."

"Thank you." Savanah fought a scowl. Every bone in her body screamed foul play. All that was missing was the spooky music that usually played when the nemesis entered a movie scene. Her family had all their negativities focused on the wrong guy. Ethan couldn't hurt a fly. This new guy looked like he sprinkled them on his morning cereal and ate them in place of granola.

"Hey—hold up. How come he can say you're beautiful but if I say she is," Ethan asked pointing a paw toward Savanah, "I get grief."

"Because we like him." Jovan bit back. "And stay the hell away from my daughter."

Ethan glanced back toward Savanah. *Not on your life.*

Savanah fanned her cheeks.

Chapter Four

"Always the charmer, Eth." Donovan turned to face the crowd. "You're a tough lot to track down. Your sister-in-law's birthing experience made national news. Raven, I felt a biting need to see you again. That little run in we had over the Christmas season wasn't enough to hold me over for another hundred years."

Donovan laughed, but it lacked that warm friendly sonance. Savanah found nothing attractive about it or the man. Matter of fact, her sixth sense was trying to get the other five to listen. Without thinking twice she moved closer to Ethan.

Raven mumbled, "This is awkward."

"Actually, Belle, I'd like to know why you never mentioned seeing him." Jonah didn't sound the least bit friendly as he, Payton and Molly entered the stables.

Payton added, "I'd like to know why you don't seem at all surprised to see him. He should have by all rights been dead, say nineteen seventy, and I'm being generous letting him live to be one hundred. Donovan, you look rather fit for your age."

"So do you, Dough boy," Donovan chided. "How's that whole werewolf lifestyle working for you?"

Payton squared his shoulders toward the taller man. "I'll let ya know firsthand the next full moon." Payton licked his lips.

"You're quiet, Jonah," Donovan prompted.

"Ever hear the saying keeping your mouth closed keeps the flies in and the shit out? I don't feel like feeding you right now, Vonnie." Sarcasm all but dripped from Jonah's lips.

"Enough," Raven snapped, "Can we deal with the mutt who wanted to kidnap me and my make-believe child first?"

"Raven, he's not going anywhere." Jonah answered. "Neither are we."

"What makes you think I can't get out of here?" Ethan barked back through his muzzle. "Just watch me!"

André screamed and the room shook. "Later, I agree with my sister. Let's deal with our new pet first." Almost everyone shut up

"Oh, I'm so not your pet." The blond wolf panted, his tail nestled between his legs.

André's look said otherwise. His gaze stymied Ethan better than an anvil. "You will be whatever I want you to be. Or stuffed and mounted in our trophy room."

"Or stuffed and mounted in my trophy room," Ethan mimicked.

André took a step toward Ethan when Savanah got between them, her hands on her father's shoulders to stop his progression.

"I have a question first, Papa."

"Thanks, Pip." Ethan added just before she did a backwards kick and clipped his breastbone. "Thanks a lot," came out in a gasp.

"How is it that a man that used to guard you now knows him?" Savanah pointed between Donovan and Ethan.

Ethan volunteered, "We had a bet to see who would find her first. I won."

"No you didn't. I did." Donovan straightened his posture and gave Raven a brilliant grin.

"Can I shift back without setting off alarms and whistles?" For a few embarrassing moments, Ethan was unable to shift. He grunted, howled, scratched at his tummy, which did nothing, and after two rounds of chasing his tail, nipping his balls, fur still covered him. Frustrated, he asked, "What's wrong with me? Why can't I shift? I've never had a problem."

"Viagra?" Savanah countered.

"Trust me, Pippy, that works. Let me out, and I'll show you."

"You can't change because I don't want you to. Not yet anyway." Savanah answered. "Remember the pretty blue concoction you inhaled? That's one of my specialty charms. It's a holding spell. The orange gel is truth potion."

"Who the hell are you people? What have you done to me, *witch*? Don't even try telling me you hexed my hoodie."

"Puh-lease—it's hooded?" Savanah's gaze dropped directly to the source.

"Only one way to find out." Ethan rolled on his back and stretched his legs out but kept his paws covering his private tidbits.

Fed up and getting nowhere fast, Savanah tried a new kinder, gentler tactic. "Just tell me all you know, then I'll release your body."

Ethan rolled onto his tummy and stretched his hind legs out. "Xanti told the Maestro he fathered a child with you." Ethan jerked his head toward Raven. "So the story goes the psycho vamp froze his brother's sperm for a hundred years."

André looked at Raven. "Lucian beheaded the bastard. We were there. Serina's got his heart in a canning jar in the Manhattan apartment to prove it."

"Okay, that's really sick," Ethan added.

Donovan asked, "Why?"

"She has a theory if his spawn ever got close to us again the heart would rejuvenate. It's a metaphysical alarm system."

"I'm going to be..." Raven darted through the stable doors. Jonah followed on her heels.

Ethan tried to ignore the gut wrenching sounds from outside the stables and the soured aromas of a mixture of blood, coffee· and—he inhaled deeply—a Boston cream donut as they whiffed their way into the stable. Days like today he didn't appreciate the extra senses his wolf offered him. Ethan would never be able to look at another Boston cream donut the same way, ever again. His bones popped, his body shifted, and he shed his hide into one matted down pile of slime and fur. It always reminded him of road-kill after a few trucks had flattened the remains. "I need a pair of pants," Ethan proclaimed, standing butt naked, his loins covered by his hands.

Julian disappeared and returned with a pair of jeans that easily could have fit Ethan and someone else. In no position to squabble, Ethan said, "Much appreciated," as he donned them. More than aware he had Savanah's attention, he flashed her a quick view of his backside as he turned to get his personal parts adjusted. When he turned back, Savanah no longer looked green, but a misty shade of pink.

After Raven and Jonah came back, Jonah asked Ethan, "How long have you been searching for Raven and when did you find her?"

"Hmmm…Xanti found her ah—you," he pointed to Raven, "in Boston. Some girly store."

Raven protested, "Wasn't me."

"Xanti never came back to the car. He called and told me to pick him up the next morning. Personally, I'd have bet ya a million to one odds that guy didn't have sex with a woman."

Raven nodded to Donovan. "You showed up and marked me at the cash register that day."

Arrogance cloaked Donovan as he stood, arms crossed, chest puffed out, and a smug smirk thinning his lips.

"Did you know Xanti was there?" Raven asked. Anger pulsed behind the question.

Donovan gave a nod yes.

"So you knew, but you didn't bother letting her family know she was in danger?" Payton took a step toward him.

Jonah grabbed him by the shoulders. "Hold on."

Donovan answered, "I got to her first. So you can thank me for saving her from that psycho anytime now."

Raven strut to Donovan with the falsest smile she could muster. She looked him dead into his olive-colored eyes, and placed her fist there as hard as she could. Her vampiric strength careened him across the stables through a wooden gate landing him next to a mare.

Donovan glanced upward to his assailant, his nose misaligned. "Aren't you a rough little wench?"

"You can go straight back to Hell, Donovan." To Raven's chagrin, she turned and left.

"Savanah, *Cherié*, go with her. We'll be in just as soon as we can figure out what to do with this mess." André grabbed Jovan's hand in passing and kissed her.

Savanah whispered, "Be nice to Ethan, Pops. He may not be the brightest star, but I can feel it in my bones, he's going to turn my dull life upside down."

"He's off to a great start then, isn't he? Go." André hugged his daughter hard to him.

"André, may I say something without getting clobbered yet again?"

"Bugger off, Donovan. You knowingly placed our family in jeopardy. You, of all people knew what Raven went through, what Sinclair put her through. That's the main reason we moved to the states. To get the hell away from his family." André pulled up a spot on a bench, straw stuck to it better than cat hair to a black wool coat and dropped his head into his hands. "Where the hell's my brother?"

Donovan offered, "I did it to keep her safe. I knew Xanti wouldn't get to her. He took some woman who looked like Raven. Xanti has no idea how to use his powers, and he kills without remorse. Just like dear old dad."

"So this other woman is, in all likelihood the poor mother of the child you were hoping to kidnap, Ethan?" Julian asked.

Ethan went to argue the term kidnap, not at all liking the sound of it. Maestro made it sound so much easier on the ears. Total seduction. Semantics at this point. "Uh, yes."

André mumbled, "That also means that Xanti may

not be as stupid as you make him out, if he was that close to her."

Julian bent at the waist and got right in Ethan's face. "You do know, don't you, that I'm calling the cops tonight and reporting an intruder."

Julian's voice cut through Ethan harder than a silver semi-automatic could have. "Dammit, whatever your name is, Uncle Jules. It's my death sentence. I'll change in jail on the full moon, and then they'll skin me alive. Have you seen it on TV? It's incomprehensible. How can you do that to one of your own?"

Julian closed the distance. "You are not mine. You are not one of my own. You came here with malicious intentions. Buddy, you're lucky I don't kill you myself."

When he was done barking at Ethan, Julian's saliva dripped from Ethan's face. Julian walked into his office located at the back of the stables.

"When I don't come home, Hell's bells will ring," Ethan yelled. "You are no longer safe here. In two days' time this house will be leveled. The Maestro will personally see to it. And I can't stop it."

André straightened and crossed his arms. Biceps bulged, biceps Ethan never achieved no matter how many hours he spent at the gym. Yeah, he was in great shape, but this guy could've put the movie star gone Governor of California to shame back in the day.

"Ethan, you overestimate your net worth. Everyone is expendable. Guaranteed your Maestro won't look for you because you will draw undo attention to him. You just became public enemy number one."

Julian stuck his head out of his office. "The authorities are on their way."

****

From a sofa in east Tim buck-two, an old man with sparse silver hair, trapped in a skeletal frame caught up on the current plays of the week on the sports channel. His crippled fingers were all but welded around the tiny device that could cause a war in the wrong hands, the remote. The television blared loud enough that Olivia Spencer heard them in the next room. The first, an announcer recounted blow-by-blow freeze-frame shots of the birth of an infant girl at Yankee Stadium with a filter over the lens giving the woman back her dignity, and the second story, the world nightly news, telling an incredible to impossible story of a set of conjoined twins who were half lycan/half vamp, stolen from the hospital in Tennessee. The PEON's, the Preternatural Exterminating On-sight Neutralizers, put out a BOLO for the babies and a shoot to kill order—no questions asked—on the babies, not the abductors.

The baby story caught Olivia's attention better than the catcher did through the first few innings. The man had butterfingers today. Olivia padded into the room silent as a great cat, with deadly intent. Seeing the birthmark on the baby girl stirred an emotion deep within her. With a quick glance from the corner of her eye, she scowled seeing the old man she'd married, remote in one hand with a bottle of cheap beer in his other, nursing it. He reminded her of an over-grown baboon suckling at his mother's tit. Oh, how she loathed his very existence.

Oliver sneered in her general direction then tipped his beer toward the television spilling a few drops.

"Buffoon." Olivia stared in disbelief at the television without so much as another word. The black casing surrounding her heart crumbled, like an icepick hacking at a glacier.

She had a granddaughter. Guilt consumed the new grandma and rightfully so. Had she known there would be such a strange expansion of her heart, she'd have released the curse she set in place the day after she condemned Lucian and André to being childless for one hundred years. She hadn't meant to include André, but being Lucian's identical twin, well, she'd gotten a two-for one special.

"Oliver, that's Serina, my baby. Remember her?"

Oliver looked at his wife, tipped his head to the side, shoved the bottle of ale through his pursed lips and gulped. After a loud, wet belch, he swallowed the fluids back down and went back to watching the game, ignoring Olivia.

Olivia's body tightened with revulsion as she listened to his disgusting body functions. It was only a matter of time before the beer found its way to the other exit. She went in search of a can of air freshener, and a phone book.

****

Cherié, I just spoke with Lucian. Everyone is fine. They'll be staying a few more days in the city. Where are Raven and Donovan?

In the library. Well, Jonah and Payton are with Raven. Donovan's disappeared. Nothing's broken yet.

Other than a few hearts.

André, I'm going up to the nursery. Join me?

I'll be up soon. Jules and I are going to the police station to make certain Ethan is out of the picture for a few days. A few of the guys owe us a favor or two and we're going to have them hold the kid until we can straighten this mess out. We won't let anyone skin him alive. That'll be my job if the little bastard doesn't straighten up. Lock up.

André, you know don't you? About Ethan?

Yes, I know. Time will tell, my love. If it is meant to be between Savanah and he, then he's got some serious changes to make. And we must help him. I know this goes against my every instinct to put the kid to the curb and slap a free sticker on him.

André you horde things. You'd never get rid of him. What of the two Ethan traveled with?

That's the other stop Jules and I are going to make. I'd hoped to sidestep this part of the conversation with you.

I want to come.

Jovan, you are pregnant with our child. Please, mon amour, stay put, just this once, for me? For our child?

Children.

Gasping, André asked aloud, "What—did-you—say?"

I found out at the doctors yesterday. He had to give me the okay to fly home and he found two heartbeats instead of one.

This is all the more reason for you to stay put and me to lock you up and throw away the key for the next five months.

André, get a grip.

Does Savanah know yet?

No. I wanted to tell you first.

Overflowing with pride and astonishment, André announced, "Julian, Jovan's having twins."

That declaration left André alone outside. Julian

disappeared into the house. Through the window he saw Julian pick up his sister and swing her in circles, both laughing.

André sauntered into the kitchen. "Motion sickness ring any bells, Jules? Hates merry-go-rounds and roller-coasters!"

"I'm sorry, Blossom." Julian set Jovan down.

Jovan looped her arm through her husband's for balance until the room stopped spinning. "How long will you be out?"

"As long as it takes to secure our family. I want Jonah and Payton to stay with you. I'll take Donovan with me once we find him. We shouldn't be long."

****

Awkward silence permeated the car like the aroma of burnt popcorn. It was there, stinkin' up the ride. What do you say to someone who failed to protect your family? That knowingly put them in harm's way? That you had no idea even existed? That was a vamp turned by your sister? "What ya been up to the past century?" sounded so trite. André was saved by the bell, literally. The cop car's whistles and sirens added more colors to the sky than the Aurora Borealis and more noise than a kid band in the garage armed with a guitar and drums, a keyboard and no knowledge of how to play them. Flares along the side of the road burned a brilliant orange and blue. Further down the street, a cluster of ambulances, fire trucks and more cops blocked the road. A man wearing a fluorescent orange vest stood out better than a fully dressed man at a nudist colony as he swung a neon light and waved them down.

"Dead end, boys," he told them as he stuck his head in the window of their SUV. "Two cops transporting an intruder were just slaughtered. Another damned vamp attack."

André and Julian looked between themselves and then at the toppled van, the wheels still spinning. The doors to the back of the van lay in the road, the werewolf that occupied the van moments past, MIA.

"We think the monsters are in that home. We got a call from the neighbors. Heard a lot of ruckus. I want these rogues eradicated." The officer turned and headed back to his partner.

Immediately, André contacted his wife. *Jovan? Ethan's escaped. The cops are dead. Vamps. Get everyone into the tunnels. Lock down now.*

Keep me informed and, André? Don't try to be a hero. Your daughter, two babies and I need you.

I thought I was one, a hero. You make me sad.

Stop quoting Monty Python movies, you goof.

Cherié, I'll love you forever.

You better!

"Ands, I'm going to slip around the back side of that home and see who's on first." Julian vanished before André even had time to think about protesting.

Donovan suggested, "I can dematerialize and enter the home. They'll never know I'm there."

"Way too risky, Donovan. If you get caught the cops will think they've got their man and you're tomorrow's news. Do the perimeter only."

"My Prince, you need to stay put. You needn't risk your life here and now. You have so much at stake at home. Julian and I are more than capable."

"Donovan, stop calling me that. I don't need any attention."

"I'm sorry. Old habits die hard."

"Let's make certain this old habit, me, doesn't die hard. I'm going to walk up and casually butt in. I don't believe you and I can read one another's minds can we?"

"No, but if you have need of me, contact Raven."

André rolled his eyes. "How long have you been able to read her?"

"You might want to let her tell you."

Frustrated he bit, "I don't have the luxury of time on my side. How long?"

"Too long."

****

Crouched low to the ground a few homes over from where the cops were Julian found Ethan bundled not so nicely in roughly twenty pounds of silver chains. "Can you move?"

"Not really. I don't even know how I got this far. Behind you, Julian," Ethan yelled a second too late.

A blurry figure slashed through the night and cut Julian wide open. He took in what his eyes allotted before he inevitably viewed the backside of his eyelids. *Ands, a young man with reddish-brown dreds just ripped into me. He has snake eyes. He's carting a Kris. Got me good.* Julian stumbled onto and then over a lounge chair and landed flat on his back.

Jules? Where are you? I'm coming.

No! Julian wanted his brother-in-law away from the danger. Being a werewolf he'd heal much faster than humans. Even though André had the benefits of longevity and speed being bound to his siblings, mortality still owned his ass, and Julian took a vow to protect it, from the day his sister took her vows and married him. *Ands, I mean it, leave.*

Not without you. I just spoke to Raven. Donovan's coming.

There are three cops closing in on us as we speak. Guns are drawn, Ands. If it's silver, Ethan and I are toast.

Relax, Grimmy, I'm coming.

Four rounds of gunshots reverberated through the air. Sickening, cracking noises exploded behind each blast. André slammed into the dirt hard, then his face met the dew covered grass with an abandoned thud. Pain radiated across his chest and wrapped around to his back. He wasn't certain if Julian got shot or him. He didn't know whose pain he was experiencing as he lay there bleeding.

"Son of a bitch," he muttered before the night went completely black.

Chapter Five

Without time to blink, darkness swarmed Savanah in the same fashion locust covered a cornfield, all-consuming. Jovan stumbled then collapsed, and Savanah caught her mother before she hit the floor. Savanah turned to say something to her aunt Raven, but instead watched helplessly as her aunt did a face plant with as much accuracy as a penny would hit the ground being dropped from the Empire State Building.

"Holy shit!" she screamed. When no one told her to watch her mouth she began to cry.

****

Donovan stumbled over Julian, curled up in fetal position covered in blood and crying like he'd never seen any man do.

"He's gone, Donovan," Julian gasped. "God forgive me, I just got him killed. I just got my best friend killed." Julian grabbed Donovan by his shirt and pulled his face to within an inch of his. "It should have been me."

"Who's gone?" the tall, dark vamp asked.

"André—I can't feel him. I heard the shots. I felt them as if they hit me. Get me up." Julian fell forward holding his stomach.

"Julian, you're watering the lawn with your blood. What the hell happened?" Donovan peeled off his coat then his shirt, and shredded it into strips. He jammed the material into Julian's side to try and slow down his blood loss.

"I'll be fine. We have to get Ands." Julian shoved Donovan off him in an attempt to get up. He went sideways and fell again.

Behind Julian, Ethan waited bound in silver, spiked chains. A sadistic razor sharp garrote decorated his neck and made his jugular veins bulge on both sides of the choker. "Get me out of this shit, and I can help."

"Eth, I'll be right there," Donovan assured him.

"Julian, I'm putting you in the shed with Ethan until I find André." Donovan helped Julian sit beside Ethan and then removed the metal noose from Ethan. "The two of you—don't blink without my permission."

"I feel drained. Silver sucks."

"You'll be fine in a minute, Eth. Hold tight." With one seamless, fluid spin, Donovan disappeared into the night just as easily as he'd appeared into everyone's lives a little earlier.

Once he evanesced, he found the cops converged in a circle, all weapons drawn on André. Why—he didn't understand. André wasn't breathing. Donovan contacted Raven.

****

In their Manhattan studio, Lucian set Elyza down in haste, with no good night kiss or lullaby. He turned to Serina and said one thing before becoming one with the floor.

"Ouch!"

Serina glanced around her penthouse and did the one thing she'd vowed to never do again.

Panicked.

Hated it when it happened because nothing good

ever came from losing control of emotions, but this time she surrendered to the chaos.

All of her family's pain, frustrations, fears, and doubts, time's infinity swallowed her whole. She now knew what it felt like to be inside a boa constrictor fighting to get out.

Two hundred and forty pounds of dead weight lay sprawled out in front of her, bleeding and barely breathing. Lucian and Raven seemed to be sailing on the same ship, the Titanic and Serina didn't fancy the ending to that particular tragedy.

Whoever orchestrated this got their monies' worth. Tenfold! Every single member of the St. James' family were linked together like pieces of a jigsaw puzzle. With one missing piece, the puzzle didn't work. The picture wasn't complete. For one hundred years it's how this family survived, all eleven of them. All for one and one for all.

****

Jonah squeezed a wet cloth out across Raven's face and neck to bring her out of her spell. Raven's eyes ricocheted like a pinball being flipped around as she came to.

Savanah sat hysterical with her mother wrapped in her arms. Once Raven had her equilibrium back she crawled to Savanah and held them both.

Serrie? André's been hurt. Donovan just contacted me. I can't do this again.

I know, Raven. Lucian's face down on the floor too. I felt it as well, the second the bullets penetrated André.

Serrie, Jovan's down. She's having twins. What the hell's happening?

It seems the devil came knocking on our door, and we stupidly let him in.

The devil's advocate, Serrie, and his name is Ethan.

Serina screamed, "Damn you, Mum, for never teaching me how to evanesce. I could be up there by now helping everyone, but *n-o-o-o!* I'm stuck here. Some witch I am."

Serrie, Donovan told me he can bring André over. He said it's the only way to save him. What will happen to Luce and Jovan and the babies if they feel him really gone from us?

Keep talking to them, Raven. They can hear you. It will give them a bittersweet hope to cling to. Do it. Allow Donovan to do this.

Serina? Do you need me? I heard some ungratuitous words related to my wellbeing roll from your lips.

Oh, Mother, you brain beep me now? In the middle of trying to save the world and you are like Typhoid Mary spreading the plague. That was you, right? So if you've nothing constructive to offer other than criticisms...

Serina, I'm in Saratoga. I followed the news trail, and I came looking for you. I want to meet my granddaughter. I know something's happened. Tell me. I can help. I owe your family a great debt. Let me start to repay them.

That stopped Serina in her tracks and without further hesitation Serina filled her mother in on the details and directions to the house.

Serina, care for your husband. Place your child in his arms. Once he feels her presence his life will once again be on a forward path.

She's a baby. She doesn't have the powers to heal yet.

Never underestimate the eternal bond and love a parent feels for their child, Serina. She will heal his heart without medicines. He will feel her and realize if his brother does not survive, he will and he has the most important reason in the world too. Tell André's daughter to hold closely to her mother until I am there. Tell her to not let go and continue talking to her parents. I am close by now, crossing the small bridge. Keep your mind open to me. Together we are of one mind, one goal. Life.

Mother, don't hurt them! Habit or fear, the words hit the airway. Would she always have a chunk of animosity reserved for her mother? Serina silently made the sign of the cross against her chest as she prayed. "Things really can't get any worse, can they?"

Savanah, don't have a conniption fit when you hear this. I'm sending someone to help you until we can all be together. Reluctant to say the least, Serina didn't want to tell Savanah her mother planned on riding in on a broomstick and saving the day.

When my mother gets there…

Excuse me? When who gets here? No freaking way, Aunt Serina. Have you lost your mind? I thought we made a pact to never let that woman in your life, let alone ours again.

She's the only chance we have at keeping your mother alive. Trust me?

You, yes. Her? No. Hell no!

Good. It's agreed. We're running out of time.

Aloud Savanah screamed, "I must be certifiable. I

can't believe I'm going along with this. If my parents survive this night somebody's going to bloody kill me come morning. What am I allowing here?"

Hope.

Hope my lily-white ass.

Mouth, Peanut.

****

Donovan returned to Julian and Ethan. "I've found André, and I've asked Raven permission to bring André over. He will die soon if he isn't."

Drenched in blood and sweat Ethan crouched in the small shed surrounded by a lawn mower, a gas can, rakes, hoses and bicycles. Opposite him, Julian had already pretty much healed up.

Without notice Julian grabbed Ethan's arm, put his lips to Ethan's wrist, and with a jerky motion bit off a clump of skin.

"What the hell?" Ethan yelled trying to yank his hand away from Julian. "Sick bastard."

"There is a silver barb meshed into your wrist. If left in, you'd die from septicemia. Trust me… My tongue on you… I'd rather rip out your throat, but that doesn't seem to be an option at this juncture." Switching gears, he added, "Donovan, Ethan tells me that two vamps tore into the van. He only recognized Xanti. And Xanti called the other by the name, Junior." Julian gave Donovan a weighted gaze. "Well then, Donovan, go kill our prince with kindness. I'd rather have one more mouth to feed than miss his ugly mug and ridiculous jokes. But once this deed is done you will release any power you have over my brother-in-law. He will not be your fiddle you string along, because by the Gods, if you don't, I'll be the last person you ever see, nightmares included." Julian pushed his body from the floor, and loomed over Donovan.

Donovan backed up. Julian followed, and pressed him against the wall. "Do we have an accord?" Julian asked.

"What is it with you and that word, Uncle Jules?" Ethan asked.

Julian leaned backwards and without missing a beat, dug his fingers into the area of flesh he'd just gnawed off Ethan.

Ethan twisted trying to get out of Julian's grasp.

"The next time it shall be your balls I shred, young man. I'm not your uncle, and I'm not your flesh and blood, but it'll be mine if I so choose."

Donovan bowed. "I mean André no harm, only to save him from a certain death."

"And you believe bringing him over to become one of the undead is saving him? It's leading him to damnation if you ask me," Ethan added astonished at the turn the conversation took. "Have you people lost the meaning of life? You can't continue to cheat death. At some point it will catch up to you. None of us were intended to live forever."

"Try telling that to the vampire community, Ethan." With that Donovan vanished.

Chapter Six

Serina, I'm with your family. I don't believe I've ever seen so many knives held at my throat at the same time. You did tell them I was coming, didn't you?
You mean warn them.

Savanah gave the woman the once-over, disgust and distrust evident by the snarl on her lips. The woman looked just like her aunt except matured; weathered she'd decided and bonier—hardened, nothing soft or feminine about her. She'd only ever heard nightmares of this woman and now here she stood in front of her, about to spiritually enter her mother. "Hurt her, her unborn babies or anyone in my family, and I'll read a charm to you from my prized possession, *The Blackest Dreams*." Savanah watched Olivia's eyes widen, but she wasn't certain whether it was fear or curiosity. "Not what you expected? Yes, Olivia, I possess *The Bound Grimoire* as well. Both the light and the dark to our worlds. The books are as different as you and I."

"I see you have your mother's and grandmother's temper. Good, we'll need a feisty one to get through this. Now allow me passage." Olivia skirted around each person carefully until the pointed end of a dagger greeted her.

Raven prodded, "Why now? You've had a hundred years to kiss and make up."

"I want to see my granddaughter, and I owe your

family more than you know. This is wasting precious time."

"Ya think?" Raven turned away from Olivia and led her toward the stairs.

****

Ethan suggested, "Donovan approach the cops and use your voice to draw their attention away from André. Julian and I will skirt behind the officers and get to André." Ethan watched Donovan close. He should've been used to the creeped out feelings he always got in the Maestro's presence, but now Donovan had the same slimy feel to him. Already he was second-guessing his entire life the past years with the vamp and his companions. Regardless of the circumstances around him, he saw things clearer, was able to think for himself again. Being on another continent helped. Falling for the woman of his dreams? Literally? Remained to be seen.

"Lock your safeties and holster your guns. You have never seen this man. The man that killed your brothers-in-arms has long since been dead. You cannot kill something twice. All right, maybe you can. Semantics. Your work here is done. Return to your precinct and tell of your bravery and triumph," Donovan instructed the officers.

Ethan watched each man robotically lower his piece. The guns' safeties clicked, they were holstered and the cops swayed in the light breeze while Donovan knelt beside André.

"Time's up, my prince. Your destiny has yet to be decided. I can't believe I'm the one doing this dirty deed," Donovan whispered as he closed his mouth over André's neck and drank his life away one devastating drop at a time. Dirty deed or not, Donovan's groin became rock-hard.

"You're fucking sick, Donovan. You got hard killing him."

"Forgive me, Ethan. Did you forget I'm a vampire?"

Finished, Donovan placed André's lifeless body in the back of the SUV. He walked off to the side of the vehicle and vomited almost every last drop of blood he'd just taken. "No blood bonds, Jules," he professed before wiping his mouth on his sleeve.

Julian approached him. "You did what you had to do."

"Is Ethan right? Did I just damn the man?"

"Donovan, do you honestly believe he wanted to die tonight? He just found out he's having twins. You saved his family from an eternal hell. Thank you for saving my brother-in-law and my best friend."

"Let us go." Donovan got into the back seat of the car with André's body. "What are we doing with Ethan? He can help you now that Xanti has shown his true colors. He'd be insane to go back there and stay with them."

"He's tied to Xier. He said it himself. He's dog food. He's on his own."

"Oh—no I'm not. I'm coming with." Ethan jumped in the front seat of the truck and locked the doors.

"Ethan, locking doors won't keep the boogie man outside. They come in all shapes and sizes. Get out."

"Nope. I am as good as dead if I go back to that house."

"Then you risk all of our lives. Get out. Now!" Julian growled and showed a full set of canines. His grip pierced the steering wheel. Reddish brown fur rippled down the length of what used to be his arm and at the same time his nose elongated into a muzzle. His ears became perky—elf-like in shape and covered with fur.

Donovan suggested, "Ethan, if you have an ounce of self-preservation in your hide, get out of the car now. Julian will finish shifting in 'bout one minute and then you'll be lying next to André. Allow the family time." Donovan tapped Julian's shoulder. "Julian, timing is everything and now sucks. Let's just get away from here first? Then you can kill him if you must."

Ethan exploded, "Thanks, Vonnie. Fine! I'm out. You're on your own, all of you. Good luck warding off the Maestro."

Ethan jumped from the car and before his feet hit the ground he'd shifted into his wolf. He disappeared between a row of arborvitaes that separated two homes. Looking around he knew he had to return to the Union Avenue home. His future lay beyond the walls. Just what his future held he had no clue, but he had no more control of his life than the planets did rotating around the sun. The woman hidden within the fortress ruled his very stars. The Maestro's power paled in comparison to this strange tugging at his heart.

Sitting on the back gate of the Alabama training track, he called, "Savanah!" as a hawk soared above him. "What is it you've done to me?" Ethan found the track tranquil now, no horses running circles, no trainers snapping whips, just a quiet loneliness he couldn't shake. Eyes closed he saw those long legs, thick black curls and huge bluish-black eyes and a smile he recognized as trouble when she looked at him.

Oh, yes, he thought, we will get into some trouble together.

****

A chain reaction of events began the moment André's heart stopped. Jovan's heart followed the same path as her husband's as did her unborn babies. Olivia was swift to shed her soul and energy and enter Jovan's body. She set the pace for all three hearts. She'd come to weather the storm, and by the Gods, what a tempest.

Serina coached Savanah, telling her to follow her lead while she cared for Lucian. *Savanah, continue to monitor your parents. You can do it.*

Auntie, I can't feel either of my parents. Are they lost to me? Savanah teetered on the hysterical precipice. Not only did she feel orphaned, but betrayed by a man she'd only just met. Despite undeniable feeling for the man, she no longer cared if Ethan lived to see another sunrise, nor would he if her parents didn't survive. She would personally snuff his last breath.

No, Peanut. You will not lose either of them. My mother has no use for the word defeat.

As if everything that just happened to her wasn't bad enough, Savanah heard Ethan call her just as clearly as if he'd stood beside her. And she thought she was shaken up a second ago. Savanah walked to the corner of the room, and rested her head on the cold brick wall. She contemplated the idea of banging her head against it to knock out Ethan's soft, soothing voice. "Ethan, how can I hear you? What is it you've done to me?"

Running laps around the track, Ethan's footing became four left paws, all going in opposite directions, taking him in one direction, down.

Savanah, you and I have no blood ties and yet we can hear each other? This can't be good. Are you all right?

No, I'm not all right, you moron. My father's been shot and ravaged by a vamp and my mother's collapsed.

I'm sorry. I never meant for any of this to happen. If I could've helped you I would have.

You just so happen to be the very reason all this has happened. If you didn't show up here with some asinine excuse none of this would have happened.

You're right…

No shit, Sherlock. Please…just go away. Savanah sighed.

I can't.

Don't stick around on my account. Whatever this thing between us is will fade out in time. It has to because I'm not having anything to do with you no matter… Savanah clammed up. She found no need to inflate his ego and tell him how gorgeous he was or that he made her blood boil or that he made her feel things she'd never experienced just being in the same room with him. From everything she'd just witnessed, his ego had his own personal helium tank to pump him up whenever.

Savanah, you may not have said it, but you thought it. Thank you.

Go to hell, Ethan. Go find another child to kidnap.

Savanah, it's not like that. I don't know how to explain it to you to make you understand.

Ethan, I don't want to understand anything you could possibly say or do. My parents are dying in front of me.

Savanah cut herself off from him, or at least she thought she did. She ignored the voice in her head telling her he was sorry. She ignored her own voice telling her this man had so much more to offer if she'd only give him the chance. Finally, she told herself to shut up.

****

In the tunnels far beneath the home, soft cries crept through the layers of earth and stone. Savanah's heart fragmented as her uncle carried her father's limp body into the cool, dimly lit room. This, the pain, consumed her. She'd never felt anything as horrific as seeing the one man she idolized, loved with every ounce of her soul, cherished his smiles, his laughter, his simple silliness, laid out before her, lifeless. No! Not lifeless. She almost bit her tongue for such a negative thought. Transposing, that worked. Three days. She had to keep it together three days. For her mother and her siblings, yet to be born. And deep in the back of her heart for the moron that created all this ruin. *Fuck you, Ethan.*

Day one was about to turn into three days of ugliness Savanah wasn't certain any of them could survive and come back whole.

****

After he placed André next to Jovan, Julian's claws protracted. He pointed to a stranger amongst them. "Who are you? And what are you doing to my sister?" Julian looked to his brother, vengeance on the tip of his tongue. "Jonah?"

Jonah got between Olivia and Julian. "Jules— before you do or say another word, listen to me. This is Serina's mother…"

Introduction over. Julian bent and plowed his

102

shoulder into his brother and shoved him across the room to get within inches of the woman.

"I'd hoped I killed you the night Serina hung from the cross. Get away from Jovan and her babies, wicked hag." Julian ripped Olivia from her chair and slammed her against the brick wall. Following her down to the ground, he found a resting spot on the hollow of Olivia's throat, and he squeezed until his knuckles burned. Olivia lay there blue, listless.

Jonah and Donovan each grabbed a shoulder in a feeble attempt to pry Julian from her, but Julian heaved both of them aside.

"Uncle, no! Mum will die without her." Savanah touched Julian's shoulder.

Julian jerked and lost his footing. He stumbled backwards, and landed squarely on his butt.

Angry words bellowed across the room. "You won't harm my sister, cowardly crone. I'm going to end your life here and now. I know you killed our mother."

"No, Uncle! Think of the babies, and Mum, please? You're like a madman right now." In her uncle's eyes, Savanah saw fear for the very first time. She'd never expected that, because he was the man villains always ran from in her nightmares. She knelt, cupped his cheeks and told him in a guarded tone, "I read her. She means no harm."

Julian stared as Savanah helped him stand. "Are you certain?" He could barely speak. His eyes held moisture he refused to let go.

Savanah nodded. "I wouldn't have allowed her in otherwise."

Jonah lifted Olivia from the floor, and gave Julian a wide berth when he brought her back to Jovan's side.

Olivia looked to Julian. "Am I going to meet yet another hard, immobile surface if I begin?"

Julian ushered out one last thing to her. "Your heart for hers!"

"Julian, you're bleeding again," Donovan motioned to Julian's side.

"What's a little blood-shed between friends?" he asked, mockery trampling his words.

"This is going to be the most tumultuous three days the lot of us have ever spent together," Payton mumbled to no one in particular. "We're going down like flies high on bug juice."

"It's my fault, Jonah." Julian confessed, his voice sounded strange even to him. "If he didn't come after me, if the stupid bastard had just listened and stay put, none of this would be happening right now." Julian covered his face from everyone's curious stare. "I'm so sorry."

"Jules, if that little shifter Ethan hadn't shown up here trying to kidnap a spawn of Sinclair, none of this would've happened. You take no responsibility for this." Payton rested his arm around Julian's shoulders. He looked directly at Olivia, and added, "We don't call him Grimmy for nothing. You'll be wise to remember that.

****

Refusing rest until her father rose, Savanah watched over her family. Somehow in the midst of all this, she found a smile, a small lopsided curl of her lips as she watched Molly, Jonah and Payton rest. The sight of them brought back memories of when she was a child. Her toy chest overflowing with dolls and stuffed animals melded into one large clump of tangled arms and legs and body parts just as these three were, oblivious to their surroundings.

Julian had made certain they were armed to the hilts with spear guns that launched wooden stakes at ten per second, crossbows that shot silver-tipped arrows, and Smith and Wessons loaded with both silver and lead, ready for anyone—shifter or not. Savanah eyed her uncle. His bloodshot eyes read better than any book. He too had sat a vigil vowing to protect everyone. His fingers caressed his favorite gun, his own version of a stun gun he'd amplified to the point of ridiculously illegal. He'd dipped two of his four darts in Sodium Pentothal and the remaining two in Versed. Both were anesthetics with different uses. The Pentothal worked as a truth serum. The Versed worked by giving the sucker a mild case of amnesia afterwards, no recollection whatsoever of having been tased, thus getting his ass out of knee-deep trouble. Savanah watched her stealthy uncle slide Donovan's paintball gun from his grasp as he slept. It took talent to one-up a vamp. The fully automatic Dye DM7 gun was loaded with tiny baubles of concentrated garlic juice and holy water. The gun worked like a charm every time. It reduced snarling vampires to harmless, squashable mosquitoes. Julian aimed the sights of the gun on Olivia's face, his finger trigger-happy.

"Jules!" Savanah whispered her demeanor fed up.

He just smirked at her then winked. "I got your back, Peanut."

Chapter Seven

With the subtlest twinge, André stretched his fingers, one at a time. They were stiff, rigor mortis had set in. He attempted to lift his arm, but it was dead weight. His gut clenched and for a brief moment he thought he would vomit, but then a hunger pang like nothing he'd ever experienced or wanted to again, rode him like a cowboy on a bull, gripping him for dear life. His hand snaked across the bed, and with a crushing force, latched on to the first thing he found.

Jovan.

****

"Three hours tops, my saucy little tomato." Duncan told Molly, "One quick stop at the morgue to pick up blood products for André's replacement when he comes out of his slumber, and we're good to go. Serina says a transfusion will hopefully ward off the initial shock of being bloodless. The one thing I've learned living with vamps is that they aren't a fussy bunch. Blood is blood, no matter where it comes from. I mean look at me! Who in their right mind would want a piece of this?" Duncan grinned to his reflection in the rear view mirror. Serina and Lucian burst out laughing. He stuck his tongue out at them. "Other than you, of course, my red-hot momma." Duncan laughed into his cell phone.

Savanah grabbed the cell from Molly and begged, "Duncan, just this once, drive like me and get home fast?"

"Molly? Savanah? Did one of you get another speeding ticket?" Dial tone!

****

By the time they reached Saratoga, André was wide-awake, and busy battling his own demons as well as everyone in the house. He gnawed Jovan's wrist open the way a starved animal would ravage his prey, ruthlessly. Feeling a heavy blow in the back of the head, André turned to see Julian wielding the base of a tall, iron floor lamp. As he lifted his arm to defend himself, talons burst out from beneath his fingers and replaced nicely manicured nails.

"What the hell is happening to me," he screamed in agony and disbelief.

Julian dropped the lamp and took one step toward him. "Ands?"

André unleashed one powerful blow in the center of Julian's chest. Not a second passed before Julian's shirt turned a wet crimson color. André watched with a newfound enthusiasm. He rolled his eyes the length of his brother-in-law. His nose twitched like a rabbit, scenting a sweet, coppery aroma.

"Oh shit," was all Julian said.

"Papa?" Savanah took a step toward him.

André heard the word *Papa* and started to laugh and like the clutch on his car, he switched gears and began to cry. He stared into his family's faces and screamed, "Who in hell are you people?"

Savanah clasped her hand over her mouth, shocked at her father's apparent amnesia. She expected the bloodlust, but not knowing her or her mother was incomprehensible.

"André? It's me—your wife." Jovan pointed to Savanah. "This is your daughter." She pleaded, "Please remember us."

With André distracted, Jonah and Payton jumped in and tried to wrangle him to the ground, but André spun on them. He grabbed Jonah by the forearms and dropped backwards, bringing Jonah down with him. As he hit the floor, André jammed his foot into Jonah's groin and pushed up sending Jonah sailing over his head and into the wall. "One down." André brushed off his hands. With his next breath of air, Andre did a scissor kick and took Payton's legs out from under him. Payton tumbled to the floor and slammed his head on the edge of the coffee table. "Who's next?" André stood and struck a boxing pose.

"You, Ands." Julian aimed his taser gun at his brother-in-law.

Jonah protested as he stood, "No, Jules, that thing is inhumane," and stumbled into the line of fire, intercepting the four darts into his own hide.

For a minute no one moved, spoke or bit anyone.

Jonah turned to Julian, a mixture of pain and disbelief plastered all over his face. He lunged awkwardly to the left and landed on a small winged-back chair in front of the window. His hand automatically went to the darts, trying to pry them from his skin, but his entire body writhed with supercharged volts of electricity. Before he passed out his last words were, "Could someone find my balls?"

Donovan rushed Andre, but André used his forward momentum to his vantage and hoisted Donovan up over his head, across the room, into and then over Julian, ending at the foot of a dresser, breaking a large antique mirror atop it.

****

"Hello, hello!" Duncan shouted, as he shoved open the front door with a foot. "Molly?"

From the second floor landing, Raven stuck her head over the railing and screamed, "Get up here, now. Duncan, Luce—André woke up with a vengeance." Raven ducked as a chair went sailing past her and over the balcony. The chair shattered only feet from where Duncan stood.

With their next breaths, Serina took the stairs, Elyza cradled to her chest while Lucian and Duncan passed her taking five and six steps at a time. At the end of the hallway they were greeted by an anxious mob of family members.

"Papa's gone bonkers, Uncle Luce," Savanah cried. "Auntie, get Elyza out of here. He doesn't recognize any of us."

"Lucian, go to your brother now." Serina started to follow, but hands from every direction grabbed her. "Let go of me," she protested. "I know what I'm do—" Seeing her mother, her words caught in her throat like insects in a web.

"You are not going in there with that baby?" Olivia's question to her daughter sounded more like a direct order.

"Hello, Mum. Nice to see you too," she added, intent on sounding sarcastic.

"Can I hold her?" Olivia asked her arms out.

Serina gave her a vexatious glare. "Are you insane? How do I know you won't evanesce with her?"

Olivia's arms dropped limp to her side.

"I'll be joining my husband on the other side of

that damned door. Excuse me." Serina shoved open the door and found her husband, who'd hit the stairs running when they'd entered the house, and brother-in-law on the floor, André on top and Lucian the bottom. Getting mauled.

Broken furniture, shattered glass, and blood-splattered walls now gave the room a morose ambiance. All that was missing was the crime scene investigating team. "André?" Serina whispered, "I have someone who wants to meet you. Look at me. *Pssst!*" She tried again and when no one answered she yelled, "André, it's me, Serina. You need to listen to me. Stop biting your brother."

When he lifted his head and turned to her, she gasped. His sunken, blood-shot eyes looked right through her. Bloody tears splattered his cheeks. His hair, which he always kept neat, was a cluster of angry curls and new fangs rested over his bottom lip, stained red, but Serina was thankful he recognized his name.

Serina, the true optimist. If she'd had a free hand, she'd have pat her own back.

"Serina!" Lucian's voice spilled onto the floor, along with his blood. "My brother sits on the brink of madness and here my wife and daughter stand, like a fresh milk and cookie snack. My wild rose, you wouldn't go to the zoo and play with the lions, tigers and bears before they'd been fed, would you?"

Lucian, it will be fine. You need to trust me.

"Serina, André isn't himself at this moment. He's not feeling well. I have to wonder about you too, bringing your baby into this." Jovan spoke up as she pulled the darts from her unconscious brother.

Serina asked, "Jovan, come to me. Now please."

Jovan didn't budge.

With a bug-eyed glare and nod of her head Serina urged, "Take the baby and walk to your husband."

"Serina, no!" Lucian screamed again, louder.

"I'm not deaf, Lucian," She snapped. "If Mohamed won't come to the mountain… Jovan, meet Elyza, your niece. Elyza, this is my stubborn, older sister, Jovan." Serina skirted around the broken glass and objects and placed her little angel in Jovan's arms.

André methodically followed her every step.

Jovan met the little girl's curious gaze and tears fell. "This baby is a miracle, a new beginning—a lifeline to carry on our love and families. She brings us hope, when we have had none for so very long." Jovan blew a kiss to her sister.

Jovan stood and carried the baby to her husband and in a soft tone said, "Look who I have in my arms, André. See what you and I have to look forward to in five months. André, she is so beautiful and full of life. She needs both her parents just as the two babies I carry will need you."

André swung his head back to Lucian then glanced at Serina, his head off to one side, his giant bluish-black eyes void of life.

Lucian tapped his arm. "André, do you remember when I first turned?"

André followed the sound of Lucian's voice back to him, and rested on all the blood covering his twin. He licked his lips then gave pause. "Ask me first if I remember you."

"You will. Serina is going to set up a few things and give you blood. You are a little anemic right now. It's why you're having trouble concentrating."

"Anemic? That's what this is called now?" A gurgled laugh crawled from André's throat.

Apprehension still very apparent, Lucian looked at his wife and nodded. "Serina, ask Raven to get the blood ready."

"André, what do you think of your niece?" Jovan gingerly put her hand on her husband's shoulder to keep his train of thoughts to more pleasant things.

He turned, and she jerked back her hand. The blood oozing from her wrist caught his attention.

Speaking in a low monotone pitch, Lucian suggested, "André, if you take her wrist to your mouth, two things will happen. You will get a small taste of what your wife has to offer you and your saliva will coagulate the wounds you've given her. You can heal her right now. I didn't have anyone to help me when I first turned. You have all of us."

"You are a sick son of a—" He inhaled. The scent of blood exploded in his airway; he doubled over, a tight grip on his abdomen. "Why would anyone want—" André squeezed his eyes shut and shook his head. In what felt like a lifetime to him, memories of his previous life flooded his circuits. About to say something he gagged, then spit-up some gooey, black sludge that looked like something drained from a 1920's pick-up truck all over his twin.

Lucian wiped the mess from his eyes. "And I thought Elyza's spit up was foul!"

André reached for Jovan.

Jovan readily stepped back.

Wiping his mouth off with his sleeve André tried again. His voice raspy he asked, "Lucian, what did you do this room? Who pissed you off?"

Lucian choked back a mixture of tears and laughter.

André turned to Jovan. "Cherié? What happened? Did Lucian hurt you?" More sanguineous tears rolled from his cheeks. "I'm so confused. Please tell me what the hell has happened. I don't recall anything. I feel like Jack Nicholson in *The Shining*—completely insane."

Trapped under him, Lucian coughed a few times. "Uhm, what about me? Forget who you've pinned to the floor? And for the record—"

"I know. I haven't been able to do this in years. So why can I now?" André shifted his weight to allow Lucian to move out from under him. He plopped down on the floor beside him. "Luce, what happened? Can I hold her? She's so little," he said reaching for Elyza.

The three of them screamed a collective, "No!"

André recoiled. "Explain to me why you are both covered in blood, and I can't remember a damn thing."

"What is the last thing you do remember?" Donovan asked his garlic gun aimed at André.

Looking cross-eyed down the barrel of the gun, André asked, "What have I done to deserve this?"

"Point the gun at the floor, Donovan." Lucian slapped the weapon out of André's face.

André shrugged his shoulders. "Donovan, Jules and I went looking for the vamps that killed the cops and Ethan."

Lucian answered, "Maybe it's a protective brain mechanism. Amnesia or something like post-traumatic stress."

André stood, aggravated. "You still haven't told me what happened and why can't I hold my niece?"

"Jovan," Serina said, "it's all right. Let him hold

her."

Within a heartbeat, Lucian wormed his way in between them. "Oh, I think not."

Serina walked around Lucian as he turned with her trying to block her, which proved futile. Serina placed Elyza in her brother-in-law's arms. "Lucian do you honestly think I would endanger our daughter?"

"Why the hell am I a danger to anyone?" André asked, exhausted. He immediately covered Elyza's little ears. "Oh, Elyza, I'm so sorry. Uncle André isn't used to holding babies, or his tongue."

"Papa, mouth," Savanah slid in as she crossed the room to sit beside her father.

André glanced at Savanah out of the corner of his eye. "Good one, Peanut."

Elyza produced an all gums smile before curdled milk shot onto his shirt. "Uncle André isn't used to that either." Jovan handed him a towel to wipe up the mess.

Lucian said, "Listen to me carefully. Ands, you and I are now identical in all matters of life and death and all that falls between. Welcome to my world."

The words didn't register at first. André thought they were pulling a fast one on him until Jovan wouldn't look him in the eye, nor his brother. He noticed Donovan disappeared again, literally. Without thinking he bent down and kissed Elyza's forehead, lingering momentarily, enjoying that new baby smell because she definitely had a fresher scent than he did.

Lucian lunged, but André held his hand up. "She's fine." Seeing Lucian so distraught, André handed Elyza back to him. Even though he knew the answer he asked, "Tell me you are joking?"

No one answered. André looked at himself

lengthwise, touching body parts randomly, making sure everything was intact and where it should be, including his manhood. He took in the room, the damage done to his family and the furniture. Bending over, he picked up a piece of broken mirror and peeled his lips back. The reflection sliced into his sense of self. The glass fell through trembling fingers back to the floor, and shattered to even smaller pieces, just as his heart did seeing a new set of dents.

"Oh sweet mother of God. Who did this to me? I'll kill them."

"Actually, Ands," Raven came in with all the paraphernalia to set up a transfusion, "it was me."

"You, Beauty? Why?"

"She didn't do this, my Prince. I did." Donovan stepped out of his shadow and got between Raven and André.

"But she just said…"

Cutting Raven off, Donovan finished, "I had no choice. You'd have died otherwise. I asked her permission."

"I've got a mammoth headache, and I feel like Grimmy—the real one, had his way with me."

"He did." Julian rubbed the newly formed lump on his head. "You think you've a headache. Look what you did to me."

André turned toward Julian's voice. "Grimmy, you tried to kill me."

"Yes—I mean no, André," Julian confessed. "I got you killed. You were shot four times by the locals."

"So what constitutes you getting me killed? I remember you telling me you were attacked, and I started after you. This is not your fault, Jules."

Donovan butt in, "Sire, I bit you to bring you over—to save you." The lanky vamp dropped to his knees before André. "If you wish my life, take it now." Donovan bowed his head.

Raven caught her breath.

"Breathe, Beauty," André said as he ran his hands through his sister's hair. "Odd way to go about saving people don't you think? Doesn't this constitute killing them with kindness? The twenty-first century does have hospitals and doctors, all though we've never had a real need for them. Get up, Donovan. I cannot kill a man who brought me back from the brink of death even in the most unorthodox manner." Once he noticed Jonah and Payton still out cold he asked, "Is that my handy work?"

Julian nodded. "Jonah took the brunt end of the taser gun. He's gonna be mad at you when he wakes up."

André had the audacity to smile until he realized all the blood, tubing and needles were really for him. In a flash his smile vanished.

Savanah took one look at her father and burst out laughing. "Oh, Papa, you're green. Well, honestly not green but grayish-blue."

"Ands, we need to get you taken care of. Sit." Lucian helped Serina set up the blood transfusion.

"Lucian, I'm sorry I hurt you. All of you. Can you forgive me?"

Jovan snuggled in to his other side and kissed his cheek. "You did nothing wrong, Bebé."

"Oh, Cherié, but I did." He took her wrist, and carefully inspected the damage.

When his lips met her flesh, she asked, "You sure

you know what you're doing?"

"We'll have fun finding out, won't we?" André kissed the length of her arm, his tongue soothing the wounds.

****

"Jovan?" Olivia's voice rattled as she pushed the bedroom door open and stepped in.

Each and every member of the St. James household turned on her like a pack of starved wolves. "I—I—I'm going to go. Yes, right now. If you ever need anything, just call out to me." Olivia back peddled to the door when a triad of ill-fated events went off more accurately than dominos tumbling.

Julian crossed the room and blocked the door before anyone saw him move. The bump on his head torn open and bleeding didn't slow him down one iota.

"Olivia, come—" Jovan stopped and said to André, "You've gone white yet again for no apparent reason. He needs more blood."

"Oh, I need blood all right! Hers!" André spat.

"Where do you think you're going?" Julian shouted right in Olivia's face. "You and I made a deal. Your heart for theirs, ring any bells?"

André ripped the tube from his arm spilling blood all over the carpet and headed for the strange woman.

She swung around to face him.

Head cocked to one side and eyes focused on Olivia as if no one else existed, André said, "I know you. You invaded my dreams for years. Your face—it tormented me and does so to this day." He crossed the room with sure-footed steps. "For nearly twenty years." He stopped one step from her. "Every night I lay awake afraid to go to sleep because I knew you would be there…waiting, in my closet, under my bed, in my head. You're a dream snatcher. But instead of stealing away a young boy's dream you stole me. Why? What did you want with me? Who are you and what are you doing here now? Answer me!" He grabbed her shirt collar.

"Stop it, André. You'll scare the baby." Serina said.

"You're the one who should be scared, Serina. She's the devil in disguise. Don't let her near your child." André closed the gap between them. "Tell me you are not Serina's mother. Tell me that you did not touch my wife and children. Any of them!"

"Ands, you're freaking everyone out. What's going on?" Lucian asked.

"Do you want to tell them or shall I?" André poked Olivia in the chest.

"André, enough!" Serina pried her way between her mother and her brother-in-law, her back to Olivia. "What are you talking about?"

Julian tapped Serina on her shoulder. "I suggest for the time being you remove you and your daughter from what might very likely turn into a war zone."

Serina spun to Julian landing squarely face to face with her mother. The two women locked their emerald eyes.

"Serina, he's right. Get away before anything happens."

One step short of hysterical, Serina pleaded, "Please just tell me. It can't be that bad, Mum."

"Don't bet the house on that," Julian chided.

"What the hell do you two know that I don't?" Serina asked completely aggravated.

Olivia cleared her throat, and wiped beads of sweat from her forehead. "Please don't make me do this. Not here—not like this." She looked between both men. Neither looked sympathetic.

"Okay, can we focus on the good things she's done? André, she saved Jovan. For the three days you were lost in space, she monitored your babies and kept Jovan alive, because she wouldn't had made it other—"

Before Serina finished and anyone could stop lightning from striking, André ripped Olivia off her feet and hurled her body through the wall. Not into the wall, through it, clear into the hallway. The aftermath—a jagged hole in the plaster and broken beams to boot. Pandemonium followed Olivia out the door.

Savanah headed for Olivia, but her father grabbed her.

"No," he said anxious. "Don't touch her or allow her to touch you. Ever again."

"Why, Papa? What could she have done? She saved Mum and the babies."

Serina passed the baby to Lucian and ran to her mother's aid.

André nudged Olivia with the tip of his shoe. When she moaned a grin spread across his face. "She's a poisoned apple. Sweet on the outside and then you take a big, juicy bite and find you've bitten a lethal snake in half."

Delirious, Olivia spilled a century worth of her secrets. "I didn't mean to kill your mother, Julian, Jonah, Jovan. I swear it was an accident. André, I needed the money your aunt Chyna offered me. I've had a lifetime to regret stealing you away from your family, for ruining the relationship you should have had. I'm sorry I lost faith. Thomas has been the only man I ever allowed in my heart, in my bed. I'm sorry I ruined Oliver's life as well. And I'm so sorry for not allowing either of you children. I'm just sorry."

"No!" Serina backed away from her and tripped on the top step of the stairway. Inches before her head slammed into the stairs Serina froze, suspended midair like a flyer in a circus, minus the life supporting ropes and net below. As blood rushed to her head veins bulged in her temples. Gravity took over control of her skirt and shirt and left one very exposed upside down woman. No panties on and her breasts spilled free of her bra. No one said anything even though they all took the time to peek.

Reaching out for Serina, Olivia found André's hands reaching at the same time for her neck, full throttle.

No longer able to control the beast screaming inside him for retribution, André's temper exploded. His fingers burned white from pressure as he gripped and squeezed the life right out of the hag. "You ruined the relationship I should have had with my siblings, with my parents. What you did is inconceivable. They died without ever realizing I was their son. God will never forgive you for what you've done, and I sure as hell won't." Crouched over her, he enjoyed watching her struggle to breathe. "If you've marked my unborn children in any way I'll come to hell to find you."

In between gasping and choking, Olivia slipped in, "Get—in—line. Julian wants me…"

Ooh! Words were spoken. Too much air getting in. Tighten the grip! André waited. Waited for her to stop bloody breathing once and for all. He felt nothing and

120

that should have bothered him, but it didn't. It bothered him that he *should* feel bad killing this woman, killing Serina's mother in front of her and his family, but still, zero remorse. He tried to think up reasons that it should affect him that he was indeed killing someone, but still, deeper inside him sat a black, empty cave of nightmares and repugnancy that saturated his soul and would not wither away without revenge. So, he gripped her a little tighter and watched. Killing her might actually feel good. Just as she passed out, vice grips bore into him.

Donovan tugged and yanked, but André's powers were a force to be reckoned with. He clung to Olivia's neck more determined. Lucian joined Donovan, but together they were no match for the newly turned vamp.

"We need the Jaws of Life to get him off her," Donovan yelled.

Lucian disagreed, "Right now, he is the jaws of the life."

Frightened beyond words, Jovan had seen enough. She would not stand idly by and bear witness to her husband about to become a cold-blooded murderer. She grabbed Donovan's gun and took aim. "I'm so sorry, Bebé." Jovan squeezed the trigger on the gun.

Thunderous popping sounds echoed as garlic and Holy H2O bubbles peppered André. He jumped, shocked when he saw the woman responsible for sautéing him.

"Jovan? Son of a—! This stuff burns." André stripped his clothes off in a matter of seconds, with the sole exception of his black silk boxers.

Jovan stepped toward Olivia to check on her, but André covered the distance, placing his body between his wife and Olivia's.

Welts formed from the close range shots. He yelled, "You are not helping that crone. I mean it, Jovan."

André followed the path of where Jovan rested her eyes.

Destination south, his black silky boxers with a subtle rise he couldn't contain.

Yes! It still works! Happy dance later.

He realized she was staring at him and somewhere in the midst of his trying to murder a woman and then getting almost naked, the two of them got excited.

Or he did.

"A little help please? Aunt Serina's a little top heavy," Savanah squeaked as she turned an aneurism shade of red. Veins in her neck jutted out like weight lifter's trying to pick up a car with one hand tied behind his back.

Duncan bound up the stairs and snatched Serina midair. "Well here's something you don't see around here every day, even with the talented lot we've got. Bottom's up, Doc! Literally. Savvy, nice job levitating, but you could have lowered her." Duncan set Serina down next to her mother.

"I haven't learned that yet, Duncan." Savanah fanned her face. "I pick things up, just can't put them down without breaking something." She gave him a small, lopsided grin.

André slid away from Olivia, but Julian continued to hold the stun gun aimed at her heart. André pointed down the stairs to the front door. "I want you out of my home. Out of my life. Out of my families' lives. Now." He straightened his stance, turned to Julian hearing his voice.

His eyebrows arched and aimed, Julian said, "She's not walking out of here on her own accord. Furthermore, she's not walking out of here breathing. I'm not playing this time." With his finger shaking in André's face he said, "Notice I didn't try to stop you from strangling the wench."

André pushed the barrel of the gun down. "Okay, everyone out of what's left of my room. No one will kill Olivia today. Sorry, Grimmy, not even you. Tomorrow? We'll see. I want Payton and Jonah out of here too. Donovan, if you'd be so kind as to keep your distance from my sister until her men come around I'd appreciate it." Glancing at the carnage of his room, André broke out in manic laughter like someone on the verge of leaping from the ledge into a bottomless pit. Quite possibly he already had.

"André?" Lucian's concern weighted his words. He stepped toward him.

"I'm fine, Luce. Why wouldn't I be? A few days ago we met a shifter, Ethan Kitt, who said Xanti and Xier Sinclair were back in town. He told us Raven had Xavier's and Xanti's child. Thank God this isn't the case, but nonetheless Ethan's out doing the blue light special for a baby. Then Donovan pops up out of the last century and takes a whopping chunk out of me. We send Ethan to the pound, but he never makes it there and I wake up a few hours ago, feeling like death warmed over. Found out I'd died three days ago, came back as a vamp, attacked my wife, you, and anyone else in close proximity. And the icing on this stale, fruit cake? I find out the one person on this planet I never wanted near my family is not only inside this house, but inside my wife doing only God knows what to her. You guys now know that she was the one responsible for my alternate life with you and our parents, and that she killed Jovan, Julian and Jonah's mom. Nice lady. Everyone should have a mum like her. Not! Serina almost takes a dive down stairs and if weren't for my Savvy doing that freeze-frame thing on her, she'd have broken her neck and died as well. It just doesn't get any better than this!" André never came up for air.

Olivia got up slowly, and rubbed her neck. "Savanah, thank you for helping my daughter." Olivia went to shake Savanah's hand, but Julian wrapped his arms around his niece and held her, hostage-like.

"You don't touch her, ever. Did you not hear her father?"

Olivia gave a sullen nod.

"Olivia, since my dear brother-in-law won't allow your death, I have an alternate plan everyone can live with. Unfortunately, even you. Jovan, please bring me the *Bound Grimoire*? Olivia, Serina, Lucian, Savanah and I will be in the library waiting."

Jovan shook her head a fast *no*. "Jules, you can't be serious. Not the book."

"Jovan, the woman just admitted killing our mother. Why would you seek to protect her now?"

"Because, dear brother, my babies and I would not be here this very instant if it weren't for her. I owe her nothing, but to kill her would be pure evil, and I'm not inclined to believe that you or anyone else in this family could kill with complete disregard for someone's life. An eye for an eye isn't always the answer. What is it you're planning?"

"We'll talk downstairs." Julian did a one-eighty and disappeared.

When the last person filed out of their room, André slammed the door shut and twisted the old skeleton key, locking the door to their bedchambers. Noting the hole in the wall, he wondered why he'd even bothered. He ripped the bed cover from their mattress and hung it to cover the hole. He turned, then crossed to Jovan, and knelt before her. He reached his arms around her, leaned his head on her abdomen, hugged her close and wept. Jovan's dress became saturated with tears of blood.

Chapter Eight

Lucian made his way into the library and noticed Savanah and his wife hogging the leather couch so he plopped down between them. "Where's Lizzy?" he asked, as he nuzzled his chin into Serina's neck.

Serina's eyes widened. "Her name is Elyza! Molly and Duncan stole her. Where are André and Jovan?"

"Hiding in plain sight."

"Savanah, do you know where your Mum keeps the book?" Julian interrupted.

"I thought you were waiting for my parents."

Julian whispered, "They seem to be taking more than the three minutes my mind allotted them."

Savanah slapped his arm in passing as she got up to get the coveted white book of charms.

Olivia began to follow her when Julian took two steps toward her. "Nope. Don't even think about it. You and I will finish this here and now, Olivia. This is payback for all the misery you've put our families through."

Olivia snapped, "Stop with all the drama, Julian. You tried to kill me once and you see where that got you. What are you planning?"

Julian strode with heavy steps toward her. Leaning over her petite frame, he got in her face. "No drama, queen of darkness. This is the ultimate reality show. And you're the witch no one wants on their island.

You're about to get cast off."

André walked in with Jovan at his side. "Cherié, please go take a seat by Serina. Where's Savanah?"

Savanah answered, "Right here, Papa. I just grabbed the book."

Julian extended his hands, his fingers wiggling impatiently.

Eyebrows raised and head cocked, André asked, "All right, Grimmy, what have you got us all corralled for?"

"Olivia, I'd like you the center of attention. Make a hexagon around her, please."

Closing the odd-shaped circle around her, Olivia spun and took in each and every person that surrounded her, shoulder-to-shoulder, fingertips touching, palms prone. She wiped her sweaty palms down her legs.

"Why aren't you fighting this? Why aren't you trying to scurry under some rock?" André asked.

"Because I want to be a part of my granddaughter's life. I told you I'm willing to do whatever it takes to make amends."

"Shame you never felt that way for me," Serina whispered. Lucian squeezed her fingers tighter.

"Enough!" Impatient, Julian opened the book to a blank page. "Give me your dominant hand."

Olivia's glare never wavered as she placed her right hand in his. In a flash, he produced a rusted scalpel. Olivia never winced as the corroded metal separated the layers of her derma. Blood ran from her wrist and dripped onto the page. The fluid soaked into the parchment like a dry sponge painting the page.

"She whom is compelled by one of the cardinal sins never wins. For your avarice, you now must pay the price. You are a bad seed, driven by greed to perform hurt-filled deeds. Allow me to be precise, not once nor twice, here, today, you shall pay."

Julian pulled a feather from his pocket and dragged it through the droplets of blood across the paper. A single word appeared, *Mortal.*

Olivia shrieked, "*Noooo!*" in one long hollow inflection.

"The gifts bestowed upon you, beseech you now. You are—mortal, I beshrew you. No more powers, no more spells, only time will tell, where you will spend eternal Hell." Julian slammed the book shut and walked to the window. He rested his forehead on the cool glass.

Olivia swayed back and forth. "Bathroom!"

Never made it.

She vomited on the floor, a thick green puddle. Holding her chest and retching toe-curling sounds, she vomited again.

"Tell me we didn't just revoke her powers as a witch. Tell me we didn't just make her a human." Serina didn't feel so good. "She'll age and die."

"I said I wouldn't kill her today!" When he turned back, Julian's sinister grin resembled Damien Thorne's in *The Omen.* "Tomorrow? Those were your words right, Ands?"

Seeing Olivia reach up to touch her, Serina backed away, scared the spell would leach over to her as well.

Olivia tried to speak, yet nothing audible came out. She covered her ears with both hands and screamed until she passed out.

Molly and Duncan walked into the library carrying Elyza. Molly asked, "What happened this time? We walk out of a room for two minutes and all hell breaks out."

"One of Hell's outstanding members just had a meltdown, and we didn't even have to toss water on her. I no longer have a witch of a mother-in-law." Lucian tossed his hands in the air.

"Now what do we do with her?" Duncan asked.

"Send her back to Oliver," André added.

Jonah wobbled in holding his ass, and uttered, "Ewh," seeing Olivia. "Who finally got her? Jules or Ands? Oh, Ethan's outside by the stables. He's sound asleep in the last stall. He's a lousy shifter. He never heard or scented me when I came in."

Savanah's ears perked up.

"Me either," Payton added, coming in behind Jonah. "Where's Donovan?"

Lucian shrugged his shoulders as Julian walked out. "Jules?"

"I'll be right back. I'm going to speak to Ethan."

About to follow, Savanah stopped fast when Julian spun on her.

"You—stay put."

"But—"

"But nothing!" he shouted then noting the sad look in her eyes he offered, "I'm sorry, Peanut. It's not you." He turned again and left.

"Donovan disappeared into thin air with all the commotion. Time will tell Ethan's fate," Lucian told Payton. He held out his arms, giving Molly his biggest pout. "Mine!" He winked playfully as Molly handed the little turquoise-eyed beauty over to him. Lucian sat in a chair beside Olivia, and held the baby at arm's length from her grandmother as she came around. "You may hold her now, but only for a moment. Your help here has been noted. When you leave my home you will not return unless you are invited."

"Highly unlikely," Julian mumbled as he walked back in.

Olivia sniffled and took her granddaughter from Lucian. "Thank you." She tried to squeeze out a smile, but it never materialized. Holding Elyza close, Olivia pressed her lips to the baby's forehead. "My precious, you are as beautiful as your mother was when she was a babe. I am only a thought away if you ever need me." Olivia turned to Serina. "I hope you can live with what you've done to me. At some point, you'll need me and when you do, you'll give me back my powers, my life." Olivia gave Elyza back to Lucian and wobbled unsteadily away.

Jovan's voice followed her out the front door. "Thank you."

Julian chided, "Don't play into her bleeding heart, Blossom. She's looking for someone to side with her and your heart's way too generous. She killed our mother." To Savanah, he said, "Ethan is staying with us. We need info, and he's the one that can give it to us. Nor does it hurt that he's completely infatuated with you."

Savanah babbled, "*Nofreakingway!* I'm not playing monkey in the middle to help that mutt. He's not marking me as his property. Three days ago you were ready to plant him in the back yard. You toss out the woman who just saved your sister yet allow the man that brought such travesty to our home in it? You make no sense, Jules."

"I'm not asking you to have sex with the guy, Savvy. Although from what I've been told it's pretty much a given. Just remember you're not a praying mantis and try not to bite his head off in the meantime. I want to do that!"

"What the hell do you mean, pretty much a given?" Savanah gave her uncle a cold glare. "I'm not a loaner, like some used car he gets to take for a test drive." She stomped out of the library.

Just as André opened his mouth to speak up, Duncan beat him to it, carrying all of André's thoughts. "Julian, I didn't think I'd ever live to see the day you'd piss off the one person on this planet that worships the ground you walk on, ever! Actually, the only person!" Duncan looked around at his family. Gesturing with his hands, he asked, "Am I right?"

Each one of them mumbled a collective, "Yes."

"That woman loves you, you giant ass. Don't you dare place her in a position she feels she has to do something against her morals or beliefs to get information for us."

"Couldn't have said it better myself, Duncan." André added.

Duncan smirked. "That would be why I spoke up."

"I'll spay the bloody mutt if he so much as sniffs in her general direction," Jovan bit out. "I don't trust him."

"Neither do I," Julian added as he sat on the floor, his legs crossed. Looking up at all the members in his family, he finished, "Savanah likes Ethan. She won't come right out and say it, but she does, and Jovan, if you'd taken the time to talk to her you'd know."

Hands on her hips, Jovan answered, "Been a bit preoccupied, Jules. Took an extended three-day holiday that I hadn't planned. Remember any of this? Been to

131

hell and back." She kicked her brother's thigh.

"I'm sorry. You're right, of course. Trust me? If things work out between our peanut and Mr. Kitt, then we'll have insider info and forgive me for what I'm about to say, even though you're all thinking it, and none brave or stupid enough to say it, another person to donate to our new vamp. André, I'm sorry. I mean it from the bottom of my heart. But it's true, we're running low on donors around here."

"You are a giant ass." André stormed out after his daughter.

"You can be so incredibly callous, Jules." Jovan swatted the back of her brother's head, turned a quick heel and left.

Jonah squatted in front of Julian. "You know how to clear a room, don't ya, Bro. I'm not following your thinking. If you don't trust the guy, why allow him near Savvy?"

"We're giving the kid shelter. Who here hasn't seen the painting Jovan did?" Julian waved his hand in the air like a kid in school trying to get the teacher to pick him. "Serina, do a quick scan of the two of them and see what you come up with. See if Jovan's scrying is on the money. Bet ya the next ten dirty diapers I'm right." Julian's smirk quickly washed away when Savanah came back into the room with Ethan on her heels and her father one heart beat from him.

Serina looked into Ethan's soul and then her niece's and found an unequaled match. "Julian, oh how I hate admitting when you're right." Serina slumped against Lucian.

Savanah entered into the center of the room. "Would you look what the cat dragged in." The second she said it she knew she'd left herself wide open. Turning quickly, she placed her finger to Ethan's lips, to shush him before he had the opportunity to swallow his foot, which she somehow knew without a doubt, he would do.

"Are you saying you're my little pussy, Savanah?"

She picked off her lime green flip-flop and clobbered him. "Get away from me you giant hound."

"You started it. I never would have finished that if you didn't..." Ethan held his arms wide open, unprotected, to which Savanah took full advantage of, punching him in the stomach. Her fist hit solid muscle that didn't give. Ethan smirked adding, "Two hundred sit-ups a morning."

"Two hundred sit-ups a morning," she mouthed back sarcastically.

In that moment, Ethan professed, "You are irresistible. The way your blue eyes blaze, and the way that little turned-up nose twitches, makes me want to kiss it, but more so, you should unleash the smile you fight to keep hidden."

She couldn't continue to look at Ethan. He was beautifully dangerous and a romantic at heart and having him this close drove her to the brink of madness. "You're a giant sap!" She turned her attentions to her uncle Julian. "And you, you're a giant ogre. You owe me an apology."

"What is with you and apologies?" Ethan playfully asked.

Savanah went to say something to him, but bit her lip instead. Mad or not, he found a way to bring out a smile in her and make her crazy at the same time.

Julian offered, "Someday, Peanut, you'll thank

me."

"That was so not an apology. That was your smugness talking out your a—"

"Savanah—mouth," her father chided.

Savanah crossed her eyes. "Good to have ya back, Papa."

André offered his daughter his hand. "Savanah, I'm going to the wine cellar. Join me? Let's go crack open a really good bottle of chardonnay. I think after the tense few days this family's been through we need to relax." André raised his voice, "I want you to be very cautious where Ethan's concerned. You know the saying, Savanah, keep your friends close, your enemies squashed under your feet. He's here because he has nowhere to go, and he knows it."

Savanah followed her father down the spiral stairway, through the heavy solid oak door to the climate controlled wine cellar where barrels of vintage spirits begged to be tapped open. She ran her hand across the smooth surface of the rich, warm, mahogany bar then reached up and grabbed a few glasses from the wine rack, then watched her father uncork a one-hundred-year-old bottle of champagne.

"That's not chardonnay, Pops." She tapped the bottle with a grin.

"Savanah, I've had a death-defying week." He pulled up a stool next to her and poured the bubbling liquid into her glass.

"Hey you two, wait for me." Jonah grabbed a glass and sat down beside Savanah.

Serina trotted down the stairs behind them and said, "Hey, hold up. We all need to drink a glass of this before you tap out the bubbly." Serina walked behind the bar to a portrait of her and Jovan's father and pulled the frame away from the wall. Behind it, a safe.

Savanah asked, "Do you remember the combo?"

She watched her aunt give her a slight questioning glance before she rubbed her hands together and then twisted the knob to the left, to the right and to the left again. The door unlatched after one solid *clunk*. Inside the solid cedar cavity, Serina pulled out a glass bottle with a corked stopper and handed it to Savanah.

Savanah read the label aloud, "*Eden's Sins*. Tell me this doesn't conjure up some vivid images?"

Serina giggled. "You, my dear niece, missed your calling as either an erotic author or a porn star. You pick."

Savanah's jaw dropped but not one word fell out. André tapped her mouth closed.

"It was our father, Father Butler's homemade wine to be used only on special occasions. I think this qualifies. What I'm going to tell you stays within these walls. This is a diluted version of the original Eden's Sins that I have safely stored for a rainy day or an all-out blood bath. The bottle held the blood of archangel Raphael, the healer and if it's true what my dear mother, Olivia, told me, Raphael is mine and Jovan's grandfather. Drinking this will ensure that you, André, walk in the sun. It was how Lucian, Raven and I do, but there is one catch. Your soul has to remain pure. You can't ever go on a blood lust killing a single person. This includes my mother. If that happens you shall venture over to the dark side, and trust me, there are scarier things there than Darth Vader."

"Well then cheers on that lovely note. We bid fare thee well to our old lives or mine anyway. To new beginnings. I think this moment should be followed by me dancing on my grave." André clinked his glass to each of theirs.

****

Pacing the outside of the North Broadway, Queen Ann home, Xanti couldn't relax. Without the Maestro's hot rancid breath scorching his skin, and orders being sputtered in his ear, the vamp had no clue which direction the sun rose.

Adrenaline, caffeine, and sugar-laced blood of the two cops he'd executed three days past still surged through his veins. *Maybe*, he thought, *cops should become a steady protein replacement to my diet.* He couldn't remember the last time he'd reaped such rewards for such a sustained time.

Nervous, his fingers played with the deep cleft in his chin as he tried to plan his next move, namely, how to get home without his pilot, Ethan. His only saving grace had been he hadn't killed Ethan. Getting the wolf back would be harder than proving the Immaculate Conception was really immaculate.

The post-storm night air weighed down the atmosphere better than the cement shoes Xanti had used to dispose a few of his victims after he'd been a tad greedy with their blood supply. The clouds hid both the moon and stars, and gave Xanti that extra edge of jitters. "I can do this. I can go for a walk alone. Ethan doesn't know diddly," he said to no one as he memorized each mansion along the pristine street with their manicured lawns, and gardener's dreams of overflowing flowers. Enthusiasm piqued as a few college students walked toward him, headed back to Skidmore College. *A snack? Couldn't possibly.* He was still running off the high test the cops infused him with, but then again… The women amused him, laughing as they moved little lawn jockey statues from one home to the next in jest. Xanti tried to make eye contact with the two women, to bespell them so he could quench his thirst, but more times than not he lacked both the power and charisma needed to seduce one into his arms, hence the reason his father always served him sustenance.

He trudged along.

Before he knew it he'd walked the length of Broadway and entered Congress Park. He stopped in front of the carousel to watch people ride the painted horses in nauseating circles, getting nowhere fast. The motion made him dizzy. He ventured further back into the park toward a couple of teenagers wading in the Spit and Spat fountain. The two playful sculptures sat on opposite ends of the fountain and waged a water war between each other while the two teenagers exchanged a youthful hunger in sex.

Looking between the pair, Xanti guessed neither were older than sixteen, both barely dressed. The young girl's jeans cut into her hips showing a perfect plumber's crack. Her bottom reminded him of the past century when women were robust and plentiful. This girl had meat on her bones, meat that Xanti *really* wanted to sink his teeth into. Stuffed into a push-up bra, her voluptuous breasts overflowed from every angle. On her lower back, Xanti noticed a large yellow celestial sun, surrounded by tiny stars. Her cotton candy, lavender-lilac-colored hair had spikes, as did her necklace—spiked, some turned inward, pinching her creamy-white flesh. In the center of the necklace, hung a large silver cross. Xanti twisted his lips, annoyed. She was obviously smarter than she appeared. Children of the Goth era would be his demise. Xanti shifted his attentions to the boy.

The boy's low-riding jeans revealed a pair of boxers sporting Batman. Having the exact same pair on tonight, Xanti became instantly smitten. With every step the boy took, the water weighed down his pants. His enthusiasm built waiting for them to sink.

Xanti casually glanced at his own outfit and smiled. He thought he looked—*nifty*. Tonight, he donned black leather pants with a carefully wadded up sock tucked strategically down the front of them, giving him a plumper perception. Image first. His black tee shirt's logo read, "Save A Horse, Ride A Cowboy." And to top off the look, he wore a black felt cowboy hat, the string tucked neatly under his chin, and black cowboy boots with a thick heel, embellished with copper spurs. Xanti's infatuation with cowboys never wavered. Having lived through it, he held fond memories of the Wild West era.

On the edge of the fountain he teetered, drooling with one repulsive snaggle-toothed grin. "Boy, you might as well put your little toy soldier away. That's just not right."

In a gutless rush, the young man, Jacob, backed away from the vamp, as he engaged in a tug of war with wet jeans.

Xanti snarled. "Would you like to see how it's done boy? Want the Maestro the second to show you a few pointers?" He tapped his fangs.

For all the good it did him, Jacob whispered to his girl, "Dylan, run to Ben and Jerry's and call the PEON's."

"You can bet your pathetic little poker I'm calling the PEON's and the cops."

"Madam, Dylan, is it? Come here." Xanti looked the young girl directly in the eyes trying to lure her to him. The boy stepped forward, not out of bravery or loyalty to his friend, but because Xanti snared him instead.

Giving the vamp the once-over Dylan blurted out, "Listen you freakish cowpoke, I wouldn't come to you if you'd just waved two front row tickets to the Korn concert this summer at the *Saratoga Performing Arts Center* under my nose. I'm so outta here." Dylan swung her leg over the edge of the fountain and squeaked with each and every step she took away from them as she headed back toward Spring Street.

"Are you going to let her go? Just like that, after calling you a cowpoke?" Jacob's voice cracked with fright.

He looked Jacob over. "Not to worry, mate." Xanti grinned. "Right now it's all about you."

"Look, Howdy Doody, this ain't Brokeback Mountain, and we ain't doing anything to the tune of it."

"You say that now."

His copper spurs scraped against the pavement as he strode down Caroline Street's hill with a newfound self-assuredness. He took in all the scents from the men and their colognes, their pheromones scenting the area better than a bull during mating season, to the pizzas being baked, to the stale beer permeating from the bars, and he smiled. He was doing just fine on his own. Xanti lurked outside Sperry's listening to the music tumble out onto the street. His feet found a rhythm, and he danced a lonesome two-step on the sidewalk.

"Vampires dance with death Xanti—not country music. Those twangy tunes will make you die a slow death. Even slower than I could drain you."

"Maestro, what brings you to this neck of the woods?" Xanti asked through chattering fangs.

"The fact that your mouth continually finds necks to ravage." On thin air, Xier glided to him.

"But Father, it is what we do."

"No Xanti, it is what you do without proper supervision. You are out of control and this needs to be fixed. Now. Where is my wolf?"

Xanti shrugged his shoulders. "I'm not a child, Father. You can't keep treating me as such."

"You're right, Xanti. Children grow up and gain responsibilities. You just grew up. The plane is waiting at the airstrip. Come now."

"I don't want to go home. What of the baby? I'm so close."

"I have no use for more children to raise, especially yours. Get into the car."

"No."

Xier dragged his son into the limo by his ear, spurs sparking against the pavement. "What? Have you been watching reruns of *Big Valley* or *Little House on the Prairie* in the short time you've been here? I'll be the laughing stock of the century."

"Father, I don't understand why you're upset."

"That's the problem in a nutshell. When we get home, Xanti, I've a surprise for you. I've found Dracula's casket. Would you like to sleep inside it?"

Already forgotten the fact he didn't want to go back to jolly old England, Xanti blurted, "Splendid.

Can I sleep in it indefinitely?"

"Definitely."

Twenty-four hours later, Xier touched his son's cold, sallow cheek lightly. He looked at Xanti, so content, so child-like and trusting as he lay there wearing yet another T-shirt he despised, "Some days it's just not worth chewing through the restraints."

Xier wondered aloud, "Will you feel like this tomorrow?"

"Like what, Father?"

For the first time in nearly a century, the Maestro found his tears still ran blood red as he closed the lid to the casket and bound it in silver chains.

Chapter Nine

At four in the morning when the phone rings, you have three scenarios and pray for the latter two, really bad news, wrong numbers or a dear friend in another time zone who's drunker than a skunk and has forgotten the time difference.

The ringing in the background of Savanah's dream intensified the longer it went on. Talking into her pillow, she repeatedly asked someone, anyone to get up off their lazy *derrieres* and answer the annoying device. Desperate for silence, her hand crawled out from underneath the cozy warmth of her blanket in search of the *soon-to-be-flying-through-the-air-to-its-death* nuisance. No such luck.

The shrill pitch hammered into her head more so than the drinks she'd consumed earlier. *Ring! Ring! Ring!* Savanah held her head with one hand and groping wildly, found the phone's cord with her other. She followed the line back to the wall and tugged—hard. The end of the cord broke free from its socket.

"Ah! Silence." Falling backwards onto the bed, she hit her head on the wrought iron headboard. Her unruly curls caught the intricately detailed scrolls. Blinded by pain, she attempted to untangle her mane when her cell phone rang even louder than the damned landline she'd just dismembered. "My bologna has a first name…." the cell phone sang its little ditty.

"Oh, for Goddess sake! Who the hell wants me at this ungodly hour?"

"I don't know, but I wish you'd just answer the thing. The ringing woke me as well."

Savanah's heart did triple time as she tried to free herself. Her mouth went bone dry. Not a drop of saliva to spit at her intruder. Her voice failed her miserably, etching out pathetic scratchy sounds instead of the really loud, horror movie scream she intended. The bed shifted as the stranger sat beside her, and covered her mouth to halt any further attempts of her trying to wake the dead.

Kicking and swinging wildly into the dark, while still anchored to her headboard, did nothing to rid the stranger. It did however increase her anxiety.

"Stop, you'll hurt yourself," he said. "I'm not going to hurt you."

"Yeah, right! Said no serial killers or rapists ever."

"I'm serious, Savanah. Stop. I'm going to untangle you from your bed, although seeing you tied up here is pretty sweet. The tables have turned—and in my favor."

"See—see what I mean. Get away from me." Tears blinded her. She tried biting his arm, but that was over before it began. She even went as far as sending little zingers of electricity through his arms.

He held her firmly. "Would you stop? Jesus, your uncles and father would shred me to pieces if I hurt you. I like the jolts, though."

"Ethan?"

"Good morning, Pippy."

Savanah slumped on her pillow allowing the adrenaline rush to burn off. "What's so good about it? And what the hell are you doing in my bedchamber?

My Mum'll kill you."

"Answer your phone first and then I'll answer you."

"I can't see the obnoxious thing."

Ethan snapped open the lid on the cell, silencing the noise. "Nice ring-tone." Ethan placed the phone in her hand and then climbed over her, fiddling through her hair. Savanah looked into his eyes, eyes that seemed to light up the room, despite the dark hour. Inhaling, wild musk tickled her senses and made her nipples tingle. It was when a warm sensation traveled to her groin that she clamped her legs tightly shut. *I'm so screwed.* Without sensor, she thought about Ethan naked, touching her as he did now, this close to her and for the first time in her life, she had never wanted or needed anyone more.

Yeah, too much wine still circulated through her system.

She shook off the first idea that she really liked him being this close to her. Letting her fear and temper back into the equation, she bit out, "Just because you're being a gentleman, doesn't let you off the hook for being in my room. I want answers." She went to tap him on the nose, but missed, and jammed her finger into his eye. "Ewh! I'm sorry. Not to worry. Maybe Xier's got a spare marble Xavier used to wear after my Aunt Raven gouged out his eye. And why not? He's got the dude's hundred year old sperm..." She mocked. "Don't forget, I can tell a lie a mile away."

"For a split second I'd have sworn you smiled."

She grunted.

"You're even cute when you make piglet noises."

She grunted louder. He placed the phone to her lips

and coached her. "Speak into the phone. Do I have to do everything for you?" She went to shove him away, but he retained possession of her hand. Savanah tried to pull away, but again, his strength won out. He tapped the phone one last time.

"What?" Her voice cracked into the little cell. A voice sounding a lot like *Charlie Brown's teacher* trickled out of the phone. "Who is this?" She huffed a chunk of black curls out of her vision, not that she could see anything other than green eyes hungrily devouring her. She covered the phone's mouthpiece. "You done with your appetizer yet?" Ethan shook his head no. She shoved at his chest, purposefully letting her hand linger. She caught her breath when her fingers hit a wall of solid muscle. *Sweet!*

Ethan smacked his lips together and whispered in her free ear, "You're more like a happy meal, all wrapped up in one juicy box, babe."

Savanah loved the idea. Her thoughts spiraled down the gutter, dreaming up ways Ethan could devour her, until her cell phone started talking to her again.

"Miss Savanah? It's Mr. Colwell, from the museum, dear. I have some very disturbing news for you."

"Then call me back tomorrow, after ten." Savanah hung up the phone. There was no sound logic to waking a person mid-dream to give them bad news. As far as she was concerned, the bad news would be there, like a fish that jumped out of its bowl, all dried up on the floor, waiting to be found, or flushed, come morning.

The phone rang again. Savanah sent *Oscar Mayer* sailing to his death. Tomorrow she'd speak with the gallery and not a second sooner.

Ethan got up and walked over to the light switch, and flipped it on. He retrieved the cell phone from the floor.

"Forget the bloody phone. What are you doing in my room?"

Sitting beside her once more he answered, "Well I was sleeping, but that time has ended and rather abruptly."

"Answer the damn question."

"No need for huffiness, dearest."

"My God, what's with you? Get out now!" She pointed to the door. "Did cupid shoot your ass with a little arrow?" She shoved harder at his chest. "I can shoot your sweet, little tush full of silver." She leaned toward her nightstand, knowing she kept a small pistol in there. She never loaded it, but he didn't know that.

"Is that anyway to treat someone *you* invited in?"

"What? Are you—I most certainly did not, *would* never—not in a million years invite your furry little hide in here."

"Liar!" he countered. "How much wine did you drink last night? Do you do this often? Invite strangers to your bedchamber? *Bedchamber?* How ancient is that word? It's like you and your uncle snuck out of a Shakespeare novel."

"Nightly, there are strange men in here, so get used to it." Savanah tried to get up, but with Ethan sitting on top of her blankets, he had her pinned. Savanah balled her fists and shook them in his face. "Out!" She pointed to the door a second time.

"I thought you wanted to know why I was here."

"You just told me I invited you, although I don't believe you."

"Try me. Am I lying?"

Eyeballs bugged, she asked, "Do I look like I remember? My uncle got me so riled up, I had two glasses of wine on an empty stomach."

"More like two bottles with your father and uncle. Your Aunt Serina is a light weight. One glass, and she got carted off."

"No way!" Savanah tried to concentrate, but the only thing she got was a shooting pain between her brows. Once refocused, she noticed a large purplish hickey on Ethan's neck. "Sweet! Who got you? Did you stop off after that tart from the restaurant? Oh crap, it wasn't me, was it?"

"Wish it were you. Your father got me, thanks for the concern though. Said he'd finish me off if I got out of line." Ethan shrugged his shoulders. "Lucian carried him up stairs. Your uncle with the yellow eyes…"

"Jonah."

"He too told me if I touched you, he'd watch me die a slow death. He said your other uncle—the one I met in the restaurant, is a marshmallow compared to him."

"Julian."

"Personally, Julian needs to get laid."

Savanah couldn't help but smile. "That's the general consensus. And yeah, Jonah can be deadly if he's cornered. He worked with a vamp a long time ago that made him do things he never dreamt he'd ever do."

"Trust me, I know the feeling! I'm dog food on a daily basis."

"Ah…more like prime cut!"

Ethan bit back a smirk. "Anyway, I got the short straw and carried you. You're much heftier than you look. You hungry?"

Savanah eyed Ethan curiously. "Why? I probably should watch my diet."

"Get dressed. I'll be down stairs waiting in my car."

Savanah laughed this time, so hard, tears pooled in her eyes. "Not! Uncle Jonah's got your keys. It's no longer your car. That much I do remember. You can kiss that little put-put *so long*." She twitched her nose at him.

Ethan dug into his pocket, and produced a shiny gold key, with a black rubber protector around it. He dangled the keychain in her face wiping her smile away. "You really don't remember anything do you?"

Embarrassment shrouded her. "No," she said with a defeated attitude as she sank back onto her pillow and attempted to cover her face.

"Get dressed and meet me downstairs. I'll fill you in over breakfast."

Savanah's heart screeched to a halt. That was the second time he told her to get dressed. She peeked under the covers praying there was more to her than her birthday suit. "Where are my clothes?" came from under the blanket.

"Couldn't tell ya, sweet cheeks."

"What did you do to me? And don't ever call me that again."

Ethan jumped up off the bed, hurt, his arms going up and out to his sides, appearing as if someone held a gun to him. "Look," he protested, "Savanah, for as much as I would love to take advantage of you, and trust me, I would love to run my tongue up the length of your soft—leg and those—" Ethan pointed to her breasts—the urge to crawl under the covers with her was all he wanted. He took a deep breath. Stifled his actions. "I am not a rapist. I will not put a woman in a position she didn't ask for. *Ever!* Once she consents, all bets are off, but not until she says those three beautiful letters that spell *y-e-s*. And before I covered you up, you were dressed. What you did in your sleep is none of my concern."

"No. You're just a lying-would-be kidnapper."

"Let me explain over breakfast."

"There's no one open at this ungodly hour."

That wasn't a no. "You don't go out much do you?"

"With kidnappers, no."

"I honestly tried to get out of this."

"Yeah, and tomorrow you'll sell me the Brooklyn Bridge. I'm hungry. Get out for the last time. I'll be down in a few minutes."

This close to her, Ethan thought he'd won the lottery. Her exotic fragrance, cardamom, and rosewood drove through him faster than his beamer could go from zero to sixty. *Behave, Ethan. For once in your miserable life, behave. What happened to luv 'em and leave, Eth? I'm going to love this one all right. Leaving is no longer an option.*

Ethan walked out into the hallway as quietly as he could. Not five feet from her door he spotted articles of clothing strewn across the hallway. He leaned over and picked up a pink sweater, then a pair of jeans, next a pair of fluffy pink socks. When he reached the top of the stairs, Savanah's pink lacey bra and her pink— whatever the hell it is, hung on the banister. Ethan held the scrap of material out in front of him to analyze it.

Why she would even bother wearing it befuddled him. It looked medieval, torturously uncomfortable. A pink leather triangle patch of fabric, attached to a rhinestone-covered shoestring-of-a-thing dangled from his fingertips. Ethan had seen thongs before, but this little thing didn't have enough thread to be called that. He bit his index finger thinking about where the rhinestones disappeared and how pretty her little derriere would look decorated in it. And then he would take it off her and he'd decorate her.

Without sensor, he brought the material to his nose and sniffed it and set it down in a pile on the bench in the hall. *Breakfast in bed would have been a delight.*

Forty-five minutes later, Savanah meandered to Ethan's car where she found him sound asleep behind the wheel, the stereo softly playing Creed's, "One Last Breath." Tiptoeing next to him, she leaned over and pressed the horn hard. An eardrum-shattering noise blasted into the wind. "Hey, wake up. You didn't drag me out of bed to watch you sleep did you?"

Ethan didn't flinch.

"No, but I didn't think hell would freeze over before you got ready either. Get in."

Savanah returned to her side of the car and didn't budge. She tapped an impatient finger on the door.

Ethan looked curiously at her and said, "Oh! You're kidding, right?"

She shook out her thick curls and feigned boredom. Ethan got out of the car, walked around to the passenger's side, opened the door for her and then slammed it shut after she got in. "Happy now?"

"Yes, thank you. A real gentleman wouldn't need

prompting, Ethan."

"A real gentleman wouldn't need prompting, Ethan." He mimicked as he settled back behind the steering wheel. He threw his car into gear, stepped on the gas, the clutch, shifted and the car all but did a wheelie as it rocketed forward. Savanah's head hit the headrest.

Her hand choking the door's handle she bit out, "Do you think you're Nick Cage in *Gone in 60 Seconds*?"

"You think you're Angie? Nah! You're way too…" His voice trailed off.

"Way too what? Don't do that. What?" She poked his side.

"Beautiful."

****

Parked in front of Compton's Restaurant on Broadway, Savanah admitted, "I've never been here." She entered the small yet cozy place decorated in knotty pine and immediately took a liking to it. The eatery barely had a table open. People chatted quietly over fresh brewed coffee, some looking like they were ready to go to work, some ready to go to bed. All the bacon, sausage and egg aromas got her peristalsis geared into action. A cat lover, she enjoyed the different arrangements of kitty portraits decorating the walls. The ambience gave her a warm and friendly invitation to come back. Ethan led Savanah to a table in the front of a large window that overlooked the street.

"Two coffees and menus. Thanks," he said to the waitress who still looked half asleep herself. "This place is a relic. Great breakfast and lunch and even greater hours. I love sitting here watching the people go to and fro when I'm in town."

"Really?" Savanah studied Ethan as she relaxed in her chair. "You're really quite different without an audience. Possibly even pleasant."

"What was I before?" Ethan leaned across the table on his elbows, giving her his best come-hither grin.

"You really don't want to know." She winked at him. "Tell me about the baby. I don't see you as the doting daddy."

"So you're a woman who puts business before pleasure, after all." It was Ethan's turn to wink at Savanah.

She gave him the one scrunched up eyebrow look that said it all: No pleasure today, tomorrow or ever for you.

"The Maestro told me your aunt Raven is a deranged, psychotic woman who isn't capable of raising herself let alone his grandchild and that's why she lives with her family. He said her looks would indeed be deceiving due to her beauty and that her family would put up a fight, because of his last name, but on the sharper side of that knife, they wouldn't want the child either because it was Sinclair. Savanah, he's got my balls pierced and chained to him. I can't get away from the guy. He's bitten me every week for the past year. Not that I've tried to get out. He's given me everything I've ever wanted and then some. He treats me better than his son, but now with Xanti killing the cops, Xier will never take me back. I just became his second biggest liability. And I honestly pity that dumb son of his. Xier's been looking for an excuse to rid the planet of him, and he just got it."

"You sound as if you like this Xier."

"What's not to like? He's incredibly wealthy and shares it and the only thing he ever asked for was blood. You don't get that from the Red Cross. They take your blood and toss you cookies. I got a plane, a car, cash…"

Savanah cut him off, "The Red Cross saves people's lives every day, Ethan. Can you say that about Xier? Did he murder people?"

"Yes and no. There's a fine line between being alive and being a vampire. Yes, technically they die. Everyone goes to the funeral, cries hysterically…but hold the fort!" Ethan lunged across the booth making Savanah jump. "The next thing ya know, there's a dead guy banging your door down, trying to get back into his house. That's Xier in a hundred words or less. He's the opposite of GE's slogan—We bring great things to life. Xier brings dead things to life."

Savanah burst out laughing and accidentally spit her coffee across the table at Ethan. "Oh, I'm sorry, but I didn't expect that."

Grasping at napkins he said, "Me either."

She shot him a wad of paper napkins to clean up the mess. "So, you really thought you were being the hero in this plot? Careful how you answer that. The next thing aimed at you may very well determine your future health." Savanah picked up and held a silver steak knife loosely in her hands.

"Do your little lie detector mumbo-jumbo on me, my Mistress of the night." Ethan reached across the table, and grabbed her hand, the silver knife solid against his palm.

Savanah wrinkled her nose and dropped the knife. "The singed skin isn't anywhere near as appetizing as the bacon cooking in the back kitchen. All right, so you're not lying. What happened to me last night? How did you get Uncle Jonah's keys back? And please tell me I had clothes on at some point."

"Whose keys?" Ethan dug into his pocket and flashed his pride possession. "Jonah came looking for me and dragged me down to the wine cellar to join you. He may have drank as much if not more than the two of you combined, crying in his glass about Raven and Vonnie. And then about destiny and you and I. The three of you tried sneaking out of the house like teenagers, trying to take *my car* for a ride. Let's not forget the saying, drinking and driving is for the dead. I drove everyone to the donut shop for some much needed caffeine and afterwards you managed to keep possession of *my* keys until I dug them from your pocket."

"For the record, I think Uncle Jonah likes you. You're kindred spirits of sorts. You have the same lousy history. Brainwashed and bitten by bastards. He sees himself in you when he was younger."

"That's exactly what he said."

After the waitress set down their plates, Ethan's eyes grew wide with delight. A three-egg sausage, spinach and cheese omelet, home fries and rye toast, rested in front of him. Pancakes, dripping in warm maple syrup, whipped cream covering them like a snowy mountain and a large glass of chocolate milk waited for her. She dove into her stack, barely coming up for air.

"You're not like most women," Ethan mused as he watched her food disappear. "Most women are petrified to eat in front of a man on their first date."

"Well this isn't a date and I'm hungry and I don't

care what you think of me. Women should go to the gym more, then they wouldn't worry about their weight and the exercise is good for them and speeds up their metabolism so they *can* eat like this. Which is where I should be in one hour." With the mention of that Savanah yawned, wide and long.

"Come on, sweet cheeks, I'll take you home and tuck you in."

"You can take me home and that's it."

Ethan dropped his chin into his palms and gazed up to Savanah. "How did your parents meet?"

"Random! Why would you, of all people care?" Ethan's hurt glare made her want to kick herself. The man had been nothing but honest with her this morning and for the most part a true gentleman, other than the car door getting opened. "I'm sorry—again. Ethan, I don't know how to take you. You show up in our lives with the vilest of intents and now you're living under our roof, and I'm sitting here having breakfast with you? My father got turned because of you." She squinted and a tired little tear rolled off her cheek. She swiped at it. "Sorry. It makes no sense to me that my parents are allowing you to breathe, let alone stay in our home."

"Me either. And have you noticed the way everyone looks at me? I feel like a freakin' ghost. Come on." Ethan got up and threw a wad of bills onto the table.

Savanah glanced at the amount of money and then back to Ethan. "You're one hell of a tipper."

"Oh, have I got some tips for you!" He held the door to the restaurant for her. As he approached his car he stroked the side in passing, wiping off someone's fingerprints before stopping and grabbing her door.

Savanah smiled, but this time walked to his side of the car and opened the driver's door.

"*Absolutely not*. You are so not driving. You'd still be blowing the top off the breathalyzer."

"Not me. I'm opening the door for you this time." Savanah motioned her hand to his seat. Ethan stood there with his mouth slightly ajar before getting behind the wheel.

Stopped at the corner of Washington Street and Broadway for a group of late-night-early-morning partiers zigzagging their way across the road, Savanah pulled her feet up onto the seat and told him the love story between her parents.

Without thinking twice, Ethan knocked her feet off the fine leather upholstery. He shot her the evil eye toward her feet on his new baby. "How long before they fell in love and had sex?"

"Ethan!" She choked. "That's none of your business. Why?"

"I just wondered how long before you and I..."

"You'll turn a ripe shade of blue before that happens. And I don't mean your face." She nodded toward his loins. "My parents actually liked each other, had respect for each other, and it was love at first sight. They were together three days and then apart nearly four years, because of a cruel vampire."

"Of course," he teased. "What else would ever get in the way of *twoo luv*?" He laughed.

"I get it. Billy Crystal in the *Princess Bride*. Great imitation. You even resemble, *the old wizard*." From the corner of her eye, she saw him quick peek in his rear view mirror, and she had to bite her cheeks to not laugh. "Actually, my great aunt got in their way. My Uncle Lucian told me she had both female and male sex organs, a hermaphrodite."

Ethan tried to peek under the skirt Savanah wore. "Genetics, shit. I hope it doesn't run in the family." Savanah tried to slap his hand away, but he caught her and held on. "I know you have feelings for me, Savanah. I'll work on the other stuff, but I know there's something there."

Savanah fought for her hand. "Which one of your deranged personalities told you that? Me, myself or I? Me—the one who sits there and tries to act so cute and innocent? Or myself—the one who has excuses for each day of the week, or I—I am God. I am handsome, irresistibly charming… I, Ethan, can get you into bed, Savanah." She raised her eyebrows to him, waiting for his rebuttal.

"Definitely, I will get you into bed, and you'll be rather pleased with the outcome. I will be the last man you ever invite into your bedchamber!"

Somehow, she had no doubt he told her the truth. She leaned across his seat, getting kissably-close to his lips and whispered, "It's on."

It took his every ounce of self-restraint he owned not to close the distance to those luscious lips of hers. Less than a breath away, he asked, "What's on?"

"The bet, you loony tune."

"One week tops and you're mine, but, Savanah, you can't fight me if you really want me, just to win."

"Oh Ethan, you're so going to owe me."

"What's the bet for?"

"This little car." Savanah smiled, as she rifled through the dashboard glove box. "All this junk will have to go," she said with a wicked sexy grin plastered across her face.

"You're insane. You really don't play fair do you?"

"No one said life is fair, baby." She turned her blue almost black eyes on Ethan, and he caught his breath. She blew him a kiss with her perfectly heart-shaped lips, and his dick went solid. He prayed she didn't notice.

She prayed he didn't notice her staring.

Parking the car in the lower lot of the rose garden, the two of them snuck in the back door, took their shoes off and padded across the kitchen floor in stocking feet, trying to be as stealthy as the plane itself. Reaching the stairs from the kitchen, they quickly realized they hadn't squeaked in under the radar. Heading up the angry lynch mob, stood André, holding all of Savanah's clothing, undergarments dangling from his knotted, angry, fingers. Jovan perched behind him and Julian brought up the rear.

Ethan burst out laughing, knowing everyone thought the absolute worst. "You three look like the *Mod Squad.* Mike, Julie and Linc. Ya know, with the exception that Linc was this really cool African-American dude, and Julian is just beastly—I bet shirts have to be made special order to fit that massive set of shoulders."

Savanah gave Ethan an unhealthy glare.

Ethan crossed his eyes. "I'll shut up now."

Mortified, Savanah prattled, "Papa, I promise—it's not what you're thinking."

"Really? Because right now, little girl," her father's voice rose in octaves, "it's not looking all that promising."

"Papa, how old am I? Shouldn't I be allowed to date a man without you breathing fear down his neck?"

Each one of them answered a collective, "No."

Ethan peered over her shoulder. "Ah! So it was a date after all."

Savanah swung around and put her finger to his mouth to shush him, trying to look stern. He returned her gaze playfully and Savanah lost out, smiling. "It was not a date. We had breakfast. Harmless, Pops," she said turning back to her parents.

"I swear, André, on your daughter's behalf, she behaved."

"It's not her I'm worried over, Ethan. And you still haven't answered me about these?" He shook her pink rhinestone string-of-a-thing in her face.

Savanah snatched her undergarment midair from her father's hand, turned and walked away.

"Savanah, you didn't answer me."

"Come on, Mr. Kitt. I'm going to the gym to work off my breakfast and some anger. Today seems to be starting where last night ended."

Ethan shrugged his shoulders in the general vicinity of the *triad of justice* and turned, following happily on Savanah's heels.

As soon as Savanah and he were out of everyone's hearing range, he offered, "Savanah, I've got a better way for you to work off your frustration and breakfast."

Savanah took in his brilliant smile and wanted him all over again. "Yeah, Ethan, I'm sure you do," she teased, as she ran her finger from his abdomen to his chin and stopped just before his lips.

Ethan grabbed her hand. "You've a one track mind woman. That idea never crossed my mind."

"Liar."

"All right, so maybe it did, but I'm thinking more along the lines of going up." Ethan pointed his finger skyward. "Let's go to the airport. I'll take you for a tour. We can go anywhere you want for lunch and dinner. My treat. I'll even let you play with my joy stick."

"See, I knew that's why you wanted me to go."

"Could you for one second get your mind out of the gutter? I know it's impossible to do this with me standing here in front of you," Ethan chuckled, "but I call my controls on my dash board my joy sticks, because flying just does it for me. One-track mind. Yep!"

Savanah tugged at her hand, but he brought it to his lips while he gazed into her eyes. Once she smiled, he kissed each finger and then worked his way up her arm. His lips nibbled on her neck.

"Now who is it with the one track mind?" Savanah turned away from Ethan, afraid of her feelings for the man. A large vacant hole sat where her self-confidence once resided. She'd declared herself a failure in love and wasn't too keen on proving herself right yet again, but this man tested her, made her want to take chances, to live, to love.

"I'd love some jambalaya. A frosty hurricane drink and for dessert, a *beignet* or two."

"*Café du Monde* it is. Your flight will depart when you are packed. Would you care to spend the evening in the French Quarter or return home? Before you jump to any conclusions, I'm asking because I need to have a flight plan, not to get you alone in a hotel room. That'll come soon enough."

"You are too cocky for your own good." Savanah looked around her room, nervous, anticipating the day. "We can come home tonight if it's not too much trouble. I don't want you tired and passing out, leaving me to play with your little stick."

Ethan's eyes lit up. "Trust me, Savanah, if you play with my joy stick, I promise I won't pass out. And it's not little, not by a long shot."

Savanah couldn't wait to find out. "I'm going to shower and get ready first. I won't be long."

"I thought you did that before we went out for breakfast. What took you so long then?"

"I sat on the other side of the door debating whether or not to join you. For the record, I'm glad I did. Won't be long." The door to the bathroom closed.

Ethan made himself at home on her bed, and closed his eyes with a smile on his lips.

With her cell phone ringing, and Ethan not answering it, Savanah crawled out from her warm, steamy retreat, wrapped her body in a big, white towel and opened the door. A cool blast of air swarmed her. The phone bellowed away right next to Ethan's head, without so much as a twitch from him. Was he deaf? Or quite possibly her father snuck in and off'd him. She impatiently waited to see the rise and fall of his chest. With the flare of his nostrils, she answered the phone. "Shit," she said perturbed, when she noticed the time. Ten o'clock. Mr. Colwell was punctual if nothing else. "Hello, this is Savanah."

"Miss Savanah, I'm sorry to bother you, dear, but something dreadful has happened." Savanah sat on the bed and shoved Ethan out of her way. She slumped beside him, pulled her knees to her chest to brace

161

herself for whatever the museum curator offered. She'd had so much fun all morning with Ethan she'd completely forgotten about the call.

"Spill 'em."

"Your display at the museum has been cancelled."

"What—why—who? What the f—?" Savanah screamed into the cell.

Ethan jumped as if ice had been poured down his shorts. "What is it?" he asked. Savanah shoved her hand in his face abruptly.

"A good morning to you too," got tossed at her. Ethan ruffled her hair.

Savanah grabbed his hand, in no mood for games. "Who pulled the plug? Is it that slime-ball Radcliff? He's doing this to get back at me for the injunction right?"

Mr. Colwell interrupted, "Miss Savanah, it wasn't him, dear. All your relics have been stolen. The museum was vandalized late last night."

Tears filled Savanah's eyes. Ethan looked helpless at his new friend? Girlfriend? Soon to be girlfriend? Hopefully soon to be under him, begging him to take her, *roll-in-the-hay friend? Wife? What?* He reached for a box of tissues and handed her one, wondering who the hell Radcliff was.

"More," she said gruff, pointing to the box. "Oh, I cannot believe all my work is gone. Was anyone hurt?"

"I dare say all your treasures are lost. Even your prized possession, the casket is gone."

"Shit no! Don't even tell me that old bag of bones is still flying high and wanted his bed back."

"I've never heard it put quite like that before, Miss, but that is the general assumption. We have the I-

PEON's searching, but I wouldn't hold my breath."

"Those morons? I wouldn't either."

"To answer your question, two guards were killed last night. Vampire attacks. Our guards were taken to the morgue and disposed of."

"Lovely term that, Mr. Colwell. Disposed of? Like they were trash? They were humans, men with families."

"Not after they were bitten, dear. You—better than anyone should know they become monsters. You've unearthed them."

Savanah hung up the phone swearing, "You're a giant ass, Colwell," before she sent the phone into the wall again. She warned Ethan, "Don't you dare get up and bring it back to me this time."

Ethan didn't budge. "Do you want to talk?" he asked concerned for her obvious state of dismay.

"That man dismissed two guards killed last night as monsters because they were bitten by vampires." Savanah threw her hands wildly in the air. "When are people going to learn not all vamps are evil? Are all humans evil because a few are serial killers or rapists? It's so—so—I forgot the word I need."

"Stereotypical? Racist? Prejudiced?"

"Precisely. Look at my family, Ethan. We're not out murdering people to get blood."

"Savanah," Ethan grabbed her hands before he ended up on the receiving end of one of them. "Not everyone is like your family. Trust me. Your family is so not the norm. Most fangers really are ruthless, demented, bloodsuckers. From what I've seen in this short time is you live in a peaceful commune surrounded by people who look out for each other."

"It's called family, Ethan. It's what people who love each other do."

"Is that all that happened?" Ethan grabbed a tissue and dabbed at her tears. "Your nose is runny. Blow." He held the soft cloth to her nose, but she shooed his hand away.

Turning her face away from him she fought a giggle. "I'm capable of that, thanks, Mom."

"It's Dad, or haven't you noticed?" Ethan pulled her into his arms, and held her trembling body. He grabbed more tissues, wiping not only her eyes, but his. He brushed a few unruly curls behind her ear, allowing his thumb to slip across her cheek. Her skin was as delicate as rose petals. Having her this close, he found it impossible to think straight. His mind wondered about every other part of her body and what she would be to touch and explore with his fingers and then his tongue.

"Ethan? Can we go to the airport now? I need to get away from here."

"Yeah, once you put some clothes on. You enjoy doing this to me don't you?"

Despite the body heat produced as he held her, she continued to shake. Ethan held her tighter, rubbed her arms and tried to regulate her body temperature to get her blood flowing. It worked.

On him.

His pants tightened. He fidgeted, trying to get a position he could sit in and not cut off his circulation.

"Just because you got me on my bed doesn't count toward our bet, Ethan."

"Just because I have you right here, right now, like this on our first date, tells me more than words, Pipster."

"Pipster? Mr. Smugster." She wrinkled her nose at him.

He quickly kissed the tip of it, and watched her blush. "Yeah, I am, but you like that. And you didn't try discredit this was our first date."

After she caught her breath thinking he was going to aim for her lips she proclaimed, "You're FBI."

"A what? Am not."

"A full blown idiot, Ethan Kitt."

"Yeah—but, Savage, look where this FBI is. Sitting beside the most beautiful woman on the planet who is wearing only a towel, no less."

"Savage? You want savage?" Savanah closed the distance between their lips and drew his bottom lip into her mouth and nibbled.

He broke away. "I'm in real trouble here aren't I?"

"Yeah, I'd say a hell of a lot of trouble, Ethan. Get the hell off my daughter."

Savanah whipped her head around to the door. There her father stood, red-faced with a miserable puss on his lips blocking the entryway. "Papa? What the heck? Don't you bother knocking anymore?"

Ethan pointed out, "Technically, André…"—He made a few hand signals, pointing to their body positions—"She started it."

Savanah shot him the, *there's-a-reason-I-just-called-you-a full-blown-idiot* look.

"Savanah, I said keep him under foot, not attached at the hip. There happens to be a significant difference. Out!" André had one hand pointing to the door and the other a balled up mass of white knuckles.

"Papa, you have to stop treating me like a teenager. He isn't the first man I've slept with."

"You've slept with him?" Every vein in her father's neck and temples pulsated with anger. His new dents shot out from his lips. "Fuck!"

"Not that it's any of your business, André, but no. Your daughter—"

"Shut up, Ethan. I don't need you speaking for my daughter. Get up and get dressed, little girl. Savanah, he's just another dumb blond. It hasn't been that long since you and the crypt keeper broke it off. This is a rebound fling you'd be best to fling out the window."

"Papa, there's no need to bring Radcliff into this."

"Radcliff?" Curiosity would kill the cat. "Should I be worried? That's the second time I've heard that name. And did you just call me a dumb blond, Pops?"

Savanah whipped her head back at Ethan. Every ounce of color André had recently regained vanished. Savanah covered her mouth in shock and awe. "I can't believe you said that, and you're still breathing."

André turned and, with authoritative thumps, strutted to the door.

"Papa, please don't leave me like this. I'm a grown woman. You do need to knock from now on. I haven't done anything with Mr. Kitt to disgrace you or the family."

"Yet," Ethan whispered.

Savanah slapped Ethan upside the head lightly. The door rattled the hinges when it slammed shut. They both listened to her father screaming for her mother.

"Oh, I'm in trouble."

"Wow! I didn't expect that." Ethan wiped the salty little beads of water from his brow. "Savanah, I'll be downstairs. Get dressed, go talk to your father and then we'll go. You don't want to leave him like this. Trust me. Sometimes we don't get second chances to make things right. So, New Orleans for the day?" Ethan attempted to get up, but someone still had him pinned against the headboard.

Angry, Savanah stewed over her father's temper tantrum and the way he still treated her. Savanah studied Ethan. Did she trust her instincts in regard to him? Did she trust herself? Ethan's breathtaking eyes never left her baby blues until she stood and dropped the towel. Turning lightly on her heels, she walked into the bathroom. "I'll be out in a bit." She peeked over her shoulder to check his expression. It was just what she hoped for…bright red cheeks, jaw hanging, but not drooling, and eyes welded to her behind.

"You don't play fair, woman," he said sporting a giant grin and an even larger hard on. "I'm not going anywhere. I couldn't walk right now even if your father brought the entire gang back to string me up. Look what you've done to me!" He pointed to his pants. "And you're walking out, all over a silly bet. You can have the damn car, just get back here."

"Ah, so the tables have turned." Savanah smirked. "It's good to want, Ethan. It gives you a reason to live."

"Savanah, I've found my reason. It's you."

Savanah stopped dead in her tracks, and faced Ethan, in only her birthday suit. With her hand on her hip she said, "That's a very nice compliment or an exceptional come on."

"Savvy, I'm not the one naked standing in front of a man whose restraint and will power is almost nonexistent. Please, do something. Either turn around and get dressed or walk to me, but one way or another end this torture."

167

Savanah didn't need to read his mind to find him sincere. That actually scared the daylights out of her. Could her father be right? Could Ethan be a rebound relationship or were her feelings for him real? Everything about Ethan caught her off guard, made her second guess her judgment. Yes, she worried about getting hurt again, but more importantly, she didn't want to hurt him. She knew what that felt like, and she wouldn't do that to him. "Ethan…" She turned abruptly, walked into her bathroom and closed the door. She slumped against the cool wood and even with her eyes closed, tears etched their way out.

Ethan slumped back onto her bed and watched the ceiling fan spin as wildly as his feelings. In less than three days his ideal life of a woman in every port had capsized. He'd entered into a realm where he was the proverbial fish out of water. Love had never been part his vocabulary. Lust indeed had a solid stage, but love? He rolled his eyes. He'd just confessed something to her no other woman had ever heard nor would any other women ever hear. And she walked away from him.

"Love stinks!" Praying he'd find the strength to survive her, he yelled through the closed door, "Are we still on for New Orleans?"

"Hell, yeah!"

After she came out of exile, Ethan got off her bed and extended his hand. "I promise just this once to be a gentleman, but if you ever tease me as you just did, your scrumptious little ass is going over my lap and I'm gonna do more than paddle it. Do we have an accord, Miss Savanah?" He brought her hand to his lips, and kissed her.

"Goddess help us both, Ethan, we do."

Chapter Ten

After four hours of smooth sailing, blue skies and fluffy scattered clouds, the jet touched down on the tarmac of Louis Armstrong International Airport. Strapped into her co-pilot chair, Savanah's fingers were numb from gripping the controls. A light mist made her face glisten.

"Ethan, thank you for letting me fly this tub…"

"Ahhh! She's not a tub. She's a Cessna 750 CJ1+. She's brilliant in the air."

Amusement danced on her lips. "Does your girlfriend have a name?"

Savanah! "You'll never guess it."

Savanah pondered every name she could fathom, without cheating and reading his mind, which is what she really wanted to do since she drew blank after blank. "How about sovereignty, or joy, or elusion?"

"Remind me to never let you name any of our children." The second he said it, Ethan almost bit his tongue off.

"Children? What?" She asked wide-eyed.

He played it down and ignored her. "Her name is Nut."

"You named your plane after a nut?"

"Not an edible nut—Nut, the Egyptian Goddess. Come on, Savanah, you're supposed to be the archeologist. She is the mother of Isis, Osiris, Set and

Nephthys. She personified the heavens and sky. She is known as the lady of heavens, the mistress of earth gods."

"I haven't given you enough credit. How much do you really know about ancient Egypt?"

"That's a whole different day, Pip, but feel free to call me Dr. Kitt. I have my PhD in archeology and anthropology. I was writing a book on mythology until I became the main character. Werewolves? Right now, you and I have a date on Bourbon Street. You hungry or do you want a cocktail first?"

"Wow, Doc! How about a car to get us there? Then it's on to the restaurant. I'm famished."

"I love your appetite, woman."

"Ethan, you haven't seen me in action yet."

"No, but I'm looking forward to seeing a lot of you and very actively under me."

"Not this week you won't." Savanah stepped closer to Ethan. Close enough to kiss him, but instead she whispered, "Once the keys are mine, I'll take you for one, long, slow ride," as she ran her fingers from his lips to his belt buckle. "It'll be fun seeing who I get a smoother ride from, who packs more horsepower beneath their hood…"

"It'll be a bumpy ride and there's no hood. Trust me, you won't make it a week. You'll be mine by this evening."

Savanah tugged at his belt. "You're delusional. Come on, you promised me food."

****

The black coupe corvette had all of three miles on it when they drove off the car lot. Savanah sank down into the buttery, soft, black leather interior. Getting comfy, she put her feet up on the dashboard, only to have them knocked down immediately by Ethan, a scowl etched into his very being. "I can't believe you bought this car."

"I can't believe you just put your feet up on my brand new baby. That's twice in twenty-four hours!"

Savanah gave him an indignant nose twitch and asked, "How are you planning on getting it home?"

"It? I'm leaving you here and flying her home with me. At least this way I'll get to ride one beauty."

Savanah waited to see if he was joking... Mr. Poker-face gave up naught. "You were teasing? You're not really going to leave me?"

Ethan grabbed Savanah's hair and tugged her toward him. When she was close enough to kiss he whispered, "No, little nut, I'll not leave you. You can ride in the back seat of my car on the way home."

"This thing doesn't have a back seat, Ethan." Savanah shoved him away.

"My bad. No, but my plane has a little compartment you can stretch out in. It has all the amenities of home. Bourbon Street Blues or Pat O'Brien's first. Your choice."

"O'Brien's has the hurricane's right?"

Once in the parking lot she watched Ethan pay the attendant for three spaces so no one would get near his newest toy. "Are you always this anal?" She pinched his backside.

"Don't start something you don't intend to finish."

"Oh, Ethan," Savanah yawned. "I have every intention of finishing you."

Ethan perked up instantly.

"Give or take one hundred sixty-eight hours." Her

grin reeked mischief as she bumped into his side with her hip.

Inside Pat O'Brien's restaurant the Creole crab steaming in the kitchen instantly flipped the switch on Savanah's appetite. Her stomach started a loud rumble that made Ethan laugh.

Catching her, he threw his arm over her shoulder and brought her close.

She slipped her arm around his back, torn where to rest her hand. On his hip—boring! Or his ass? Her lips curled upward. Savanah slid her hand into the back pocket of his jeans and with a hint of stealthiness, copped a feel at his firm glutes.

Ethan kissed the side of her neck. "I'm glad you picked my pocket," he teased. "I love this place. It's rustic, old-world gentlemanly." He pointed to the beer steins that hung from the ceiling and empty champagne bottles that doubled as lights on walls.

One foot inside the piano bar, Savanah's jaw dropped. "This place is fantastic. Papa and Aunt Raven would kill to play here. Look, Eth, two copper-topped baby grand pianos. Oh, they'd so be in heaven. So would you if you heard the two of them play together. They're better than Billy Joel and Elton John together until my dad sings, then the hooks come out." Savanah walked to the edge of one of the pianos and ran her fingers across the top of it, gently stroking each ivory key. Melodies sifted through the air.

Envy struck Ethan with more accuracy than her fingers did the keys. He wanted her delicate hands tapping out tunes on him instead of the piano. His fantasy disintegrated when a young man in a green waistcoat, and a velvet green bowtie carried two tall, fruity, concoctions with oranges and cherries skewered onto tiny swords to them.

"This way," the waiter said as he led them through to the patio where they could be in a much more private setting. Outside, Ethan admired the flaming fountain, another hallmark of the restaurant. In between jet streams of water, flames sparked into the atmosphere defying the water's ability to extinguish it. The fountain became his metaphor for Savanah, warm and wet, or at least she would be later in the evening if all things in their universe symmetrically coincided. Otherwise, he'd be cold, wet and alone in the shower!

"They're potent, watch yourselves. One usually does the trick. More than that and you'll end up like this." The green coat shot his thumb over his shoulder to the table beside them. People weighted down with strands of beads, masks covering their faces and a table full of empty glasses, hooted and hollered and did what tourists do best, they enjoyed themselves.

Savanah clinked her frosty glass to Ethan's. "Cheers, Ethan. Here's to a lifetime of making up our own bedtime stories."

With a subtle cock of his head, Ethan tipped his glass to her. "May each one be sensually erotic with a happily ever after." Unable to stay away from her one second longer, Ethan reached out, hooked under her chin with his index finger and slowly brought her across the table to him. "No more teasing, Pippy, kiss me." He puckered up. Every muscle in his body tensed with anticipation. With Savanah's warm sweet lips caressing his, all he could think about was what the rest of her would feel like to kiss, suck and lap at from her pouty mouth to her private lips. Solid as a rock took on new meaning. There he sat, trapped between pleasure and pain and more than happy to be in the predicament. Ethan grabbed Savanah's chair and dragged her next him. There was too much space between them. Shit, he didn't want air between them.

Their kiss transcended time. Ethan wondered how he'd gotten her on his lap, straddling him, her private lips grinding into him with unrestrained fury when only moments prior he complained about the vast horizon that had separated them.

Savanah's eyes glistened like black diamonds under the starry night. He tangled his fists in her thick curls, and tugged. "By the God's you're beautiful!"

Savanah pressed a soft kiss against his lips. The warmth of her skin against his blasted through him like electricity slamming against the breakers, waiting for the switch to be flipped and let loose. Tingles were replaced by rigors. The stars he saw were no longer in the sky, but behind closed eyes. She relaxed and gave herself to him as his tongue swept through her mouth. He wanted all of her and damn any consequences that happened their way.

"I'm so hot." She picked up her glass and finished the last drop of her hurricane. "Did we scare everyone off?"

A quick glance around the patio, all the tables were empty. Before, when they first arrived, scattered couples basked in the late day sun. Now, just the two of them sat under a canopy of glistening gems with the moon glimmering overhead.

"Savage, how long have we been here? I don't even recall the sun setting. I don't remember drinking all these drinks either." Ethan pointed to six empty hurricane glasses. "You and I should be trashed right now, Savage. Savage? I spoke to soon. Shi—"

Savanah's eyes rolled backwards. Her long slender body slumped away from him, and she slipped out of the chair, heading toward the floor.

"Oh no you don't. Savanah don't pass out on me. Please? *Nooo!*"" Ethan tipped one of the glasses over, and trickled melted ice over her face, trying to get her to come around, but his attempts proved futile. "Out cold. You're a cheap date."

The green coat returned. "Mr. Kitt, there is a car waiting out front for you and your lady, Miss St. James."

Funny how certain situations can sober a person instantly. Fear being one. Ethan asked, "How the hell do you know our names?" He searched the perimeter. Nothing.

"Sir," the man answered, "I do not know you, but the gentleman outside seems to. He bought you the drinks and personally brought you them. You spoke for quite some time. Before that, you and your lady sat at our piano singing, some, *Sonny and Cher,* melody. Poorly, I might add. You remember nothing of this? The gentleman left a calling card with you."

"I sing quite well," he mumbled as he scraped up the tiny soggy, ink-smudged black card stuck to the bottom of one of the glasses. He read the inscription:

Draque. Thanks You For Your Indentured Services. Flipping the card over, scribed in meticulous penmanship it read: *What you stole from me, has now been stolen from you. How does it feel? I want it returned, and just possibly I'll spare the rod.*

"What the hell? I don't know any Draque. Do you

keep a video camera surveying the restaurant?" Ethan hoped to see the person who bought them drinks and now had a car waiting for them. Call it a hunch, Ethan had a sneaky suspicion this new turn of events didn't get the happily ever after ending he'd wished for.

"This is a public establishment, a place where people come to relax and enjoy themselves without anyone's watchful eyes. Just as you and your lady were doing."

"Just how much *were* we doing?" Ethan's chest tightened. A few vague memories swam in his head of Savanah gyrating on his lap, pressing her breasts into his chest, her hardened nipples rubbing against him. Was it a dream? Please say no.

"Not enough to get you kicked out. The lap dance cleared a few people, but you two kept your clothes on."

Ethan wiped the sweat from his brow. "Do you have a back door?"

"What about the man?"

"My lady and I came here alone. We told no one where we were headed. Do you understand?" Frustrated, Ethan gripped the green coat's velvet collar. "I'm sorry. Please? Get us out of here?" He released him and smoothed out his collar.

The waiter brushed him away. "I have explicit instructions, Mr. Kitt, that states…"

"Screw your instructions. Now, get us out or the only tip I'll ever give you is how to get your head out of your ass once I put it there. Although, I can't tell the difference anyway." Ethan shoved the waiter out of his way. "Come on, Sleeping Beauty, over my shoulder." Ethan started toward the back of the patio with Savanah flopped over his shoulder. The waiter bolted toward the front of the restaurant, shoving people out of his way. Holding onto Savanah tightly and running, Ethan took off, like a cadaver dog chasing down a zombie. In the car lot, Ethan noticed his newest baby had been tampered with. He continued past. The gas cap lay on the ground next to a puddle of pale yellow, fluid. Bending over gingerly with the girlfriend out on his shoulder, he sniffed out the substance on the ground and backed away. A sweet fragrance permeated the area. He looked around to see if anyone watched him or the car. Oddly, he found no one.

"Come on, Savanah. You have to wake up. Just long enough to start a fire. Oh, I can't believe I'm doing this," he whispered to no one conscious. "Up you go, Savvy." Ethan leaned Savanah against a Hummer parked about fifty feet from his 'vet. Kissing her for lack of anything better to try and get her to come 'round, he gave it his best shot. Savanah sloppily returned the gesture. "Open the baby blues for me, Savage."

Savanah squinted then began to laugh and continued until she vomited all over the Hummer.

Hanging on to his shoulders she asked, "I don't feel so well, Eth. What's wrong with me?"

"I'm pretty certain we were drugged, Savanah."

"How come you don't feel like I look?"

"You said that backwards, sweets, and I'm a shifter. The drugs wear off much faster in me. About three times as fast. You, on the other hand are going to be out of it for a bit. Can you walk?"

Savanah shook her head yes, but she slid to the ground the moment Ethan let go of her. He scooped her up and flattened her against the vehicle with his body.

"Can you start a little fire for me, my little witch?"

"Just aim and shoot. Pick a finger, any finger, and we'll see." Savanah huffed a large curl from her vision and wiggled all ten fingers at him. "Are you cold? Is that why you want a fire? Ethan—I can warm you up." Savanah tried wrapping her legs around his waist, but lost what balance she owned and tipped sideways.

"Oh, Savanah, not now." Saying no to her was the hardest thing Ethan ever did. "Right now we need to get away from here so later—yes later, you can warm me up, but first ignite that puddle under our new car."

"Our car? Oh, I've always wanted a 'vet."

"And a beamer. Anything else you want?" he asked still scanning the area for trouble. He hoped if someone wanted them dead seeing the car turn into a fiery death trap it would satisfy someone's fatal attraction.

"You. That's three letters, Eth. So's your name." Savanah giggled. She leaned forward and tried to kiss him, but she missed and continued forward until he caught her in his arms.

The bulge in Ethan's pants spiked. He couldn't help it. She'd said the one and only thing he needed to hear come from her lips. Granted she'd been drugged and the alcohol factored into the equation, but she'd said she wanted him. Right now, even blowing up his car didn't bother him.

Ethan lifted her finger and aimed it at the yellow oily puddle. Some bastard added instant *Kaboom* to his gas tank. He knew because chemistry had been his saving grace in college. He understood the world very clearly from a molecular level. The tiniest details mattered. $C_3H_5(NO_3)_3$ or dinitrooxypropan-2-yl nitrate aka Nitroglycerin. The numbers would forever be engrained in his gray matter. Archeology and anthropology became a passion later in life, one that he could share with Savanah, if they lived that long. "Now, Savage. Let's heat things up. Kiss me and light my fire."

Savanah kissed him. Her lips were magic in the making against him, but no big boom came from behind. No rush of heat or flames. The car sat beautifully intact. However, the heat and flames inside his body now threatened spontaneous combustion. All he wanted right then was her but as his luck would have it, Ethan noticed a shadow crawling toward the car. The giant ink-splat seemed to soak up the pavement better than paper towel soaked up spills. "Come on, Pip." Ethan grabbed Savanah's finger, flicking it toward the car in a last ditch effort.

Savanah held her belly and laughed. "That's not how it's done, silly. I'm not a lighter, Eth. And don't pull this finger," she wiggled her pinky finger under his nose, "It'll make me toot."

At that point Ethan just wanted to kiss her again, thinking she was the cutest drunken and drugged witch alive.

She wiped her mouth off with the back of her sleeve then flicked her nail off her fingertip. "You're such a sloppy kisser."

Ready to protest he kissed better than Casanova, a bluish-red spark seared across the lot toward the car followed by a thunderous clap, which shook the earth they once stood upon. Savanah and Ethan went air born almost twenty feet, only to land in a soured, rotted-meat stench of a dumpster. The vet rocketed into the night sky like the space shuttle lifting off, with bright orange flames pushing the car higher into the sky. The brilliantly crafted automobile exploded and chunks of fragmented metal filtered through the night like a firework display gone awry. Ethan covered Savanah with his body as the debris rained down, and bounced off their invisible shield. Ethan looked at Savanah, perplexed.

How did she do that unconscious, because she'd passed out again. And he didn't do it. Being a werewolf didn't give him magical powers, just some serious strength. Ethan checked her pulse. Nice and strong. Picking her up, and brushing off gooey leftovers of people's lives, he inspected every square inch of her, making certain she wasn't broken or bleeding. One beautiful piece. He let out a long slow breath and then jumped when his cell phone started chirping at him.

The caller ID came up unknown. One ring. To answer it, or not to answer it, he pondered. Could be the mystery man from the bar. Two, three…four rings later, Ethan growled into the phone, "Who is this?" hoping to intimidate whomever was on the other end and sounding just like Savanah earlier this morning.

"Get my daughter out of there right now."

"Jovan? How did you…?"

"Listen to me, you little mutt," she screamed, "get her away from there now! Get back to the airport and get your little tub…"

"It's a plane, not a tub, and stop calling me a mutt," Ethan screamed into the cell. "What's happening?"

"Semantics, Ethan. Call me when you're in the air." Jovan hung up.

"But I don't have…your number, Mom, and your

daughter's not really in a chatty mood!" Ethan flipped the lid on his phone, and jammed it into his pants pocket. Looking at Savanah, he wondered what possible feat it would be to get them to the airport with her draped over his shoulder and not end up in the big house.

"Come on my edible nut, wakey, wakey. Your mother just called. We had a most pleasant chat as usual. I really think she's warming up to me because she sounded pretty hot on the phone!" Unable to do anything else at the moment, Ethan laughed at the ridiculousness of the night. His girlfriend was down for the count, his brand new vet resembled the last car left on the field after a demolition derby and some random man, Draque, left them his calling card and they were up to their eyeballs in only God knew what. It was best left that way. In the far distance the piercing screams of sirens echoed through the vacant lot.

"Yeah, Pippy, your mom's right. We're outta here." Ethan picked Savanah up, draped her in his arms and held her tightly to his chest as he climbed out of the bacteria-ridden tin box and navigated the back alleyways. Coming out onto Bourbon Street, he realized they blended right in; lovers and drunks alike enjoying each other and the night, dancing in the street to their own tune. The street didn't have the flavor of Mardi Gras, but it came close. Holding Savanah, he wished they could enjoy the ambiance of the evening like this instead of fading into the darkness. This was not how he envisioned their first date. Oh—far from it. Pushing and shoving through the maraud of people, he finally scoped out a vacant patch of sidewalk where he sat down with her draped in his lap. He leaned over and rested his lips on her head.

"Come on, Savanah, you're giving me a complex. Most women don't pass out until I've thoroughly worn them out." His heart melted, all the rough edges smoothed over as he cared for the woman in his arms. Without thinking his lips found the tip of her nose, then her cheek and then the corner of her mouth. Behind closed eyes his free hand caressed her cheek. He whispered, "Savanah, I don't know how, but I'm in love with you. God help you, baby, because I've never loved anyone and that's the truth."

Hearing the whinny of a horse, he glanced up the street. A horse and carriage waited by the edge of the road. Both the driver and the mare wore hats with a giant daisy growing out of them. He hoisted Savanah's *not-so-fragrant* deadweight and bee-lined toward it before anyone beat them to it. Ethan gave the driver a wad of bills and pointed in the opposite direction they'd just come from.

"Can you take us to the House of Blues? But first a little ride around 'til my *belle au bois dormant* comes too?"

"She is a sleeping beauty." The driver pocketed the cash. With a little 'chic-chic,' the horse jerked forward bringing the carriage behind.

"Too many hurricanes, Sir?" the driver asked.

Ethan nodded, then realized the driver didn't have eyes in the back of his head, the way his mother always swore she did. "You could say that. How late do you run your service?"

Savanah stirred. Looking around, she found herself safely tucked into Ethan's arms, his jacket draped over her shoulders. She cuddled closer. "Where are we?"

"Hello, sleepy head. We are outside the House of Blues. Thought you might enjoy a bit of music before we headed home."

"Oh yeah," Savanah perked right up, "I love dancing. Let's go."

"Sweetie, not two minutes ago you were viewing the backside of your brain and now you want to dance?"

"Um hum! I like the carriage. It brings back some fond memories, but where's the new car and what's that smell?"

Ethan sighed. "It's a long story. Let's get inside and I'll tell you everything. What did you mean about fond memories?"

"You still don't know how old I am, do you? Later, we'll trade stories."

"Bed time stories?" he asked behind a wide grin.

"No X-rated ones, Eth." Savanah gave him an all-teeth grin, and then chomped at him.

"Sir, 'til three in da morn," the driver interrupted, "I'm easy ta find."

Once inside the building, Savanah looked around awestruck. "Did you ever see the movie *The Blues Brothers*? It's one of my favorites. I went one night by myself to an all-night theatre and sat through every showing, and I laughed harder each time I saw it."

Ethan grabbed her hand. "It's playing at *Canal Place Cinema*."

"You're a tease."

"No really, it is. I saw it on the marquis as we drove into town. Come on, we'll dance a bit and then make our way there."

"Eth, you still didn't answer me about the car or

the"—Savanah sniffed and made a face. "I feel like I'm blanking out on half the night."

"That's one way of putting it. Come on—slow dance. That's all I'm good for. Rest your curly locks on my shoulder, and I'll tell you what you've missed in the past two hours."

"What?" Savanah yelled over the music.

Ethan dragged her out to the floor where he snuggled as they danced to Tabby Thomas, *I Need Your Love so Bad.* He held her cheek to cheek through the song telling Savanah the wild events of the night.

She yelled in his ear, "Why aren't we on the plane heading home?"

"I want some distance from my plane right now. Whose Draque?"

"Who's—who?" Savanah asked, unaware her hand went to her heart for protection. She visibly paled before Ethan's eyes again once the name registered.

"You're not going to pass out again are you? You get that look just before... Son of a bitch—Savanah." Ethan picked her limp body up from the dance floor and carried her to the men's room. No one objected and a few people were even nice enough to hold the door for them. With one sweep of his arm, Ethan sent all the little bottles of toiletries crashing onto the floor. Laying her down on the countertop, he grabbed a towel and soaked it with cold water, then soaked her.

Spitting and sputtering gibberish, she came around. "Now what? One second we're dancing and now I'm soaked. What did you do to me? Trip me up and knock me out?"

"No, Savage, you're pretty capable of that feat all by your lonesome. Why do you always pass out?"

"I have a genetic disorder called Myotonia Congenita. It's a neuromuscular meltdown. When I get startled or excited my synapses light up like a board on Wall Street just before everything bottoms out and goes belly up. So, I'm not sitting upright until you've told me all the bad news."

"That is the smartest thing you've said. Okay, we were drugged by some dude named Draque." Ethan produced the small calling card from his jacket and held it above her head so she could read it. This time she didn't pass out—she vomited.

"I'll never get to the punch line at this rate." Ethan grabbed some paper towels and washed her face off again. "You okay?" He walked over to the second sink where additional toiletries lined up. He grabbed a small paper cup and grabbed a bottle of mouthwash and then handed it to her. "Swish and spit."

Savanah did as asked then turned the faucet on full blast to rinse out the sink.

"Draque wanted us to go somewhere with him."

"Straight to Hell is my guess."

"What did you steal from him? You're really not telling me this Draque guy is the real deal? The procreator of all vamps?"

She nodded. "We pretty much took everything. Uncle Jules and I wiped out his tomb. That's what the call was about this morning. Someone stole the entire collection from me. Doesn't that feel like a lifetime ago?"

"We blew up the car."

"What car? Draque's? Bet he drove a hearse."

Ethan shook his head. "Not Draque's."

"No. Don't even tell me we no longer have the

'vet."

"You really don't remember?"

Savanah pouted.

"Someone tampered with the car's gas tank and added Nitro to it. Had we gotten in and started the car…"

"We'd be on the TV show, *Without a Trace*," Savanah finished. "Now what?"

"For now, we'll lay low and get to know each other better. One more dance?"

"I think I better just listen. Did we eat at O'Brien's? I'm starved."

"We had a liquid lunch. Come on, we'll go get some popcorn and watch your movie."

Sitting up, Savanah gave him a pain-filled glance. "Ethan, why do I feel like I've been riding a horse?"

"I've been compared to a stallion a time or two, but honestly…"

She slugged his arm. "Shut up and answer me. Did we or didn't we do the dirty dance?"

"I have not sullied your reputation as of yet, Missy, but the night is young." Ethan found himself unable to stay away from her, and subsequently, found his lips engaging hers in a passionate, molten hot, blood-scorching kiss that left them both breathless.

"I think you're still feeling the after effects from the drugs, Mr. Kitt."

"Come, little nut, and we'll see what I'm feeling in a nice dark theatre."

Despite everything that had gone utterly wrong: being drugged, the car blowing up, and the God Father of Vamps wanting to breathe down her neck, or chomp on it, Savanah smiled. She was having fun. She hadn't felt this alive in—when? She couldn't recall ever feeling this way or wanting to spend so much time with one man, regardless of his antics or hubris. Yes, he was relentless in his pursuit of happiness, his, but he seemed smitten and cared for her with both passion and precision. No other man had ever done that.

"Ethan, if I tell you something will you promise not to laugh?"

"No guarantees, sweet cheeks. Whazzz up?"

"Never mind, then." Savanah grabbed Ethan's shoulders for balance. "Ethan, go slow with me tonight, until I get my feet under me?"

Ethan slid his arm around her waist. "And here I thought I'd end up under you!" An elbow to his rib cage stole his breath.

She was feeling better!

****

Inside the movie theatre, Ethan noticed couples scattered about the theatre, slurping large fountain drinks through skinny sippin' straws. The aroma of popcorn was as subtle as a cat in a canary cage. He led Savanah to the front row of the balcony where she sat and dangled her legs over the edge.

Ethan got down on one knee and whispered, "Would you like something from the concession stand? I did promise you dinner."

"Oh no you don't! You owe me a real meal, but, for now chocolate covered raisins and water and popcorn smothered with butter and salt." Ethan got halfway down the aisle when she yelled, "Napkins!" The other couples cranked their necks upward, giving her the rude-how-dare-you-yell-in a-theatre glare. She bit her cheeks trying to control her mouth, but when she had something to say... "Lighten up. The movie hasn't even started yet."

Upon his return, Ethan piled everything into Savanah's lap and got comfy, with his arms securing her body to his, his feet up next to hers and his head nestled on her shoulder. Looking at her he wiggled his eyebrows and asked, "Feed me?"

"Would you two keep it down?" Some man shouted from below the balcony.

"Not a prob bud," Ethan yelled back.

"We're going to get kicked out of here before the movie even starts."

"Trust me, Savage, we'll get kicked out, but not for any of reasons you're thinking. The noise level could reach record levels. Yours, not the antiquated sound system in this joint."

Savanah bit her tongue, as he teased her with his words. She really hoped he'd come through with all his innuendos.

"What did you want to tell me, without me laughing at you? I'll behave."

"Yeah, right. It's not important."

"Come on. No secrets between us."

"It's silly. Really."

"Hurry up, the movie's about to start."

"I've never been to a movie on a date."

Ethan inhaled, lodging a little, white, corn cork in his airway. Coughing and choking of course followed. Savanah shoved him forward, and slapped his back hard. One lung-tossing hack later, the kernel soared through the air, over the balcony and onto Mr. Mouthy below. "Sweet cheeks, have you ever heard of the Heimlich? If someone's choking you don't whack 'em.

You give 'em the ultimate tummy tuck, bringing it up and in to force the air and obstruction from their body. But that's only after they've turned a putrid shade of blue. But thanks for saving my miserable life."

"I got it out," she said in her own defense. "You all right?"

Ethan nodded before he placed a water bottle to his lips and chugged. "So finish your tall tale. I find it impossible for someone as beautiful as you to never have been on a date. What—did your Papa scare every suitor off?" Ethan grabbed Savanah's hand and ran each finger past his lips, then popped her pinky finger into his mouth and then sucked on it.

"You going to choke on that as well?" She yanked her hand back. "No one's ever asked me."

"So, I'm your first?" Ethan straightened up in his chair.

"Yes, in that sense, I guess so." Savanah leaned onto him, and rested her head next to his. "I want to make-out in the theatre."

"Oh, I love a dirty girl."

Someone once more screamed, "Would you two shut up?"

They didn't have to be asked again because Ethan effectively took control of her lips.

Tilting her face to his, he whispered, "Close your eyes. If you don't want me to do anything just say *heel.*"

Savanah burst out laughing, but at least her laughter coincided with the movie. She whispered, "Heel as in good doggy?"

"Should work like a charm. Close 'em, sweets."

Excitement welled in her gut as Ethan's breath

feathered over her skin. His fingers tugged her shirt off one shoulder and his lips worked their magic over her breasts. He made no contact, just his hot breath against her cool skin and a promise of what could be. Savanah nipples swelled under her bra, which now became an unwanted item of clothing. As his hand skimmed along her thigh, Savanah's blood heated her from her head to her toes. Her breath burned from the inside out. She was a dragon spontaneously combusting. When he stopped just short of the juncture where her thighs ended and her treasures began the little voice inside her begged, *Goddess please don't let him stop*. Now it wasn't just the bra she wanted off, but everything.

Not only did Ethan hear that little voice, he listened to it.

Someone's timing stunk. With that annoying sixth sense of eyes burning into her, Savanah peeked out of the corner of her eye and gasped. "Ethan, heel!"

Ethan produced a low guttural growl. Nothing human about it. "What is it? Did I hurt you or not about to fulfill your wildest desires?"

Oh, how she wanted this, wanted him on her in a dark public area, making love to her, but…

"Get off the lady, Mister."

The flashlight blinded them, and stopped Ethan's lips in his tracks, puckered around her nipple.

Nipping her swollen bud lightly once, he snarled. "Don't you have some popcorn to pop? Other patrons to spy on?"

"Nope. Get up and go quietly, and I won't call the authorities."

"Sir," Savanah cringed. "We weren't doing anything illegal." *Yet*.

Ethan sat up wearing a scowl that Scrooge would have envied. "Savage, why is it every time you and I— you know—get close, someone happens by and pulls the plug?"

Savanah stood, yanked her shirt back onto her shoulder, and gave the man an intense glare. "Mister, we'll behave if you'll forget you've ever seen us."

"What did you say?" The manager asked his voice gruff.

"Ethan, would you close your eyes for one second? No questions."

Ethan did as he was asked.

Savanah leaned into the flashlight wielding man and in the blink of her eye, gave him the flash of light. Her deep baby-blues created a beam of sheer power so intense it bore into the manager's retina and bounced through to the back side of his brain, redirected his thoughts and in the long run, kept them from being tossed out of the theatre on their butts.

Dumbfounded, the man asked, "Do you people need more drinks or candy?"

"No, thank you," Ethan answered, giving his date a curious glance out of the corner of his eye. "Some privacy? We're on our honeymoon." Ethan laughed when he heard Savanah gasp.

"That's it, I'm calling the manager," someone from below the balcony yelled.

"I am the manager and these two are on their honeymoon. Leave them be."

Savanah gasped again and looked around for a paper bag to breath into. *Honeymoon?*

"Don't you dare pass out, Savage."

"Congrats," the guy yelled. "Now get a room all

ready and rent the damn movie there so I can watch it here."

"A room really isn't a bad idea, Ethan."

"Huh—what?" Behind closed eyes and a tightly closed fist, Ethan jerked his fist triumphantly in the air, mouthing the word, "*Yes*," into the darkness.

"I still haven't seen a movie with a date."

"And with me, Savage, you probably never will."

"I need to use the restroom, Eth."

"You don't mind if I tag along? I'm not letting you out of my sight. Safety reasons, baby."

"Perverse and deranged is more like it. No golden showers!" Savanah pushed open the door to the restroom and dragged Ethan in behind her.

"Never even heard the phrase before."

"God you suck at lying."

"Not all I suck at." Once behind closed doors, Ethan snaked Savanah to him, turned and slammed her against the door, his body pressed solid against her. Brushing back soft jet-black tendrils from her face, his lips met her neck. With a subtle graze of teeth he sucked on her neck. She squirmed and giggled until he released her. With a slight lift of his head he came face to face with his tall dark beauty.

When Savanah turned into his lips it unraveled every fiber of Ethan's genetic makeup. Ethan pressed his hips into her so she could feel what she'd done to him. Once more, clothing became an unrelenting obstacle. "Savanah, I'm on untested grounds here. As God is my witness, I don't know how to handle my feelings for you."

Savanah leaned back from Ethan. "So, what usually happens on one of your dates?"

"Sweets, it would have been over this morning. One of two things would have occurred. First scenario, you would have had an orgasm to end all orgasms, and I'd have left you alone fully sated, and probably never would have seen you again. Second scenario is you wouldn't have let me touch you, and I'd have left. I'm not the type of guy to stick around. Shoot and score's been my goal for the past few years. It beats getting hurt once someone finds out you're a shifter tied to a vamp."

"So let me get this straight, you love 'em and leave 'em so *you* won't get hurt?" Savanah scratched her head. "I'm sorry your life has become so forlorn. But Ethan, you're no longer alone. You and I have similar pasts and futures. My entire family are characters ripped straight from a quirky horror novel. And let's not forget, I have the king of vamps hot for my blood. You have a vamp almost as evil and disgruntled, not to mention my mother."

Ethan cringed. "Oops! I forgot to tell you she called. I'm guessing you two have some serious psychic connection because she saved us when it rained car parts."

"What, the protective shield?"

Ethan gave a little nod.

"Yes, we do have a bond that gains strength each and every day. For the past one hundred and fourteen years to be exact."

Ethan searched Savanah's face waiting for her punch line. And he waited… With the knowledge she wasn't joking, his eyes grew wide. He managed to squeak out, "No freakin' way. How?"

"I stopped aging at twenty-five. We, Sydney,

Avery and I started donating our blood to Uncle Lucian, Aunt Serina and Aunt Raven then, but for some reason Sydney and Avery never stopped aging. They were hexed by my mother's half-brother, William. We haven't seen him since the night my Auntie Serina was almost stoned."

"As in pot? Illegal drugs?"

"As in the witch hunts. Long story."

"You're pulling me leg."

"Not."

"Who are Avery and Sydney?"

"My cousins. Uncle Lucian and Aunt Serina adopted them. Avery died in the First World War although we never found his body. Syd lives in Georgia on a large reserve for endangered animals. I miss her dearly. We stay in touch, but she doesn't come around too often to see her mom for safety reasons. Kinda hard to call her mother—mom when she looks old enough to be a great grandmother."

"And you've never been on a date to the movies in how many years?"

Savanah released a long pent up breath. "I can't believe you didn't flip over my age."

"So I really am your first? Virgin?"

"At the movies, yeah!"

"I don't care about the other men, Savage, as long as I'm the last. I hate being the first anyway. Too emotional. Women cry, get freaked out, then feel guilty and get that look in their eye like they're petrified you won't call them. Did they perform to my satisfaction? Did they lay there and play dead? They never orgasm the first time because of all those questions screwing with them and honestly, I'm not that nice of a guy to stick around and hold hands. Sure as hell won't tell them they made the right decision to hand over their virginity to me. Let someone else deal with it."

"I don't think you give yourself enough credit. If nothing else you're brutally honest. I like that. I don't know if you're right about other women and their first time making love, but you were right on the money about me. I made a huge mistake. Capital "*H*" huge. I worked with a guy and we had just unearthed a mummy nearly a thousand years old, and we both got excited and one thing led to another."

"No details, Babe."

"No, you have to hear this."

"No, seriously, don't want the blow by blow."

"Seriously, you do. A few hours after he walked off with my virginity, he told me he needed a cold stiff one. I thought it was due to me being so hot." Savanah fanned her cheeks. "Well, I didn't take him literally. I found him in the cooler an hour later with his nob stuffed into the mummy we just unearthed. I cried my eyes out in my father's arms."

Ethan attempted to shake off the disturbing visual. "Sick bastard. You told your father? Did he kill him? I would have. You really told your dad you had sex?"

"Eth, if you're going to hang out with me, get used to it. There are no secrets at our home."

"Except the one with your Aunt Raven and Vonnie. Dirty little secrets! That blew a few fuses."

"That it did. Anyway, you okay with everything so far?"

"Savanah, I've never been okay. Let's go get a room somewhere so we can get some rest."

"Rest?" Her bottom lip jut out.

Ethan immediately kissed the pout from her lips. "I think I'm going to need some rest before you and I engage in any other activities. I want to be at my best."

"Right now, I'd take your worst. My body is in an uproar."

Ethan produced a smile that purred sexy promises. "Hands on my shoulders until I say otherwise. No questions."

Savanah did as he asked. With his knee he nudged her thighs apart, only to place one of his legs between hers. Pulling up her shirt inch by slow-maddening inch he lapped at her belly, mixing kisses with nips along his path. His tongue traced each and every rib. Through the bra's lace, Ethan's lips moved circles with a hint of pressure over her areola. Savanah moaned and dug her fingers into his blond mane. Tantric foreplay, nothing like it. Taunt and tease. Bring her to the edge just to let her down a notch and then drive her over. He had a plan.

Ethan suckled at her nipple and tugged slightly with his teeth until he had her doing what he hoped, grinding her hips and private lips onto his thigh. Little murmurs she had no control over filled the room.

"I am becoming so addicted to the sounds you make as I touch you. You make me so hard."

"Don't start talking now." She grunted one long, "Ummm! A delicious tingle worked its way from my gut to my groin."

Ethan grabbed her ass pulling her groin against his where she felt him solidly waiting.

"Here, Eth? Like this?"

"No, Baby. Our first time will not be here." Ethan slipped his hand between her thighs and with some pressure, pressed into her jeans.

Savanah started to say something, but when his fingers pressed into her mons, he'd found the correct button to push, pushing past her limits.

"Ugh! Eth? This is torture. I want you."

"I know, Baby. It's good to want. It gives you a reason to live."

"Thief. That's my line."

"Put your arms around my neck and hold on for the ride."

"But I still have my pants on."

"Don't worry. You'll still feel me. This is safe sex at its best." Ethan picked her up, and pressed her up against the door. "Wrap your legs around me." Moments later Savanah resembled a living painting. Ethan drove home his point over and over, pushing into her private lips. The movement relieved some of the tension from him too.

"I love the feeling of this"—she admitted—"in public. It feels so naughty."

"A little voyeuristic. I'm with you. It adds the element of danger to the excitement." Ethan carried her to the countertop. "Lean back."

Savanah leaned back on her elbows, and watched as Ethan pressed his bulge into her. "Sweet rapture, Savage. This is hot." Unhooking her bra, one handed, he gave a subtle grin to her.

"Multitasking I see." She giggled.

Too busy to answer, Ethan found her creamy flesh warm. Inviting. He trailed circles around her areola, sucked until her nipple burst in his mouth. His penis swelled to a point he feared if he never had release he'd be blue for months, but watching her face full of pleasure, he'd wear the unnatural color as a badge of honor. He waited for the change in her breathing and once her pattern deepened he cupped her womanhood. Her contractions were strong enough to feel through cloth and rocking her.

"Ethan!" she gasped. "Something's happening to my body. I'm shaking from the inside out. This is wild."

Ethan stopped everything and looked at her. In his arms, he held the most beautiful woman he'd ever seen, and she was clueless. He drew her closer still and held her until the shakes subside. "Baby, tell me that wasn't your first O. You told me you've been with men before. This never happened to you?"

Savanah shook her head, no, embarrassed.

"Oh, Baby! I didn't hurt you, did I?"

"That is the nicest thing my body has ever experienced. Thank you."

"Savage, don't thank me. How many times have you had sex?"

"Only a few. I told you of my first time. The second wasn't any better and trust me the third was a complete disaster."

"I can't see anything worse than your first time. So three times? Three different guys?"

"Uhm, no. Two moronic mistakes. Why?"

"Because I wouldn't have let you walk away from me until you were washed out of every ounce of energy you had. I wasn't even trying hard."

Savanah slowly rolled her eyes to meet his, grinning. "Oh you're hard, Eth."

Ethan blushed. "Not any more. I guess your body was saving itself for Mr. Right."

"Do you think you foot the bill?"

"You got a pretty glass slipper I can try on, and we'll see if it fits?"

"If anyone gets the pretty glass slipper it's me."

Savanah's smile left Ethan defenseless. "Come on Cinderella, let's get cleaned up and then back to your carriage and find a nice room for the night."

"I don't recall that line in the movie." Savanah cupped Ethan's cheeks with her hand, and got lost in the beauty of eyes. "Maybe I just wasn't privy to the X-rated version you were."

****

Back at the carriage, Ethan asked, "James, would you take us somewhere quaint and exceptionally nice?"

Savanah smirked. "Are you just assuming all chauffeurs are named James?"

"No, Cinders. I asked him while you were under your enchanted spell."

The chauffer answered, "Sir, I've just da place for you and da Misses."

Savanah's eyes went wide. Before she could protest the new prefix on her name, Ethan's mouth covered hers with a soft kiss.

"How many people are you going to tell we're married?" she whispered.

"Only one or two more."

Looking at him out of the corner of her eye she asked, "Who?"

"The hotel concierge and your Papa."

"What?"

"I'm teasing. I really don't have a death wish."

As the horse drawn carriage skirted the waterfront, Savanah watched the moon's glow dance on the waves of the Mississippi River. People strolled along the boardwalk moving to and fro from the Canal Street Market, holding hands, some loaded with bags, whispering, laughing, watching ships port, as others set sail. As the carriage rolled to a stop at the hotel, her jaw dropped. "St. James Hotel. How did you even know there was a place down here with my name?"

"Don't look at me. You heard what I told James."

"I don't know about you, Eth, but this is freaky. Coincidence?"

"Let's hope so. Come on, let me help you down."

"Such a gentleman. Wasn't it only this morning you wouldn't even get the car door for me?"

"Take full advantage of me like this coz tomorrow's another day."

"Oh, Mr. Kitt, I do plan on taking advantage of you."

"Promises, promises. Shall we?"

Out on the curb, Ethan held his hand out waiting for Savanah to accept…waiting…still waiting….

"Hello! Savanah? You with me?" He gave her his best eyebrow-raising-double-wink-wink-come-hither smile he could muster.

Teeth chiming out a rat-a-tat tune, knees shaking, Savanah found herself huddled, too petrified to move.

"Ethan, it's not you. It's—I—I don't know. I feel—a presence. It's the only way to describe it."

"Misses?" The carriage driver interrupted, "Can I tell ya something?"

About to argue with the prefix to her name, she quit before she started. And honestly, she'd developed a fondness for it (Ethan and the idea of being his wife).

Ethan jumped into the back seat and hugged

Savanah while the driver told his story in a spicy gumbo accent. After a long rant that spoke of a lifetime of living in the Bayou, Ethan and Savanah got a little glimpse of some of the mystique that surrounded New Orleans. All the Voodoo and black magic fit right into their lifestyle.

"Dis place is a portal for spirits and energies. 'Tis why I brought ya here. I can feel it in your aura. You are familiar with dese entities."

"So—this place is haunted?" Ethan exclaimed jumping back out of the carriage. "Sweet! Come on, my blushing bride. Let's go have us a séance."

"Ethan, can I borrow your phone?" Savanah watched Ethan's eyes light up and just then, Savanah knew without a doubt, she'd gone and done it again, she'd set him up, hook, line and dial tone. She could all ready hear the music in her head. "Don't…" she teased.

"Who…?" Ethan spread his arms wide.

"You…" Savanah pointed her finger at him, warning.

"Ya…" He egged her on. He placed his thumb and pinky finger to his mouth and ear, making a phone.

"Dare…"

"Gonna call?" he sang.

"Say it." She cracked up laughing.

"Ghostbusters!" Ethan tossed her over his shoulder and headed for the lobby beboppin' away. "If you're all alone, pick up the phone…"

"You are a moron, Ethan."

Patting her rump, he said, "Yeah, but I'm the moron going into the hotel with Cinderella. I'll bet ya Prince Charming didn't make it this far on their first date."

Jaclyn Tracey

Once in the lobby, energies bounced off her like moths converging on a bug zapper. This place had an infestation of spirits, pissed off little goblins that left her with goose flesh. Creeped out, didn't cut it. Nightmares were in her future.

"Room 214, misses." Ethan tossed the card key into her lap and held his hand out yet again. "Our room has the same date as Saint Valentine's day."

"Go, Cupid! Let's just pray for no bloody massacres. Seriously, can I use your phone?"

"You calling home?"

"Yeah. I don't want to use my psychic channels in case someone tries to hack me."

"What's that mean?"

"Body snatch. Spirits are sneaky little shits. I need to let my parents know we're okay, because if they don't hear from me, I can guarantee they'll be pounding our door down in a few hours."

Ethan gave Savanah a quick gyration show of his hips. "The only pounding happening tonight is between you and me, baby."

"Such sweet words, Elvis!"

"Savvy, hold on—I think his spirit's got me!" Ethan revved up the hip action. People in the lobby pointed, stared and whispered amongst themselves.

"Oh my God!" With the cell pressed close to her ear, Savanah was unsure whether to hit him or kiss him. She leaned against the wall and crossed her ankles and watched Ethan charm the hotel concierge and everyone around him with his handsome looks and unbelievable wit, and by the Goddess, he charmed her with no magic or potions, just him. Yes, he was now in the thralls of doing an Elvis impersonation and laughing his way through it. When no one answered, she snapped the cell shut and waited for Ethan to finish his debut.

****

Walking through the square-shaped courtyard, Ethan took in all the sights, getting a feel for the place, looking for an escape hatch if they needed one. All the room's entrances were outside. The courtyard had old world southern charm to it. Each window held overflowing flower boxes. Each door had intricately painted hex symbols. A black wrought-iron fence lined a gray slate pathway to a pool filled with majestic turquoise water. Wedgwood blue wrought-iron tables held pink-crackled crystal vases filled with fragrant bluebells. Wisteria trees with their delicate bluish-lavender flowers added both color and a sweet fragrance to the patio. The starry night illuminated the area.

Hearing footsteps fast approaching, Ethan glanced over his shoulder only to see the bell hop with a tray of food and a bottle of champagne. He swept Savanah off her feet. "Come on."

"That's ours?" Savanah's smile inched its way across her face. "Dinner?"

Ethan finagled the card key through the slot and the little green light winked to life. He pressed down on the latch and shoved the door inward using Savanah's butt. "Your room and dinner, Misses." Ethan carried her across their threshold, his lips welded to hers.

His hand outstretched like some pathetic slob on the dole, the waiter coughed once and when neither of them came up for air, he set the tray down and excused himself, uttering one word. "Newlyweds!"

Savanah and Ethan burst out laughing. Savanah

didn't relinquish her grip when Ethan tried to toss her onto the king-sized bed. The two went down atop the purple and orange flowered coverlet oblivious to everything but each other.

****

"Family meeting, everyone front and center, pronto!" Jovan screamed from the second floor of the house.

"Cherié, you don't have to holler. Use your mind messenger. You'll wake the dead with that tone."

"I felt like screaming, so let it be, André. And as far as waking the dead? Trust me, they're up and up to no good."

"What's happened to get your knickers in a knot this time?" André approached his pregnant wife with caution, wearing a grin that only a mother could love and since Jovan wasn't his mother...

"Back up. And for the record? I stopped wearing knickers long before I met you."

"Fibber. You had those silly little bloomers on the first night we met. I remember seeing the sexy little garment and remember wanting it gone more so."

Jovan ignored him even though she was impressed he remembered her outfit one hundred fourteen years past. She couldn't remember what she wore yesterday! "Have you not felt any strange vibrations coming from your daughter in the past fourteen hours? She's in trouble."

"Family meeting. Front and center!" André yelled louder than Jovan.

Julian stumbled into the hallway half asleep. "What time is it?"

André shrugged his shoulders.

"It's midnight," Jonah answered as he came out his room, Raven tucked under his arm. "What's got you two crazy this time?"

"Savanah's in trouble that's what," Jovan spouted. "She and the mutt were about to get blown up by someone, and I had to throw a shield around them to keep them safe."

"Why—ah—couldn't Savvy do it?" Raven asked through her yawn.

"Her brain patterns are off, and she's making no sense. I called Ethan's cell hours ago and told him to get her home. I haven't heard from them since. The little prick never called me back."

"Cherié, did you give him the number? You come up unknown on cells."

Jovan went to say, "Yes, of course I did," but shut her mouth when she realized she'd hung up on him before that little tidbit of info was given. "Well our daughter should have called us back by now. That only proves something's wrong."

"Who tried to blow them up?" Lucian leaned into the hallway, Elyza cradled in his arms whimpering with giant-sized teardrops rolling off her little red flushed cheeks. Her baby-soft curls were matted down to her head and her eyes were wide as she looked around at everyone. "Next time you guys have a shouting match, do it outside. Remember the rule: Let sleeping babes sleep."

"Come here, my angel." Raven snagged her from her father's arms. "Your other very loud, inconsiderate aunt and uncle are sorry they woke you."

Jovan walked to Elyza and kissed her. "Not to be a nag, but someone's got to go to New Orleans. Tonight.

Now. This very instant." Jovan scratched her nose and then rubbed her eye to try and alleviate the twitch working its way in.

"How do you know where there are?" Raven asked.

"I'm her mother. I know when she sneezes and has to sit down so she won't pee her pants afterwards."

"TMI, Jovan." Jonah added.

****

Within an hour and a half Lucian, André and Julian sat on a private jet, headed for the Big Easy. Thirty minutes after they were in the air, Savanah phoned home again.

"Mum? Hi. Don't speak yet and whatever you do, don't channel me."

"What's going on? Are you all right? Did that stupid thing you're with hurt you? I'll castrate him."

"Mum! I'm fine, other than being drugged, doing a lap dance…"

"What?"

Her mother's shrill voice made Savanah jerk the phone from her ear. "Never mind that part. We had to blow up Ethan's new corvette. That's the most painful thing we've been through tonight."

"Your father's going to kill me. You're really not hurt?"

"No. Why? We're fine."

"Then what took hours to call me back? You should be home by now."

Savanah smiled. Her mother was her best friend, and she loved her with every ounce of her soul, but the woman had the most viable umbilical cord on the planet still strangling Savanah. Her mother's voice sounded shaky. Savanah needed to quell her worries before the posse was unleashed. "I tried a bit ago but you never picked up."

"Savanah, I panicked."

"No, not you Mom. I don't see it happening." Savanah giggled trying to tease her mother. Her mother didn't laugh, giggle or even breathe. "I swear, Mom we're fine."

"You won't be in a little bit. I sent your father and two uncles looking for you when you didn't return my call in the thirty seconds I allotted you to return my call after I spoke with Ethan."

"Oh, Mum." Savanah shook her head. "Listen, my artifacts at the museum were stolen from me last night. My exhibit has been kiboshed. That's the reason I took off. I needed a bit of space, so Ethan—oh, Mum, you'd really love him if you gave him a chance." Savanah heard her mother gasping into the phone. "Mum?"

"I'm here, baby. Keep going. Did you say love?" Jovan's eye twitched like a frog in a science experiment hooked up to a battery juiced up enough to drive a stock car.

"Are you sitting down?"

"Should I be?" Jovan sat regardless.

"Draque is here somewhere. He bought us drinks, drugged us and then left his calling card with a note on the back, basically telling me he wants his shit back."

"Savanah! Mouth."

"Sorry. Someone put Nitro in the gas tank of Eth's new car. Ethan found it and blew up the car. The explosion gave me a concussion. Other than throwing up and passing out, I'm fine. If it makes you feel any better Ethan hasn't let me hit the ground. He's strong, sincere, funny, and one heck of a kisser. Mum, don't let anyone channel when they get here. This hotel we're at is loaded with spirits." Savanah yawned.

"Where's your escort? You have separate rooms right?" Jovan crossed her fingers.

Savanah giggled. "He's in the shower. We just had dinner. So how long have I got 'til I can expect my door being broken down?"

"You're safe for at least three more hours. Behave and for Goddess sake, don't sleep with the man tonight."

"You did with Papa."

"Yes, my baby, and we have you to show for it. Please, just be careful?"

"I love you, Mum. I'll see you tomorrow. Sweet dreams."

"Love you more, Peanut."

Chapter Eleven

Soggy, gray nimbostratus clouds smothered the horizon and threatened a good ringing out. The sun wouldn't come out tomorrow and with that thought Lucian would be stuck with the ridiculous *Annie* song all day. His nose pressed against the chilled glass of the leer jet, he fought gravity to keep his eyelids open. Between his two traveling companions acting like Chatty Cathy dolls, and the turbulence he'd gotten no rest.

Julian cursed and paced the entire flight. A box of Dramamine didn't take the edge off his fear of flying. If anything, the medicine acted more as an antagonist. Just hearing the term *near miss* brought the man to his knees, and André had whispered it to him more than once. *Johnny Damon nearly missed that ball... Jeter nearly missed the throw to first base... Did you see that flock of geese we nearly missed?* That's when Julian cuffed him upside the head. Julian believed each and every time he boarded a plane—it would be his last. A friend of his, an air traffic controller, constantly told him stories of close calls—the things no one wants to hear before boarding a plane. Once Julian's feet were firmly planted on soil, he bent over and kissed the ground.

A few steps in front of his brother-in-law, André turned back. "So it is true," he teased, "you do worship the ground I walk on." The next few seconds of André's life became a complete blur. He found himself on the runway, air knocked from his lungs, and crushed into the pavement. After André caught his breath he yelled, "The truth hurts doesn't it, Grimmy."

Julian never looked back as he walked to the limo. "Not as much as I could've hurt you."

Lucian picked his brother up from the ground, snickering. "You two are far worse than you and I when we were boys, Ands. All this time and you guys never quit."

"We're just fooling around, Luce. It's harmless."

"Yeah, and that's why you're bleeding." Lucian pointed to the red stain crawling across André's white linen shirt.

"'Tis just a flesh wound!"

"All right, King Arthur! Where's the cell phone? We should call the hotel and give your daughter a head's up we're here. You don't want another episode like yesterday, do you?"

André's smile vanished. "I didn't handle that very well."

"You think?" Lucian asked as he shoved him forward toward the car.

"I think my cell phone is what's crushed into my chest. Either of you bring one?" Both Lucian and Julian gave the official "no" nod.

Driving down Magazine Street, André asked the chauffer, "Can we hit Decatur Street first? Savanah loves beignets. We can pick up breakfast for her."

"André, you're planning on killing her with kindness aren't you."

"Something like that, Luce."

"He's planning on stuffing the little dough bombs down Ethan's throat is what he's planning," Julian added. "And if he doesn't I will."

A mere few feet from her room, a box of *Café Du Monde* coffee, and a bag of piping hot beignets in hand, André's stomach went queasy. He wasn't quite certain whether he needed blood or he smelled it, but either way it couldn't be good, and it sure as hell didn't smell as appetizing as Savanah's food. He turned and looked over his shoulder. Lucian's dents hung over his lips, his silvery-blue eyes had become roiling mercury. André looked at Julian and cringed. He could already see the headlines on the cover of the *National Geographic*. *Shoot First. Don't Bother With Questions.* An elongated nose and the shift of bones that make more noise than corn morphing into fluffy white kernels is never a good thing.

André whispered. "Are there any surveillance cameras? We're toast."

Julian dropped his voice. "Knock on the door or knock it in, but do it now. I hear footsteps."

André banged on the door three times and waited. "Savanah, it's Papa. Open up, Peanut."

"Again," Julian urged a second later.

"Move, Ands." About to slam into the door, a member of the housekeeping popped her head out of an adjacent room.

"Sir?" she asked, "Can I help you?"

Julian spun away from the woman so she couldn't see his facial fur. Lucian threw on sunglasses and yanked his bottom lip up over his top teeth leaving him with a sad under-bite.

André rolled his eyes. "My daughter checked in

here last night, and she's not answering her door."

"Well, Sir," the woman blushed, "neither would you if you were on your honeymoon."

"Wha—uh, oh shit—did you say?" Julian choked.

André held up the wall and turned ghostly white, and Lucian? Lucian had tears in his eyes, laughing.

"Oh bloody hell, brother. Your baby's finally gone and done it."

"Bust the door down!" André pointed to Julian.

"Sir, really, you must let them be."

"Lady, you don't understand. That's my baby."

"And babies grow up, Ands." Lucian slapped his brother's shoulder.

"I can't wait for Elyza to get married. Then don't come to me looking for help, because I'll laugh in your face." André turned his attention back to the locked door. "*Savanah!!!*" André screamed. The silence that followed might as well had been death lurking in the darkness. Or at least that's how André saw it. His heart hurt. Something was wrong, and he knew it wasn't due to the nuptials between his daughter and Mr. Kitt.

Jovan? I know you told me not to channel, but, hon, we are standing in the hallway of Mrs. Kitt's room, and she's not answering the door.

Mrs. who?

Kitt. He married her, Cherié. Our baby got married!

Oh bloody hell.

That's exactly what Lucian said.

Bust down the door and let me know the second you do. She didn't tell me that little detail.

I'll talk to you later.

The maid pried André from the door. "Sir, let me

go first. She may love you, but I don't think she'd appreciate seeing you if she and her husband…"

"Don't—say another word! Get in there." André bit out, "Thank you," as his foot tapped impatiently.

The maid disappeared behind the door. "Misses? It's housekeeping, dear. You descent?"

André pounded his fist into the wall. "Is she descent?"

The housekeeper raised her voice to carry into the room. "Mister? Misses? You two in here?"

The three men waited in the hallway looking more like thugs in a Martin Scorsese movie than a doting, overprotective father and two uncles.

Thump.

Three stooges squeezed through the door at the same time. Taking in the dismembered room, André ran to his daughter's side. His heart sank seeing Savanah bound, her hands and ankles duct taped with silver shackles as a secondary binder. Her mouth was stuffed with a sock. Copious amounts of blood covered the bed she lay in, yet the only visible wounds on her were a few scratch marks and two very distinct puncture marks on the right side of her neck, centered over her jugular.

Savanah's eyes filled with tears. André tenderly removed the tape from her.

"Oh princess, who did this to you? Where's Ethan? Where's Lucian now?" André pulled her into his arms, and rocked her back and forth.

Dizzy and confused, she tried to answer them, "They gave me Foxglove. It could've killed me, Papa. It's a cardiac stimulant. Why would they do that? I threw up all over before they taped up my mouth to stop me from yakking up any more shit."

"Mouth, Peanut," Julian said.

Both Savanah and André turned, giving Julian an irate glance.

"What?" Julian threw his hands in the air. "Sorry. It's habit. She swears and someone always says, 'Mouth!' Jesus, Savvy," Julian turned from her and wiped his eyes.

Lucian entered the room breathless. "Ethan's not here. I evanesced and covered this hotel. There is a trail of blood going out the bathroom window and up the side of the wall on the other side of the breezeway. Scratch marks are gouged into the stucco. From the looks of things he put up one hell of a fight. But someone got him."

"Savvy, what happened?" Julian knelt and took her hand. "Don't worry, Peanut, we'll find your husband."

Savanah snapped her head to face Julian and started laughing hysterically…until she passed out.

"Call the cops. Now. Get the maid up off the floor and don't touch a thing," Lucian ordered as he looked around the room. Just as Julian picked up the phone, Lucian picked up a small black business card from the table. He read the card: "Draque, Thank you for your Indentured Service. What in blazes is this?" Flipping the card over, Lucian finished, "How does it feel to have something stolen from you that you love? We'll be in touch. I'll call. You'll come." He turned to Julian. "Put the phone down."

André went to the bath, grabbed a wet a cloth came back and sat beside Savanah. He dabbed it over his daughter, cleaning the dried blood from her. "Peanut, tell us."

"I ah, I—don't—I can't." She began to shake with

tense involuntary rigors. "What did you say before I passed out?"

André held her tight until he relaxed. "Lucian, does she need blood? Is she in shock? Someone took a chunk out of her."

Savanah looked between her father and two uncles blankly. "What makes you think he's my husband? Papa, I met Draque. The big guy himself paid me a visit. You know all those movies, all the books, all the folktales ever depicted about the guy don't hold a candle to the real deal. He's actually beautiful. His eyes are black, his hair is so very white and straighter than a pine needle and as soft as a feather. Look." Savanah dug into her pocket and pulled out a chunk of blond hair, roots attached, showing them. "We didn't exactly see eye to eye on a few things. Things got physical. He's bigger than you, Papa. A lot bigger. Six-six or even six-seven and comes in about three hundred pounds of death-defying brutality."

Not one of them said a word, but instead gawked at Savanah, jaws dropped open like nutcrackers waiting for a token to crunch.

"Ethan is gone, Papa. He took him from me. I tried to stop him. Ethan tried to protect me. He really tried." Tears filled her eyes again. "Draque had some bloke with him that's bigger than the *Hulk* on steroids. He and Ethan got into it pretty good. Most of the blood is Androgen man's. Eth may not be as big as you three, but he got the guy, that is right up until Draque sank his choppers into me. Then Ethan started bargaining for my life, using his as bait."

André dropped his head. The mere thought of Dracula biting his daughter drove him to the brink of madness.

Julian bent forward fast. Speaking with his head between his knees, he asked, "What happened to Ethan?"

"Draque tag-teamed with Androgen man and knocked out my would-be lover, squeezing him through an all too tiny window and flew off into the night. Who's the lady on the couch?" Savanah pointed to the maid.

"Housekeeping."

Savanah!

Savanah spun toward the door. "Did you hear that?"

"No. What?"

Savage? The voice whispered to her in the wind.

"That! Ethan!" Savanah bounced off the bed and into the breezeway just in time to intercept Ethan. Julian followed on her heels.

Ethan didn't have time to apply his brakes and ran both of them down.

"Come on, Savage, we gotta get the hell outta here. Come on, baby. Please tell me they didn't hurt you." Ethan spoke so fast he never noticed Julian under him. His lips went in search of Savanah's and when they met he thought he might devour her in one single kiss.

Savanah gave him the quick once over and cringed. "Ethan, slow down. God, you're one bloody mess."

"Nowhere near as bad as Androgen man."

Savanah cracked a subtle smile. "That's what I called him too."

"Really?" Ethan stood and helped her to her feet, and then realized she wasn't alone. "Uncle Julian, I'm actually glad to see you."

Ethan put his forehead to Savanah's. His hands trembled as he struggled to hold her. "Are you really okay?"

Savanah shook her head yes. "Are you?" She kissed the tip of his nose.

Ethan drew her to him and clung to her with a thread of his sanity left. "I am, sweets, but we gotta get outta here. Draque's got a lair over in the City of the Dead. How *apropos*! The vile mosquito bit me and then Androgen man came at me with a silver prod. Use your imagination as to where he lodged it."

"Oh, Eth, no. Can I do anything?"

Kiss my ass better, was the very first thing that popped into Ethan's head, but he'd finally learned some restraint and kept his mouth shut. "I castrated the steroidal-mutant. I got him good."

"Ethan, TMI," Julian added.

"I shifted after the vamp climbed into his casket for the day and ripped the mutant's nuts off him."

"Ewh!" Savanah's stomach tightened.

"I thought they'd be more like brass beach balls, looking at the dude, but his were more like Q-tips. Seriously, Savvy, they were this freaking big." Ethan spread his fingers out less than an inch apart, showing her what he meant. "He can't reproduce now. Thank God."

"Ethan! Don't really need the gory details." Savanah covered her ears.

"My bad?" Ethan looked up, and noticed the maid staring at everyone. "Probably shouldn't have said all that aloud. Can you blink at her, you know, do your, *I Dream of Jeanie* sexy move?"

Savanah turned to the maid and did as she was

asked, knocking the maid on her feather duster.

"You saw me asleep on my bed. Thank you for allowing my family in."

"You're welcome, Misses." The maid got up, straightened her skirt, turned and walked out of the room rubbing her rump.

"That is so cool," Ethan said.

Savanah could have sworn she saw stars in his eyes. Hearing a loud crash in the bathroom she turned and ran. She found her father slumped over the toilette, clammy, pale and disoriented.

"Papa? Can I help you?"

André barely whispered, "Blood."

"Take my wrist, Papa. Take what you need."

André swatted at his daughter. "Get away from me."

"You can have mine," Ethan offered.

In a voice that no one recognized, André pleaded again, "Get her out of here. I think some pissed off spirit is messing with me."

Julian guided her out the door. "Go, Peanut. He needs blood and doesn't realize it." Turning to André, Julian explained, "You haven't been invaded, Ands. You're just low on fuel. You'll be fine."

"You sure? Jovan told me I could get possessed."

Julian pat his shoulder. "You're fine. There isn't a spirit stupid enough to screw with you. Shifters are a whole other story." Julian gave Ethan a look that asked without words, "Death wish?"

Ethan shoved his wrist under André's nose. "Here you go. This little mutt's your meal ticket, so ask politely or you won't get seconds. You want to be able to trust me? I'm all yours. Be careful. It packs a wallop.

Second time's the charm all right. One more and I might as well be the choir boy."

"I want your throat, boy." There was no humor indicated behind his obsidian eyes.

Looking between the three men, Ethan realized this was one test of wills he couldn't lose. He had to be stronger or respect would never be his. He'd just be considered fodder. Those days, he thought, are through.

"It's my wrist or nothing. My neck is not an option. There's only one person getting her lips on this, and it ain't you. And don't forget—Xier may very well be able to track you from this, and Draque. Jesus, I feel used." He attempted to crack a smile, but no one else seemed to understand his humor. To his astonishment André bowed before him.

Emerging from the bathroom, Ethan glanced at his reflection in the mirror. He had a pasty pallor, and André held a healthy rejuvenated glow. Funny how that worked, he thought.

"Ethan, if at any time you're up to no good, I'll find you."

"You're welcome," Ethan finished.

André walked to Savanah, dropped to his knees and kissed her palm. "You are everything to me, little girl. Why don't you lie down and rest. You looked exhausted. I'll be right here."

****

After a short restless nap, getting clean and fed, Savanah asked, "So what time to do we head to the City of the Dead? We're going after Draque right?"

Ethan waggled his index finger *no* in Savanah's face. "We? We—your father, Lucian, Julian and I will head out just before dusk. You, Pippy, are not included in this."

Hearing his concern for Savanah's welfare, André gave Julian, *the nod,* behind her back.

"Oh, you're so not leaving me here alone. We are a team, Eth. Papa, tell him. Tell him I'm coming." Savanah bat her big baby blues for all she was worth at her father.

"Ethan's right, it's too risky. It's hard enough to take care of ourselves, let alone worry for your health."

"Oh because I'm so much safer here alone? Really? I'm quite capable of caring for me." With an exaggerated huff one black curl lifted and landed exactly where it began; in her eyes.

Studying her, Ethan decided, "You look like you could cry at the drop of a dime. That's blackmail, Savanah. Don't get all girly on me." Then her bottom lip started to quiver.

Julian, Lucian and André sat back, eager to see how Ethan would handle this, having lived the past century with the little woman, who in her own right was a skilled actress.

I'm so bad. I can't believe I have to resort to this. Savanah bit at the evil little grin trying to work its way onto her lips.

Ethan gave her a soft kiss. He swept her tears away, and pressed his forehead against hers, watching her through crossed eyes.

"Savage," he murmured, "I grew up with five sisters, sweet cheeks. You're gonna have to do better than this to get what you want."

André, Lucian and Julian got up abruptly and walked away, all suddenly finding busy things to do.

Appalled, Savanah pushed him so hard Ethan did a

backwards dive off the bed. He landed squarely on his feet.

"Ta-da! I seem to have nine lives these days with more agility than a kitten."

"Come here you little fur ball." Savanah tried to sound angry, but she grinned regardless.

"Why?" Ethan teased, backing away from her as she stalked him across the room.

"I want to give you a good licking."

Savanah's smile wasn't the only thing to spring to life.

Ethan's pants took on a new shape. "Oh, from the lips of a Goddess! Go lock the door on your sentinels."

"Only if you let me go with you." Savanah sat down on the edge of the bed, crossed her arms, and purposefully plumped up her breasts.

"Let me guess, a slight diversion tactic you've learned from the other women in your home."

"When all else fails use what you are born with, be that beauty, brains, boobs or a combination or magic if all else fails miserably. Tell me one of the three is working."

Ethan knelt at her feet.

"Groveling—love it when men do that. I really should've been the queen."

"Sweet cheeks, when I get back I'm going to eat you alive, my promise to you. Behave. Here's a stun gun your pops brought and some Holy H2O balloons. Aim and shoot. See you tonight." Ethan pushed Savanah backward onto the bed. Climbing atop of her, he crushed her into the mattress. From his new perch, he admitted, "I love you," then covered her lips with his, kissing her with a passion he'd never experienced.

Before she had a chance to say another thing, he added, "When I return, I'm going to kiss you like that starting at your toes and then I'm going to make my way up your luscious thighs and pause where your dreams await me. Dream of that while I'm away saving the world, Savage." Ethan sprinted toward the door and her sentinels.

Savanah watched his perfectly shaped *derriere* scoot out the door, too flabbergasted to have any type of comeback.

****

Inside the wrought-iron gated pillars to The City of the Dead, each man paid respects to all those who entered before them with a one way ticket. Ethan took in the orange fireball hogging the sky as it descended toward western lands. The sun cast shadows on different tombs and headstones, adding that *spooky-spine-tingling-nails-on-chalkboard-effect* he neither wanted nor needed. He'd gotten more than his fair share with Draque and his albino sidekick.

Claustrophobic from birth, the passageways through the cemetery grew more narrow and confining than a straight jacket. Beads of sweat adhered Ethan's shirt to his chest. Cemented souls lay stacked like pancakes some five or more high, reaching toward the heavens. Others crypts were but a single dwelling, enclosed by intricate iron gates guarded by angels and gargoyles alike. Nothing lay beneath the surface due to the city being at least eight feet below sea level.

In passing Marie Laveau's tomb, the Highest Voodoo Priestess, Ethan bowed. The tomb seemed too small, too ordinary for her larger than life persona. Scattered flowers lay like a worn carpet around what was left of her little piece of earth.

Hearing a shuffle of gravel, Ethan looked forward. Coming at a good clip, a grisly mutation of a man with a distinct limp closed not only the distance between them, but the exit out.

André looked over Ethan's shoulder. "Shit, Grimmy, he looks like you when you wake up."

With a quick spin Ethan wound his way around Julian. "Guys, that's Androgen man."

"How the hell did you get away from him?" André asked mesmerized by the giant *it*.

Ethan shrugged his shoulders. "The bigger they are, the harder they fall."

André nudged his brother. "Luce, got the spear gun?"

"Aimed and ready. How close should he be?"

"I'd say another fifteen feet. Grimmy, got the taser charged?"

Julian flipped his braid behind him and tucked in all the stray strands of hair behind his ears. "Got more juice flowing through her than the Sunshine state's got oranges, baby."

Androgen man stopped, his head cocked to one side, thick white hair covered his shoulders. His piercing orange eyes mimicked the sunset. "Well aren't you a shifty little bastard?"

Palms in the air, Ethan chided, "Suppose I've been called worse."

"Where's Draque? We've come to pay our respects." Lucian added, sounding less than respectful.

Androgen man jut his tree trunk of a neck out, and blurted, "Holy *voodoo-up-my-arse,* if it aint royalty starin' me in the face."

"Do we know you?" André asked the stranger. He turned to Lucian. "Do we know him?"

Lucian shook his head *no.*

"Probably not, but trust me, people here know of you and my guess is your radar's going right off the charts as we speak. St. James, right? One of you two almost became the King, right?"

Ethan nudged his way around Savanah's father and Lucian. "What's he talking about?"

"Didn't Savanah tell you our past?"

"André, in the past thirty-six hours, your daughter's passed out on me at least three times, we've been drugged, chased and abducted by vampires and assholes," Ethan tossed his thumb over his shoulder pointing at the mutant. "And been pursued by an overly protective family. We haven't, as God is my witness, even had time to consummate our relationship yet."

Lucian's grin got the best of him. He whispered, "Pity," as he turned on Androgen man and without warning, exercised his trigger finger on his spear gun. *Thud, thud, thud,* sounds sailed through the air as each spear impaled the disfigured man, and left him pinned to someone's mausoleum.

André approached and stopped roughly three feet from the mutant. "Where's your boss? And no, for your own curiosity, neither myself nor my brother were to be king. You've mistaken us."

"Liar," he gurgled. "My master makes no mistakes—ever." Blood dripped in lines down the large man's lips and pooled on his shirt. "Draque's flown the proverbial coup."

Julian strut to him, pressed the stun gun into his groin and asked once, "Where is he?"

When the man laughed at him, Julian pulled the trigger and watched the man's body dance the electric slide, without the need for twangy music. Spasm after spasm jerked and contracted his muscles involuntarily. The foul aroma of burnt flesh filled the air like a barbeque gone awry. Smoke poured out from under his waistband and zipper. When his head slumped forward, Julian removed the gun.

"Is he dead?" Ethan asked, hoping it was so.

Lucian shook his head. "No, but he'll wish he was in a few hours. See his lips?" Lucian moved Ethan around to view his face. "Can you imagine how his balls are going to feel? Blue!"

"They already are, what's left of them."

"Ethan, did the guy shift on you or is he just bound to this Draque character?" André poked him. "This guy's solid."

"He didn't shift per say, but he's able to crawl up the side of walls just like an insect, even with me fighting him. He's also able to do the long jump, about forty feet or better. Check out his hands. They look like suction cups—tentacles. *Super-fly!*" Ethan jumped into a surfer position, legs spread and arms out to his sides for balance.

He was ignored.

"Luce, how the hell did the guy know us?" André asked.

"Maybe he's psychic?"

Ethan jumped in André's face. "Whoa—are you two saying you really are royal? So when Savanah tells me to kiss her royal rump, she really means it?" Ethan found the only trace of humor to be found. "Cripes, I really did get Cinderella and I'm Prince Charming."

"You definitely are not Prince Charming. And yes, you will kiss her royal little rump when she tells you to or you'll deal with me chewing yours off. Do we have an accord, Mr. Kitt?" André asked.

Ethan tapped on André's cheek in passing. Two visible fangs hung down over his lower lip. "Fix the smile, Pops. Come on, let's get outta here. I got some royal ass-kissing to do."

Julian nudged Lucian. "I like the kid."

"Me too."

Chapter Twelve

Day 7, New Orleans

After being in New Orleans one long, drawn out week, there wasn't an inch of Louisiana Savanah and her family hadn't scoured and come up clean. She now knew more about the bayou, Creole cooking and voodoo than humanly possible. She also knew without a doubt Draque had moved to sunnier horizons. Okay, not so much sun, but less people tracking his each and every move.

If only Draque had taken Savanah's sentinels with him! That would have been splendid. As far as her relationship, Savanah told Ethan they were worse than fugitives. At least prisoners were given conjugal visits.

Wide-freaking awake with a need she couldn't explain, Savanah tossed and turned. She curled around Ethan, chucked her leg over his, tucked one arm under his, and played with the blond curls on his chest while her dear, sweet, meddling uncle Julian, slept soundly ten feet from them on the couch behind a wall divider strategically placed for privacy. No other rooms at the hotel and no other options! They made due. Her father and other uncle booted him out of their room for snoring.

"Ethan!" Savanah groaned. "Eth, wake up. We need to find somewhere alone. I can't wait another minute."

Ethan cranked his neck around to see her. Not a bad wake up call. Couldn't let her know he felt the same if not worse.

"You just did, sweetie. Forget I can read minds?"

"Ah, Savage. This is unfair. All of it." Ethan dropped back to his pillow and lowered his voice. "I just want to make love to you. Is it so wrong?" Ethan flipped over and cupped her cheek. "Kiss me for now, pretty lady, since we can't do much more. Being this close to you is torture."

She shoved at his chest. "You don't have to sleep next to me," she teased.

"That came out wrong. Not taking you in my arms and making love to you is torture. Sound better?"

Savanah wrinkled her nose. "I feel the same way, but…" Savanah's grin reached ear to ear. "It's been a week. Know what that means?"

Utter astonishment slapped Ethan's face. "You did this on purpose. You had your uncle rooming with us all week just to beat me! Just to win my car! You really were going to hold me to a week just to get my car. I've been beat at my own game."

She protested, "I did no such thing. I swear." She leaned into him, and pressed her lips against his hard, until hers tingled.

He pulled away. "Trying to charm me out of it?"

Eyebrows raised and fighting a smirk she asked, "Is it working?" before she lost it and started to giggle.

In one swift move, Ethan covered Savanah and pinned her under him. Her arms, he brought up in one slow, seductive move above her head, and held her captive.

"This all you got, Mr. Kitt?" She feigned boredom and huffed a curl from her face.

Ethan whispered, "We'll see." He leaned a hair's distance from her lips, licking his.

She watched his tongue trace the outline of his lips. Suddenly she wanted to do that with her tongue, starting with his tongue and working her way down his muscular body to the protrusion poking into her thigh. Savanah pressed her hips into his groin. "Just what are your plans here today, Ethan?"

"This." Ethan puckered and waited and waited and waited until his arms started that slow burn, holding his body weight up over hers. "Shit, woman, are you gonna kiss me or…"

"Love it when men beg!" Savanah met him. With her eyes closed her other senses took hold to enjoy this moment with this man. His lips were warm and soft. His kiss drove her insane, a feeling she oddly enjoyed. Getting a major itch that needed scratching, she pressed her hips into his. A warm fire ignited low in her belly faster than a button on a gas fireplace exploded flames.

He let one arm go, and trailed his fingers down the underside of her arm, tickling her. His lips met hers once again, with a little more oomph. He pushed her back onto the pillow, while his knee nudged her thighs apart.

With the sudden change in position her eyes blew open. She wasn't in any position to fight him off, nor did she want to, and there in laid the problem.

She broke away from him and licked her lips watching him seemingly mesmerized by the movement of her tongue. "And here I thought you were saving me for your mile high club."

Ethan's green eyes glistened with mischief. "Who said I'm not? I'm just getting comfy."

"Your comfy leaves me in a precarious position, Sir. One a lady might not like compromised." Even as Savanah spoke, her actions told a different story. Her free arm trailed around Ethan's back. Sinew rippled beneath her touch. She slipped lower still to the top of his pajama pants and slid her finger just under the waist band, finding nothing between him and his pants. "Commando?" she asked in a playful tone.

He winked. "All-natural, babe."

I am so screwed.

His erection hit her right between her private lips, and she groaned. "Ummm…"

In a low melodic voice, Ethan asked, "Ever hear one of my favorite songs from the Black Eyed Peas, "*Let's Get it Started*?" He brought his hips up to meet her vulnerable spot, and pressed one solid shaft into her.

Savanah closed her eyes, overcome from the sweet, hard sensation. "Tell me you're not going to sing that song." She fought the laughter.

He added a punchy swivel of his hips. "I'll make sweet music to you without the need of actual words. My tongue shall be preoccupied anyway!" His eyebrows shifted a few times.

"It'll be fun seeing who I get better mileage and a smoother ride from," she teased as she slid her hips across his hips and groin. "We'll have to see which I want more—you—or the car." In one swift turn she rolled out from under him and straddled him.

"You little minx. You are going over my lap right here and now. I don't care if Julian wakes and kills me.

You won't get my car without a fight. " He pushed up from under her taking her with him and over his lap she went, laughing as he paddled her bottom as gently as he could.

Savanah made no attempt to get away, more than happy to be receiving his affections. She curled around him like a boa, and buried her face in the covers of the bed, to drown out any sounds. Didn't work. If anything she giggled more.

"Shush!" Ethan pleaded as he slid his hand under her pajama bottoms and fondled the delicate folds of skin in between her thighs. After a few intense minutes he had her sinking her teeth into the pillow to muffle hefty pleasure-filled notes. "I need you all to myself. You still have yet to see my one surprise I've got for you."

Savanah's dimple graced her cheek. "What is it all ready?"

"That's one visual I'm not spoiling."

"Ethan, you've been one giant surprise, a most pleasant one."

"Morning you two," came from behind the separation screen. "I'm going out to get some tea and beignets. Any takers? I'm walking…slowly, all the way there, all the way back…" Julian stuck his head around the makeshift wall and winked as he tip-toed past.

"We get the hint, Uncle." Savanah looked at Ethan, her cheeks a brilliant shade of red. "I'd love one or two. Ethan gets some only if he gets to actually eat them!" Savanah gave her uncle a knowing glance. She knew what they'd planned for Ethan.

"You're just like your mum. Nothing is bloody sacred," Julian shot back. "I'll be a few hours. Behave!"

Julian walked out the door still half-dressed without so much as a glimpse back.

"Alone at last." Savanah grinned. Every hormone in her body stretched and woke up. She was certain beyond a doubt her body was in a constant state of estrus. Suddenly the room didn't seem big enough, or her clothes. Everything was tight, constricting, along with her airway. Hyperventilating, Savanah looked at Ethan humiliated.

Ethan reached for a plastic bag off the floor.

Savanah tried to make light of her predicament. "You going—to suffocate me—with that thing?" she asked in between gulping down air molecules.

Ethan handed it to her. "No sweet cheeks, I've got something a lot more fun I can choke you with." Ethan got down in front of her and kissed her knees. "Savage, we don't have to do this today just because your uncle so blatantly left us. I'm more than willing to wait for you. When the time's right, you and I will meet on fair grounds. Not a second sooner. When you're positive you won't pass out on me, we'll go for a walk along the river and get some exercise that way. I'll go get your shower ready." Ethan grabbed his jeans, dropped his pajama bottoms in front of her and flashed her a quick peek of some make-your-heart-run-a-marathon-cheeks. He glanced over his shoulder and winked before he crawled into his jeans.

At that moment, Savanah couldn't have loved him more. It wasn't just the ass, even if it was sweet, but his patience and tenderness took her by storm. Never, had any man shown such a caring, genuine concern for her happiness.

Ethan walked around the half wall that separated

the shower from the rest of the bath and set the temperature of the water, got her towels ready and even hopped out the window of the room, instead of using the door to surprise her and stole some roses from a nearby vase. He spread petals on the floor when he returned.

Savanah started to cry.

"Not quite the outcome I'd hoped for. Did I do something wrong? Are you allergic to flowers?"

"No. It's just that—this is beautiful. No one has ever done this for me."

"Savage, I'm still reeling over the fact you never went to the movies on a date. How I found you leaves me breathless."

"Do you need the plastic bag now?" She ruffled his curls tenderly. "Some things were meant to be." She slipped the top to her pajamas off slowly, without turning away from him.

Confident global warming would never melt him, Ethan stood frozen. He followed her fingers as she undid the string that kept her pants in place. With a slight tug the knot unraveled and gravity took over. Her pants slipped down to hug her ankles.

Ethan's hot air balloon began to fill. Lift-off in ten, nine, eight…

Savanah walked to him with a graceful swing of her hips. "Join me?" She held her hand to him.

"You certain?"

"What was that thing you needed to hear? *Y—E—S*. I believe that's how it's spelled. I love the rose petals. Nice touch."

"No, my tall, dark queen, you're nice to touch." In one swift move he grabbed her and pulled her sensual body to his. Walking her backwards into the shower, he trapped her against the cool tile of the shower.

His kisses were hungry and offered her a delicious *entrée*.

She broke away laughing. "Foolish man. You're still dressed."

"It's okay for now."

"Eth, no more safe sex. *Okayyy*, that came out wrong. Get undressed."

The way the shower turned Savanah's skin into one long glimmering gem left him in awe. Each droplet of water held the fire of a diamond as it danced across her.

He traced every curve and outline her body offered, with as much restraint as his will allowed. Grabbing the mass of curls draped down her back, he swung her around and braided her hair in one loose tail. From the backside, Ethan caught his breath. Savanah's ass had two more little dimples his tongue had to trace. Had too. Dropping to his knees with his eyes shut, Ethan kissed each of Savanah's curves. He blew his breath over her delicious *derriere*, as a whisper in the wind could caress someone's soul. His fingertips memorized each nuance her body held with a slow march up her legs. Feathering his finger lightly up the inside of her thigh, left Savanah laughing and squirming.

"I see I've found one ticklish spot." He nudged her thighs apart and began to kiss her inner thigh. Goose bumps appeared.

Savanah jumped. Looking over her shoulder, she pleaded, "Eth, please. Are you going to get out of your clothes?"

"Eventually, baby. You warm enough?"

"I feel like a chocolate bar stuffed between two

graham crackers, melting over a fire."

"That you are, sweet cheeks. Did I mention I love chocolate?" Ethan latched onto her bottom and sucked giving her a large purple love bite. With a guilty grin, he admired his handy work. He stood and leaned into her, his chest against her back and curled his head into the crook of her neck and kissed her.

Savanah wiggled her bottom backwards into him. There sat a very solid lump under his soaked pants. "Ethan, I want something to play with. A rubber ducky or a floaty toy…something." She pressed harder. "Take your pants off."

"Stop whining and enjoy this." He dragged his nails up the length of her legs inching upward to the juncture of where his wet dreams were stored. His fingers tangled in her maze of curls, purposefully missing the one spot on Savanah that would turn her inside out. Later, he'd go back to that little nubbin. First things first, he had to work her into a lather.

She wiggled, scooted, tried to direct his fingers to the *right spot* to no avail.

Ethan stilled her hips. "I want to do it my way."

"Okay, old blue eyes. But if you're going to do it your way you better sing to me whilst you do it."

Between Ethan's voice, his hands caressing her, Savanah did a better job at steaming up the bath than the hot water.

Ethan turned her face to meet his and kissed her, his lips hard on hers, his tongue in a heated duel with hers.

His thumb feathered her jaw. "Don't close your eyes on me. Your eyes see a side of me I never thought would see the light of day again. You fill me with hope,

Savanah, and I haven't had that luxury in a few years."
He grabbed the bar of soap and washed her breasts, ran
it down her abdomen, through her thighs from front to
back a few times to tease her. A little trail of bubbles
clung to her. With a quick glance, Ethan saw light,
passion, and heat in her eyes, waiting for him with a
hunger he'd never seen or experienced or believed he
deserved.

Her skin was on fire, wherever he kissed her. He
cupped each breast and rolled her nipples between his
fingers. Two perfectly plump, succulent-sink-your-
teeth-into-nipples he had to have. Right then. With a
quick spin, he pinned her against the wall of the
shower, the warm spray bathing her. Ethan took her
ripened bud between his teeth and switched between
sucking and nipping. Her pleas, "Just get naked
already," made him harder each time she begged. He
grabbed her ass, and brought her toward him as his
other hand caught her. He stroked her private lips,
rubbed softly through the center, trapping her mons.
With a delicate pinch and just the right amount of
pressure, he had her grinding in his hand. He sang some
jumbled song to her while he continued changing the
rhythm until her legs shook.

"Ethan, I adore your voice. You missed your
calling even with a mouthful!" She melted into one
giant puddle. Of course his fingers gliding over her
mons might have had something to do with her soggy
state of affairs, not the shower they were submerged in.

The more he touched her, the more anxious she
became. Savanah didn't know whether to cry or scream
from the storm this man brought out in her. Tiny little
zingers scurried down her every nerve, from one

synapse to the next, spreading her fiery little hot and bothered hormones to every dark sacred place in her body.

"Please take your clothes off."

"Soon, Pippy," he answered. "Right here, right now, I want you to turn and face the wall and spread your legs."

Savanah did as she was asked. Within seconds Ethan's tongue traipsed around her ankle and headed north. The second his mouth covered her clit, a tantalizing quiver rode her.

"Ummm," she groaned. She grabbed the control to the shower and clung to it. She cried out one shrill, "*OohGoddessthatfeelsrapturous…*" The little zingers were no longer little, but rocking her. Her nipples pressed against the cold marble as Ethan's scorching mouth worked its magic, Savanah soaked in the fabulous conflict. Ethan lapped at her as she came and didn't quit even when she cried, "Eth, air, I need air. Would now be the time to get naked?" Desperation took on a whole new meaning.

With his teeth attached to her private lips he shook his head *yes* and she came again. Sliding inside her warm haven, his finger started a little dance of its own, tickling her insides and hitting something Savanah never had tickled.

Tears streamed down her face as she pleaded, "*Please*, Ethan."

"That's what I wanted. Groveling. Love it." Ethan stood, laughing at the surprised expression Savanah wore as she looked over her shoulder at him. With one free hand his pants met the floor leaving only air between them. "How long has it been since you've been with someone, Savvy? I don't want to hurt you."

"A while, but Eth, this is torture. Just try, now!"

"Turn around, Savage. You have to see this before you and I go any further, otherwise you won't appreciate it afterwards."

Savanah turned to meet Ethan's gaze. His lips hit hers hard. Their tongues mated, tasted one another. Loved one another. Life or death. He needed her, and he'd never needed anyone. He broke away from her and pointed south. "Check it out before it runs out of hot air."

Eyes wide, she said, "That is the coolest thing I've ever seen. It had to hurt like hell getting it."

Discretion is a wonderful tool if used wisely. In the hands of a moron, it can be more precise than lethal injection. Ethan's first thought, tell how he got the tattoo and how it really didn't hurt afterwards, flew out the window. No, no one would accuse him of being a moron. Not today, not ever again.

"I survived." He bit the smile off his lips. "Hold on my little nut, coz I'm about to crack you wide open."

She wrapped her hands around Ethan's back and began her descent. She cupped the firm swell of his cheeks and tugged him closer still. Between her thighs, his erection pressed firm against her and quite frankly, his size took her breath away. All soft on the outside, solid on the inside, she wanted to sink her teeth into him just to find out if he was as sweet as he looked and felt. She reached down to find his shaft a velvety sheath more than ready to impale her. Her fingers trailed around the tip of his head. Ethan shook like a dog coming in from the rain. She squeezed him again just to relive the reaction.

"Tease."

"Payback." She pried backwards and peeked at his offering. The first time Ethan pushed his penis through Savanah's private lips she thought she'd died. Her little itch festered into an uncontrollable need to be rubbed raw. The second, third and fourth journey through as his head bumped into her quim, she pretty much thought she'd entered heaven, but when he entered her, her body rocketed into a new Milky Way. In one swift plunge, Ethan filled her, with his body and love. The three times she'd ever been in this position (well, not this exact position) she'd never experienced anything other than heartache and loneliness. Right here and now she knew she had found Eden!

"Ethan, whatever you do, don't stop, okay?"

"Not 'til I'm out of ammo. And trust me, there's more than seven rounds in this pistol." Ethan splayed his fingers across her mons, pushing in as his penis tickled and taunted her sweet spot.

The fire in her belly erupted and spread through her groin, down her legs, curled her toes and jumped to Ethan.

The moment her contractions gripped and squeezed his shaft, his seed sailed into port. For what seemed an eternity, neither one moved. Muscles deep inside them were working off the effects of their magic.

Pulling away from her, she cried out, "No, please, Eth, don't leave me."

Odd moment for him.

His heart skidded to a stop recalling the conversation they'd shared over his love life earlier in the week about him loving and leaving women. At that point he wondered how he could've been such a callous, insensitive, fool for so long and not died of stupidity or someone's revenge.

"Baby, you're stuck with me. I'm not leaving you today, tomorrow or ever."

"Promise?" Savanah sniffled.

"Savage, marry me. I'll make my promise to you and God. I won't leave you."

Choked up and crying at the same time she still managed to ask, "When?" She fished around outside the shower and grabbed a towel to wipe her nose and eyes.

"October's end, under a canopy of glistening stars in the rose garden on your property. The end of fall. So…is that a yes?"

Savanah shook her head yes.

"Doesn't work that way, baby. Need to hear the letters, remember?" Ethan hooked his fingers under her chin and brought her teary eyes into view.

"*Y—E—S*. Ethan, I—"

Ethan devoured her words, kissing her with every ounce of compassion he could give to her, leaving the two of them licking their lips and gasping for air.

"I promise, Savanah, I'll do my best to make you smile every day."

"You're off to a good start, Mr. Kitt, but I'm famished and the water's gone cold. Now what?"

"Come on, hopefully Julian's back with food."

****

Savanah rifled through a few outfits still in bags from their trip to the mall a few days earlier, trying to decide what she'd like to wear. "You really have five sisters?" She held up a black lacy boxer and matching bra in front of him and gave a little wiggle. "You like?"

Ethan nodded. "I think it would look better on you."

Savanah swatted him.

"I was the baby. Got picked on relentlessly from the day I popped out."

"I can see why," she teased. That teasing got her naked little butt tossed onto the bed and pinned under Ethan in a flash. It did nothing to halt her laughter.

"I've learned a few tricks about getting picked on since then, Savage. Revenge can be so sweet." Ethan lowered his mouth over hers and kissed her, rekindling the fire in her belly. He moved to her neck where his lips lingered, his breath sweeping her away to places only her dreams allowed her to venture.

"Savanah, I know this may sound silly, or even old-fashioned, but when I'm with you I feel different about myself. Every instinct I have just wants to spend an eternity making love to you and protecting you."

"Nice to know this. And you'll get your wishes, all of them because we seem to have longevity working with us. Ethan, I—"

"Hey you two, good morning. Am I interrupting? Sleep well, Peanut?" André came through the adjoining door, oblivious to the layout of his daughter and her lover as he headed for the couch and the remote.

"Good morning, Papa. Slept wonderfully and no, you're not interrupting us. You're too late. Don't look, still naked." Savanah gave her father an evil smile as she lay under Ethan thinking of the credit card commercial. Private jet from New York to New Orleans—two thousand dollars. Limos and cabs all week—another grand. Food and hotel for the week—an easy two grand. Look on Papa's face after finding his daughter under Ethan both in birthday suits—priceless.

The remote hit the floor and separated into shards of metal fragments and plastic. André turned without so much as another word and walked through the door. The entire wall shook when he slammed it shut.

"Wow! Didn't expect that. Why did you piss him off?"

"Because, if I didn't he'd just continue with his little off color comments trying to get a rise out of me. I beat him to the punch line." Savanah looked away from Ethan, tearing up.

"Is this the first time you two have head butted each other, except for the first day he found me in your bedchamber? There seems to be a pattern here." Ethan wiped away her tears. "You'll both be fine, baby, unless, of course, he really hates me."

"He doesn't hate you, Ethan. He just doesn't want me to grow up and move out."

"I won't take you from your family, Savanah. I know what it's like to lose your family. I lost mine when I turned. For all it's worth, I would've had an easier time of it telling my parents I was gay. That, they could understand since my oldest sister is. Being able to shift into a werewolf—well let's just say they've seen *Were-Wolf in London* and *Resident Evil* too many times and have no idea the movies are fictitious. It hurts. I have one sister, Edan, she's eight months older than me. She dragged me wherever she went from the day I was born until the day I almost died. She was my best friend. There isn't a day that goes by that I don't miss her. We were as close as you and Julian."

This time Savanah sat swiping tears from Ethan's face.

"Eth, we met a girl at Lillian's the night I met you. Her name was Edan. Come to think of it she looks just like you. Maybe together we could go and see her and invite her to the wedding and to meet our family. Give her a chance to see you're really all right, despite the monthly fur coat."

"I had no idea she was in town."

Ethan gave her a hug that stole her breath. Seeing movement from the corner of her eye, Savanah jumped, only to slam into Julian trying to sneak in.

"Hey, mister voyeur, how long you been standing there?"

"Too long. Your Pop and uncle are packing up. So, did I hear wedding bells are going to ring?" Julian bent to eyelevel with her. "Congrats, baby. I mean that from the bottom of my heart." He planted a big kiss on her cheek. "I hear you sprang a good one on your Papa. Don't you know if you're going to do things like that I have to be around to witness them? Come on, Savvy, what is it I live for?"

Savanah smiled despite the fact she felt horrible.

"You, Peanut, need to get dressed and go talk to your father. I know you feel awful. You've red puffy eyes to show for it. But cover up the purple patch on your neck before you go in. Telling him you two were together is one thing. Telltale signs are another slap in his face. And don't mention any wedding yet. Let him warm up to Ethan on his terms."

"I thought you lived for this sort of torment."

"I'm your father's lunch today. I don't want him ripping me to shreds while he's thinking of Ethan. Self-preservation and all."

Once more a steady stream of tears broke the

floodgates. Dragging one of the sheets off the bed left Ethan scrambling for cover. Savanah wound the sheet around herself and with a quick spin of her heels, she turned only to land in her father's arms.

"I'm so sorry, Papa."

"No, I am." André crushed her to his chest. "I don't know what came over me. You're the one pure thing I have left in my life, and I don't want you hurt or gone from me."

"Papa, I'm not going anywhere. I was out of line."

"No, I was, butting in. I realize I am an imbecile on occasion, but it's only because I'm genetically linked to Lucian. He's the real imbecile." André turned his attention to Ethan sitting there with nothing more than a lacy, black boxer draped across his lap. An eyebrow shot up.

He didn't apologize or welcome him to the family, but he didn't kill him either, so as far as Savanah's concerns went, life was like a bowl of cherries, sweet 'til you broke your tooth on a pit.

"Hey, Ands, come on. Limo's waiting." Lucian hollered from the adjoining room.

"Where you headed?" Savanah grabbed her father's hand lightly.

"If we don't come home with gifts for your Mum and Serina, there will be hell to pay. Lucian and I are going to hit the Canal Street Mall while you guys finish packing. And dressing. We'll be back in one hour." André kissed Savanah's forehead. "I know he asked you to marry him this morning," he whispered. "And I know you accepted. It's not him, it's me. Give me time?"

"Papa, we have all the time in the world. And trust

me, once you get to know him, you'll love him."

"Let's not push it. Let me get past wanting to kill him first?" He winked. "The lacy boxers would look better on my daughter, Ethan." André broke out in laughter as he left.

"That's what I said."

With preternatural speed Ethan got dressed and threw his belongings into a duffle bag. "Do you mind if I go with Lucian and André?" he asked not even out of breath.

Savanah's eyes grew outrageously wide. "Got a death wish? Why would you knowingly put yourself in the mix with them?"

"Gotta start some time, sweet cheeks. Might as well be now. Besides, I want to hit up a little store we passed the other night when I carted your little ass around town."

"Oh, so now it's little? Weren't you just last week telling me how heavy I was?"

"Engaged men are smarter than that, baby. I know when to hold 'em and when to fold 'em."

Savanah giggled. "You and I can play some poker some night, and we'll see how well you fold."

"Strip poker only. Be prepared to lose your shirt…for starters. See you in a while." Ethan kissed the tip of Savanah's nose and scooted out the door on Lucian's heels, belting out one of his favorite songs about making love slow and easy.

Lucian stopped dead in his tracks leaving Ethan no room to brake. With a snail's turn and a deadpan glare Lucian suggested, "You might want to find another song to sing Ethan, unless you really do have a death wish." Then he continued as if nothing happened.

Ethan didn't care. Nothing or no one was going to mar this day for him, even if his subconscious tried reasoning with him that there was an overabundance of testosterone and vamp pheromones living under one roof. Didn't matter as long as the one woman he loved lived there. Nothing else mattered. He felt another song coming on.

****

The flight home went off without a hitch, with the exceptions of the bumpy skyways. Ethan couldn't find an altitude where turbulence wasn't waiting like a rickety, broken roller coaster.

Lucian and André fought like schoolboys over who rode shot-gun in the co-pilot's chair. They both wanted to test their piloting skills and Ethan, being an incredibly quick study, decided it was better to butter his bread than toast it. André reigned control of the co-pilot throne. Savanah whispered the words, "brown-noser" in his ear, and he chuckled. He wasn't above reproach at this point. When the plane did its first loop-de-loop, Julian's voice flooded the cockpit with a horror scream that put scary movie screams to shame. André yelled over the loud speaker, "To the moon, Grimmy." The second spinning dive Julian counted, "Hail Mary, full of grace, please get me the hell out of outer space so I can rip the smug smile from my brother-in-law's face," over and over.

Ethan attempted to explain that the aerodynamics of the plane weren't built to do things jet fighters did, but did it stop André?

Hell no!

Soaring toward the heavens like a rocket, the plane's engine cut out just as André pulled back on the throttle and did a backwards dive. Ethan's gut did a weightless, flip-flop as the plane hung suspended for a second before it plummeted toward the earth.

Julian cried out, "Ands, you're a dead man if we land."

André laughed like a madman, and resembled one as he hung on to the controls, and restarted the plane. Staring into the horizon, he sang, Aerosmith's, *Back in the Saddle*. Ethan joined him. Shortly thereafter, they lost Julian. Cookies were tossed and vows of retribution were once again sworn. The last hour of the flight, Ethan handed over his controls to Lucian. Ethan grabbed Savanah's hand and ventured to the back of the plane.

****

"You weren't kidding when you told me you had a little spot to get laid in. I mean lay in." Savanah's smile purred sex. A plush double mattress just begged to be bounced on. "Can anyone see us from here?"

"Not unless they really have eyes in the back of their heads. You're not really thinking what I hope you're thinking are you, Misses?"

Savanah's grin widened. "A real quickie? They'll never know."

"Baby, they'll know. Trust me. The altitude does things to you and makes you sing louder than your Pops. But, hey, who am I to look a beautiful gift in the mouth and deny her ecstasy?"

Savanah jumped on the mattress. "How do we do this?"

"Did I teach you nothing this morning? You need your pants off, I need mine down and then?" Savanah attempted to swat him, but he caught her hand, brought it to his lips, and kissed each finger. Before she realized what he was up to he led her hand down the inside of his pants handing over his personal joystick to her. "Trust me?"

Savanah gave a quick nod. "Yes."

Not seconds went by and Savanah's pants were around her ankles, exposing her own personal heaven to him.

"You can play with my throttle only for a minute or two, but then let up on the pressure or we won't get a clean landing." After a moment of silence Ethan's lips found Savanah's private lips, kissed her, sucked her, and lapped away at her as her body let him know she was very happy he'd chosen a personal flight plan for her, because she was gliding above the clouds. Ethan's fingers slipped in and out of her velvety haven time and time again, hitting that one sweet spot she'd become very fond of in the recent past hours of her life.

"This is truly heaven," she admitted when her knees started their little dance with the crescendo of the orgasm. "Ethan, are you going to join me or is this a solo flight?"

"I'm coming, baby. You ready?"

"Possibly passed that point."

"You are not. I'd know." In one well-timed move, Ethan moved atop of her, nudged her legs apart, and slid his shaft in deep, bumping her cervix. A loud hiccup echoed in the small room.

Savanah's breath caught in her throat and in that one look, Ethan had her. Covering her mouth and muffling her scream, he knew they were so caught. Her voice flew faster than the speed of sound. Her orgasm followed, climbing higher than the clouds they sailed through and all he could do was hang on for the ride. He pumped into her faster than the pistons in his car worked and with more precision. Being a werewolf had a few redeeming qualities. Faster and harder could be taken seriously.

Laughing and thoroughly exhausted, they crept out of the little cabin. Julian acknowledged the two of them with his putrid green pallor and red eyes. "Aye, Captain Kitt. Inducting the new flight attendant I see."

Ethan's temper hit a new altitude, a cross between anger and embarrassment. "What the hell's wrong with you? It's one thing for you to know what we were up to, but it's not right that you announce it like it's her coming out party or something. She's not a debutant. It's no wonder it took her this long to bring someone home."

As Julian asked at point blank range, "You don't get it do you, Ethan?" the vile vomit breath flew across the span of the plane as easily as and accurately as dog farts.

Ethan gagged. "Uncle Julian, there are mints in the closet and mouthwash back in the bath. Ugh! Use it, now."

Covering his mouth, Julian excused himself. On return, he smelled minty-fresh.

André swung his captain's chair to face the rear. "Ethan, we believe there is only one person for each of us to love. From the day we meet that person, we know, just as Savanah knew when she saw you last week. That is the reason she hasn't brought anyone home, not that she hadn't found anyone in the past. It's why Julian is still searching."

"How do you know these things?" Ethan sat down,

grabbed Savanah and pulled her onto his lap. Once she settled, his arms wrapped around her, his fingers locked with her hers.

"Trust your instincts, Ethan. It's brought you this far. You asked Savanah to marry you this morning after only being with her a short seven days. And she said yes. My guess is you knew the minute you saw her in Lillian's."

"Honestly? I knew when she accosted me in the airport."

"I did no such thing," Savanah protested. "You did the accosting."

"She took my breath away." Ethan smiled at his fiancé.

"Really?" Savanah leaned into him, angling for a quick kiss.

Ethan obliged with a soft kiss on the corner of her lips. "If you guys are finished, I should probably take over and land. The airport's calling in the runway patterns." Ethan gave a little nod to the twins. Without missing a beat he said, "This means one of you has to give up a seat."

With a challenged glare, Lucian and André shot odd/even fingers at each other. Lucian grinned in triumph as André moved to one of the seats in the rear. "Thank you, Ethan, for this opportunity. I've forgotten the freedom this offers."

"Anytime, call me, and we'll come up."

Savanah wiggled her nose into Ethan's neck and whispered, "Brown-noser," one last time and then kissed him lightly.

Chapter Thirteen

One foot in the door, Ethan stifled the thought he'd just been tossed into the lion's den. He wondered why they even bothered with the *Welcome Home* mat outside the front entrance. A meat-grinder would have been more appropriate. His soon to be mother-in-law's blistering glare oozed retribution. Standing beside Jovan, her side-kick—Doctor Serina with a lethal injection hidden somewhere on her person he was certain, and next in the firing squad's line-up, the totally, non-lactating—Raven, and members of their chain gang, Payton, Duncan, and Jonah, all shoulder to shoulder like great starving cats, snarling angry, because they didn't like the piece of meat offered to them—him.

Savanah grabbed Ethan's hand and dragged him in. Lucian, André, and Julian brought up the rear. Jovan walked up to Ethan with a viper's grin and slapped his face. Ethan didn't flinch even as the deep red welt formed.

"What the hell, Mum? What the hell did he do to you?"

"Jesus, Blossom. That was out of line, even for you." Julian added.

"It's okay." Ethan said as he rubbed his cheek. "We know now where we stand with each other. For the record, I'd have called you back, but you never left a number."

"You put her in harm's way. You could've gotten her killed. Absolutely nothing good has happened since you crawled from under your rock and into our lives."

"Mum, he had nothing to do with Draque chasing me. He kept us alive."

"No, Peanut, I kept you alive when you were unconscious in the car lot."

"Thank you. It's a comfort knowing that Savanah has a family that looks out for her wellbeing. Jovan, I hope that someday soon, you can trust me with her because I plan on taking care of her for a very long time." Peripherally from the corner of his eye, Ethan saw André giving him the universal sign to shut up as he waggled his hand frantically across his throat like it was slit. Being a quick study, Ethan stopped talking.

"Not now, kid," Lucian mouthed.

"Ethan, I didn't like you when I first met you. Nothing has changed. Stay out of my way and don't ever place my daughter in a position that could harm one hair on her head." With an abrupt turn, she stormed out of the entryway.

"*Cherié,*" Andre chased after her. "Wait up." Jovan turned back to them.

"We just spent a week with the man, and we didn't kill him. That has to tell you something."

"All it tells me is your judgment is poor. Did he let you fly his plane home? Is that why you like him?" Jovan didn't miss a thing.

"Yes, but, *Cherié*, he loves her. It's like Serina said. They're a perfect match for one another." Desperate to get a smile on her lips he added, "They complement each other better than Sonny and Cher."

No smile, but her glare intensified. "Give your daughter some credit. She's intelligent and knows herself."

"And that's why she dated those two other scum of the earth creatures? Because she knew herself so well?" Jovan argued.

She had that point.

"Please, give him a week before you condemn the man." André walked, as if on egg shells, toward his wife.

"André, he's tied to Sinclair. Does that mean nothing to you? The family is the cesspool of Hell. We are to have our babies in a few months, and we allow this man to come and live under our roof, knowing full well he carries a larger threat?"

Not wanting Savanah or Ethan to hear him, André shot Jovan a quick message. *Jovan, you painted the damn picture yourself, little Miss Scryer. We have to protect him. I'm not asking you to be his best friend or bake him a cake, unless you really do want to kill him…* He waited for a look that could kill, but Jovan tilted her chin up, defiant to the end. Stubborn was in the dictionary just because of her. Jovan spun and headed for the kitchen. André followed.

Jovan paled. André helped her sit by the fire pit. "Relax. I'll make some tea."

"André, I'm scared. Something's going to happen, I can feel it down to my toes, and you know I'm never wrong. Our daughter's got the vamp that haunts people in movies and real life after her, and Ethan's tied to the second biggest nightmare. We need help."

"Speaking of the big picture, everyone except Savanah has seen it."

"It wasn't supposed to be like this—" Jovan wiped

tears from her cheek. "—He wasn't supposed to be like this. When I scryed I saw a caring, loving man, not someone tied to the *Lusitania*." More tears slipped past her hardened façade.

"I'll add some herbs to your tea. Possibly a shot of brandy."

Jovan's face turned an angered shade of red.

"I'm teasing. Come up stairs. I'll give you a nice massage and relax you in my own special way."

"Your own special way got me into this mess, husband."

"Ouch, Jovan. Don't be upset with me. I'm not the one that slept with the guy."

"You might as well be," she huffed a blonde tendril from her face. "You certainly sound as if you like him enough too."

André dropped to his knees and gave Jovan his best double lift eyebrow, wink-wink face. "I never said I wasn't easy. You of all people should know that."

Jovan's husky-blue eyes almost barked.

"Oh come on, Cherié, that was supposed to make you smile, not snarl."

"Enough already, Mum," Savanah entered the kitchen. "Don't go getting your knickers in a knot at Papa. You're just going to have to get to know him."

Jovan threw her hands in the air. "Why does everyone think I still wear knickers? Oh and you think you *do* know him after a week?"

"You did with Papa after three days."

"That was different."

"Why, Mum?"

Jovan's silence filled the room.

Savanah got in her face. "What? No oh-so-brilliant

comeback?"

Pushing her growing belly up from the chair, she grabbed André's hand and led him toward the back staircase.

"I thought you were going to give me a massage."

André looked back to Savanah and shrugged his shoulders. "Ah, guess we'll see you at dinner, Peanut." André followed Jovan's heels.

Savanah mouthed the words, "I love you," to him and went after Ethan.

Back at the main entry, Savanah found she was alone. Her heart raced until Ethan peered over the edge of the balcony.

"Come up. Julian just gave me a room to hang my hat so to speak."

"Where?" she hollered upward.

Ethan crooked his finger to her. "Not down there, silly."

Taking the stairs three at a time, Savanah met him without even losing her breath. However, inside the room her jaw dropped.

"This is so much better than you passing out on me," he teased as he tapped her mouth shut.

"I'd forgotten this room existed. This is my mother's handy-work. Is she or isn't she the most talented artist alive?" Upset with her mother or not she loved her and proudly showed off her talents.

"Savage, look at the back wall. It's you all grown up, in a wedding dress. Half the wall is covered with a sheet. Oh, is it bad luck to see the bride before the wedding?"

"Doesn't count, Eth. This is my Mum's dress. I climbed into it one day and she caught me. For penance she made me stand there for *hours*," Savanah fanned herself feigning weariness, "as she painted me. But she did it on a canvas. I don't know when she did this one. The canvas is actually hanging in the *Louvre* under a penname."

"What's under the cloth beside your painting?"

"Dunno. I was alone in the original painting. Shall we peek?"

About to rip the cover from the wall, Serina stuck her head into the bedroom.

"Unless you're both sitting, you might want to wait to see what's under there."

"Hey, Auntie. Who is it?" Savanah asked.

Serina crooked her head to one side and lifted an eyebrow toward Ethan.

"Auntie, out with it. How long has she known?"

Ethan looked between the women. "Known what? Why do I feel like I'm the last one getting the punch line to a joke?"

Not mincing words, Serina answered, "You are the punch line, Ethan. And it's no joke." Serina lifted the tarp. Ethan's jaw now dropped.

Painted next to Savanah's portrait was Ethan, wearing a black linen jacket with tails. A black silk tie, done in a double Windsor knot loose around his neck. His untucked white shirt left his portrait rugged. Casual. His loose curls brushed the top of his shoulders. Gawking between Savanah's real hand and the hand in the painting, he realized his soon to be mother-in-law might just be the one person on the planet to predict Armageddon. The engagement ring in the picture happened to be identical to the one Ethan had in his pocket ready to give to her. He'd seen it in New

Orleans and knew he had to buy it. A one and half carat princess-cut diamond sat nestled inside an antique platinum setting, surrounded by two trillion diamonds.

Ethan glanced at Serina. "How does she know this stuff?"

"We are born with these abilities," Savanah answered. "Aunt Serina can heal people without medicines or surgery. My Mum can see into the future and do all the things I can. I cannot see the future, which is fine by me."

"Jovan allowed herself the one luxury of seeing her daughter's wedding day, because she became a wee bit leery that it wouldn't come in the next millennium, and she saw you, Ethan."

"Aunt Serina!"

Serina blew Savanah a kiss. "Maybe now you understand where her hostility comes from. You come traipsing in here trying to kidnap a child, tell us it's a Sinclair and then run off to New Orleans with our baby. By the goddess, you totally snookered all of us. You're damned lucky I haven't tried any of my spells on you."

"She isn't kidding. Her juju ain't what it used to be!"

"Savanah!"

Savanah returned the devilish wink.

"If you two would excuse me, I'm headed down to the wine cellar. You'll hear a knock at your door and there will be a tray for you in the hallway. I think you two might like to be alone." Serina curtsied and left.

"So, do you like your room so far?"

"I get to look at you when I close my eyes and when I open them. What's not to like?" Ethan pulled Savanah into his arms, a breath away from his lips.

257

"Savanah?"

"Yes?"

"Sit down on that antique of a thing for a sec. Probably squeaks to the heavens. That's why they put me in here," he mused. "Savvy, when I asked you to marry me this morning, there was something missing."

"What?" she asked a serious expression etched on her face. "I loved your proposal."

"No, Pip—this." Ethan got down on his knee in front of her and pulled a tiny black velvet box from his jacket pocket.

Opening the box with trembling fingers, Savanah let out a little, "Holy cow," and started to giggle. "How? How—uhm—did my Mum know or you? Eth, this is the most precious ring I've ever seen. You sure you never met my Mum before this? It's identical to the one in the portrait."

"Will you wear it?" Ethan raised his voice above the chatter of her teeth.

"No. I just thought I'd put it storage with the rest of the Crown Jewels."

"Savanah, I don't know what I've done to deserve you, but I promise to do right by you and your family. And in saying that, there's something I have to do."

"I'm thinking I might not like this conversation. You sound way too serious."

"I have to cut my ties with the Maestro."

"How?"

"Come on, Savage, you've seen the movies, you live this life. It's the only way I know I can keep you safe."

"Not alone, Eth. You're a part of this family now which means you've got people to watch your back."

Feeling bad for taking away their special moment he changed the subject. "And I've got you right where I want you. Shall we give this thing a run for its money?" He pat the mattress next to her.

"In a bit. I heard footsteps a second ago. Let's go see what goodies we've got at our fingertips."

In the hallway a tray with a vase of yellow roses, a bottle of very expensive champagne, two glasses and a bowl of strawberries, raspberries and pineapple with melted chocolate sat by the door. Frozen sugar-coated grapes and some Cabot cheese slices outlined the tray. Ethan looked at Savanah and back at the tray.

"Why are they being so nice to me now? Well, except your mom."

"This is their way of welcoming you to the family. If you get Payton's specialty, chocolate amaretto cookies with orange glaze then you hit the lottery. Payton rarely makes them."

"Savanah, the day I met you, I won the lottery. Now, shall we find out if the springs on this thing need some oil?"

"Let's bounce." Savanah climbed on the mattress and started jumping up and down like a little kid.

"What are you doing," Ethan asked as he watched her carefree attitude, and lust for life and wondered how she'd lived this long and never lost it. "You're too…"

"Don't you dare. Don't you dare tell me I'm too old to bounce."

"Pippy, I'm smarter than that. You're too tall. You'll bump the ceiling."

Savanah kicked her feet out and with a hard thump on her bottom, caught air and landed next to Ethan. "Join me."

So bounce they did. First standing, then lying. For three days food was delivered. For three days, laughter and squeaky springs filtered down through the home. On day four, André and Julian lugged a new king-sized mattress up the three flights of stairs. That night, almost everyone slept like babies. Savanah and Ethan? The Sand man could have dropped a truckload of his finest granules to knock them out and rest would not come.

****

"Who's got the Sunday newspaper? Just once I'd like to read it, Duncan, before you maul it for the comics," Raven protested.

"Come here, Beauty. You've gotta see this," Payton called. "I've got the paper not the old man."

"I heard that," Duncan grumbled, as he glanced over the top of the comics through huge magnified glasses. The specs made his eyes appear ten times bigger.

Julian walked past Duncan and swat the back of his head. "Mister Magoo, in the flesh." Julian added, "There is an ad in the paper someone paid dearly for. If the PEON's see it, it could very well cost the person their life."

"Someone's desperate," Lucian continued, "Do you think it's a set up?"

"I get the feeling it's very real," Serina explained as she held her hands just above the paper, getting a psychic reading from it. "Do you remember hearing about the set of conjoined twins born the same day as Elyza? They vanished from a hospital in Tennessee. The news said that whoever stole them killed their mother."

"How awful," Raven remarked as she shimmied in

between her two brothers on the couch. "Ands!" Raven gasped seeing his cheeks bulging like a chipmunk. She pinched his cheeks together. "That's the third muffin you've devoured."

André attempted a rebuttal, but with a full mouth, his manners kicked in. He jammed the remaining delicacy into his mouth and made little yummy sounds in her ear.

"Imbecile!" Raven turned to Serina. "So, do you think this ad is about the babies?"

"I'd bet my powers on it. I think we should call."

"Hence the compulsion! M'lady," Lucian cautioned. "We need to do a little research first."

Serina began to interrupt, but Lucian stuffed a slice of the decadent roll into her mouth. "I'm not saying no. I'm saying let me check this ad out before you go committing yourself. You and I have way too much at stake. If the ad is real then we'll make plans."

Entering mid-conversation, Molly asked, "What for? You're not leaving now, are you?"

Serina swallowed her treat. "Good morning, Molly. We were just discussing plans to separate a set of conjoined twins. The ad says they're a cross between vamp and wolf. One of each. Poor little things. And they're in Mexico."

Duncan nervously tapped his fingers on the table. "I've got a really bad feeling about this. It smells like a set up."

Julian offered, "If it is the real deal, Serina, I'll help."

Lucian cleared his throat. "Slow down. Research. Decision. Fair enough?"

Serina rubbed her hand across her husband's chest

in a seductive manner. "Fair enough, M'lord. Got any other treats you'd like to stuff in my mouth?"

"You two just never stop!" Raven rolled her eyes.

Serina giggled. "I meant muffin, Raven."

Waltzing into the room with Ethan in tow, Savanah announced, "Happy Sunday, everyone."

"Oh blimey!" Duncan chuckled. "She's got it bad."

"Love you as well, old man." Savanah skipped to him and kissed the bald patch atop his head. "What's up? We haven't all been gathered in the library together in ages. This is nice." Hearing footsteps she turned into her mother.

Savanah's happy Sunday took a dismal plunge making it feel more like a dreaded Monday. Before her first tear fell Jovan hugged her. "Please give him a chance, Mum."

Jovan clung to her, trembling.

"Mum, what is it?"

"The future sometimes has bumps, baby. Sometimes we bounce back and sometimes we get lost in the crevices. I'm not willing to lose you."

Savanah tried to quell her fear. "Scrying can be tricky. You only see bits and pieces, not the whole picture. You saw your daughter happy and getting married, so whatever happens before that is null and void for the most part." With a slight tilt of her head and a shift of her eyebrows, Savanah saw the return of her mother's smile.

"As your mother, I have the right to change my mind at any time I deem fit or his if the occasion arises."

"You're talking about the blinkie thing again aren't you?" Ethan asked.

"Isn't he cute?" Savanah ruffled Ethan's curls.

Jovan tried not to cringe.

Savanah's take on the morning: Bleakness gone. Day looking better by the second. "All right, since I have you all corralled, anyone interested in going back to London for a few days with us?"

"We just got home." André frowned. "Your aunt wants to go to Mexico, you want to go to England? What's left, Disney?"

"I'm in," came from Duncan.

Savanah butt in, "I want to see if it was really Draque that stole all his belongings back or if it was some other dead beat."

After one sharp inhalation, Jovan ordered, "You will not go there and chase that demon. Savanah St. James, have you lost your mind? André?" Jovan looked desperate.

"Mum, that ghoul stole my life's work. It's not right."

"Peanut, you stole it from him. Did that thought ever occur to you? How would you feel if you had something you loved stolen from you?" Lucian asked, looking and sounding exactly like her father.

"What? Are you two practicing ventriloquism now!" Savanah exclaimed.

"Savage? Isn't what Lucian just said, written on the back of one of the little cards we got in New Orleans?" Ethan spun on his heels and fled the room. When he returned, he waved the small black cards under her nose. "Look. The card reads almost identically. 'How does it feel to have something you love stolen from you?'"

"Can I see the card?" Lucian asked.

After handing it to him, Ethan stopped and read the ad in the paper. "Hey, who put the compulsion in the paper? Isn't that a death warrant?"

"Only if you get caught. How do you know of them, Ethan?" Jovan's interest piqued enough to speak with the man in a civil tone.

"I've picked up a few tricks living with the one guy whose name you don't want repeated in this home." Ethan would have sworn just then he saw Jovan smile.

Jovan asked, "Food for thought, Ethan. You said Xavier's child was born the same day Elyza was. If the ad's the real deal and the babies are really half-vamp, half-lycan what are our chances that these two babies are the devil's little spawns?"

"Still want to go separate them, Doc?" Duncan asked.

Serina answered, "Think about it, Duncan, how many babies are born each day? And with more and more of the population being turned, the chances are pretty good they're just two babies who need our help."

"M'lady, even with all the ghosts and goblins in this world you refuse to see the possibilities that these two babies could have ties to Sinclair?"

Serina scratched her head. "Lucian, that's just it. They're babies, they're innocent. Whoever kidnapped them obviously wanted to keep them from either the science labs or Sinclair as well, if all this is true. If you didn't tamper with Elyza's labs we'd be in the same predicament! The PEON's would be hunting her down. It is the age-old question, is it Neo-Darwinism— genetics or environment that makes a person do the things they do? Nature versus nurture. Here's a quick tangent: Pit bulls. Beautiful, intelligent, loyal animals with a bad rap because some slimy, scum-of-the-earth bastards raise them to kill and fight, so the innocent dogs get tagged a bad breed. They weren't born like that. They were raised that way. We won't have answers unless we go see for ourselves. Innocent until proven guilty."

Jovan spoke up. "Serina, last week I told you something bad was going to happen. Do you see where I'm headed with this? Between Savanah, Draque and Ethan and his ties to you-know-who and the possibility of the two babies, this isn't trouble, this is the last chapter in the book without a sequel. This is not a good idea. This is a very, *very* bad idea. Please, I beg you, don't go there. Let someone else do the surgery."

"Sis, if you're so worried, scry. See what it brings."

"No." Jovan offered no more, then left the room.

"Why is your mother scared of her gift, Savvy?" Ethan asked.

Julian answered, "When we were young Jovan used to rely on her foresight, but one day she played around and saw our mother on the couch, dead. A few weeks later her vision came true. She's used it twice since then. Once, on the day she met Goliath, she cast a spell and scryed," Julian bowed to André, "and two, to make sure Savanah was actually going to have a wedding. No offense, Savanah, but you're maturing as we speak."

"I live with a group of really bad comedians."

"Ethan, has anyone taken into account that Draque is spelling his name differently these days? As long as I can remember it, the suffix was "*cula*", not "*que*." This guy's a fraud. Yeah, he may be big and scary, but he's not the Godfather. He's more like an extended uncle three coffins over." Lucian took the card without thinking, and stuffed it in his wallet.

"Uncle Lucian, I stole Dracula's casket and all his goodies. Trust me, it's him. I need to get out. Anyone want to go shopping?"

Raven perked up. "Oh, I hoped you'd say that. Serina, come on. Molly? Up and at 'em. Let's go grab your mum and be gone." Raven grabbed her wallet and headed out the door.

Serina asked Lucian, "Should I introduce Elyza to shopping today or would you like to give her the finer points of relaxing with the boys?"

"She's mine. You go have fun."

"I'm going to check on Jovan before you steal her from me." André kissed Serina's head as he passed. He added, "Lucian, don't we have tickets for the game today? Front row—third-base line?"

Serina spun on her heels, the look—ready to kill. "You're not funny. Lucian, tell me he's joking. You wouldn't dare go without me."

"That was mean, Ands," Lucian said as he gave his brother a thumb's up gesture behind Serina's back.

"Lucian, there's a mirror not two feet in front of you. Imbecile! Are you blind?" Serina punched his arm and walked off.

****

After shopping for close to five hours, Molly asked, "Who's hungry? Want to go to the new restaurant on the lake? I hear it's to die for."

"As long as that's not taken literally. What's the menu?" Serina asked.

"Seafood?" Savanah asked, hoping.

Molly pulled a small menu from the console of the

truck and read it while they waited for the light to change. "No seafood from Saratoga Lake. But they have bass, northern pike, walleyes and black crappies."

Serina scrunched her nose. "Sounds too much like Elyza's diapers. No thank you. What's the name of the new place?"

"Sinsations. It's a cross between a high-end restaurant, and a trendy night club with three different floors with a phony dungeon to boot."

"What's the clientele? Humans or shifters? Molly, how do you know so much about the place?" Jovan's curiosity piqued.

"Heard it's mainly humans, but shifters are getting in and behaving so the PEON's aren't inspecting the place. Jovie, you've been in England and Paris for the past few months now. Serina's always off either saving the world or having sex. I had to find something to keep out of trouble. Food works wonders."

Serina defended herself. "You are so bad! I'm not always off saving the world."

Jovan slid in, "Notice she didn't argue the sex part."

"A girl's got to have priorities, Jovan. And you, Missy, are in the wrong shoes to argue this point with me." Serina rubbed Jovan's belly.

"Anyone up for hitting the furniture store on the way home? I'm going to do our bedroom over. Not the walls though, Mum. They're beautiful. So are you."

"Oh, does she want something!" Raven nudged her niece. "Will you wear your mother's wedding dress, Savvy? Actually, it was your grandmother's."

"I'm too tall."

"No, she won't wear that," Jovan spoke up. "She'll

wear something original and outrageously expensive that her Papa will pay out of his nose for."

"Good line, Savanah." Serina gave a chin nod to her niece. "You once again worked your charms."

Savanah's grin crawled across her face. "Putty in my hands."

Serina slapped her arm. "You are a conniving child, and I pray mine doesn't follow your footsteps."

"Auntie, you don't have a prayer. Elyza's not only got me to corrupt her, but Ray and Molly. Can you imagine the trouble if Sydney came up to stay with us?"

Raven shrugged her shoulders. "If Sydney were here? What's that saying...no rest for the wicked? That girl is a spitfire. I miss her."

Serina went solemn. "Me, too."

Jovan squeezed Serina's hand. "No worries, Sis. We'll take the family down after my two are born, and we'll overstay our welcome."

Trolling the parking lot, the women spotted a young man waving them down with a heavy metal spiked ball and chain.

"Killer valet! Do we trust him with this monster truck?" Molly's heart raced.

"Remember *Ferris Bueller's Day Off?*" Savanah asked.

Molly answered. "Point taken!"

"Why the tinted windows in the restaurant?" Jovan asked.

Molly answered, "How long have we lived with vamps? No amount of sun block will protect most of the nefarious ones. We may be able to walk with the living, but there are others less fortunate. We've been blessed."

Serina, Savanah, Jovan and Raven all said, "Blessed?" at the same time.

****

Pacing, Ethan found, passed time and gave him a bit of exercise. He also found it stretched Payton's last nerve too thin. On his umpteenth trip through the kitchen—stopping and looking in the pantry to see if anything miraculously appeared to eat, Payton pointed one of his favorite knives at Ethan.

"Can you not see it's Sunday? Considered a day of rest for most around here. Try it out," Payton suggested his tone stern.

"Where is everyone?"

"The women for all intents and purposes won't show up here until we're rightfully broke. The guys go down to the theatre and watch porn."

"What?" Ethan's ears perked up.

"Joking. The game's on. Hope you're into stripes coz it's the only thing we watch from April through November. If you're a Boston fan, there's a telly in the stables."

"Funny."

With a deadpan stare Payton replied, "That time I wasn't joking."

"What are you making?"

"Dinner."

"Are you always this chatty?"

"Only with people I don't trust yet and, Ethan, there's a few of us that don't trust you here. Just because Jovan scryed into the future and saw you with our baby, it doesn't mean you've got free reign here. You have to earn the trust. It's not just handed over as easily as the front door key. You come with more baggage than any of us did. Even Jonah and he had enough to put Samsonite out of business."

"Ya know…" Ethan picked up an apple, shined it on his shirt and bit a huge chunk off. With a mouth full he finished, "Just because your love life is on the brink of extinction and mine's on front burner heating up, don't blame me for Vonnie showing up. He would have sooner or later." He swallowed one huge gulp.

"Ethan, if you think for one minute I need you in my face talking to me about something you have no clue over, or right to discuss you're dead wrong. Stay out of my business. Stay out of my love life…"

"What's left of it…"

"And my kitchen, for that matter. You came here with the intentions of stealing a baby. What perverse person would do that?"

Ethan tossed his hands in the air. "For the last time, I was under Xier's stronghold—compulsion—whatever you want to call it. The vamp made me believe I was doing the right thing. That's the last time I'm telling that tale to anyone." Ethan spun on his heels and headed toward the theatre. Hand on the knob to the room, Lucian, André, Julian, Duncan and Jonah's voices bounced off the walls. Ethan opened the door and stepped back in time. In the corner of the room sat an old popcorn machine overflowing with steaming buttery kernels. Next to it was a light blue Formica countertop. Deep sapphire vinyl covered stools lined the length of the counter. A soda fountain and old Coke glasses took up part of the surface. At the other end sat a stainless steel beer lever, the handle a deep red ceramic glaze. Steins hung from pegs on the wall behind. Red, plastic baskets of popped corn waited to be eaten. Ethan helped himself.

"Keep it down. You'll wake the baby," Lucian yelled to Duncan who was shaking an accusatory finger at the umpire in a loud boisterous tone.

"What? And you're not yelling you giant buffoon?" Duncan whispered. "Give her to me. She needs her uncle." Duncan walked to Lucian and took the little girl from her father's arms. With a gentle sway and rocking motion he calmed the infant down. A few minutes later Duncan and Elyza sat in one of the leather recliners and settled in for the game.

Lucian pointed to a seat once he noticed Ethan. "You a Yankees fan?"

"I'm told my television is in the stables. Boston."

"We should have killed him the first night we met him." André grinned, giving Julian—the nod.

Ethan laughed it off, but the thought bit at him like an annoying little sand flea stuck in his shorts. "Any of you meet the Yankees?"

"I did. Elyza was born on the field behind home plate," Lucian bragged. "Ethan, I don't want to rain on this parade, but how did you meet Sinclair and are you willing to stop him? Our family, which you will soon become a part of, cannot have that carnivorous cannibal or his brethren breathing down our necks or worse."

"My furry tale of woe began when I ended up on life support after being turned. My parents and family disowned me and the X-man showed up and rescued an abandoned wolf at the eleventh hour from lethal injection. The rest is bad karma I 'spose, although I don't know why. I've never hurt anyone. I told Savage I am going to finish my business with him."

Jonah shot in, "He won't let you just cut your

apron strings and waltz off. He'll kill you. Been there, with an old associate of his, actually."

"Not if I get him first." This was the part of the conversation Ethan prayed one of them would kick in and say, "We'll help you, Eth." Instead everyone silently bit the bullet. "Savanah wants to help me, but that's a no-brainer. She's not getting within a continent of that man."

"I'm in." Lucian.

"Me too." Julian.

André added, "We were coming with you one way or the other, Ethan. We just wanted to see your reaction. You didn't whine, which is what Grimmy would have done." André never turned to see his brother-in-law's reaction.

Ethan saw Julian though, and fought not to laugh as the two men went down on the floor wrestling. The camaraderie, love and respect in this home stymied Ethan. They each had a defined personality, no one more demanding than the next, and they each truly put the other person first, no matter what the cost to themselves. And the fact these fine people opened their home to him blew his mind. He needed to show them he'd never get them in a tight spot or let Savanah or any of them down, again.

After eight innings of listening to pitch-by-pitch plays of his least favorite team, Ethan gave in to his eyelids. Gravity would close this inning, not the Sand man. Fine by him.

****

"Hey, ladies, who owns this joint? And who's the handsome man on his way over to us?" Raven purred better than a cat.

Noting the bedroom eyes Raven shot the man, Savanah waited for her aunt to start licking her paws or other personal parts as a little foreplay, if she was nimble enough to crouch and curl into that position. Seeing the returned gaze from the new gent, possibly he'd get her hard to reach spaces for her. A sexual awareness oozed from him better than a bottle of two-dollar cologne.

Blinding white teeth grinned at each woman. Thick, lush lashes encased his almond-shape black, lifeless, eyes. His black, tailored, Italian suit screamed obscene money, and the body hidden beneath it, hinted the man spent some time in the gym or with a plastic surgeon.

Savanah's aunts smiled as a very distinguished gentleman with dark olive skin, salt-n-pepper hair and a matching goatee, approached, a bottle of wine in hand.

"Good afternoon and welcome to Sinsations. My name is Seamus. I see I may have been hasty in bringing only wine. I'll return with drinks for the two mothers to be." Once the bottle was down, he excused himself.

"Who else here is pregnant?" Jovan looked directly at Savanah.

"Ah—no—not me," she choked out.

Molly waved her white napkin in the air. "Guess with everything that's happened it slipped me mind to tell you. Do I look pregnant? I'm only two months. What's going to happen at nine months?" Molly's face turned into one giant moue.

Serina grabbed Molly's hand and gave her a squeeze. "Who's busy having sex all the time?" Serina teased. "Congrats, Molly."

Seamus returned with a carafe of lemonade, fresh, with thin yellow slices of lemons floating like lily pads in the pitcher. "Ladies, this is on me. Enjoy. And Madame, when you reach nine months your radiance will be everyone's envy. I see you're new here, as am I, and I'm trying to get to know all my patrons."

"Thank you, Seamus," Jovan replied. "Your restaurant is wonderful."

Seamus bowed before them and then retreated to the bar.

Raven watched as the tall man walked away, then went on her rant. "Gone are the days of chivalry and romance. Today's world is more dog-eat-dog, an unpleasant mixture of reality television, court television, rap music dissing everyone and little actresses and heiress with too much publicity and money and no brains to brag of."

Serina glanced at Jovan, Savanah and Molly. "She's been reading the tabloids again."

"Haven't seen gallantry like that since the dark ages," Raven boasted. "He'll do well here. He's a flirt. He reminds me of that sexy actor, the one who played a Godfather in some shoot 'em up flick."

"Yeah, he does, and Ray, it was you he was flirting with if you didn't notice." Molly added.

"No, it was Savanah."

"Oh *puh-leeze*," Savanah bat her eyelashes playful. "It was Mum. Or her boobs."

A hand came out of nowhere and ticked the back of Savanah's head. From a sideways glance, she gave her daughter the evil eye. Jovan sputtered, "Serina, it was all you."

Serina nudged Molly. "Hell no! Did you see the

way he eyed Red? Her radiance will be everyone's envy?"

"Me?" Molly asked. "Are you blind? He probably thought I'm the over ripe tomato. He's just waiting for the precise moment to pop me into his sauce."

"Or give you some of his special sauce."

"Ewh, Savanah," circulated the table.

"Yeah, he's a player all right. He worked our table in under a minute. He's good." Raven smiled. "Older men can do that."

"We have some older men at home that can do more than that. Lest not forget that." Jovan jabbed her finger in Raven's arm, driving home her point. "Ray, you're the flirt still, after all these years."

"Doesn't hurt to look. It's when you bite them that you seem to get in trouble." Raven threw her hands in the air, gesturing, "Who knew?"

"Oh, Raven!" Serina cajoled. "What are you going to do with all your men?"

"Serrie, if I knew I'd be one happy camper. Right now, Murphy's ringing out his dingy, black cloud over my little tent, and I'm drowning in it all alone. I inflated my air mattress and it's now flat. Jonah and I attempted to make up this morning. After an hour of exhausting all other avenues other than talking, Jonah left upset with both of us. I suppose mad make-up sex is better than no sex! Payton and I tried to make up last night. The sex was hot. The conversation afterwards had an artic chill to it. And then Donovan disappeared the same day André had his rebirth."

Savanah added, "If he comes back he'll be sorry. I don't see what the big deal is with him, Aunt Ray. He's creepy."

Raven chugged a second glass of wine. "Peanut, he's my problem, not yours." Raven grabbed her niece's hand. "I'll take care of what's left of my love life. Will you excuse me? My eyeballs are floating. It's four seventeen. If I'm not back in five send a search party."

Molly asked, "Savanah, go see that she's ok. Raven could go the wrong way on a merry-go-round. She's no sense of direction."

"She's no sense, period."

"Funny." Molly high-fived Savanah as she passed by.

Savanah didn't want her aunt thinking she was incapable of going to the lady's room alone so she stayed back and watched from a distance. She watched as her aunt stopped, looked left and then right for the restroom. A maze of hallways led her to a back spiral stairway. Savanah tiptoed behind being as stealthy as possible. Raven's hand turned white as she gripped the banister, and she took her time going down the steps. After descending two flights Savanah played catch-up and found a door with a picture of lamb on the front. She peeked inside and found the room coed. A man wearing a nice suit had his back to her next to a sink. Savanah jerked her body back to hide behind the retaining wall.

I've descended to level of a snoop. Fabulous!

"I'm so sorry," Raven said, "I must have walked in the wrong room."

"No, Ray, you're in the right room."

The man's voice sent a chill down Savanah's spine. She compared it to being blasted with liquid nitrogen. She rubbed her hands up and down the length of her arms when she realized whose grating voice it was. Nausea clawed its way through her gut.

"I wondered how long it would take for your drink to go through you."

Raven asked, "Would you mind turning around so I know who I'm talking to?"

Seriously, Aunt Raven, Savanah wondered, *how can you not know who this is?*

"Come on, Beauty. Gone one week and forgotten. And here I thought abstinence made the heart grow fonder."

"Donovan? What are you doing here and in the ladies room no less? Perv!"

Yeah, perv works and I feel like one eavesdropping.

"You never were a rocket scientist," Donovan answered. His tone, condescending.

Raven's no better. "Screw you."

"I plan to. You that is."

Savanah froze; her knees went weak as she heard Donovan's footsteps clinking on the marble floor headed toward her aunt. Did she intervene? Did she let her aunt take care of herself like she said she could? She held out in hopes her aunt would stop whatever repulsive consanguinity they had between them. It would make her day if her aunt released the man of the blood bound ties between them. Fists clenched, Savanah prayed, *Please, Aunt Ray, tell him how to intercept the next stake to hell.*

Donovan grabbed Raven's hand and pulled her to the front of his pants where the linen stretched taut.

With a little gasp, she tried to pull away. "Let go of me. I'll give you two seconds before I scream for help."

Do it and I'm all over the leech. Savanah waited, her breath caught in her throat.

Donovan pressed her hand in a slow circular motion over his pants, into his erection. Low-and-behold, her fingers wrapped around his bulge like kid gloves. "One-one-hundred, two-one-hundred," he counted, sarcasm most evident.

If Savanah ever had doubts about the man prior to today, listening to him here and now convinced her to trust in her instincts. He probably had a grin smeared across his lips identical to the one that made Charles Manson famous.

Pure evil.

"Cat got your tongue? I want you to look at me, Raven, as I screw you. Right here, Right now."

"You can't vamp me, Donovan. It is impossible. I made you."

"You gave me the after-life, Raven. From that point on I made my own eternal Hell. A challenge then? And, Beauty, if I do vamp you, I don't want to hear you go cry rape, because you know what you're getting yourself into."

"There's no need for a challenge. I'm tired of hiding my feelings and living one giant lie. I have such passion in my heart for you it leaves me breathless. For so many years I worried over you and wondered what your life had become."

"Hell without you beside me, Beauty. My heart too refused to let go of you."

How did that happen? Everything got turned around. Damn Aunt Raven! Savanah rolled her eyes and headed back to the table, absolutely disgusted and enraged by her aunt's behavior. Midway up the spiral staircase she stopped, stewed over the situation before she turned back around, not about to let this slide. Raven had to come clean. Hearts were at stake. Literally.

"Aunt Raven!" Savanah's voice blared. The door to the stall opened again and Raven exited. Seeing Savanah her cheeks went brilliant red.

"How much were you privy to?"

"Too bleeding much. Wow! That man is dangerous, and I can't believe you can't see that. I can't believe you just did that. Here!"

"Savanah, I said I would handle my love life."

"Yes, and what a beautiful job you're doing, Auntie." Savanah turned and headed out. "You coming? Again? Try being a tad more discreet the next time."

"Savanah, this is none of your business. Leave it be."

"Really? You of all people taught me to trust my instincts and trust me, they're screaming obscene things over that vamp and you just allowed that—that whatever he is into your life. Literally!"

Savanah watched Raven climb the steps even slower than she went down. If she had a tail like a few of the werewolves in their home it would have been tucked securely between her legs. Back to the top level of the restaurant, Raven looked around the bar through guilt-ridden eyes and turned away from Savanah's scorned gaze. An awkward silence suffocated Savanah. It had never been there before, and Savanah didn't like it one iota. Having a sneaking suspicion the bastard hadn't vacated the vicinity as easily as he did the restroom, Savanah pointed to the bar. And there

Donovan sat, next to Seamus, his arm around the owner making idle chit-chat.

"You should go talk to him. Talk, you know the meaning of the word. Please keep your clothes on this time though." Savanah couldn't contain her anger or hurt that her aunt would place herself in this man's vice and bring with it the possibility of more foul play. Or hurt Payton and Jonah. Was she being too critical? Too judgmental? Possibly, but she knew with every breath the man at the bar was rotten to the core. Making her aunt see the light of day might take some finagling.

"Did you get lost? You don't look so well." Serina looked at Savanah and without saying a word or needing to she stood in haste. Savanah's emotions and thoughts were plastered all over her face better than a billboard with big bold letters exposing Raven's exploits out there for the world to see.

"I think I might like spend some time with my daughter," Serina said as she stood and walked toward the exit.

"Works for me," Oblivious, Jovan babbled through a yawn. "The two in me tummy have been kicking all day. How you feel, Molly?"

Molly rubbed her belly. "Gaseous."

"Get used to it." Jovan winked.

Raven made it as far as the door and turned back. "I'll meet you in a minute."

Savanah was on her heels better than a wad of gum on a hot sunny day.

Raven approached the bar and stood between Seamus and Donovan. "Seamus, I just wanted you to know—"

Seamus cut Raven off. "Raven St. James. Heard

oodles about you over the years. You are very much as beautiful as the tales I've been told. Meet my junior partner, Donovan Drake. Donovan's more like my silent partner."

Savanah cozied up to the bar and wormed in between Seamus and Donovan. "I could stifle him on a permanent basis if you'd prefer, make him truly silent." Savanah's frosted glare met Donovan's surprised look, and Raven's seething cast. At that second, she had two things she wanted. One, to grab her aunt and run. And two, to rip out Donovan's olive-colored eyes, drop them in a martini and chomp them to bits. Instead, she picked up Donovan's shot glass and downed the smooth bourbon in one long gulp.

Seamus' amusement spread across his face. "I happen to like my partner, Savanah, and I think I'm not the only one"—he nodded to Raven—"but if the time comes when I want him staked, I'll call."

"Promise?" Savanah asked. "Aunt Raven? Let's roll." She grabbed Raven's hand and proceeded out the door, laughter chasing them.

****

The sound of the Payton's engine revving, wheels spinning, and gravel spitting out raced up the stairs faster than the car could flee down the driveway. "Did you hear that?" Savanah asked Ethan. "That can't be good."

"I have a feeling our meal ticket just drove off with the family recipes. I'm never getting those cookies now!" Ethan pouted.

"I knew this would end badly."

"I can't believe you found her in the restroom with Vonnie. Wow! Do me a favor, Savage? If you ever feel like you want another lover, don't sneak off and do it. Invite whoever it is into our bed. I'm not saying I'm willing to make us a threesome permanently like your aunt did, but curiosity wins out sometimes."

"Not to worry, Mr. Kitt. There's no need for third parties in our bedchamber. Ever."

"Toys?" The ever-present twinkle in his eye glistened. Angling his head into the side of Savanah's neck, he nibbled.

"What toy have you stashed away under here?" Savanah bit at her bottom lip as she tugged at the zipper on Ethan's pants. It didn't budge. "What? Is this thing crazy glued in place?"

"You're joking right?"

"Hell no! You're glued shut." She tugged harder at the zipper.

"I'll bet your father and uncle did this to me when I fell asleep during the baseball game."

Laughter bellowed through their room. "That'll teach ya for nodding off during the game. That's almost as bad as going to church and napping."

After a minute of struggling with his zipper, Ethan gave up.

"Come on, Savvy, tell me you've never crashed in church. That's how I survived most of my Sundays as a kid. It was that or fake sneezing when Father came down the aisle with his incense and left everyone in a hazy cloud."

"Eth, I haven't prayed in church in eons. My Mum always told me I could pray anywhere I deemed fit."

"Pip, help me out of these things! Can't you use some magic on them?" Ethan tried to wiggle out of the pants.

"Eth, you'd be naked all day if I could do that. My mom has that ability. She can fashion up a wardrobe in a split second. Me? I can make Holland's flowers look like a little roadside stand. I have the original green thumb."

Ethan's half grin appeared. "What of God? Do you believe in him?"

"That's a loaded question. I want to believe there is someone up there looking after my family, but then you flick on the telly and all you see is doom and gloom and how people blow each other up, children shoot their friends in schools or malls or even worse, all the sickness and death, it's hard to trust in faith. Doesn't sound like God, but more like the Devil, if you ask me. What about you?"

"Complete believer in heaven and hell, the devil, the antichrist, the archangels, cupid...the tooth fairy, Tinkerbelle. I'm a freakin' werewolf, Savanah, what's not to believe? Everything is a balancing act. The sun, the moon. Some days God's got the scales tipped in his favor and other days Lucifer's tampered with the weights. 'Course you'd have to expect that from the devil. We can't control the weather any better than we can control our neighbor's actions." His face red, he still struggled to free the zipper.

Savanah cleared her throat.

"All right, Mother Nature's helper, but for the most part...when we were created we were given free will and each one of us made our own Heaven or Hell. That, of course, impacts everyone else. How we deal with the situations tossed at us is what counts. I think everything is fate related. It's what brought me to you."

Savanah smiled as Ethan babbled and finally got

the zipper apart. Broken, but apart.

"Let me change, and we'll go for a ride and grab some dinner."

Savanah pouted.

"There's a pretty face," he teased, as he ran a gentle finger across her lips.

"I wanted to blow up your balloon."

Ethan stopped dead in his tracks and with a fist pump, mouthed the word "Yes" to her.

"Looks like I'm getting a little help. Your balloon's rising on its own." Savanah stood by the side of the bed, and slipped out of her sweater. With a slowness only a sloth could appreciate, she undid her pants and wiggled them to her knees. With a quick turn she flashed him her bottom.

Enthusiasm high, Ethan watched. After getting the pants down around her ankles, she slid onto the bed and kicked her feet in his face.

"Would you be so kind as to remove these pants?"

In a flash her pants and panties disappeared.

"You cheat, Eth. I was going to finish my little dance and get the undies off for you."

"Another time. Right now, my balloon's ready to set sail." Ethan pointed south.

Savanah dipped her head toward him. Licking her lips in a slow seductive manner, which almost cost Ethan the ride.

"Come to me, baby, *please*?" Hands clasped in front of him.

Ethan closed his eyes when her lips met his flesh, and she trailed kisses down his shaft. He threw his head back and relaxed to the rhythm of his woman while she worked her magic and sucked the very life out of him.

"Jesus, you know what you're doing."

"I'm cheating, Baby…"

His fingers tugged her hair. "No—no talking yet." She couldn't stop. He'd never experienced anything in his life like this.

Savanah tightened her lips around his shaft as she went down, then she released pressure and dragged her tongue slowly up his pleasuring tool. He wasn't going to last long at all with this attention. With pursed lips, inch by slow inch she swallowed him down. At the base of his penis she feathered her fingers over his balls as she sucked his shaft and in the next breath of his air a sensation started right where her lips were…Coincidence? Not this time. Pleasure pulsed throughout his entire body. She had him. It was over that fast. He lost his control and felt his body come. Savanah's eyes watered when his seed spilled down her throat. One huge gulp and it disappeared.

"So you swallow?"

She licked her lips. "I was taught it isn't polite for women to spit, ever. I'm pretty sure my mom didn't have this in mind when she said it though!" She produced a sinful grin.

Ethan pinned her to the bed on her back. With one hand he slid his fingers between the folds of her private lips, and he tapped out his own tune on her mons. Savanah's hips danced with Ethan's fingers slow, intimate as her orgasm built.

Ethan kissed her through the soft murmurs, and shakes her body delivered. "You've taught me the meaning of love, Savanah St. James. And I'm going to spend eternity practicing it on you."

From the tip of her nose to her toes, Ethan kissed

every square inch of Savanah's body. A few ticklish spots were stored for a rainy day; behind her ear, inside her thigh, and the bottom of her foot.

"Eth, do we have to go out tonight? I'd just as soon stay here with you all night. I can go raid the fridge if you like."

"I got this one, Baby. I'll be back soon."

"Eth, I…"

He placed his finger to her lips, silencing her. He winked as he finished pulling the belt through his new pants and headed out the door. "Don't move. And dear God, don't get dressed."

****

Two hours later empty cardboard cartons covered the floor. Savanah lay draped over Ethan's exhausted body, both of them spent from a marathon lovemaking. His arms held her safe within his, his lips pressed to her forehead, sound asleep. Lying beside him, she'd never been more fulfilled, complete. Savanah focused on the television's pretty blue screen and listened to Korn's, *Tearjerker* sifting through the vents from Julian's room. She finally gave in to the need to close her eyes. She didn't want the day to end, it had been so perfect.

Chapter Fourteen

"I smell steak and eggs. Payton's back! Come on, Eth." Savanah sprang out of her retreat rejuvenated, headache she'd acquired earlier—gone, her appetite voracious. She tugged on Ethan's limp arm.

"Sweets, save yourself. I need sleep. I can't keep up with your body's demands. You're trying to kill me, aren't you?" Ethan growled as he dragged her back into their bed and under the covers. "Get over here you little minx."

Without struggle, Savanah scooted under Ethan's large frame and angled herself for easier access to anything he had planned or more importantly, what she hoped he had in mind. Legs were spread, her tummy growled, but no longer for food.

"Hey, you," she teased as she slid her hands over his muscle-clad buns of steel. A wee bit lower and around his front she found her personal vibrator solid, warm, waiting to be inserted and ready to pulse. "Who's trying to kill whom?"

"Good morning, little nut. My plan today is to love you to death." Ethan's lips met Savanah's gently. "Want to work up an appetite first?"

"What? You want to go to the gym?"

"No. I thought you could be my work out buddy. We could pump a few things…" Ethan pressed his hips into her groin, his erection in hard contact with her more sensitive areas. "Then maybe we could lift a few weights." This time he fondled her breasts, flicked her nipples and watched them pebble. Dipping his head, he said, "Ah, an appeteaser."

"A what?" she asked, watching his eyes go dangerously dark.

"An appeteaser. Kinda like an appetizer, but more fun and zero calories." He traced circles around her areola, enticing her nipple to the point it could explode. "Then I thought maybe we'd work up a sweat, ya know, get really physical and then hop into a nice steamy shower and relax. Then round number two…."

Savanah laughed at his antics. "Hum…. Do I really need a workout?" She felt his hand move between her thighs to work out the one area the sun wasn't going see, not even if she was on a nude beach—alone. His fingers were meticulous, delicate, stroking her in sweet tantalizing brushes. Breathless she said, "A—workout—seems most doable."

"Ah—one—and—a—two."

"All right, let's get physical," Savanah grunted back.

Ethan began to sing, and Savanah laughed. His voice melted her even more so when he slid his microphone in between her legs. Ethan's female impressions of one of the 1980's notorious pop queens left a lot to be desired.

"Stop with the singing, Eth, and just do me like an animal."

"There's another one of my favorite songs in there."

"When isn't there?" she teased. "Stop those flapping lips and mount me, you animal."

And he did. One hour later the two of them were in the shower, on the floor, both too exhausted to stand.

****

In the kitchen Savanah found all sorts of dishes stacked in the sink, waiting for some unlucky sod to tackle them. On the counter a warming plate held an authentic English mixed grill of sirloin cooked rare, plump golden brown sausages, with grilled mushrooms and tomatoes. Next to the meat, a dish of scrambled eggs, smothered in cheese lured Savanah near. Blood pudding, sliced thick had fresh pineapple slices around it. Fresh bagels, grapefruit juice, yogurt, granola and blueberries decorated the countertop.

"Payton?" Savanah yelled ecstatic her friend came home.

When Payton didn't answer, disappointment snuffed out the scrumptious aroma of breakfast. A crunch of something on the floor made her turn. She slammed directly into Kyle, Duncan and Molly's youngest son. With a joyous screech, Savanah jumped him. Before the young lad had a chance to react, she had her legs wrapped around him, in a stranglehold. "Kyle, what are you doing home?"

"Let me go, brat," Kyle pleaded as he tried to peel her off. He plopped her down atop the countertop, but she kept her legs secured to him. "I came home for two reasons. First is to meet Elyza, but I can't find anyone and secondly, because I heard from Da trouble's brooin'. And cartin' your bum about isn't on me bucket list, Lass."

"Listen to you with your little Scotty accent. What's that school teaching you? You're a limey. Dunna forget that." Savanah mimicked him.

"So, brat," Kyle ran his fingers through Savanah's maze of twisted tendrils, "you look fantastic, cousin. Where's Pay?"

"That's the hundred-thousand dollar question." Savanah's smile faded. "I thought when I smelled all the food he'd come home."

"Where's my black bird?"

"Raven's locked herself in her room. Jonah left too with Aunt Serina, Uncle Lucian and Jules. They're in Mexico. Left early this morning to separate a set of conjoined twins, who happen to be a wolf and vamp. Ya, Kyle, trouble's brooin'."

"I also hear that you have a new roommate? Tell me everything, Savvy. I want details." Kyle hugged her.

As the saying goes, timing is everything, and Ethan wasn't so pleased with his. He rounded the corner and found his fiancé with her legs securing another man to her body, and the two of them looking rather intimate. Jealousy was not on his menu for breakfast, but he found he had to swallow a good lump of it regardless. Savanah's new friend reminded Ethan of the kid on the cover of Mad Magazine, red hair ruled by cowlicks, brown eyes and string-bean thin. The only thing Ethan couldn't find fault with was his shirt—a dark gray T-shirt with the *Boondock Saints* movie logo across the front. Ethan respected the movie. *Take care of your own and screw all the consequences*. It pissed him off his parents didn't feel the same way about him!

Savanah answered Kyle, "He's the best, the greatest, no not the greatest…"

"I get the point. You're smitten."

"Good morning, Savage. Mister?" Ethan cocked his head sideways; a grimaced look disfigured his handsome appeal.

Savanah smirked. "Your color's draining onto the floor." *Jealous!*

"I am not."

"Liar."

"Stop! Just please tell me this isn't Radcliff."

Laughter filled the kitchen. "You must be the new kid on the block." Kyle stretched his hand to Ethan's. "Call me Radcliff ever again, and I'll introduce you to Sweet Pea."

Ethan's blank stare was filled with dark thoughts. His hand stayed in his pocket.

"Sweetpea, my love, is Kyle's alligator." Savanah released Kyle, jumped off the counter, strut her long legs to Ethan, and kissed his lips softly. "Eth, meet Kyle, Duncan's son, my cousin." Ethan's lips trembled beneath hers. Cupping his face between her hands she kissed him again, with a little more umph behind it. "You okay?"

"I'm fine. Just seeing you in someone else's arms, well, it did nothing for me." He shook his head and flexed his arms.

"Eth, he's family. He is really. He's my third cousin."

"Yeah, but isn't royalty known for trysts with those closest? And did you know it's legal to marry your third cousin?"

"Ewh, Ethan." Savanah swatted him. "Incest? I think you've read one too many books or seen too much telly." One more kiss had Ethan kissing her back with vigor.

"Hey, brat, forget you've company?"

Savanah ducked her head to Ethan's shoulder, her

cheeks a new shade of red. "I'm sorry."

"No you're not. Ethan, nice to meet the man who finally swept this one off her big feet." Kyle pat his shoulder. "I'm going to the stables. Da doesn't know I'm home. I woke Mum up a while ago. Pregnant again? We're a prolific bunch if nothing else!"

"How long you home?"

"Just long enough to get under everyone's skin and then get out. Get a few bucks in me pocket for spendin' and then I'm back to Europe. You, Missy, are not the only one with a buddin' love life." With the wink of his brown eye and a quick kiss on Savanah's cheek, Kyle left.

"Does he really have a 'gator?"

"Yes. Sydney gave Sweet Pea to him about six years ago. She'd found the little thing all wound up in a wire mesh, left to die. The poor thing crawled out from the canals in Florida and the local residents took a baseball bat and tire iron to her. Knocked all her teeth out, broke her jaw and amputated one of her hind legs in the process."

"I'm not the Crocodile Hunter, but I wouldn't want it hurt."

"Fear, Eth. People are scared of them so they tried to kill her. Sadly, it's the same mentality as shifters and vamps. If people would just take the time to educate themselves about whatever it is that scares them, there would be a lot less prejudice. Ignorance has to be erased from this earth or there won't be one." Savanah leaned around Ethan to the plate with the sirloin and inhaled. "Sorry for the rant. I've gotta eat. After this morning I'm famished."

"Sit. I'll fix you a plate."

"I lo…"

Kissing her faster than a lightning bolt could strike, Ethan stopped her in her tracks. "Do me a favor?"

"You look way too serious. Name it."

"Don't tell me what you just tried to until the day we're married."

"Why?" Savanah's eyes grew wide.

"Because everyone who has ever said that to me has left me. My mother, my father, my sisters, all the freakin' people who are supposed to love you unconditionally. It's a load of crap, Savanah and I can't take you telling me it and then leaving me."

"Ethan?" Tears welled behind her eyes. "I'm not going anywhere. If I can't say it, I'll just have to find ways to show you."

"You were off to a great start this morning." He gave her a playful wink.

"No, we were off to one, and we still have the rest of the day to ourselves."

"Want to go speck a few places out for our wedding?" Ethan set a plate full of eggs and steak in front of her. "*Bon appetite*, my sweet one."

"Thank you," she managed to say with a mouth full eggs and a tight-lipped grin. "Join me? Have some fresh pineapple. You need it." Savanah devilishly shot her eyebrows up.

"What's the look?"

"You don't know about pineapples?"

Ethan shook his head no. "I did wonder why your fridge is always stocked with it."

With a slight giggle, she explained, "It alters the juices flowing from you. Makes everything on you sweeter than you already are. More palatable, if you get my drift? Want some?"

"My semen gets sweet? Hmmm... Guess I won't die today. Old saying goes, if you learn something new each day you won't die that day. And if you keep swallowing we won't get preggers."

Savanah handed him a slice of the yellow fruit. "*Bon appetite* back at ya!" Wiping toast crumbs from her lip she asked, "How'd you feel about it? I mean we only just met. Would a baby smother us at this point?"

"Funny you should ask that, Savage. Last week, if anyone other than you told me I was going to be a father, I'd have hopped on my plane and headed for the Outback. If you shoved one of those home pregnancy tests in my face today and it came back with two lines instead of one, I wouldn't run, but the little things..."

"Babies."

"Babies," he said with all his pearly whites showing, "scare the daylights out of me. They're so little and breakable and what happens when that new baby smell wears off?"

Cracking up, Savanah answered, "You give them a bath."

"I don't have the first clue what to do with one."

"Thank someone Raven really wasn't pregnant. I can't imagine you stealing a baby, Eth."

"Me either. I can't believe the Maestro hasn't sent a hit squad after me. Or had me dancing from a distance. It's got a feel to it, Savage, I can't place. It's like I'm waiting for the eye of the storm to pass, and then I'm going to get sucked up and whirled off."

"All right, lover, this conversation's going downhill fast. I'm the only one sucking you up. I'm going to brush my teeth and then you and I will go for a ride. We can check out the Hall of Springs, the Casino, and then our rose gardens. I loved your idea actually of the ceremony in the gardens. I'll be right down."

"Yeah, I've heard that before."

The kitchen was spotless and still no sign of Savanah. Just as Ethan opened the fridge to put the food away the phone jingled. He pulled the antique of a thing off its cradle. The phone had to be over a century old. He placed the black earpiece to his head and talked into the mouthpiece hung on the wall. Suddenly he felt like he'd stepped back in time. "Philly International. Whose up?" He answered.

The voice on the other end of the phone paused.

"*Hello*?" He sang into the phone.

"This is Sinsations. Is there a Savanah St. James there?"

"Can I help you? She's busy." Ethan decided upon discretion. No need telling some unknown his fiancé was in the bathroom leaking body fluids.

"We found a wallet here with her name on it."

Ethan scratched at the thickened gel in his hair. "Thank you. I'll be right out to pick it up."

"*Bring her to me*."

"What? Who is this?" The hairs on Ethan's neck launched from their follicles with more accuracy than missiles taking to the sky.

"Sorry, Sir. We need her. Our policy."

"We'll be over." Ethan hung up the phone in a new pissy mood. And to top it off, he thought he was hearing things. The man's tone… The man's words… *Bring her to me?* "Did he really say that?" He *was* hearing things.

"Who called, Ethan?" Jovan asked, leaning against

the doorframe entrance to the kitchen.

"Good morning. The restaurant you went to said they have your daughter's wallet."

"That's funny. Savvy doesn't carry her wallet anywhere if I'm with her. Never has. Get used to it."

"How else would they get it?"

Jovan tossed her hands in the air. "I suppose she could have carried it in. Did she call you while we were there? Maybe it fell out of her purse."

"Nope. No phone calls. Her phone's in pieces anyway, and I was busy meeting your husband and his clone's sense of humor."

Jovan smiled, a big wide grin. Ethan did a second take, when he saw how similar Savanah's smile and her mother's were. And that's where the similarities ended. André's genes made up ninety-eight percent of Savanah. Jovan's two percent contributions were her female anatomy and her smile, both of which Ethan could have kissed Jovan for if he thought he's live to see another day.

"I heard about your nap during the game."

Her hand covered her mouth, but Ethan heard her giggling regardless. "Yeah, you and all of Saratoga by now."

"I'm sorry."

"You look sorry." Ethan smiled this time at Jovan.

Jovan backed away, annoyance clearer than the nose on his face.

"Did I just do something, Jovan?"

"No, Ethan. It's me. You and I got off to a very bad start."

"That was all me."

"Yes, it was. And from what I'm told it was also

that other vamp."

"Ah yes. The one you don't want mentioned. Jovan, I swear, I'm going to rid him from our lives."

"You do that and I'll walk my daughter down the aisle to you. And quite possibly I'll even smile." Jovan glanced back at him as she walked out with a well-maintained poker face. "And don't look at my ass."

A grin spread across his lips. Ethan sat there on the stool trying to figure her out. He wasn't certain if she was trying to be cordial on barest-of-bones of extremes or if she still loathed his very presence. Making him forget all about his soon to be mother-in-law, Savanah walked right up behind him, slid her arms around his neck, covered his eyes and kissed his cheek.

"Hi, you. Miss me?"

"Hi back. Yes. Your mother and I just spent some quality time together."

"And look at that—there's no blood anywhere, and you're still breathing." Savanah teased.

"Funny. Hey, yesterday, did you take your purse into the restaurant you had lunch at?"

Savanah scrunched her face into a crooked disarray as she thought it over. "Possibly. Why?"

"The place called and said they've got your wallet."

"Well, I guess I took it in, but Eth, ya know what— I have no need for one. I'm broke. But hey, if they've got it, let's go get it back. I'm just going to tell everyone we'll be gone for the day. Meet you in my car?"

Ethan backed Savanah up against a wall. "Whose car?"

"I believe I said mine. Oh, look at this, I've even

got the keys!" Savanah did a little victory dance, bumping her hips into his pelvis. She dangled the keys under his nose.

Wearing the grin of a hungry lion, just before he pounces, Ethan shackled her.

"Ethan...I don't think it's in your best interest if you—"

"Put you over my knee? Oh it is, Savage. The car's mine, little nut." He tangled with her as he sat on a stool and got her across his legs. He slapped her bum once, playing with her.

"Mine, you big oaf. I won it fair and square." Another pat and she was laughing like there was no tomorrow.

"You and your sentinels swindled me."

"All right, I give. I'll let you drive it *today*. Feel any better?" She peered around him, her face pink her eyes leaking happy tears.

"Oh, thank you. See if I let you in the next 'vet I buy."

"You will. Because I look extremely hot sitting next to you."

"Personally, I like you sitting on me."

"Easily arranged." Savanah peeled her body from Ethan's lap and stood up.

"You're so beautiful." Ethan cupped his hand to her cheek, his thumb brushed her flushed skin. "Come on. Let's go find us a place to get married. Lucky for you, I've still got money. I guess lunch's on me."

"I'll lick it off you if it is."

"Music to my ears, sweet cheeks. Let's ride."

Chapter Fifteen

"Savanah, really, can we put the top up? It's gonna downpour, and we're going to get soaked, not to mention this baby will get wet. Please?"

"Eth, the sun's shining, its eighty-two degrees and there isn't a black cloud in this hemisphere. Stop worrying about *my* car."

Ethan's lip twitched. Whether it was to be a smile or a frown remained to be seen. "Can I drive? You said I could." Ethan put on his best *I'm-adorable-you-can't-resist-me* face with clasped hands in front of her.

Tossing him the keys, she hopped over the door and slid into the seat.

Ethan dropped to the ground gasping.

She called back to him, "Come on, drama queen."

"That's king to you. Buckle up," he chirped as he too jumped into the car, slid the key into the ignition, turned it and closed his eyes in rapture as the engine came to life.

Savanah's jaw dropped. "You just got off, didn't you?"

"Keep it between us, okay? Sliding the key into the snug slot and giving it a little twist made me think of you this morning when I slid my cock inside you and gave you a little joust side to side and your engine revved up beneath me and left us both out of gas. That's the hottest feeling, Savage, knowing I can turn you on and have you purring beneath me." Ethan blew her a kiss before he turned the wheel right and peeled out of the driveway. Destination—Saratoga Lake. "First stop, your wallet, then the state park? Did you tell your parents where we are headed?"

"Yes. Why?"

"Do you think now that I've given your Pops my blood a few times, he can read my mind and me him?"

"Try it. Can that other ghoul you're mixed up with do it?"

"Yeah, he can. So how do I get your Pop?"

"Try saying, 'Can you hear me now?'"

"Aren't you funny!"

"Crack myself up, actually. Someone has to!"

"All right, all right. Hey, André you out there?"

Savanah's smirk traveled the length of her lips and cheeks in a flash.

"Don't you dare laugh at me," he scoffed. She turned her head, pretending to look out the window, but Ethan watched her body shake through silent laughter regardless.

****

Sitting at the piano, playing Beethoven to his wife and her belly, Jovan said, "You're off key. What's wrong, Bebé?"

"Ethan brain-beeped me. I forgot he'd be able to do that. Is this a good thing or are we never to have a moment's privacy ever again?"

"André, look at me belly. In a few months you won't even remember the word privacy let alone your name. Answer him. Could be important."

Ethan, is everything all right?

"Shit, Savage, it worked. He answered me."

"Answer him back, Eth. You don't need to talk aloud to do this."

"Got it."

André. Just checking out the wiring. Guess it works. Sorry to bother you.

Just don't send me any viruses, and we'll be fine. Did you get to the Hall of Springs yet?

Ethan punched Savanah's arm. "This is so cool."

No. We're just crossing the bridge to retrieve Savanah's wallet. See you later tonight.

Tell Savanah Lucian informed us that the surgery is set for tomorrow and the children are indeed your ex-boss's grandchildren.

Wow! You probably shouldn't have told me that. Ignorance isn't always bliss, but it could save your life. Let's hope the nameless vamp doesn't ask me about them.

"The twins are Sinclair's." Ethan informed Savanah. He waited for some sign from his fiancé that the earth was going to come crashing to an end, or at least his life for bringing all this drama back into their lives.

Savanah said nothing.

"You okay with this?"

"You'll make it okay."

Ethan did the only thing he knew how. He hit the CD player's button and rocked the car with one of his favorite Dave Matthews songs, *Crash into me.* He reached across the tiny front seat and rested his hand on her thigh and attempted to do the 'let your fingers do the walking move' up her thigh with zero stealth. He grasped the zipper on her jeans, at the same time she latched onto his hand and squeezed. With a subtle shake of her head he found an instant pout.

"The faster you can get me to our destination the faster we can get home and those precision timed moves you were thinking of tuning me up with will have my engine purring better than a pussy. Now, dear fiancé, drive with intent and watch the road instead of me.

"If I get pulled over, it's up to you to change the officer's mind." He winked as the speedometer soared past absurd legal limits.

Savanah tied the scarf tighter around her wild dark curls, adjusted her sunglasses and returned a mischievous grin of her own. "What a sweet ride, Mr. Kitt. I may let you drive more often."

In Sinsations parking lot, Ethan glanced around. "Looks like a wild place."

"Wait 'til you see the inside."

"Hold up." Ethan pointed to the rear of the lot. "Isn't the mini coop your aunt's? Plates read 'Cooped up.'"

"Hmmm… She came back. Damn." Savanah waved to the valet as they passed by.

Ethan jammed the keys in his pocket. "Not on your life buddy."

The valet rolled his eyes.

As they approached the door to the restaurant, it burst open. Ethan looked at Savanah with caution.

"Ah, Miss St. James!" The man greeted her. "We've been expecting you. If you'll join us."

Savanah glanced to Ethan out of the corner of her eye, flashing him a warning sign. The moment the man placed his hand on her shoulder goose bumps formed and just as quickly ducked for cover. Sweat seeped from her pores and her mouth went bone-dry. A quick glance at Ethan proved he didn't appear any better. Savanah watched a blond beard sprout quicker than a child's dough machine could push one out. *Keep it together, Eth.*

I'm fine. My five o'clock shadow came five hours early, that's all.

"Do I know you?" she asked the doorman her tone guarded.

"No, Miss St. James, my name is Jacob. I'm one of the bouncers." Jacob shied away from the direct sunlight coming through the door. "The boss said you'd be coming and to look out for a gorgeous tall woman. He even showed me your license photo so I'd know who to look for."

Vanity struck, Savanah let down her guard. "Oh jeesh, not that old photo. It's a mug shot really. Doesn't even look like me. Feels like it was taken a century ago." She glanced at Ethan and winked. "Pathetic really," she rambled.

"No, Miss, you're much prettier in person."

Savanah took an instant liking to Jacob. "So, if you'll just get me my wallet, we've much to do today."

"Lunch is on the house today. Boss said so himself."

"Eth? You hungry?" Savanah rubbed her tummy. "The food is excellent."

"I love your appetite, woman."

"Have a seat and your waiter will be over with menus and drinks." Jacob started to walk off.

"Jacob, excuse me. You didn't happen to see the woman I was with yesterday come in did you? Her car's in the lot."

303

"The other pretty woman with jet-black hair? Yes, she's with the owners doing some business."

"Would you show her to our table when she's done?"

"Yes, Miss."

"Wonder what type of business? Wink, wink, nudge, nudge."

Savanah bit her cheeks and dug into the breadbasket. "Dear God, don't tell me. Another Eric Idle fan?"

Ethan answered her with another wink, wink, nudge, nudge.

****

Three hours later relaxed in their chairs with an empty wine bottle and a full stomach, Savanah watched people file in to the club, each dressed to the nines in short skirts, skimpy tops, spiked heels, spiked hair, spiked jewels, pretty much spiked everything. The men looked like models from *Play Girl*, all pretty toy boys. Ethan could've been the cover to that magazine a hundred times over. Savanah took one good look at her wardrobe and cringed.

"Eth, we gotta go. Look at them and us."

"You're beautiful. Who cares if you have the same holier than thou jeans on that I first saw you in? Your toenails are pretty. Your hair's done and if you were to take off the outer shell you threw on over your tank top you'd be good to go." Ethan bent down to her feet, and slowly skimmed the length of her leg to her shoe. "And what's this? No flip-flops? You wore grown-up, spiked, ankle-breakers making yourself at least three inches taller than me. Yeah, baby, I noticed." Ethan kissed her ankle. "Let's go dance and work off a few of our drinks." Ethan stood and extended his hand.

"Lead the way." Her other hand on the handrail for balance just as her aunt had the previous night. The music shimmied its way through her feet, up her legs, down her arm and resonated in her chest. It was one of the things she loved about rock music, the intensity and pounding, the way it made her feel alive—part of the music itself. She watched people sardined onto the small dance floor grinding, swaying, tangoing, some really out there, dancing to the beat of a different drum altogether. With that she could identify.

Ethan pulled Savanah to him, her back against his chest and he wrapped her in his arms. He had to have her touching him. He couldn't explain the need, but the moment she touched him, everything in his universe became symbiotic. His chin on her shoulder, he thought back to their first night together at the House of the Blues. He yelled in her ear, "Not quite the same is it?"

She yelled back, "Why? Just because I haven't passed out yet or vomited on you? The night is young, my love." She turned, angled her face to his lips then puckered up and made kiss-kiss noises.

Ethan laughed and squeezed her tighter. "Oh, my little nymph, I want to make love to you right here. Right now."

"Who's the nymph?" Savanah yelled a second after the song ended. All eyes on the dance floor momentarily focused on them. Some bowed, others cheered, "Just do it."

"Savanah, you turned a delicate shade of red." Grabbing her cheeks between his hands, Ethan cupped her face and met her lips with his in a soft kiss as they danced.

Savanah tightened her arms around his back and ran her fingers under his shirt, exploring. That was all it took for him to wind up rock hard. He rubbed his fondness for her into her tummy.

She broke away from his kiss and offered, "Shall we ditch this place?"

"Not so fast, Pippy. Anticipation is a beautiful thing. Dance with me. Slowly."

Ethan nudged his way through people, Savanah's hand in his as she trailed behind. He checked out his surroundings, watched other couples on the floor loving each other, some in the same fashion he loved Savanah, others in a most peculiar manner, body-slamming into one other, almost to the point of fighting. Others still, were concealed in darkened corners huddled together being sucked on and bitten…by vamps. Ethan wasn't too worried. Being surrounded by vamps for the past few years he knew most weren't killers, just thirsty.

But just to be on the safe side he sashayed Savanah away from them. Once they had enough room to move he brought her close to him, wrapped one arm around her back and his other hand, he rested inside her back pocket. He bumped her purposefully during their dance to remind her they had unfinished business to attend to at some point.

Sooner rather than later.

With each bump and grind, Ethan grabbed her derriere a little harder, his fingers cupping her. He pressed his erection harder into her Venus and watched a mist glisten on her. Dirty dancing had its finer points. He wasn't sure whether this was one step short of torture or one step closer to heaven, because all he could think about was taking her down on the floor, right here and doing it. Yeah, the idea of an audience intensified the fantasy. When Eiffel 65's, *Too Much of Heaven* played, and she began to sing to him his fantasy almost blew the top off his hot air balloon.

Her voice was that of an angel, soft, flowing, sexy as hell and doing things to him he had zero control over. He stopped dancing and watched her mesmerized, the graceful sway of her hips, the soft curve of her breasts slipping under her silk tank top, her nipples peeping through the material begging for his attention, and the radiance her blue-jeweled eyes dazzled him with. Before the song ended, Ethan hoisted Savanah in the air and had her legs wrapped around his waist headed for the first vacant room with a couch, desk, anything he could take her on. Never—ever had this much raw passion possessed him. This woman had turned his life upside down and fast. In less than one week he'd done two things he swore he'd never do. First comes loves, then comes marriage, then comes the baby…

Topsy freaking turvy!

Savanah's head on Ethan's shoulder, her legs securing her body to his, she slid back and forth in a seductive tease against him. Her nipples pressed across his chest and the fire he ignited in her made its way between her thighs. He definitely had the anticipation thing right.

She closed her eyes as she moved with Ethan's body, and continued to sing to him. Ethan's touch caused an insatiable itch wherever she offered herself to him. She raised her arms above her head, her hands clasped together swaying with the music. She opened her deep blue eyes and smiled. So badly, she wanted to tell him she loved him, but he'd asked her to wait. So, instead, she continued to sing and put up with the aching in her heart.

If she couldn't tell him, she'd show him.

Chapter Sixteen

Opening the door, Ethan found the room pitch black. No windows, no light switch on the wall and no one home. *Perfect!* Ethan felt like a young boy with his first girlfriend sneaking off to cop a feel, only this was different. This wasn't some cheap thrill; this was the luxury of love.

"I'm going to make love to you now, Misses. No guarantees on how long I last. You're killing me, baby." Ethan had her pants undone and down around her ankles in the blink of an eye. His disappeared even faster.

"Eth, where are we? Kinda spooky in here."

"You afraid of the dark, my beauty?"

"No. It's just eerie. Isn't there a dungeon down here somewhere?"

"A what?"

"A dungeon, Mr. Kitt. Miss St. James, I suggest you pull your panties back up and then your pants. The same for you Mr. Kitt. The owner of this establishment isn't very fond of people having conjugal visits in his office unless he's the one being visited."

Savanah's heart, she was certain beyond a reasonable doubt, stopped. She fumbled to get dressed. Ethan helped her, then dressed himself. Neither one said a word, both mortified.

"Descent yet?" The tapping of a pencil or pen on a

desk could be heard.

Savanah," Ethan whispered, "Run, baby, and don't turn back."

Savanah shouted, "Like hell! Not without you."

"Neither of you are going anywhere so if you're both dressed there are few people dying to see you."

When the door to the room reopened Ethan shoved Savanah through it so hard she fell on her hands and knees. Not by any means what he'd intended, but with adrenaline flowing and werewolf strength, he wanted her safe.

Standing on the other side of the door a man waited. Well, not exactly one hundred percent man, more like ninety-nine percent mutant... Savanah strained to focus as the giant's tentacle-like hands gripped her and brought her to her feet. She opened her mouth to scream yet nothing came out. Oh, how she hated when shit like this happened.

The ogre resembled a Redwood tree, solid. And yes, she decided, if he fell alone in a forest, someone would hear him. The earth would shake. Savanah's first thought was the baseball leagues were spending way too much time worrying over their players using steroids. This thing was probably bottle-fed the life-altering drugs.

Savanah looked into his red snake eyes and could not look away. She'd never encountered anything like *it*. He appeared part reptilian. Taking in the spiked gray teeth, yeah they fit right in here. Probably venomous, as well. And getting a whiff of his breath, she gagged. The fumes, she swore smelled like a neglected cat's litter box. Ethan yanked her back to him. Mr. Redwood followed, his hands suctioned on her.

"You're like a fucking leach."

"Savage? Get your filthy paws off her," Ethan yelled over the loud music.

From behind them the strange voice ordered, "Release her, Angus. She is to be untouched…for now."

"She's to be untouched, period," Ethan interjected.

"Mr. Kitt, please silence your lips or I'll have them sewn shut. Thank you."

"Who are you?" Savanah yelled.

"Miss St. James, follow me please. I believe your aunt would welcome your company right about now."

Savanah turned in Ethan's arms. "Eth?" Her eyes filled with tears.

"Come on, Jeanie, don't do that. Blink your fears away." Ethan kissed her forehead hard, his lips glued to her praying she could read his mind now.

Behind Ethan stood the man who found them in the office. He too had snake eyes, red. Reddish-brown dreadlocks with purple highlights fell from under a skull and cross-bone's bandana. No shirt to speak of revealed six pack abs, biceps that put every gym junkie to shame. His jeans clung low on his hips showing off a tattoo or birthmark on his left hip.

Savanah tried getting a better peek at the tattoo, but the man saw her and with a subtle change in his stance made the tattoo disappear.

"Done devouring your eye candy, Miss St. James?"

"I am so on a diet! Besides, I've got my breakfast, lunch and dinner right in front of me." Savanah ran her hands purposefully down Ethan's body.

"Well then, he's going to be busy, because I do believe he's already on someone else's menu. You'll get left-overs, although I doubt there will be any other than gristle."

Done with this line of BS, Savanah called her powers and unleashed them on the man with a vengeance. A brilliant white heat pulsated from her eyes and slammed the half-naked man in the face.

He stumbled back off balance. After a deep breath he snarled. "You pack a rather good wallop. You're good, but it won't work on me. Or Angus. That's what the contacts are all about. Save it for someone else."

Instincts taking over and years' worth of self-defense classes, Savanah kicked her leg back behind her, the heel of her spiked shoe sinking through his pants into his flesh and popping Angus' private jewels. The sound twisted her stomach into a nasty knot.

Having become all-too familiar with the look on his fiancé's face before she vomited, Ethan stepped back.

Gone was her lunch as it covered the Red Oak. She didn't apologize. Savanah tugged to get her heel out of Angus' loins. "Embedded, Eth! *EWH*!!!" After two tries her foot came out of her shoe. Ethan reached around Savanah and ripped the shoe from the man's crotch, and handed it back to her. Shaking her head frantically, she prattled, "This is why I wear freakin' flip-flops."

It was as if having a three-inch spike driven into his genitals never phased him. Angus' wide grin displayed his gray, pointy, cusps.

The man calling all the shots casually explained, "Mutant."

"Oh, no kidding!" Savanah answered, tone dripping sarcasm.

"As I was saying before I was interrupted yet again, Miss St. James, these men were designed without the need for extra baggage for just the reason you tried. He neither needs nor wants sex nor does he need to defecate or urinate in the same fashion humans do."

Although she thought she had a pretty damned good idea she knew the answer—Angus' breath being a direct giveaway, she said "Do tell."

"He eats like humans. Everything moves through his digestive tract and then it's rerouted back up the same way it went down."

"He pukes shit?" Ethan's grimace gave away his disgust.

The man gave a nod yes and then hastily nudged both Savanah and Ethan toward the stairs, but instead of going up, they headed down two flights. "He isn't a vampire. His bite is designed like a cobras. He injects a poison into his victims."

André, get out to Sinsations on the lake. Now. Bring help.

Papa? We're in trouble. Help!

I'm on my way, baby. Talk to me. Let me know what's happening.

****

André was up and moving to find Duncan and Kyle. He'd known in the back of his mind this would happen. He knew—hands down—this day would come. Ethan was his catch twenty-two. His daughter's destiny came with baggage. Bad baggage.

Jovan followed on her husband's heels. "André, have you tried to contact Lucian? Tell him to abandon their ridiculous notions of splitting the two little spawns from hell apart." Jovan gave André a vehement glare, mad at the world for her daughter being placed in danger. Just as she went to reach for his shoulder an unwelcome pain penetrated her abdomen like a knife only sharper. Jovan grabbed her belly and doubled over.

André had her in his arms and on the couch before she knew what happened to her.

"What is it?" he asked, worry mapped across his face.

"I don't know, but it hurts like a mother f... Please get Savanah safely home to me."

André ran and grabbed a glass of cool water for her.

Lucian? You out there? Serina? Jonah? Grimmy? Come on guys. We need help. Now! André waited for a reply from Lucian and as he did, the sinking feeling he had in his heart smashed on the rock bottom abyss. For the first time in one hundred plus years he couldn't reach his brother through their mental channels.

Savanah? Raven? Ethan? Anyone?

Papa, What's going on? Some people are taking Ethan and I to what appears to be the dungeon in this place. Ya know what? It's looking pretty damn authentic from my point of view.

Savvy, for whatever reason, I can't reach your uncles or Serina. I'm beginning to fear the worst. You need to keep your temper intact. I know if you get upset, trouble follows.

Papa—already in trouble. Can't use the flash of light. Angus has contacts and so does bandana man.

What? Who?

Just get here before anything really bad happens.

Baby, I think the really bad thing all ready did. Your mother's getting sharp abdominal pains. I think she's experiencing premature labor.

Forget me and Ethan. Get her to the hospital. Now, Papa! You two have waited an eternity for these babies.

And, my sweet child, I've spent the best years of my life loving you. I'll not abandon you. Not now. Not ever.

André's heart fragmented. Torn between helping his daughter and his pregnant wife, if he helped his wife did he condemn his daughter and possibly risk her life? If he left Jovan was he putting her and their babies' health at risk? Praying for the first time since his change of life, he asked for guidance and strength.

Savanah, I love you. I will make it to the restaurant.

Savanah's head throbbed. Nothing he said made sense. He sounded like a radio that's tuner dial got stuck between stations. *Papa?* Panic welled. "Papa!"

Ethan shoved Savanah behind him and threw one punch into the giant's nose and crushed his fist upwards. The mutant's ethmoid bone crumbled easier than breadcrumbs. Angus staggered. The mutant went face first down like a ton of bricks. Triumphant, Ethan turned toward Savanah only to see bandana man with a knife to her throat.

"Impressive paws, Mr. Kitty. Guess that's one design flaw we overlooked. Thank you for pointing it out. Now as I said, proceed down the stairs or this will be your last good-bye. Miss St. James, screaming will do you no good. Your mind-to-mind channels have been disconnected. Granted it takes a few minutes to figure out the frequencies your family uses, but your signal has been dropped."

Mum? Are you all right? Please answer me! Savanah tried one last time to reach out to her family with no luck. Emotional overload, she passed out.

Ethan lunged after Savanah before she hit the ground. "Do you have a name?" Ethan yelled.

"Devon."

"Devon, before my fiancé and I leave this unholy place you won't be breathing."

"Pick up your wench and move."

With Savanah limp in his arms, anger blurred his vision. All of this happened due to his poor judgment. Had he not shown up on her doorstep attempting the unthinkable, kidnapping a child, she'd be safely at home with loving parents and family. Never mind mentioning Xier and his involvement in Ethan's life.

"Devon, who wants us?"

"Take care of your wench." Devon walked into a room not much bigger than a pantry and showed Ethan a cot. With the snap of his fingers, a teenage girl in very snug jeans sauntered in.

"Dylan, get some water and rags for Miss St. James."

"Why? He's only gonna kill her. I don't get what the big fuss is all about. And she's not as pretty as everyone keeps saying." Dylan twirled her lilac/lavender hair around her finger, and smacked her lips together on a wad of raw beef.

Devon gave a fallacious grin to the girl with cotton-candy hair. With a crooked finger he called the girl to him.

Ethan cringed. *Seen that look a thousand times on the Maestro, and it's never good.*

Ethan stepped back.

Dylan smiled as Devon approached her. He gently brushed the hairs from her neck and inhaled sharply.

Before Ethan's eyes, Devon's jaw elongated into something Ethan couldn't take his eyes off. Quentin Tarantino would've killed for the special effects for his movie, *From Dusk Till Dawn*. Devon's skin became a transparent-blue road map of veins. His fangs lengthened a good two inches before they stopped sprouting and with no warning and unfathomable speed, those fangs disappeared into Dylan's neck. Ethan watched his reptilian eyes shrink to slits as he sucked her dry. Her body convulsed in his arms until it didn't. When he finished he dropped her to the floor and kicked her aside.

"Get Miss St. James up and ready, Mr. Kitt." Devon exited the room, the door behind him locked.

"Pippy? Wake up. Baby, we got us a dead girl in the room. We need to find an escape hatch to get us outta here. Maybe we, all right you, can torch the place, set off the alarms and get the fire department here. Sweet cheeks, wake up." Ethan shook her limp body.

"And just maybe we'll all die down here, Ethan."

Ethan looked around the room. No one. He looked at the dead girl. "Did you say that? Please say no!"

"No, Ethan. I'm one cell over."

"Aunt Raven?" Ethan's voice squeaked.

"Yes. *Aunt?* Kid you got brass kahunas*.*"

"What happened?"

"It's a long story with a bad ending, Ethan. I am a giant ass. I've lost the two men in my life and now I've placed my family in jeopardy as well. How is Savanah? He hasn't touched her has he?"

"She's out cold. Raven, have you been able to reach any of your family?"

"No."

"Who's behind this madness?"

"I made it this far when I came to see Donovan this morning. My big plan backfired."

"What big plan?"

"I wanted him out of my life so I tried to stake him mid orgasm."

"Whoa! Where is he?"

"Below, in the freezer, healing."

Ethan closed his eyes trying to shake the thought when Savanah's hand flailed through the air into his cheek. The pain was instant.

Savanah looked up dazed. "Eth? You okay? What happened? Who hit you?"

"I'm fine," he said as he rubbed his face. "Babe, Raven's in the next cell."

"Cell?" Savanah spun around taking in the tiny, windowless room they were locked in. "Do I want to know?" she asked pointing at the dead girl on the floor.

Ethan shook his head no.

"Auntie Ray?"

Raven whispered through the metal bars in her door, "Peanut, listen, in a few minutes this guy's going to be back. When he does between the three of us we should be able to take him."

"One can only pray," Savanah answered.

****

With a body-curling screech, the doors opened and barrels of guns protruded into the cells. "Out," one deep raspy voice ordered. Three men pushed and prodded Ethan, Savanah and Raven down two more sets of stairs. Coming off the bottom step, the first guard jammed Ethan hard in his flanks with the butt of his rifle, forcing him off balance and into yet another room.

Savanah took one look at the guard, wearing the same pathetic outfit the valet had on, and silently whispered, *"Disintegrate pro mei eyes,"* before she had a chance to comprehend what the consequences of her words truly were. The phrase came from the book she'd gotten the day before she left England. She wasn't kidding when she told her mother the book's first chapter could cause someone to die from a broken heart…and then some.

A menaced glare shot over Savanah and Raven as the guard began to hyperventilate, one deep, labored breath after another. Steam blasted from his nostrils with the same intensity a pressure cooker exudes before it explodes. His mottled flesh bubbled and dripped like melted wax into one big puddle.

"Help me!" The guard screamed before his tongue turned into a glob of black jelly, and dripped in one long chunk to the floor.

"Doesn't he sound like some movie about a fly?" Raven giggled.

"Oh crap! I just killed a man. I'm a black witch now. I'll probably grow freaking warts too, only they won't be hanging off the tip of my nose—oh no—I'll end up with genital warts for this deed."

"He and Androgen man were related so it doesn't count, Savage." Ethan assured her. Looking between the dead guard and Savanah, Ethan realized at that very moment she could have the car, and anything else she ever desired from him—no questions asked.

The second guard turned a ghastly shade of blue and exited the room in haste. Guard number three wasn't the third wise man. Savanah pointed her finger toward him, about to give him the same fate when he grabbed Raven and yanked her to him.

Raven replaced her fingernails with talons, reached backwards and tore through his chest.

Raven—one. The guard—dead. The heart—writhing and squirting blood everywhere as she tried to hang on to it. Getting filthy, she gave up and tossed the defiled organ on the floor. Nerves shot, she giggled. "I might pick that up on my way out and pickle it. Serina's all ready got one."

"Shall we?" Savanah grabbed Ethan's hand and tugged him to move.

He didn't budge, his eyes fixated on the melted body and then the man's heart a few feet away. "Remind me to never piss you off. Either of you."

"Ethan, you were damn close the first day I met you." Raven added.

Ethan's green eyes went wide. "Auntie Raven, from the bottom of my heart, I apologize."

At the top of the stairs, freedom seemed only feet away when footsteps approached, fast. Savanah and Ethan turned. There stood Seamus between the front door and escape.

Ethan's hopes of a swift exile faded. "Savanah," Ethan whispered so low it was barely audible. "Run baby, and don't turn back. I'll stop him."

Hand on her hip, she countered, "We've already had this conversation."

Savanah's next breath caught in her throat when Jacob came up from behind and shoved her into Seamus' arms. From what seemed thin air, Jacob produced a silver garrote and snagged Ethan by the neck.

André, he…

With one quick jerk of his wrist, Jacob tugged the medieval torture device to end Ethan's air supply. Ethan hung in limbo before his head slumped to the side of his body.

Savanah's vocal cords bounced off the interior and exterior of the restaurant with pleas for help, but between the DJ blasting out tunes in the basement and the jazz band in the attic, she may as well had been in a soundproof room. Seamus secured his grip on her ponytail.

His pungent breath crawled across her skin. "One wrong move, Miss St. James, and it shall be your last."

"Eth, get up baby. You gotta get up. *Please?*"

Seamus pressed his lips against Savanah's cheek. "Shut up, foolish girl. I won't kill him…yet. First things first. Ingrid, get Raven back down stairs."

A woman equal in height to Raven with jet black hair and blue eyes, approached, a loaded harpoon gun aimed at her chest. "Give me a reason, vamp. You just give me one reason and the trigger's clicked."

Raven reached out touching her niece's hand in passing. "Show 'em Hell, baby, and then come get me." She turned to the woman ordering her around. "You should feel good right now. Today is the last day you'll ever be called an idiot. Or anything for that matter."

Seamus flagged his hand at Jacob. "Release him and take Savanah." Seamus pulled a round nickel finished, wooden handled gun from the inside pocket of his dinner jacket. He handed Jacob the weapon. Once Jacob secured his grip on Savanah, Seamus turned to Ethan. "Oh, Ethan, I missed this." Seamus took a knee and knelt over him, pressed his face to Ethan's neck and tore into him.

Coming to and trying to suck in huge amounts of air with a vampire attached to his neck, proved futile. It pretty much equaled having an elephant sit on your face and attempt to move. Ethan fought the vamp and lost on all counts. Seamus jammed a silver poker into his side. One wrong move, Ethan knew his life would end. Looking up and seeing Savanah being held at gunpoint put his adrenaline into overtime.

"Please, Seamus, let him go. He's done nothing to you," Savanah pleaded. When he smiled, and Ethan's blood spilled from his lips she uttered, "Once you awaken, the powers you have forsaken shall be taken. Blessed be to those holier than me. Your judgment day will arrive and you shan't survive." For a split second Savanah had the oddest of moments where she couldn't deny a connection to Draque. A queasy bile rose in her throat. She didn't understand anything and quite frankly, didn't have the luxury of time to figure it out.

Seamus stood, brushed off the dirt from his trousers and left Ethan on the floor, drained, white and shaking. "Stupid witch! Your little rhymes are child's play."

"Let her go. She means nothing to you," Ethan pleaded the same.

Seamus hollered, "Dylan? Have you no manners, girl? Please? Escort Miss St. James to her aunt."

"Dylan's dead. Some guy killed her." Ethan scoffed. "Or not!" He reneged as Dylan appeared absence of any personality, her motions methodical, calculated as if driven by someone else.

"So, Ethan, miss me?" Seamus asked.

"Can't answer truthfully without damaging that fragile ego of yours. It isn't polite to talk with your mouth full, Maestro."

Confused, Savanah said, "That's Seamus, Eth. Not the Maestro. Right? Oh somebody please tell me I didn't have a Sinclair with his filthy hands on me?"

"Meet my boss, Pippy. Maestro, meet my fiancé." It was the last thing Ethan said, before passing out from blood loss.

****

Hello?" André yelled at the top of his lungs. "My wife's gone into labor, and she's only twenty weeks along. *She's having twins!*" André carried a protesting Jovan into the emergency room. Duncan, Molly and Kyle followed.

A young man came to the rescue with a wheelchair.

Jovan shooed the man away. "I'm quite capable of walking if someone would put me down." Her anger rose like heat waves on sunny pavement.

"Hospital policy, Misses."

"Climb in, Cherié. Please? I need no further heart attacks."

A red-headed nurse in a florescent floral scrub set approached André and Jovan. Her tone soft and comforting, she asked, "Sir, why don't you go to the registrar's office and give them all your information, and we'll take your lady and get an exam begun. My name is Kathleen. I'm a licensed midwife. My nurse Joanne and I'll take great care of her and your babies. I promise."

As another contraction tightened around her abdomen, Jovan grimaced. "Go get Savanah. I'll be fine here. Molly will stay by me."

"How far along are you, Miss?" The midwife asked

as she typed every answer Jovan gave her into a computer screen.

"Twenty weeks."

"Age?"

Jovan hesitated. What did she tell her? The truth was definitely out. "Twenty-five, give or take a hundred years." She gave the nurse a crooked smirk.

"I feel that old sometimes too. I'd have guessed twenty. You hold your age well."

"Thank you."

"I'm going to do an internal on you and hook you up to a stress monitor. One for you and one for the babies to monitor their heart rates. Did your water break?"

Jovan shook her head no.

Kathleen explained, "Good. I'm going to hook an IV of Nalepsin to you. It's an isotonic solution of magnesium sulfate. Hopefully, it will halt the contractions. I'll have the lab do some other tests as well. Hopefully between the fluids, the medicine, and some rest we'll be able to stop this. At twenty weeks gestation, your twins would be in dire straits."

Attempting to put her best face forward Jovan grabbed André's hand when he returned.

"This IV is going to take a few hours so get comfy. I'll be popping in and out checking your blood pressure and these monitors. If anything at all changes, press this call button and people will run to you." Kathleen pointed out a small device she'd pinned next to her on the bed sheets.

"Oh, you're spoiling her. She's going to go home and expect a little dinner bell for her leisure after this." Duncan added as he leaned over André and kissed

Jovan.

Jovan gave a relieved grin. "Where's Molly?"

"I'm here, Jovie. Just getting a good book for the two of us to pass the time. Pick one." She held the books up for Jovan to see. "Love story with happily ever after, or a tragic tale of two lovers who found out they were siblings after she was already pregnant, and he'd killed his first wife?"

Jovan wrinkled her nose. "I don't need any more stress. Give me the HEA. You guys need to go get my big baby for me. Now, please?" With that said a steady stream of tears fell.

André ducked to Jovan's belly. "Hey, you two, knock off whatever it is you're up to in there and let your mother be. Stay put. I love the both of you and can happily wait the next four months to meet you. Understood?" André kissed his wife's belly twice and then moved to her lips. "I love you, Jovan St. James."

That's when his own tears started, and he couldn't stop them. "There's nowhere on this earth I'd rather be than by your side, raising our children. Where you go is where I go. I'm going to get our other baby now and give you your happily ever after. I don't care what the hospital policy is, leave your cell phone on vibrate." Trying ever-so-gently to lighten her mood he tucked the phone between her thighs. "Think of me if it goes off." André kissed Jovan one last time with a little umph behind it and left. He didn't turn back. He knew if he did he'd never be able to leave her.

Chapter Seventeen

"Son of a bitch!" Savanah screamed at Jacob when he shoved her back down the stairs she'd just come up. Her jaw dropped when she caught a glimpse of the contents of a dungeon room for which the door had been previously shut.

"That's all my bloody relics. That's all my stuff. How did it get from the museum to here? Stop, for the love of God!" She gripped the handrail, her knuckles now white and burning.

Jacob pulled up a step behind her, his breath hot and heavy on her neck.

"Ewh! Get off me!" She shoved him back and sent a little zinger through him to show she meant business. She focused on a wooden table in the center of the room and from there her eyes slowly glanced upward. Her stomach knotted and she wished she hadn't looked. A pendulum hung above the table. Damned thing looked awfully authentic. Deep grooves were gouged into the table. The crimson-stained blade had chips missing. Savanah tried frantically not to think about a person being severed in half, but the more she tried not to, the clearer the vision became. Magic shows came close, but without all the carnage.

To the left of the meat slicer, a casket stood vertical, the cover open. Silver spikes lined the inside of the box. Savanah decided she really wouldn't want to have to lie on top of those for an eternity. Then she decided that just might be the point.

A small, silver, razor-wired birdcage dangled from the ceiling like a lethal ball of yarn. Inside sat a platform just wide enough for a pair of feet. The height—Mini Me would have had to squat. Savanah could no longer focus. Overload on the brain…about to be thrown into a cell—hopefully not the room in front of her, her mother going into premature labor with the gloomy possibility of losing her babies, her boyfriend—out cold upstairs with the one man on the planet her entire family loathed and the icing on her cake—not being able to reach her father. *Think Savanah, keep it together. When all else fails, use the gifts God gave you.*

She turned to Jacob ready to charm the pants off him if need be. Not hers though.

"I found that." She pointed to a second casket secured by silver chains. *Wonder where the chains came from?* "Can you guess who owns it?" She pointed to the side of the black casket. "See the gold inlaid initials VTD? Stands for, Vlad Tepes Dracula. His casket is forged from pounded iron. Weighs a freakin' ton. It's lined with mink. Bastard, killing all those animals to surround his scrawny ass. Did I say scrawny? It's not. Trust me. Seen it, been bit by the demonic thug," Savanah prattled. She wet her lips on purpose for Jacob as he ogled and listened with a new found interest.

"The skull is a rare find. 'Tis a mix between a jackal and a human. How much fun could that mating ritual have been? Total bestiality, baby. The mandible is longer than humans. See the teeth? Double rows of dents…"

"Dents?"

"Fangs. Sorry, I'll use little words. See the smaller razor sharp canines inset? Nastier than a piranha and stronger than a bear's. The nasal passage is interesting. The opening is so miniscule that the beast barely required air. Kinda goes hand in hand with being dead, don't you think? The huge iron lattice cage is designed to fit over a casket. Keeps vamps in if they're fortunate enough to escape their first casket. It's a second layer of protection. And what girl couldn't use a little extra?" She batted her eyes at him and ran her hand down his arm to the gun.

Jacob clicked the safety on the gun and dropped it to his side.

She took a deep breath and relaxed a notch. The longer she could prolong ending up in a cell, the better her chances of getting the hell out of there were, without killing anyone else.

Savanah placed her hand on Jacob's shoulder, her fingers played lightly with the hairs on his neck. "The other casket has a mummified vamp. Her carbon tested back two thousand years. She is perfectly preserved and put up one hell of a fight. The original stakes are still in her. Her fingers were severed, as were her feet. Her mouth was wired shut so she couldn't bite anyone. Her eyes gouged out so she couldn't see and her ears removed so she couldn't hear. If we were to remove her stakes she'd come to life because her head and heart are intact."

Jacob added. "It's awful, the things they do to us. I can't believe I'm a *one of us* now. One week now."

Savanah noticed how uneasy Jacob appeared, nor

could she blame him. "It must be hard, Jacob, being a normal teen, then your life is stolen from you and you're given a whole new set of rules and values to live with. You were probably just settling into the ones your parents brought you up with. It's not easy, but you'll adjust. You see the cherry table with the books?"

Jacob nodded.

"The one with the flattened black rose trapped between the pages is *Dracula,* by Bram Stoker. It's autographed by both the author and the vampire. Had that little treasure in my grasp for some time before I handed it over to the museum and then Xier, or as you call him Seamus, swiped it." Savanah sighed.

"What's the gold cup all about? Seamus allows no one inside that room."

"Thank God." Savanah let out another sigh thinking just maybe she wouldn't be looking out from behind bars. "The golden cup has quite the history to it. It is Dracula's. As ruler, his punishment for criminals, tyrants and armies against him, was to impale them with a long stake. Be it their heads or their entire bodies. He was known as Vlad the Impaler well before he became Dracula, the vampire. In his village crime was taken seriously. As a show of faith to all, Vlad left his gold cup in the town centre next to a well for anyone traveling or thirsty to drink from. Bacteria and viruses weren't on the top ten list back then. It was the one thing that was never stolen. He swore whoever stole it would end up a human shish kabob."

"And you swiped it from him?" Jacob's eyes went wide. "Do you have a death wish, lady?"

"No! It was actually a gift. That was sent to me a few months ago with a note that said, 'Have a drink with me some night you little witch of a thief.'"

Jacob's jaw dropped. "How did he know you stole all his stuff?"

"Jacob, he's the Godfather of vamps. I used to believe he was the procreator 'til I found my *hear no evil, see no evil, speak no evil mummy.*" Savanah pointed to her mummified vamp. "He tried to blow me up in New Orleans last week. He knows where to find me."

"Think he'll come here? Can I meet him?"

Jacob had an unhealthy curiosity. "Let's hope not. Would you willingly invite the devil into your home?"

"Savanah, I think the guy I work for upstairs is the devil. His son changed my life last week and my girlfriend's and then he disappeared without a trace. Haven't seen Howdy Doody since."

"Does he have anyone else around that's blood tied to him?"

"Don't know. Trying to figure me out first and worry about everyone else after."

"Smart thing to do. Ya know, Jacob, not all vampires are bloodthirsty."

"I thought we need blood to survive?"

Savanah rolled her eyes. "Let me rephrase that. Not all vampires are murderous, leeches that get off torturing innocent people. Your new boss falls into the latter category. How would you like it if I got you out of here and showed you a better way of living with your new life?"

"Tell me more. I'm beginning to feel like an indentured servant."

She didn't bother to tell him he hit the nail on the head.

****

After a loud crash and a series of thuds and cracks, Ethan lay limp at the bottom of the stairs like a lumpy welcome mat.

"Oh, my little wolf. What am I to do with you? I've treated you better than any of my three sons and look how you repay my kindness."

If this was repaying kindness Ethan didn't want to see him pissed. Certain he would hurl any second; he turned his head toward the voice. What's a little body fluids between friends?

His head, he was positive, was about to hatch the world's largest egg. After that, a quick body part check seemed in order. He touched his face, and his fingers came away warm and sticky. Something was cracked open. Explained the headache. He wiggled his toes. They worked so he figured his legs weren't in pieces even if they hurt like he'd been run over by a truck.

About to say something, he instead spit a few teeth out. "Maestro, my two front teeth are missing. Could you get me a glass of milk to put them in until I get to a dentist?"

"Ethan, if I allow you to live you'll know what to ask Chris Cringle for Christmas now, won't you."

"If it's all the same to you, humor me?" Rancor saturated his words.

"That's what I love about you, Ethan, your optimistic view on life even when the glass has a gaping hole in the bottom. All right. What type of dog does Dracula have?"

Ethan gave him a blank gaze.

The Maestro laughed. "A blood hound, Ethan. What? Lose a few teeth and you lose your sense of humor too?"

"Maestro, let the women go, and I'll stay. Whatever you want. Please don't hurt them."

"The love-struck martyr. Ethan, we have a predicament here, son. I send you after a baby and you come home with a babe. Not quite the same thing now is it?" Seated two steps up from Ethan, the Maestro put his feet atop his body, then dug his heels into Ethan's ribs. "Tell me where my grandchild is. Xanti may be a moron, but I know for a fact I'm a grandfather. I can feel the lifeline calling me. You will tell me, Ethan, and would you like to know why?"

"Waiting with baited breath."

"Yes, it is rancid. I met a woman a week ago in Saratoga. She came looking for you. Gorgeous creature really. Tall, thin, long, curly, blonde hair, a tattoo of a Celtic cross with yellow roses entwined on her mid back and the greenest eyes I've seen since yours."

Ethan vomited.

The Maestro rubbed his palms together. "I see I've hit a nerve or two."

"Where is she? I'll kill you myself if you've hurt her."

"She looks exactly like you, Ethan except she's got a pussy instead of a prick. I didn't know you had a twin."

"Where's Edan? What have you done to her?" Ethan's leg snapped when he tried to stand.

"Shift to heal your leg, boy, and I'll skin you alive. You had every intention of staking me. Did you forget that I still can read your infantile mind?"

"Where is she?" he screamed until his voice withered to nothing.

"Safe for now. Scout's honor." Maestro made an "*X*" across his heart as he chuckled. "Cross my heart and hope to die. Oh dingle berries, Been there and done that. Ethan you slept with the enemy, boy. How am I to trust you now?"

"I'll tell you where the kid is. Just let the women go. All of them. Savanah, Raven and Edan."

"You are precious. Pick one, Ethan. Pick only one and I'll allow her freedom."

"I'm no one's judge and jury. Neither are you."

"Then by not choosing you condemn them all." The tall, distinguished vamp stood, smoothed out his linen pants and motioned Dylan to him. "Get rid of the trash." He pointed to Ethan.

****

Ethan, can you hear me? We are outside the restaurant, but there's a hitch, literally, on the door. We're locked out and you're locked in.

Not a good time, André. Place is bugged, especially me. Anything you say can and will be used against you. Case and point—the babies.

Does he know where they are?

Not yet, but I'll give them up in a heartbeat if it gets the women out. How come I can hear you, but Savanah can't?

Wards have been placed. Guess they didn't realize you and I would be allies. What's happening?

André, we're buried in a load of manure and no one's coming out smelling like roses. It was his last thought before getting conked on the head.

****

Olivia entered the maternity ward, acting as if she belonged to someone there; the doting grandmother.

She smiled as she passed new parents. She told them they had the most beautiful babies. No need to burst their bubbles or tell them Elyza was indeed the most beautiful baby. It just went without saying. Tapping an impatient well-manicured nail on the nurse's counter she asked, "Jovan St. James, please?"

One woman, with dark hair hanging in her eyes, looked solemnly at her. "Are you her mother?" she asked.

Olivia pictured Jovan's mother rolling over in her grave with her answer and for that she sincerely apologized. "Yes. Can I please see my daughter? How are the babies?"

"Her contractions have gotten stronger. If they don't stop you'll be a grandmother in a few hours and your grandchildren will have one hell of a fight for their lives on their hands."

Heartsick tears filled her eyes.

I did not spend two days in that woman's body humped over her bed with no food nor rest to have these babies die. Now...do I tell her the truth about the book and my powers or do I plead the fifth? Thinking back to the fateful moment Julian thought he'd taken her powers, she certainly had done her best acting job to date.

"Give me your dominant hand," he'd said. She gave him her right hand and with no further ado, he took her powers away. Or so he thought. She mumbled, "I'm a south paw, Julian. You should do your homework better."

Olivia stuck her head in the room. Jovan's casual elegance had been replaced by raw adrenaline and fear.

"Jovan?" Olivia tiptoed past Molly.

"How did you know where to find me? Did you hear me call to Serina for help?"

"Yes, for a lack of a better explanation." The truth be known she'd felt the babies distress. Going into their mother and saving all their lives earlier left her with a direct tie to the twins and Jovan. She didn't bother telling any of them that little tidbit. "Look, Jovan…"

Jovan cut her off, "I know you are left-handed, Olivia."

"Call me Livvy? Please? I believe we are past formalities."

"Livvy, if I'd thought you were seriously still capable of evil I'd have told Julian the second you placed your hand in his. Can you save my children?"

"Only one way to find out. Wake Molly and have her stand guard. If the nurses come in and see me slumped over your bed they'll either cart me up to intensive care or the morgue, where I by all rights should've been many moons past." Olivia grabbed Jovan's hand. "My word to you. My heart for theirs."

Jovan frowned. "Isn't that what Julian said to you?"

"Semantics, dear. Let's get to work."

****

Serina? I need to speak with you immediately. Get home.

Mum? What's happened? We just landed at Albany Airport,

Serina, get home. Yes, there's trouble. Get Lucian and his entourage to Sinsations and you need to get to the hospital.

Why?

Jovan is in labor. I'm attempting to calm the twins

down and stop this process, but I need help.

Serina grabbed Lucian's arm. "Lucian, when you evanesce can you take people with you? How fast can you get me home?"

"Fill me in on the way."

****

"Jacob, we need to get my family out of here. Can you get the keys to the cells?"

With a simple nod Jacob disappeared.

Without him glued to her side, Savanah realized she didn't like being alone. Hidden in a tiny alcove, she watched Devon drag Ethan into the cell next to Raven. She wanted to run to Ethan in the worst way, but she needed a plan. Running in blindly would only make their situation worse. *Could things get much worse?* Her father's favorite line came back to haunt her. *Don't ask if you really don't want to know.*

Peering in through a trap-hole on another door, Savanah noticed a woman with blonde hair face down on a cot. Her wrists and ankles were bound by zip-ties. Her hands and feet were deep purple and she wasn't moving. Savanah wasn't certain she was even breathing. Behind her Jacob gave a little jingle of the keys. She jumped.

"Sorry," he said earnestly.

"Not your fault. I should be more aware of my surroundings." Pointing to the door she asked, "Can you get it open? Do you know her?"

"Yes and no."

Savanah looked at him blankly. "Huh?"

"Door's open. Go in and I'll stand watch."

Savanah stopped in between the door and the hallway; the mouthy voice in her head screamed, *set-*

336

up. If she went in to check on the lady all Jacob had to do was slam the door behind her. She motioned him in first.

Hands thrown in the air, he barked, "You don't trust me. I don't believe it. Look, Savanah, if I wanted you dead you'd look like her." Jacob pointed to the blonde. "I want the hell out of here and you're my ticket."

"Fair enough, but Jacob, if you trick me so help me, I'll make payback worth my while. One more dead vamp or mutant won't tarnish my soul." Savanah covered the distance to the woman and put her fingers on her neck praying to find a pulse. "Holy mother of God. Her neck is sliced open better than something some ex-pigskin tosser could have done, might have done, probably did do and bloody well got away with!" Shaking the blood from her hand, Savanah looked at Jacob with fury controlling her deep blue eyes. "Is there anyone else trapped down here?"

"One more woman. Savanah, I hear footsteps. I'm going out into the hallway and looking like I'm doing my job. I swear to you I'll unlock the door."

"No!" Savanah pleaded as she lunged for the door. "Please don't lock me—" The door latched shut. Her fingers through the bars she rattled the door and with defiance whispered, "—in. Jacob, I'm going to kill you when I get out of here. This is the second time today I've been locked up with a dead woman. If she comes back with a disposition more pissed off than me, it'll be your misfortune because I'm telling her you did this to her." Savanah sat in the far corner hoping against the odds Jacob would keep his promise and more important, that her roommate stayed put.

"Jacob!" Dylan approached. "What are you doing?" Dylan moved to look into the cell, but Jacob turned and stood in front of the door.

"Just locking up." Jacob dangled the keys at her.

"Where's the too tall St. James chick? What cell is she in?"

About to scream in her defense that she wasn't too tall, Savanah bit her lip and allowed Jacob the opportunity to either sink or swim with her trust.

"She's back up on the second level by the dungeon. You look like crap Dylan. Why?"

"Devon got thirsty, and I looked like a cool glass of tomato juice. Devon wants the St. James bimbo. Wanna go watch her die?"

"No."

"Coward!" With a sharp turn and whip of her hand through her hair, Dylan disappeared down the corridor.

Chapter Eighteen

Footsteps approached. Raven sat up. "Savvy?"

"Not quite, Beauty."

Raven did a double take. She rubbed her eyes to clear the image. "What happened to you—Donovan? You know, other than my attempt at your life." Raven gave the man a heinous grin.

"Not quite what you're used to seeing is it? Not quite the same man."

"Oh, you could say that again—but don't. Spare me the halitosis." Raven walked a half circle around Donovan and as she took in his new appearance she found her heart beating ridiculously fast.

"It's time you and I had a chat. A real heart to heart."

"The conversation shall be lopsided then since only one of us has a heart. What exactly happened to you after I staked you today? You don't look well." Raven sat down on the lumpy cot.

"You ran a steel blade through me, Raven." He snarled. "A direct blow. What did you expect? You've seen the movies after a vamp gets his due. He fizzles away and goes out screaming." Donovan did a slow spin and showed Raven what he looked like without all his glamour and magic he'd used each and every time he'd bedded her.

"I'm going to be sick. You look exactly like—"

Raven leaned over and heaved.

"Were you about to say Xavier? Didn't he ever mention me? Not once? Your brother was his roommate in college for four years, Ray. Really? Not once?" Donovan sighed as he sat beside her.

Raven couldn't talk if she wanted to. "Ha-how? Why?"

"Let me tell you a story, Raven. It began a long, long time ago in a land far away. My identical twin brother met a gal and fell for her. She pretended he was dirt and walked all over him. When he tried to tell her he loved her she ripped out an eye and tore off one of his balls. "You're a little rough in the sack, Ray.""

"He raped me then tried to eat me alive."

"Everyone has different ways of showing their love. How's André and his new change of life these days?"

Realizing what she'd done she was certain God would strike her down any moment. "Oh no! I handed my brother over to you on a silver platter. And you killed him. You freaking killed my brother." Guilt left her heart bleeding better than a hacksaw could have.

"That's the face I wanted to see. Thank you. Yes, he was a delicacy…succulent and juicy. You've just made the past one hundred years of my life worth every dreadful second. You're about to get a makeover, Raven. Here," Donovan shot her a manila envelope. "Think quick."

Making no attempt to catch it, the envelope landed at her feet. "And here I thought you were a baseball fan. When I return I want you naked and in these."

"Die already!"

"Oh Ray! Just open the damn envelope. This is one

surprise I want to see with my eyes."

With trembling hands, Raven ripped through the enveloped and looked at Donovan horror-stricken. Turning away from him she vomited her soul onto the floor again.

"How did you get these pearls? Xavier stole them from me the night he tried to kill me. How did you get these? Was it you that tried to kill me? Not Xavier?" She yelled backing away.

Donovan snickered. "It's our little secret, okay? Lucian killed the wrong guy. I body snatched Xavier that night at the university he came to you. His body, my brutality. He'd never have hurt you. The fool loved you. Even the night Lucian killed him, he was sputtering gibberish about his love for you and you cut off his fucking head."

Raven realized he was actually more insane than his dead brother. "So everything was a complete lie? The story about me turning you, too? Does Ethan know you're a Sinclair?" Raven fought the tears. Right now she was so mad and confused that if she cried…well she wasn't going to. Not over this demon.

"I really enjoyed the sex if that's what you're worried about. You're better than a seasoned whore. Kudos, Raven St. James. Not many women can achieve that honor. I'm going to eat you alive in front of your family tonight. And no, Ethan knew naught of my name." With unsound speed Donovan grabbed Raven's arms, and twisted them behind her back and pinned her face down on her cot.

Dylan yanked the door open to the cell, the harpoon shooter pointed at the cot. "Hey," she yelled. "You told me I was the one. That you were just gonna kill her. That it was me you wanted."

Donovan inclined his head toward the door, yelling, "I am going to kill her, Dylan. After I've had my fun. Get out!"

"Over my dead body!" Raven screamed.

"That's in the works, Beauty, but for the love of Lucifer, shut up." Donovan threw a right fist into Raven's jaw. He stood and in a blur hovered in front of Dylan, holding the weapon she had seconds before.

"Why is it men always hit women in the face?" Raven shoved past the two of them, rubbing her jaw, aiming for the door only to have her foot snagged mid-air by Donovan. Landing on her hands and knees, he leaned over her, and she kicked backwards and hit his nose squarely. The weapon skidded across the floor. She crawled toward it. Dylan lunged for Donovan her fangs visible.

Donovan swatted Dylan off him as if she were an insect and watched her spiral to the floor. He followed her, grabbed a handful of her purple hair and crushed her on the cold cement, as if she were a cigarette butt.

"Hey!" Raven shouted.

Donovan lifted his head and glared into the lethal end of a harpoon aimed between his eyes. He looked past Raven, a malicious glint in his eye. "André, so nice of you to join us. You're just in time to kill your sister!"

Raven swung around an unprecedented one-hundred-eighty degrees. "André?" Raven set her sights on the silvery-blues of her brother and scratched her head.

Donovan ordered, "André, take the gun from Raven and then stake your beloved sister."

"Beauty, give me the gun please?"

Raven handed the gun over and walked out of the cell. "When did you get back in town?"

Lucian cocked his head to one side taking in everything and everyone. "Not soon enough, apparently."

Donovan screamed, "Stop her! I command you!"

"Donovan, of all the time you spent with André and myself, pretending to guard us, did you never once notice the only difference between us is our eye color?" He didn't wait for an answer and proceeded to unload the stakes into Donovan's heart with deadly accuracy.

Dylan tried to skirt around Lucian. "I was trying to help Raven. I swear to Gah—gah—god." Her arm extended, to keep him at bay.

"Then when you meet him—Gah—god, be sure to tell him you're sorry for lying." Lucian aimed the gun once more and pulled the trigger. Mercy? He had none. The force of the harpoon sent her backwards and staked her to the wall. Lucian turned to his sister, dropped the gun and held her. "Jesus, Beauty! Did he hurt you? I thought I saw a freaking ghost when I walked in."

"Xavier and he were identical. Luce, he body snatched Xavier."

"Go. Julian, Jonah and Ands are up a few levels. I'll be up after I finish this deed and you can tell me all of it."

"No, I have to finish this, Luce, otherwise it'll never be over for me." Raven approached Donovan's limp body and rummaged through his pockets for a pack of matches. Finding her treasure, she opened the little book with the logo, "Sinsations ~ a little slice of Hell."

More like the porthole, she thought. Raven tossed

the tiny torch on Donovan's body and walked out.

Lucian asked, "Where's Savanah and Ethan?"

"I'm here," Ethan answered, his voice barely audible.

Lucian walked one door down, grabbed the handle with one hand and slid his fingers between the bars on the door and one giant yank later tore the door from the hinges. Taking a good look at Ethan, he told him, "Shift and heal your leg. Double shift if you've got the strength."

Ethan squeezed his eyes shut, grunted and within a blink blond fur replaced skin and the broken bones mended before his eyes. "Where's my fiancé? Lucian, my sister's here. The Maestro kidnapped her. My leg's better."

Lucian helped him stand. "You up for this?"

Ethan didn't answer him already headed for the dungeon after reshifting. Seeing Savanah pinned down to a table, nude with black leather straps anchoring her to the table was the beginning of Ethan's demise. Seeing Devon undoing his trousers and watching them drop to the floor was the last straw. Ethan fought wildly to run to her, but Lucian picked him up by the back of his shirt and hoisted him off his feet.

"Hold up. Julian's on the other side of that door. As is her father and Jonah. "Gotta get all our eggs in one basket. Then crack them. Trust me? She can handle this for a minute."

****

"Look, Devon? I realize you were raised amongst the underprivileged, scum of the earth, but rape is wrong. Astronomically wrong. We won't even mention murder, but did you have to kill Jacob?" Savanah prattled, "I have every known disease. Herpes, had a break out just yesterday. Totally covered with big juicy blisters."

"Me too."

"Shit. You so don't want a piece of this." Savanah cranked her head around taking in her room. "You really don't want to get on this table with me. Holy mother of God—is that the same birthmark I have? Oh my goddess. No way. No freaking way!" Savanah screamed, seeing the exact same birthmark that every member of royal lineage held in her family.

"Hello, dear cousin. Nice of you to notice. Yes, my mother was Devona and I was raised by a nest of vamps. So this is going to make us truly kissing cousins."

Devon's snarl had Savanah's stomach in a giant knot.

"Still got an itch, witch? We'll knock it out of you from both ends. You want top or bottom, Devon?"

Don't pass out Savvy, she told herself. *Live first. Do as much damage as possible*. Savanah struggled to see where the voice came from. It, the *nasal-drone* voice, was supposed to be on the flip side of the pond.

"Hello, Princess. Miss me?" Radcliff walked around the side of the table, and ran his fingers up the length of Savanah's body.

"Savor that little delight, Radcliff. 'Tis the last time you'll ever touch me."

"Radcliff, do you mind?" Devon asked his tone pissy. "Little busy here. In the midst of a family reunion. You can have her after I'm finished."

Savanah hissed, "Oh my God, stop! May *vestri fingers quod penis putes*—"

When her words registered, Julian yelled, "Savvy, no!" at the same time Devon covered her mouth hard, crushing his palm into her lips.

"You recited a black charm. What did you say?" Livid, Devon spit in her face. "How could you do this to your own flesh and blood?"

"Holy crap! Are you serious? You're insane. Look at the bleeding position you're ass is in. How could you?" Savanah's evil grin matched her mood. "You'll find out soon enough. I got most of the charm out."

Devon went to point a promising retribution in her face when his index finger burned red then turned to gray ash and dropped to the ground the way a cigarette does when it burns. With each breath he took, more of his fingers disintegrated and fell to the floor like filthy snowflakes. "What have you done to me?"

Savanah added, "That's just the tip of the iceberg, you cowardice rapist."

****

Before Radcliff could cry, *Uncle*, André pinned him inside the spiked casket, and pressed the door closed for all he was worth. "You obviously have no clue what five hundred ridiculous yards is, Radcliff, so I just showed you. You need some tweaking with your wish list, Crypt-keeper. It's not what you wish for, but how you wish for it. You said you wanted a piece of Savanah's exhibit, well here it is, boy." André leaned back against the door forcing it to remain shut.

The air in the room dropped twenty degrees instantly when the Maestro entered.

Lucian walked in behind him, rubbing his arms. "Seamus Xier Sinclair, aka the Maestro. We finally meet. Hello, Peanut. Get you undone in just a sec, luv.

You okay?"

"Little chilly, Uncle."

André removed his shirt and threw it to Lucian as he continued to lean into the casket like a garlic press making Radcliff into a juicy, mess. As he aerated Radcliff he sang, "My name is André and I should've been king, but since I can't sing they won't let me wear the bling… Second verse, same as the first—everybody join me to drown out this pitiful lecher's squeals."

"Gentleman, if you don't mind?" Lucian turned to cover Savanah. He mouthed to her, "No worries. Well except your father's lost it."

Her look said otherwise.

Caught between Lucian and André, the Maestro squared his shoulders. "So I finally meet the two men responsible for murdering my son. Tremendous! I'll get two for the price of one."

"Maestro, let's make a deal." Ethan stepped in front of his boss.

"Ethan?" The Maestro spread his arms wide.

"It's not really what I can do to you. It's what I can't do." Ethan turned and released the leather buckles holding Savanah captive. "I cannot allow this. You asked me to choose." On his way to the dungeon, Ethan saw a dead blonde woman he assumed was his sister. He'd wanted to rush to her aid, but there was nothing he could do for her now. Later he would come back and give her a proper goodbye. Savanah, on the other hand, was still very much alive and screaming for all she was worth. Raven was free and told him she was going to call the authorities. "So, I'm choosing to free the love of my life. You will allow her freedom."

"Ethan, your deal expired. And you shall too,

soon."

"You know, Maestro, how you saved your trump card for me? Here's mine—Donovan's burning to a crisp as we speak. Tell me you can't smell that heavenly scent of burnt flesh permeating the stench of this sham of an establishment." Ethan held up the string of pearls Donovan had given Raven and with a hard jerk, broke the beads open. The little balls bounced, rolled and scattered across the floor.

"No!" He cried. "It's not possible." Tears of blood ran from the corner of the Maestro's eyes.

"Dammit, a Kodak moment, and we've no film, Eth." Savanah jumped off the table, as she yanked her father's shirt snug around her waist.

Ethan pointed to the exit. "Go with your aunt and wait for the police."

"Not without you."

André shook his head. "Please, baby, get away from here. I can't lose three children today."

"Papa?" Savanah crossed to him.

"Peanut, go, please? I can't—"

With her father choked up and worried sick, Savanah felt stuck between a rock and a hard place. She didn't want to make the man have a complete meltdown, but there was no way in hell she was leaving here without her family.

Devon's struggle to get dressed with only nine...no, make that eight, seven, six fingers, left Ethan's jaw hung open. Each time he counted down another phalange fell off his hand. Ethan picked a dagger up off the table and aimed it at him, willing him to take one more step; wanting him to.

Raven stuck her head into the room and yelled to

André, "Catch." She tossed him a crossbow.

"Are you serious, Raven? A crossbow? Are we stuck in the middle ages? I want a god-damned gun," he yelled.

"It's a dungeon, brother. Work with me." Raven shrugged her shoulders.

With his index and middle finger, Lucian pointed from his eyes to the Maestros'. "You and I, now. Here." Fangs bared, a snarling match began. Both men circled one another, neither losing site of the other as they twisted and turned in an oddly choreographed dance. With unfathomable speed and one cold, hard spin-kick to the back of his head, Lucian stumbled, face first. The Maestro straightened his stance, ready to strike again. On the ground, Lucian swung his foot hard and fast into the back of the Maestro's legs, to bring him eyelevel to him. Both men scrambled to their feet. Beside them Ethan and Devon were on the ground in a free-for-all throwing punches, kicks and bites. Blood, clothing, fur and fingers covered the floor.

Devon's.

Taking aim, André locked the sights on Devon and released the trigger. Hearing a whizzing noise intensify the closer it came, Devon ducked. The silver tipped arrow struck Julian's leg. In that moment all fighting stopped and all eyes were upon Julian.

"Uncle Julian?" Savanah whispered her face contorted with pain seeing his leg impaled.

André yelled, "Grimmy?"

Madder than hell, Julian yanked the stake from his leg without batting an eye. "This insanity has to stop." He stood to cross the room and slipped backwards hard and fast on pearls. Arms circling like a bird trying to take flight, he became snared on the razor birdcage.

A tap on his shoulder to get his attention back on him, Devon turned to meet Ethan's fist.

"You were going to rape my fiancé." A second blow and Devon's jaw snapped sideways. "That's a death warrant where I come from. You don't touch a woman until she consents. Did you hear her say *Y-E-S?* I didn't. Did you say yes, Pip?"

Savanah shook her head no. "That ignoramus is my cousin, Eth. Long lost cousin. Wish I'd never found him. He should have rightfully been king."

"I still will be." Devon spat.

"I think not," Ethan answered. Devon became intimately aware of the phrase *out cold* with one strategically placed right hook. Ethan hoisted then strapped the unconscious man to the very table Savanah lay trapped on minutes earlier. With the flick of his wrist, he set the pendulum in motion. "Ta, Devon."

Savanah almost had Julian untangled when the Maestro reached out and grabbed her. With his free arm, he swiped the gold challis and stuffed the treasured artifact into his pocket then fled with Savanah kicking and screaming. André and Ethan were on his heels.

The Maestro yelled, "Back off, boys, or she's dead."

"I so need a bath," Savanah muttered. "Let go of me." She stomped hard on the top of his foot and head butt him with the backside of her skull, hoping to break away. Ethan lunged for them, but fell into thin air with the Maestro's stealth. He immediately got up and followed.

Chapter Nineteen

"Jules? Let's go!" Lucian pointed as André, Ethan and the Maestro fought over Savanah like she was a *piñata*. He yelled a second time, "Come on, dammit. It won't be candy that spills from her if they split her in half."

In the blink of an eye the lot of them disappeared in thin air. Lucian tore Julian free from the barbed ball and evanesced before he could protest. They went through each floor of the establishment only to come up empty handed. Bursting through the doors like two cowboys getting tossed from a saloon, the two men landed in a parking lot crowded with vehicles. The PEON's took up most of the space. The news crews were there too, cameras fixed and lenses dilated on Lucian's exit from the establishment. Officers converged on the two men like dogs to bones. Lucian prayed for all he was worth the wards were no longer working and their mind-to-mind frequencies were up and working.

Jules, I'm disappearing. I'm not leaving, just disappearing.

One officer removed his glasses, cleaned the lenses, then rubbed his eyes. "Sir, are you all right? Did he bite you? Are you contagious?" He asked as he drew his gun on Julian.

"For the love of God." Julian grabbed the revolver and jammed it up the man's nose. "Dumb fecking twit!

351

Count your blessings I'm in too much of a hurry to deal with yet another ass." Hearing a thunderous commotion, Julian shoved the now crying man to the ground and headed to the shoreline at the lake where he found Savanah hysterical. She was pointing to a speedboat careening across Saratoga Lake and André was struggling to hold her back.

André tightened his grip on Savanah. "Sinclair had a blade to Savvy's throat. Ethan charged him and took the brunt of the blade into his abdomen. The blade was pure silver." André looked hopeless. "Sinclair shoved Savanah to the ground, picked Ethan up and fled. They're in that boat right now. Where's Lucian?"

A man in a blue jumpsuit, his face shielded by a helmet carrying a backpack loaded with weapons scurried passed them in haste, got down on one knee, took aim at the boat with what resembled an RPG (rocket propelled grenade) and launched the missile.

Seconds later the ground shook. A fireball of scorching heat seared across the lake and exploded with an aftermath of debris raining down on everyone.

Savanah broke free from her father and did a running dive into the murky water before the last pieces of debris hit the ground.

"Ethan!" She swam a good one hundred meters before arms grabbed her. Fighting for both her life and Ethan's, she turned around in the water fists plowing into an officer's nose. "Don't touch me," she screamed. She filled her lungs and disappeared beneath the surface, headed for the sinking wreckage.

A second pair of arms caught her but didn't relinquish their grasp as she was reeled up. Savanah turned and even though she saw Julian, she fought.

"Get off me, Uncle. Let me go. Help me." A wave of gasoline and oil slapped her in the face and left her gasping. The combination of fear, exhaustion and adrenaline quickly took its toll. She went under again and had trouble wading. "Please, go get him back?" she begged as tears spilled down her cheeks and mixed into the lake, vanishing, just as Ethan had.

"He's gone, Peanut." Julian tread water beside her and held her afloat until the police boat swung up to them. "I'm so sorry."

Back on land, shivering and numb, Savanah watched the boat Ethan was in vanish with the same disappearing act the Titanic did. Her knees gave out, and she dropped sobbing, mad at the world. André followed. Savanah looked at her father and asked "Why Papa? Why did Ethan have to die? I don't understand? You told me the good guy is the last man standing. Papa, he was good. I love him. He can't be gone." Savanah hiccupped and passed out.

A man in a dark black suit with PEON embroidered on his jacket's lapel emerged from the restaurant carrying a woman draped over his shoulder. "I found one more," he yelled. "Get me a paramedic. She's still alive. She's in rough shape. Been raped and beaten. This place has a dungeon down stairs. Some guy was secured to the table about to get sliced in half. I let him go."

"Fuck!" André called out, "I need another stretcher. My daughter's passed out. Her fiancé was on that boat. And the guy you unleashed was behind all of this chaos. Good job!"

The ride to the hospital sobered him. André promised Jovan her happily ever after, but instead he was bringing his daughter in as a patient because Savanah went into shock.

Approaching Jovan's room, André heard Jovan's laughter. Sticking his head in the door, his wife had a cup of tea in front of her. Molly slept in the bed next to her and Serina sat in the chair with her feet up on her bed, Elyza in her arms.

"How're my babies?" André asked. He sat down beside his wife and leaned in for a soft kiss.

Serina answered, "Fine. Hopefully you won't be seeing them for a few months. They got tied up in each other's cords and started fighting. One thing led to another and here we are. The operation of the conjoined twins never happened. The people that have them freaked last night when someone tried to break into their hotel room. They fled with no further word of their whereabouts."

"Serina, how did you and Luce know where to come and what was happening? We lost contact with everyone." André glanced between his wife and Serina, suspicion plastered all over his rugged face.

Serina swallowed the guilt gurgling its way up her esophagus. Did she tell André her mother was once again inside his wife and children? At least they were in a hospital if someone got hurt! That slice of optimism was her saving grace.

"Cell phones. Everyone has them these days."

Jovan pulled hers out from between her thighs with a little grin.

"Where are Lucian and Savanah?" Serina asked.

Hesitation in any situation is sure death. Obviously, André took a split second too long to answer.

"Out with it." Jovan ordered through clenched

teeth.

Before he was done explaining, André was wheeling Jovan down the hall to her daughter's room.

"Oh, André, how could this happen? I scryed and saw them together. How? Why?"

"I don't know, *Cherié*, but he gave his life for her."

"Where's Lucian?" Serina asked trying to keep pace with Jovan.

"He had to disappear for a bit. He's in no danger."

"*Bebé*, how do we help our daughter get over this?"

"Time and our love, my *Cherié*."

****

October 10th

"Savanah! André! Serina! Julian! Jonah! Lucian!"

Sticking his head out his bedroom door at two in the morning Lucian asked, "Jovan, how come I'm always last on your list when you call people?"

"No time for funnies, imbecile. I've sprung a leak. Please get your dead-beat of a brother up and moving."

Jovan waddled past Lucian in a way he was positive pregnant woman couldn't move—unnaturally fast.

"Savanah?" Jovan stuck her head in her daughter's room. "You awake?"

Rubbing her eyes and looking at her clock, she answered, "I am now. What is it?"

"You ready to meet your new brothers or sisters?"

Half asleep Savanah threw on a pair of flip flops and a pair of Ethan's baggy sweatpants. She buried her hair under her Yankees cap and ran down the stairs to her parents' room.

"Whose driving?" Savanah asked.

"I am." Jonah answered in passing as he went to bring the car around.

Jovan skidded to a halt in front of Jonah. "Absolutely not. I can see it now. We'd get pulled over for speeding, and I'd deliver these two in the backseat."

"'Tis only fitting dear, sweet sister. Isn't that where they were conceived?"

She snatched the keys from his hand and gave them to Savanah.

"Don't take it personally, Jonah." André yawned. "How far are your contractions, my Cherié?"

"If they're much closer there will be no need for me to get into the car and get to the hospital. Answer your question?" Jovan shoved her little overnight bag in her husband's arms.

"I'll get the car warmed up, Mum. Where's Duncan and Molly?"

Julian mumbled, "Europe ring any bells? They left two weeks ago."

****

In the car waiting for her mother and everyone else, Savanah surfed the radio for an upbeat song then twisted the button off immediately after hearing the one song that stole her heart, *Let's get it started*. She remembered Ethan's cockiness as he looked up to her, his green eyes so alive and so full of mischief. Just thinking of him hurt. For a brief moment her memories brought him so close, she could taste his kisses. Swiping at tears as they trailed down her face, she licked her lips, only to taste the bitter reality she was alone. Her heart ached; she was positive it would shatter soon if she didn't get her life back, but what was left? The one and only love of her life was dead, blown to smithereens in Saratoga Lake.

"Fish food, Savvy. He's freakin' fish food. I'm sorry, Ethan. I love you. I never got the chance to tell you. You bastard!" She pounded her fists into the dashboard until her knuckles throbbed. "You wouldn't let me and now you'll never know. Oh God, just take me now." Savanah wiped away her tears, blew her nose and put on the falsest smile she could muster when the car door opened.

"Baby, that look is all wrong on you. If you want to cry then by the gods cry. You can sit in the labor room with me, and we'll both have a good drenching and no one will be the wiser." Jovan pat her daughter's hand. "Now get me to the damned hospital."

****

All Hallows Eve

From her bedroom, her elbows propped up on the windowsill, Savanah watched the snowflakes sift down from the heavens thinking they resembled her heart; small chipped pieces of ice lost in a vast, bleak existence waiting to melt away. A freak storm. *And why not,* she thought. Everything else in her pathetic existence had turned one-hundred-eighty degrees opposite to the sublime. Savanah realized she'd missed summer and most of fall. Life had become a *dull-drag-her-ass-out-of-bed-only-if-she-had-to* existence. She got up to eat, pee, vomit every other morning and shower when she couldn't stand the stench another second and then retreat back under the safety of her covers, hiding from reality not monsters. The monsters were easy enough to kill off. Reality scared the daylight from her. Every now and then she'd glance into her mirror and not recognize the starved, lonely woman with a blank expression staring back. Daily, she waited for any sign it was time to get back into the swing of things, but alas, no winged angel slapped her in the head and told her to get her ass back out with the living. Nothing changed. Ethan was gone and her cancer-like-loneliness spread throughout her body, killing her one little cell at a time.

The silhouettes from the rose garden of leafless, thorny, rosebushes resembled skeletons crawling from a grave. "Beautiful view, Savanah."

Hours from now in that very garden, she was supposed to be marrying the love of her life. Instead, she would attempt to put her best face on and try not to break down into a million pieces in front of her family. They didn't need the stress of worrying, and she didn't want the attention.

She yawned, her eyes tearing, and she went back to bed.

****

Jovan paced by Savanah's room trying to kill two birds with one stone. Calm Rylea down and wake Savanah up. Neither of which were working. The baby cried, and Savanah slept like one.

André met Jovan carrying Rian. "Come on, wake her up. It's two in the afternoon. Besides some package just arrived for her."

"What is it?" Jovan asked eyebrows raised.

"I didn't open it. It's not mine."

"Did you at least shake it? See if it's breakable?"

"And if it is—break it? No, *Cherié*." André chuckled. "It is on the counter."

"Who sent it?"

"You're a nosey little woman."

"That's not all I am, André." Jovan got a hair's distance from his mouth and ran her finger across his bottom lip. "I miss these warming my flesh."

The door to Savanah's room opened. André flipped on the switch and set Rian down beside her in the bassinette.

"Good afternoon, Peanut."

"Is it?" Savanah asked, rubbing her eyes.

"Will you watch these two for your mum and me?"

"Do I have a choice?"

André grabbed Rylea from Jovan and set the little girl down beside her brother. He wrinkled his nose to his daughter as he closed the door.

Savanah sauntered over to the bassinette and peeked in, her nose catching some nefarious odor. "Your Papa's a sly one all right. Okay, which one of you left me a present? Probably both of you, right? Is that why they dumped you two on me?" Savanah picked up Rylea and hugged the little girl to her chest. "Good morning, my little squeaker." Savanah kissed the blonde beauty with the blackest eyes she'd ever seen and traded her for Rian. She found out fast where the odor came from. "You're the devil in disguise." Savanah turned away from the diaper. "You've a healthy appetite, don't you?" Savanah got the little blond boy with light blue eyes like his mother's cleaned, powdered and rewrapped. Feeling confident in her parenting skills, she grabbed them both and headed to the kitchen.

"Morning, Molly," she said in passing.

"Get back here with at least one of those babies, Missy."

"Pick one." An impish grin spread across

Savanah's face. Molly went to grab Rylea, but Savanah twisted from her. "Nope. Try again." Molly went after Rian and Savanah did the same thing, teasing. "Sorry, Molly. I just love them both, and they're both being so good. I promise, when one starts to cry they're all yours."

"Savanah St. James, it's a blessing seeing that smile of yours. Been way too long."

Eyeing a raspberry pie on the counter, Savanah passed Rylea to her. "I can't hold babies and eat."

"Then pass me Rian," Raven offered as she sauntered in at a snail's pace, her pregnancy weighing her down.

Savanah plunked a big kiss on her aunt's cheek. "Morning, Aunt Ray, how you feeling?"

"Fat and miserable, thank you. You?"

"Mostly alive." Savanah gave a half-shoulder shrug.

"Are you going to open the box staring at you on the end of the counter?" Raven waddled to it, inkling her head toward the mystery present.

"It's probably a razor and since I've given up shaving my legs?" Savanah yanked up a pant leg to show she wasn't kidding.

Raven blurt out, "Dear lord, girl, you're hairier than Julian."

"Shush." She turned to walk to the fridge when a strange tug at her heart gave her pause. She coughed to clear her throat, but still, something was there—lodged. "May I?" She hastily swiped Rian's bottle of milk, unscrewed the nipple and chugged it.

"That's breast milk, Savvy. What is it? What's wrong?"

Savanah's eyes watered. She pat her chest hard a few times trying to shake the idea her heart really did break, physically. Savanah eyed the box on the end of the counter and swore she could hear a heart beating! *Thump-thump…thump-thump…*

Savanah aimed her index finger toward the box. "I'm going to go. And that box is going in the trash. Now."

Savanah picked up the box and the room went black.

****

"Miss St. James, you have something I want and I have something you need. Shall we make a trade?"

"Where am I? And who am I talking to?" Savanah floated, wearing only her birthday suit in a room with windows everywhere. Bright, warm, light blinded her. She spun in the air, her hair free-floating above her as if she were suspended in a pool of water, weightless.

"Physically, Miss St. James, your body is on your kitchen floor. Your family is trying to revive you as we speak. Metaphysically, welcome to my world. Please tell me you haven't forgotten me so soon. I introduced myself to you in New Orleans."

"Where are my freaking clothes? Am I dead? Did I just have a heart attack? I died from a broken heart, didn't I? Why isn't my heart hurting right now? I feel nothing other than cold."

"Do you really want the answers?"

"I don't know. Do I? What the hell is wrong with me? Why am I so cold? Please tell me why I'm naked. Oh crap! Can you see me?" A sudden case of self-effacing panic shrouded around her. Trying to cross her legs proved impossible to do in her current state of void. She was neither here nor there, but she was both.

"You are in between life and death right now. I believe I heard you say a few times now you, 'just wanted to die.' Do you really? Choose your words wisely, Miss St. James. What caused you to give up on life?"

"Did my Papa get me drunk again? Am I dreaming? If I am dreaming I want Ethan not some voice asking me annoying questions, giving me another question in place of an answer."

"What is it about Ethan you would choose death to be with him now?"

Savanah tried scratching her head. That movement alone stopped her. She couldn't feel her hands or head or anything other than an insatiable itch she couldn't reach. She looked down. Her body lay crumpled on the floor with her Aunt Raven screaming and her Uncle Jonah doing CPR. "He has my heart, Ethan. I handed it to him on a platter. He kept me safe, made me feel beautiful and loved. And I wanted him to feel the same way."

"Miss St. James, I'll say it once more. I have something you need and you have something I want."

"What?"

"My book."

"Are you the vamp that bit me?"

"What do you think?"

"There you go again answering me with a bloody question. I'm finding this whole conversation a bit too surreal. If I say yes than I'm talking to Dracula in the nether-world. If I say no I'm certifiably dead."

"Why didn't you open the box? Where were you headed before you dropped off the face of the earth?"

"Just so you know? That doesn't have a nice ring to it. To answer you, I was going to the store to tell the woman I no longer need my wedding dress. Been in denial since Ethan died. I just haven't had the heart to cancel it. I guess I really don't have one now do I?" Savanah laughed. And just as quickly she stopped. "Is this purgatory?"

"No. Purgatory is for sinners. Your soul is pure."

"But I melted a mutant. Oh, and Devon's fingers. Not sure if his penis is still attached. He stopped me mid-charm."

"Your soul is safe. The beings you destroyed were mutants, just as Androgen man. As for Devon, the jury's still out."

Savanah found a peculiar smile working its way to her lips. "Are you really Dracula? How are you here?"

"Believe it or not, I have friends in high places, Miss St. James. Life really isn't all black and white, nor death. I must tell you, when you were in New Orleans, your Ethan did something to me that no man has done in at least three hundred years of my soulless existence. He restored my faith in man. He did nothing but go on and on about you telling me he'd die to save you. He kept his promise. He said he'd go willingly through the gates of Hell if I allowed you safe passage. Do you remember fighting me in New Orleans? You said the exact things your Ethan did even after only knowing the man a few days. That is why I released him and that is why I had to see you once more and give you this option. Now, for the last time, do we have an accord as your uncle says?"

"What deal? Am I really making a deal with the devil?"

"Pretty damn close. Trade with me."

"What do I get?"

"Your heart's desire."

"Okay, then why does my heart ache again?"

Chapter Twenty

Serina jumped inside Savanah's body as soon as she heard the screams from Raven and Molly. She found nothing at all wrong with her niece. She was as healthy as a horse—well with the exception that she'd turned a putrid shade of blue, had no pulse or respirations…and died!

"Savanah? Please, Serina—save her." Jovan knelt beside her daughter, blindsided by tears. Her hands shook as she touched her daughter's clammy face. "André," Jovan choked, "This isn't happening. Babies aren't supposed to die before parents."

André wiggled his daughter's toes. "Please don't leave me, baby," he whispered. "Please, Peanut, don't leave your papa."

In the far corner of the kitchen Julian was sheet white, except for the red eyes from crying. Lucian stumbled to him and hugged him. Duncan, in no better shape, walked in between both men and held on. Jonah sat on the floor next to Raven, with his arm around Savanah's legs.

****

With all of her family gathered around her in the kitchen hysterical, Savanah wondered what possible atrocity brought them together this time? "What's going on? What did I miss?"

Jovan gasped and passed out. Savanah sprung up

from the floor as if she not about met her death and rushed to her mother's side.

"Mum?"

No one moved, other than all eyes following her.

"Hey! Mum passed out. What's up with you guys? Some help?" Savanah yelled.

"Peanut? Are you okay?"

"I'm not the one down for the count," she yelled louder as she cradled her mother's head in her arms.

"She's fine, Savanah," Serina answered. Serina grabbed a cool cloth and washed Jovan's face. Jovan came round and smiled as if she'd been given back the gift of life when she saw Savanah.

Serina added, "You, on the other hand, Missy, died on us."

"Aunt Serina, did you screw up another spell?"

Julian answered, "Death, the final frontier, the pearly gates?"

"All right, Rod Sterling, now I know you're pulling a fast one on me. I feel fine except my chest hurts."

Jonah told her, "Because I did chest compressions on you."

Savanah inspected each and every member of her family waiting for one of them to admit this was a giant hoax. Awkward silence filled the kitchen. "My God, you're serious."

Serina nodded yes.

"Holy cow! I knew my heart ached—unbearably for the past months, but death? Guess I better be more careful what I wish for." Savanah's eyes were drawn to the end of the counter. The box struck a raw nerve. She grabbed the container and a pulse wave shot up the length of her arm making her gasp. Julian stood beside her before she finished inhaling.

"What is it?" Julian reached for the box.

"Don't touch it, Jules." Savanah opened the box with caution keeping her head far away just in case something popped out.

So slowly, André piped in, "Much longer and I'll be the next one dead." That comment immediately followed Jovan elbowing him in his side.

Inside the container sat a black lacquer box with a soured aroma permeating the area. Savanah shrieked, "It's a heart!" and dropped the box on the floor.

Spilling like a broken wheel, the rotted organ tumbled unevenly to Raven's feet. She stepped back faster than she'd moved in months.

"What sick psycho would send you a heart and better yet, whose is it or was it to be more precise?" Jonah asked.

"Open the other box, Savvy." Duncan pointed to the larger of the two boxes.

"Not really sure I want to, Duncan. Body parts weren't on my wish list this year unless it came in one package, healthy and breathing and looked and acted and sounded exactly like…" Savanah stopped and chomped on her cheek. *Ethan…*

A piece of parchment glided to the counter while her anger shredded the brown paper. Eyes fixed on the contents, she pulled out the golden cup. Covering her mouth didn't stop the scream that squeaked its way free.

Jovan tugged at Savanah's jeans. "What's the paper say?"

"Have a drink with me at midnight in the garden of Eden."

"What the hell?" André scratched his head. "Where is the garden and who wants to drink with you?"

Savanah explained, "The Maestro swiped this cup before he fled Sinsations. I saw him pocket it. I told you all the history behind it. It's Draque's cup. He wants it back."

"It'll be a cold day in hell before I let you go have a drink with that ghoul and what garden?" Julian said staunchly.

"Our rose garden, I think. It's the only thing I can think of. Why would he send me a heart?"

Serina bent down and grabbed the defiled organ and tossed it into the sink. "It's a vamp's heart all right." A little nudge and it slipped into the garbage disposal. Serina flipped on the switch.

"Okay, that's really vile. I'm out of here." Jonah walked out followed by Molly and Duncan.

"Me too. Look, I've gotta go into town. I'll be home in a while." Savanah threw her coat on, and headed for the door.

"Take someone with you. What happens if you black out again?" Jovan asked.

"Mum, I'm fine. It won't happen again unless I don't show up in the rose garden tonight. This guy wants his cup back. I got everything returned from Sinsations and have everything he owns in storage in England and all he wants is his cup?" Savanah shrugged her shoulders.

"Wait up, Peanut. I'm coming whether you like it or not." André followed Savanah out the door, wiping his eyes dry.

****

Gathered in the kitchen, the entire St. James'

family smiled when Payton turned to them holding a thirty-five pound turkey, golden brown with sage stuffing pouring out the end of the bird. On the counter sat a twenty pound spiral-sliced, honey-glazed ham and next to that a standing rib roast, surrounded by baby roasted red potatoes with rosemary and thyme.

"I've died and gone to heaven," Duncan admitted licking his lips. "Welcome home, Payton."

"Hello, family. I couldn't stay away tonight. I figured you guys might enjoy a home cooked meal versus something Raven might have tried to whip up." Payton glanced at Raven with caution. Before Payton knew it he was swarmed with hugs and kisses from pretty much everyone, *except* Raven. She gave him a chilled glare with her back against the fridge. Payton was pretty certain the fridge's cooler temp had nothing to do with her disposition.

"Are you home for good, Payton?" Serina asked.

"One day at a time, Doc. Where's Elyza? Jovan, how're the twins? I'm sorry I've only seen them once."

"When did you see them?" Raven asked her lips pursed as if she'd sucked a lemon dry.

"Shortly after their birth."

Lucian could read his sister easier than politicians could fabricate, twist and realign the truth. She was a storm brewing. "Look, tonight is time for celebration. We have our family together as it should be. We celebrate Samhain tonight. Let us eat this meal our dear friend has made because by the gods I'm sick of take-out." Lucian hugged Payton and took the turkey from him. "I've got the breast."

"Typical," André added. "I've got the legs."

"Some things never change." Duncan picked up the

ham. "I got the porker." Duncan winked at his wife.

Molly grunted.

"That didn't come out right, my little tomato. I swear I didn't say it coz you're bursting at the seams with our child."

"Now would be a really good time to swallow your foot, Duncan," Lucian added.

"Where's Savanah?" Payton looked around seeing no sign of her.

Jovan answered, "She'll be down. She's wrapping some things for our midnight gifts."

"How is she? I'm sorry I haven't been here to help her come through her loss."

Raven blew. "Hello? What about me, Payton?" She pointed to her ever-growing tummy.

Payton said nothing.

Lucian stepped in. "Ray, not tonight. Don't do this to yourself."

"That's the point, imbecile. I didn't. Two of the three men that could be responsible for this are before us and neither one is owning up to it."

"Hail Mary!" André stood up and fist-pumped the air. "Someone finally got it right." André shrugged his shoulders at his twin when he realized his triumphant shout-out wasn't done with the best timing. "Apologies, but Lucian finally got pegged imbecile correctly." He sat down immediately seeing Jovan's stern glare.

"Truly, you are identical," Jovan whispered to him.

Jonah looked at Raven. "Only one of the two of us are in that pot. One of us has nonviable sperm. When the baby is born we'll have DNA tests done to determine the father. If it's Payton's, then we'll help care for it. If it isn't…" Jonah's voice trailed off.

Raven backpedaled for a chair, and landed squarely on her bottom looking up at Jonah. "How long have you known you couldn't father a child? All these years and you never said a word."

No one else did either, all too shocked.

"Don't ever speak to me again," Raven mouthed to Jonah.

Pounding down the stairs two at a time, Savanah lugged a box overflowing with gifts into the dining room. She glanced toward the three swings holding Elyza, Rylea and Rian, and carefully tucked a stuffed animal beside each baby. Next she placed a pink and green box with yellow ribbon in front of every person at the table. Ten boxes in all.

"Happy Samhain, everyone." Savanah noted everyone at the table and for the first time in months felt joy in her heart. She looked at her uncle Julian and his gorgeous guest beside him. She went to her. "Edan, it is an honor to have you with us. With my uncle." She turned away from everyone not wanting everyone to see her eyes fill with unshed tears. She took a deep breath, wiped under her eyes and turned around. "You look so much like Ethan, in a prettier way. Anyway, thank you for accepting our offer to join us." Edan held her hand to Savanah and grasped it, tears falling down her cheeks. Her other hand covered her mouth.

"Ethan was a lucky man to have all of you in his life. Thank you for caring for him. Again, thank you for tonight and for being there for my brother."

Savanah sat beside Payton and held his hand under the table. "It's so great you're home."

Payton added, "I missed you too, Savvy."

"Any last minute wishes before we begin our

festivities? We honor our women and their gifts tonight." André said, "I finished my list." He winked then puckered up and blew a kiss to Jovan.

"Just health, happiness and someone to share your love with." Jovan stood up and walked to Savanah. Kissing her cheek, she said, "Don't give up on love, my sweets."

Noticing a van pull up to the house, Lucian asked, "Someone getting a delivery tonight? We've company otherwise."

"Who owns a van?" Serina asked.

Before the doorbell rang, twelve people crowded the main entry. They all watched as Olivia straightened her dress and used her umbrella as a guide to get her through the icy mix on the driveway. In her free hand she carried a bag of gifts. Everyone piled outside into the blustery weather.

"What is she doing here?" Julian asked in an irritated tone.

"Did you know she was coming, Serina?" André asked.

"Haven't talked to her in a month or so."

Olivia offered, "Happy Samhain. I hope I'm not interrupting, but I have a few things for your family. I won't stay long. I'm sorry for coming unannounced, but things happened so fast that I didn't have time."

"What things, Mum?" Serina walked to greet her.

"Who's the guy that drove?" Lucian asked, not trusting the woman one second.

"My driver. Would you all go inside? Please?"

"Does he need help getting anything?" Payton offered.

"Not if it's suit cases." André threw in caustically.

Olivia smiled warmly at him.

"I'll set another place for dinner." Payton headed inside for the kitchen.

"Payton," Olivia raised her voice slightly. "Would you have room for three?"

"What the hell is going on?" Julian's temper flared. He started to go to the van when he stopped. "Holy shit!" he whispered. "How?"

"Hi, Jules, Mum, Dad, Duncan, Uncle André, Aunt Jovan, Molly, Aunt Raven—you look radiant. Vanah!!!" the young woman yelled her arms flailing in the air.

"Oh my God," Savanah squealed, as she covered the distance to the woman and hugged her.

Serina's mouth dropped.

The young woman turned her head to Olivia and whispered, "Grandma, we should have phoned them."

"This is more fun."

"Mum, are you going to say anything or at least let me in? Georgia's a whole lot warmer than New York."

Serina had Sydney in her arms before her teeth could chatter again. Lucian stood beside her with his arms trapping both of them together.

"Hi, Diddy."

Hearing that, Lucian roared with laughter.

"This is the best blessing ever, Sydney. Look at you. You're beautiful and young again. How?" Lucian swatted at stray tears. He cast a curious glance toward Olivia.

"Can I tell you inside?" Sydney briskly rubbed her arms.

Serina stood in awe of her daughter. Sydney looked about twenty-five, no longer seventy. Blonde layered curls with darker blonde highlights covered her back.

"Oh my precious girl. What a beautiful surprise." Serina looked at her mother and mouthed, "Thank you."

"You've got another surprise, Serina." Olivia inclined her head toward the door.

Coming in backward, the driver kicked off the snow from his boots and gave a big tug to a wheelchair. He brushed the snow from the tires before coming any further inside.

Tongue-tied and twisted, Serina spit out, "Fa-Father Butler? Lucian, tell me I'm not dreaming."

"'Tis no dream, baby girl," Olivia answered. "His progress has been a true miracle. You said you wanted to see him."

Serina ran to her father, wrapped her arms tightly around the man and hugged him.

In a soft voice he whispered, "My girl. You haven't changed. Where's my other baby?"

Jovan knelt before the man, nervous. "Hello, I'm here."

"Jovan, you are the spitting image of Sarah. Your mother was a beautiful woman. I'm sorry it's taken so long for us to reconcile but losing your head does things to an old man's body."

The only thing Jovan could say was, "Better late than never!" before she kissed his cheek.

"Open the champagne. I'm serious." Serina chirped. "Do you really remember? Mum told me you couldn't talk or remember anything."

"I still had my memory, just no way to communicate 'til recently."

"You're a granddad."

"So I've heard."

****

With everyone jammed into the main entryway, Savanah watched the reunion, and she couldn't have been happier. She reneged that thought knowing her wish didn't come true tonight and wouldn't tomorrow either. But she'd never begrudge the joy in this house tonight. Her mother and aunt hadn't seen their father in over a century, hadn't known his whereabouts or anything. The man had simply vanished, with Olivia's help and since none of the St. James were on speaking terms with her for that period of time. Yes, she had a few stubborn-streaked people in her home.

Savanah turned her eyes on Sydney. "Hey, trouble. I've missed you."

"Vanah, we've so much to catch up on. Let's stay up all night, okay?"

"Deal."

"Okay, dinner is set up in the dining room once again. Savvy, Jovan, Serina, if you guys wouldn't mind pulling a temperature change and heating the food again, we'll be good to go." Payton pointed to the food.

At half past eleven Raven excused herself for the evening.

Jonah stood at the same time. "We need to talk, Raven." He met Raven's glare with caution. "You were not the only one carrying around lies in this relationship. I always planned on telling you I couldn't get you pregnant, but when I saw you with another man's child, my heart shattered. Even if this child is Payton's. Please forgive me." Jonah held his hand to her.

Raven studied Jonah before taking his hand.

Payton added, "Mind if I tag along?"

375

Julian stood and held his hand to Edan. She placed her delicate fingers in his without hesitation. "Edan is going to get a tour of the grounds. See you guys in a bit."

"Thank you again for tonight. Savanah, call me. We'll get together soon."

Julian's smile—Savanah hadn't seen it so sincere or fulfilled ever. She watched as he helped her into her coat and then walked through the kitchen to go outside. *Go Jules! It's about time.*

****

Sydney walked around Savanah's room and stopped by the bathroom door. "Savvy, isn't that your Mum's wedding dress hanging there?"

Savanah whispered, "I know I'm insane, but I had to have it. Something told me to bring the dress down from the attic."

"Try it on for me. Please?" Sydney gave her cousin big, brown, doe-eyes that Savanah had never been able to say no to and had led them into lots of trouble growing up.

"I'll be out in a minute. Syd, Draque wants me to meet him at midnight and give him the cup. He said he wanted to have a drink with me. How romantic can my night get with a proposal like that?" Savanah opened the door and swirled around showing off in her mother's light blue wedding dress. She glanced at her reflection in her mirror with tears filling her eyes. "Wow, if I do say so myself, Ethan missed out on a pretty dress. Too bad I can't seem to get all the buttons buttoned. I've gained weight again. Tummy and boobs, that's me."

"He missed out on one beautiful woman, Vanah."

Sydney hugged Savanah and together they cried.

"We're a useless pair. Let me get out of this thing, and we'll go out."

"Savanah, it's five minutes to midnight. One, I drove up from Georgia today and," Sydney looked again at her watch and reiterated, "And two—oh my God, it's five minutes to midnight. It is Samhain. This is your night to celebrate. Come on. Grab the cup and let's head down to the garden."

"Are you nuts?" Savanah stood her ground. "You honestly want to go meet Draque? He'll be a no-show anyway."

"Chicken." Sydney stood straight, hands on her hips, daring her cousin.

"I'm not chicken. I'm practical. One of us has to be. Goodness, Syd, you're not home four hours and you're stirring up the cauldron. Come on then. A quick stroll through the dead garden and then I'm hitting the wine cellar." Savanah chucked her black bag over her shoulder as they headed down the back stairs and out the back door in an attempt to sneak under the radar.

"Where exactly do you think you're going in that beautiful dress of your mother's in the snow with that goblet?" André chased after the girls. On his heels everyone else followed. Julian pushed Father Butler in his chair with Edan in tow.

"Is your home always like this?" Edan asked breathless.

"Sometimes worse." Julian grinned and kept going.

Olivia nudged past the pack of parents catching up to the two girls.

"Hi, Gram." Sydney offered Olivia a hug.

Olivia grabbed the girl's hand. "So, why are we

going to the rose garden?"

Sydney whispered, "To meet Dracula."

Olivia yelled, "What?" then tried to cut them off at the pass.

"He won't be there," Savanah reassured Olivia. She hiked up her wedding dress above the level of the snow. "This is crazy, Syd. How do I let you talk me into these things?"

"Here." Olivia slowed down and concentrated on the snowy path. With her eyes closed and her arms in the air, Olivia pulled the energies from the skies, and directed them to the ground. Within moments a carpet of green grass lined the way.

"Thanks," Savanah said as she let the dress fall to the ground.

"I'm only getting warmed up. Watch this." Again, Olivia lifted her palms in front of her, wiggling her fingers erratically.

"What are you doing, Olivia?" Savanah laughed.

"Spirit fingers, Savanah. Mine however, are the original. Cheerleaders stole the name quite a few years ago." As she maneuvered her spirit fingers, flowers sprung from the ground by the thousands. When she finished, black roses filled the garden with a sweet fragrant aroma. The arbor came to life with lights twinkling under the stars.

"That's beautiful. What time is it?" Savanah asked, as she scanned the gardens looking for the tall, blond vamp, only half expecting to find him and oddly wanting to.

"One minute to midnight," André answered in a shaky voice. "Savanah, please tell your old man you're really not hoping to meet the procreator of all things evil."

Not paying attention to her father's worries, Savanah's eyes were drawn to the farthest entrance of the garden like a shark to chum. No longer chilled, her flesh heated, noticing the darkly-beautiful vampire at the corner entrance to the gardens. The man blended with the crisp night air as easily as breathing. His glistening black eyes reflected the image of her lying on the floor dead. "I actually died, didn't I?" She barely whispered.

Dracula answered her in her mind. *Yes, Savanah. Your love brought you back.*

"This is way too freaky for me—to have a head-to-head with Dracula."

Savanah, you and I will have a drink, and I'll be on my way.

Savanah watched Dracula snap all five fingers, each one cutting into the night. About to say something, Savanah noticed her entire family looked like a portrait, all frozen in place. "What did you do this time?"

"It is time for our drink. May I?" Dracula held his hand out for the cup.

"I forgot the wine."

"I don't drink wine, Savanah." Dracula gave her a chilled peek at his teeth, white, sharp, ridiculously long.

Savanah caught her breath. "I don't drink blood."

"But I do. You made a deal with me. I want to taste you once more."

"It's good to want. You told me all you want is the book. Myself and the book equal two things."

Dracula's grin grew wider. "You are afraid of nothing, are you?"

"Only knowing my life without Ethan will be long

and lonely."

"Then we will make a fair trade. I am a gentleman, Savanah, above all else."

"Not in all your movies. You're down right trodden."

The tall mysterious man laughed and his voice soothed the soul. Savanah decided right then and there that's how he obtained so many.

"What do I get?"

"The book first."

Savanah reached into a small bag she'd thrown over her shoulder and pulled out the book of *Blackest Dreams*. She didn't remember even carrying it from her room. As she handed it to him, she started to cry. What if she gave him the book and he disappeared?

Dracula brought his hand to her chin and with his thumb caressed her cheek. "Such raw passion, Miss St. James. I could eat you alive." He dipped his head to meet her lips in a light kiss. Savanah backed up fast.

"Little creeped out. You don't really mean that, right?"

Brows pinched, Dracula answered, "Yes. I really could eat you alive—but I won't." Dracula bowed. Without another word he walked to the far corner of the garden once again.

"Pippy?"

Savanah spun fast, landing squarely on her bottom looking up at the most beautiful pair of green eyes. Scanning him head to toe he wore a black linen tux, his white shirt hung untucked with a double Windsor knotted tie resting around his neck. His hair was longer, curlier, but Savanah wasn't complaining. "I like a man who's prompt and doesn't keep a lady waiting." For the first time in months her heart no longer ached.

Ethan's hungry gaze devoured Savanah in seconds. Looking down on the woman he thought he'd lost, the sickening loneliness dissipated. The overwhelming need to take her and love her until the cows were smart enough not to come was vehement. Seeing her disheveled beauty, her hair wild and dusted with snow tugged at his heart. All wound up in her mother's wedding gown staring up at him with her jeweled-blue eyes trusting him with her life, took his breath away. Spending a lifetime loving this woman wouldn't be enough time for him. He even questioned eternity.

"May I help you up, Pippy?" Ethan reached down and grabbed Savanah's hand. Once her hand was in his she yanked for all she was worth, bringing him crashing down atop of her.

Between giggling, crying, screaming and kissing each other for close to ten minutes they forgot they had an audience.

Coming up for air, Savanah looked around the gardens. All her family came together. Even Raven, Jonah and Payton trudged out to the garden carrying Elyza, Rylea and Rian swaddled in warm cozy blankets.

Ethan looked at Savanah behind a wealth of tears and got on his knee.

"I made you a promise, Savanah St. James. Tonight at midnight under the stars in our garden that I'd marry you before your family and God. Will you marry me?" Ethan pulled out a small box. Opening it, he showed her two wedding bands.

Savanah sat on his knee, tossed her arms around his neck and kissed him. "Yes, Ethan. Tonight is perfect."

Ethan placed his lips to her neck and said, "Let's get it started."

Savanah burst out in a mix of tears and giggles all over again. Looking over Ethan's shoulder Savanah motioned Ethan to look behind him.

Ethan had his sister in his arms before a second passed. "I thought you died. Part of me died with you. You're so beautiful."

"Same here. Gosh Ethan, I thought I'd lost you forever. Mom and dad will be so blown out of the water when we see them."

"Edan, they want nothing to do with me. I heard Dad say to pull the plug on me." Ethan cast a glance down to his feet. Edan put her hand under his chin and tilted his face to hers.

"Eth, you couldn't be more wrong. They love you. The man who held you under his enthrallment these past years pretended he was a doctor at the hospital you were taken to and he told Mom and Dad there was no hope for you. That you were brain dead. Dad couldn't bear to see you suffer so he made the horrific call to end your life. He's felt guilty every day since. Said he still felt your presence. We'll talk more tomorrow or the next day. Right now I believe someone wants to marry your furry hide." Edan hugged Ethan with every ounce of strength she could muster and clung to him. "I love you, little brother."

"Edan, will you stand up for me? Be my best man or woman?"

If the tears hadn't begun a landslide before, they had now. Not a dry eye could be found.

Savanah knelt in front of Father Butler. "Grandpa, can you marry us?"

Father Butler answered, "With pleasure, Savanah."

****

Under the starry moonlit night, André walked his daughter down a rose petal path where Ethan and Edan waited. When he reached the arbor he leaned into his daughter and kissed her gently. "I love you, Savanah St. James. You changed my world and made it the most beautiful place for your mother and I and for that I will always thank you. I pray you and Ethan find the same love I have with your mother." André placed Savanah's hand in Ethan's. Leaning into Ethan's ear, André said, "Welcome to my world, Ethan Kitt. Love her for all your worth and you'll get more than your dreams can imagine."

Ethan kissed Savanah's cheek. "Dance with me, Savanah under the diamonds of the night. Love me as I love you under heaven's warmth. Kiss me with your heart and tell me you love me.

"I love you, Ethan."

Father Butler skipped most of the ceremony due to shivers and chattering teeth. He did, however, linger on the last part of the ceremony. "You may kiss your bride, Ethan, again and again…" Father Butler chuckled. "They follow orders well. I'd like to be the first to introduce, Mr. and Mrs. Kitt."

Ethan swung Savanah into his arms and grunted. "Mrs. Kitt," he teased, "you've added a few pounds to your body."

"You are just out of practice carrying me. And look at this I haven't passed out."

"The night is young."

Savanah attached her lips to Ethan's and her world solidified once more.

"Good night, everyone." Savanah waved to her family. "See you in the morning—make that afternoon."

****

Relishing the moment Julian noticed Olivia standing alone. "Olivia," Julian offered his hand. "You have fulfilled our deal. You have mended many a heart here tonight. You have truly given your heart to us."

"It was done out of greed, Julian. All my motives…. All I wanted was to see my granddaughter."

"That's not greed, Olivia; that's love. You are welcome to stay in our home."

Through sniffles Olivia shook Julian's hand.

****

Having Dracula in his garden unnerved André. Grabbing Lucian they ventured to the most renowned vampire of all time.

"Excuse me, Count," André bowed before the man. "Thank you for returning Ethan to us."

"You are welcome, Lord St. James. He's a fine man."

Lucian butt in, "How did you find him?"

Dracula straightened his stance. "I searched for the Maestro and found Ethan imprisoned in a silver-lined well very close to death."

"But I saw them. They died in the boat." André added.

"No, Lord St. James. The Maestro evanesced with Ethan before the explosion."

Lucian interrupted, "Why were you searching for them?"

"He walked off carrying my golden cup. That cost him his life. He didn't think I would follow through on my word. A man is nothing if his word means naught."

"So then why, Sir, did you send it to my daughter if you wanted it?"

"A gift of intent. She had something I wanted more than the cup. I had someone she'd given her life for."

"What is it you want from her?"

Dracula's facial expression turned to stone only for a moment before he answered. A shallow grin etched its way across his lips, baring a hint of dents, before answering. "Wanted. She can open the show in London with my best wishes. The publicity does wonders for my bank accounts. People see all my possessions and make more movies, write more books and keep a very, very old man wealthy and immortalized. One last word of advice. When Savanah's exhibit opens in London, tell her there is indeed another vampire in the casket with the silver chains. And yes it is a Sinclair, Xanti. I left him for your family."

"Will we see you in London?" Lucian asked starry-eyed. André elbowed him.

"No, Lucian. You are able to conceal your lives by walking in the day. I get more attention than Brad and Angelina when I'm spotted. You two men are entertaining. You wear your heart on your sleeves. In our line of work, that's dangerous. Good evening." In one fluid spin Dracula became one with the night.

****

"Savage, breakfast has been delivered to our door and guess what I got? Chocolate amaretto cookies with orange glaze and pineapple slices. Want one?" Ethan did his little *woo hoo* dance. "Savage, you in there?" Ethan set the tray down and hopped across the bed headed for the bathroom. Opening the door, he found his new bride hugging the toilette bowel.

"Isn't this how our day started out months ago?"

"Eth?" Savanah looked up to her husband disgust etched into her. "I'm so sorry. I can't seem to stop. This is getting old. Every other morning I'm in here praying to the porcelain goddess."

"Have you told anyone?"

"No."

"Want to hear something just as strange? So have I. I think it's why Dracula was so willing to get rid of me. But then, I had silver poisoning too. Hold on, Pippy."

After filling their tub with water and scented oils, Ethan helped Savanah out of her dress. "I can't believe we didn't make love last night, but holding you in my arms and falling asleep with your body glued to mine settled my soul."

Once Savanah sat in the whirlpool, he slid in behind her. Rolling the soap in his hands, he worked the bar into a rich lather and slid his hands down her arms, tickling her. Savanah dropped her head back onto his chest with her eyes closed. Unable to help himself, he cupped her breasts. They were fuller, heavier than he remembered, and he'd memorized every square inch of her body. With a little more soap and massaging them, her nipples blossomed. A grin worked its way to her lips.

He hadn't lost his touch!

He stood, stepped around her in the tub intentionally showing off his inflated balloon and poked her eye with it in passing.

Savanah swatted at his nob. "Ethan! Is this how people go blind with too much sex?"

Ethan gave her his evil eye. "Pop your leg up on

me. I'll shave your legs." When he noticed the thick dark covering he gasped. "Cripes, Misses, how long has it been since you've done this?" He'd never seen hair that long on a woman's legs.

"A day or two."

Ethan's eyes grew wide. Her giggles gave her away.

After making Savanah's legs flawlessly smooth Ethan asked, "Stand for me? I want to give your little *cresson* a trim too." When she stood, Ethan's heart stammered as he watched the water drops roll smoothly across her ripened abdomen. "Oh, Savanah, you are so beautiful." He caressed her thighs then made his way to her tummy. His fingers splayed her stomach's little bump in a loving touch. Without realizing his actions his lips pressed against her belly.

Ethan's lips on her made her forget all about wanting to vomit, so this—whatever he was doing worked until he got out of the tub.

"Ethan?" Savanah gave him her best kept moue, her bottom lip rolled over and big sad blue eyes.

"Pippy, I'll be right back. Stay put, relax, read some romance book to keep your mood right here." Ethan slipped his fingers between her thighs and teased her private lips, with a subtle taste of what lay ahead.

"Where are you going?" came out breathy.

"Promise, my love, I'll be right back."

Thirty minutes later and a cold tub of water, Ethan brought Savanah a tray with a red rose, hot English breakfast tea, a bagel, fresh orange juice, vitamins and a home pregnancy test he'd run out and gotten from one of the twenty-four hour pharmacies.

Seeing everything spread out on the tray, she

protested like a kid getting dragged to the dentist, blurting out, "I'm not."

"How do you know you aren't? When was your last period?"

"I'd know, Eth. I'd feel the little life inside me. It's been months. For God's sake, I'd be huge."

"Last period?" Ethan shoved the box under her nose.

"Eth, no." She shoved the box away frustrated. "It's never been regular. You take it. You said you'd been sick too. I think we just missed each other. I haven't been to the gym since you died. Belly fat!"

"Disappeared dearest, not died. I think your life and mine are so intertwined I'm getting your symptoms." Ethan crooked his finger inching her toward the toilette.

Savanah's eyes grew wide. "What's the bet for this time, crazy husband?"

"I want my baby down in the car lot—you remember her well—the little black beamer?"

"You're on."

For most couples it would have been the longest three minutes of their lives, but Savanah found it was three minutes well spent. She had Ethan undressed, inflated and setting sail in record time. After a very quick two minutes of their bodies tangled into different positions, Savanah lay quivering in Ethan's arms. "Eth, your balloon popped."

"You popped it, my dear bride. Don't go blaming me. That one little move you make tightening your cheeks together and trapping me…. You're killing me softly, woman."

Savanah laughed hysterically, happier than she

ever thought she'd be again. "Don't you dare sing the rest of that song."

Ethan pulled Savanah into his arms and held her. "Times up. Let's go see who wins today."

The harmless little baby detector sat perched on the sink yet Savanah and Ethan approached the piece of plastic as if it were a chunk of C4 with wires stuck out of it. Both stretched their necks out, peering at it from a distance.

"Looks like we both win today." Ethan softly kissed his wife's belly.

****

March 23

"Harder," Savanah whispered. Looking down she got more aggravated as the seconds ticked away.

"Are you sure?" Ethan asked.

Panting like a dog in the desert heat she screamed, "Yes, Eth, push harder."

"Okay, but nothing's happening. Damn hole's too small."

Ethan took off his baseball cap and plunked it on Savanah's head. He suggested in a softer tone, "Slide it *gently* and see if you can't get it in, my little diva. You're too rough."

Deja vu! Savanah giggled. "*Ohmigod*! Wow. Hey, Eth? Do you believe in premonitions?" Savanah sat Indian-style on the floor and reminisced about the dream she'd had before she first met Ethan.

"I believe in you." Ethan kissed the tip of her nose and when that didn't seem enough he caught her lips.

Savanah pulled away and bent forward to hold her tummy. "Hey, Eth?"

Ethan started laughing. "What, Pip?"

"I sprung a leak."

Ethan sprinted to the hall and screamed, "Jovan, André, Julian, Jonah, Raven, Payton, Duncan, Molly, Serina, Lucian, let's roll."

Lucian entered the hallway holding Elyza. "I want to know why I'm always the last one called."

In a huff, Serina grabbed Elyza and answered, "He saved the best for last, M'lord. Now move your ass, we've a baby to deliver."

A word about the author…

Jaclyn Tracey was born in England on an American Air Force base, giving her dual citizenship to both beautiful countries.

She spent most of her life in Saratoga Springs, NY, where she married her better half, Steven, and began their family. They have two children, both grown and now on their own, and a beautiful not-so-little Pit Bull princess, Lonny, who rules her heart and the house.

Jaclyn graduated from Ellis School of Nursing in NY, and is a Registered Nurse Case Manager, educating people on healthier lifestyle choices.